Odtaa
A Novel

by
John Masefield

Odtaa
A Novel
by John Masefield

Copyright © 2024

All Rights reserved.

No part of this publication may be reproduced, stored in a retrieval system, or transmitted in any form or by any means, electronic, mechanical, photocopying or Otherwise, without the written permission of the publisher.
The author/editor asserts the moral right to be identified as the author/editor of this work.

ISBN: 978-93-64280-87-7

Published by

DOUBLE 9 BOOKS
2/13-B, Ansari Road
Daryaganj, New Delhi – 110002
info@double9books.com
www.double9books.com
Tel. 011-40042856

This book is under public domain

ABOUT THE AUTHOR

John Masefield (1878-1967) was an English poet, writer, and poet laureate renowned for his narrative poetry and contributions to literature. His works often reflect his seafaring experiences and deep appreciation for adventure and storytelling. Sea Voyages: His early experiences at sea profoundly influenced his writing. He sailed around Cape Horn and worked on various ships, which provided rich material for his literary works. Desertion: He eventually deserted his ship in New York and lived as a vagrant, working various odd jobs before returning to England in 1897. Notable work," Salt-Water Ballads" (1902): A collection of poems inspired by his experiences at sea. "The Everlasting Mercy" (1911): A narrative poem that brought him widespread acclaim. "Reynard the Fox" (1919): Another notable narrative poem. "ODTAA" (1926): A novel reflecting his adventurous spirit and narrative skill. Masefield was appointed Poet Laureate of the United Kingdom in 1930, a position he held until his death in 1967. As Poet Laureate, he wrote numerous poems for state occasions and continued to produce a significant body of work. His tenure as Poet Laureate is noted for its longevity and productivity, and he remains one of the longest-serving Poet Laureates in British history. John Masefield's literary legacy is marked by his vivid portrayal of life at sea, his adventurous narratives, and his ability to capture the essence of the human experience through his poetry and prose.

CONTENTS

CHAPTER I 7
CHAPTER II 21
CHAPTER III 37
CHAPTER IV 50
CHAPTER V 62
CHAPTER VI 76
CHAPTER VII 92
CHAPTER VIII 113
CHAPTER IX 126
CHAPTER X 137
CHAPTER XI 149
CHAPTER XII 158
CHAPTER XIII 168
CHAPTER XIV 177
CHAPTER XV 188
CHAPTER XVI 205
CHAPTER XVII 221
CHAPTER XVIII 231
CHAPTER XIX 243
CHAPTER XX
APPENDICES AND NOTES 254

CHAPTER I

Santa Barbara, being the most leeward of the Sugar States, is at the angle of the Continent, with two coasts, one facing north, the other east. The city of Santa Barbara is in a bay at the angle where these two coasts trend from each other.

Those who will look at the map of the State will see that it contains, in all, ten provinces: three eastern, four central, three western, each of which must be briefly described. The visitor sees the land as low-lying coast, growing sugar, with immense ranges of scrub, wild land and pasture behind the sugar country, then foothills above and behind the ranges, and behind the foothills, as the southern boundary of the State, the Sierras of the Three Kings, all forest to the snowline.

The easternmost province of the State is that of Santa Barbara, which contains the capital city. This, Meruel and Redemption, are the three eastern provinces.

Meruel, to the south of Santa Barbara, has a more temperate climate than the western provinces, owing to the cold Southern Drift which follows the prevalent southerly along the coast. Meruel, the capital of the province, stands on a rise of iron outcrop which gives the earth a reddish look. The people of Santa Barbara nicknamed the Meruel land "the Red Country" and the Meruel people "the Reds."

Redemption, the coal country, lies to the south and west of Meruel. It was formerly a small independent Republic. It was seized by Santa Barbara in 1865, in the war of aggression known as the Redemption War, when a young man, Lopez Zubiaga, the son of a Meruel landowner, "wedded" (as they put it) "the Meruel iron to the Redemption coal."

The four central provinces are Pituba, near the sea, San Jacinto, in the heart of the State, and the two mountain masses, Gaspar and Melchior.

Pituba, once the home of the warlike Carib race, the Pitubas, is now one of the richest sugar countries in the world. It stretches along the northern coast for nearly two hundred miles, no mile of which is without its plantation, either of sugar or of coffee.

San Jacinto, which lies to the south of Pituba, is the most barren of the provinces; most of it is of that poor soil known as scrubs or burnt land: it is mainly thorny waste, with patches of pasture. In spite of its barrenness, it is most beautiful, because of its expanses. Its chief town, the Mission city of San Jacinto, stands on a peninsula rock above the river of San Jacinto, which rises in the Sierras and comes down in force there, in a raddled and dangerous stream (now controlled so as to be navigable).

Gaspar and Melchior, to the south of San Jacinto, are vast, wild, forested mountain masses.

The three western provinces are Baltazar, Encinitas and Matoche.

Baltazar, to the south, is a mountain mass, forested to the snowline: it is part of the Sierra, like Gaspar and Melchior.

Encinitas, to the north of Baltazar, lies between the San Jacinto River and the Western Bay. Of all the provinces, Encinitas is the most delightful to an English mind. It is mainly an expanse of grass, marvellous to see. It rises from the river into a range of downs or gentle hills, called the Encarnacion Hills, which are crowned with a little walled town, called Encinitas, because the Conquistador, who founded it, came from the village of that name in Spain.

To the north of Encinitas there is a narrow, hilly strip which thrusts out a snout into the ocean. The strip is the western province of Matoche: the snout is the northernmost point of the State, Cape Caliente. The copper found in the hills is smelted and exported at Port Matoche, on the western coast of the snout, in the deep water at the mouth of the Western Bay, the State's western boundary.

The bay is a deep, dangerous expanse dotted with volcanic islets.

At the time of this story, and for many years afterwards, only seven of the ten provinces ranked as inhabited. The mass of the Sierras, forest to the snowline, were hardly visited by white men: the three forest provinces of Gaspar, Melchior and Baltazar had not been explored. Seasonal rains made the forest unendurable from November until April: the forest fever, to which the Indians burnt copal in copper bowls, was fatal to man and beast from April till November.

At the time of the Spanish Conquest the lowlands were inhabited by small warlike tribes of Caribs who lived in stockaded settlements near the coasts. Of these tribes, the Araguayas, of Meruel, and the Pitubas, of Pituba, were the most important. When the Spaniards landed, Don Manuel of Encinitas, the Conquistador of the State, allied himself to the Pitubas by marrying the daughter of their chief. With the help of his allies he exterminated the Araguayas and drove the survivors of all other tribes into the forests of the south, where a few of their descendants still exist, as forest-Indians; that is, as the shadows of what they were.

After the conquest, vast tracks of land in Encinitas were granted to Don Manuel: other tracts in San Jacinto were granted to a Castilian noble, from whom they passed to a branch of the de Leyvas.

The colony or province of Santa Barbara was administered like all other Spanish possessions in the New World for a little more than three centuries. Jesuit missionaries converted the Indians; the owners of haciendas imported negroes. In the course of the three centuries the northward provinces became sparsely inhabited by horse and cattle breeders, sugar-growers, rum-makers and copper-miners, governed (if it can be called government) by a Viceroy in Santa Barbara city.

In the year 1817, the inhabitants, following the example of other Spanish colonists, broke the link with Spain, by declaring the land to be the Republic of Santa Barbara, with a Constitution partly modelled upon that of the United States. At the time of the foundation of the Republic the State contained, perhaps, one hundred thousand souls, of whom not more than one-third were white.

It happened that a retired English naval lieutenant named William Higgs-Rixon took a prominent part in the capture of Santa Barbara from the Spanish garrison. For this reason, and from the fact that English merchants were the only traders to and from the country, English was taught in the schools, and English people were (as they still are) popular throughout the State. After the War of Independence a good many Englishmen came (and were welcomed) as settlers in the land about Santa Barbara city. In the 'fifties and 'sixties the copper boom brought others, mostly Cornishmen, to Matoche. After the Redemption War a good many more (mostly from the northern Midlands) came to Meruel, to mine iron or coal. In the 'seventies others, from all parts of England, settled as sugar-planters along the northern sea coast in the Pituba country. These men, though they were but a sprinkling, helped profound changes in the land, which in three generations of men multiplied the population tenfold.

It is well, now, to talk of these changes.

Soon after the establishment of the Republic the two political parties in the land became defined as Feudalist and Modernist. In Encinitas and in western San Jacinto, the will of the great landowners was still law: in Santa Barbara City, Pituba and in Meruel a new and vigorous race was demanding freedom from the feudal lords and wider teaching than the priests gave. As the feeling between the two parties ran highest upon the point of Church teaching, the Church party, which was that of the great landlords, came to be known as the Surplices or Whites. For a while, as the Reds were without a leader, the governments of the Republic were White.

Mention was made of one Lopez Zubiaga, who seized the coal country of Redemption in 1865. This Lopez, born in 1840, was the first leader of the Red or forward party to count in affairs. At the time of the Redemption raid, he was a tall, strongly built, masterful and very handsome young man, with a contemptuous manner and savage courage. He was fair-haired and blue-eyed, which made some think that he was not the son of the landowner, but of an Englishman, named variously Corbet, Corphitt or Cardiff, about whom there had been talk.

After his success in seizing Redemption, Lopez was elected President of the Republic in place of old General Chavez, the White. As President he rallied the Reds, and carried through what was called "the Liberal Struggle," which made all Meruel and Redemption places of mines and factories, and took the schools from the control of the Church. After four years of his Presidency, the Whites returned to office, under the hidalgo, Miguel de Leyva, of San Jacinto, a man of burning faith, more ardent than wise, who provoked the forward party almost to the point of civil war. At the next election, the Whites were turned out of office and the Reds put in, with such unanimity that Lopez could rule as he chose. After the election of 1878, which repeated his triumph, Lopez declared himself Dictator, "while his country had need of him."

Miguel de Leyva, disgusted, retired from politics: the Whites had no other leader, save young General Luis Chavez, who was indolent, and Hermengildo Bazan, who was only a speaker.

The Dictatorship of Lopez was marked outwardly by a great increase in the foreign trade of the eastern provinces, the threefold growth of the city of Santa Barbara, and an improvement of all the ports, harbours and coastwise railways. After 1884, those who studied the land's politics felt that the real Dictator was no longer Lopez, but old Mordred Weycock, the manager of the United Sugar Company, an unscrupulous business man.

It was at this time that the oddness and brusqueness in Lopez' character changed to a madness not likely to be forgotten.

The madness began to show itself in a passion for building big and costly public works. He rebuilt the cathedral (a Colonial Renaissance building) on the lines of the temple at Hloatl. He built himself a palace of glass, having heard, though wrongly, that the Queen of England lived in one. He then built himself a summerhouse, roofed with silver plates, and added to it an ivory room inlaid with gold. Being a Red, he caused all the bread used in his palace to be coloured red. He frequented shambles in order to see, as he said, "the divine colour."

He had two favourites, Livio and Zarzas; two negro servants, Green Feather and the Knife; and one son, the child of his youth, Don José, born in 1860, a depraved youth of sickly beauty, who headed a clique of vicious lads at the court.

Late in the year 1886, the Dictator's madness began to take other forms, of hatred and suspicion of the Whites, fear of assassination, and the belief that he was god. All these obsessions were fostered by Mordred Weycock, who contrived to win, from each of them, advantages for himself or his firm.

In all his schemes, Mordred was helped by his nephew, Roger Weycock, twenty-seven years of age, who had been in Santa Barbara since 1883, after having failed for the Diplomatic Service. Roger was a tall, polite, brown-haired, fair-bearded man, with a pleasant manner and a pale, inscrutable face. He was the channel through which Englishmen knew Santa Barbara. It was through his able weekly letters to the English press that English opinion was in favour of Lopez for so long. He knew Lopez to be mad; but the Red party favoured his firm and he had no pity for the Whites: old Miguel de Leyva had once kept him waiting in the hall, and had then brushed by to lunch.

Miguel de Leyva was now dead, leaving many children, including his youngest, the girl Carlotta, born in 1868, who even in infancy impressed people as a creature from another world. She comes into this story (as into many others) as a rare thing, whose passing made all things not quite the same. She was of a delicate, exquisite, unearthly charm, which swayed men, women and children: the Indians of San Jacinto used to kneel as she passed: some have said that animals and birds would come to her: at the least she had a beauty and grace not usual.

Nearly all the province of Encinitas was owned by the last descendant of the Conquistador, Don Manuel of Encinitas, who lived at his palace in his town, or in his hacienda below it, with his old mother, whom they called the Queen Dowager.

Don Manuel was born in 1857. He has been so often described, that it need only be said of him that he was a very glorious young man, noble in beauty and in intellect. In the days of this story he was an unmarried man of not quite thirty. In his youth, before his father died, he had had his wild time in the city with other young men. He had been a friend of Don José,

Don Lopez' son, and had practised black magic with Rafael Hirsch. All this ceased when his father died in 1879. Since then he had lived at Encarnacion, breeding horses, for the men of his State, who are among the great horsemen of the world. He took his stature, beauty and masterful fierce eyes from his mother, the Queen Dowager, who had been a Peralta from Matoche.

In October, 1886, Don Manuel met Carlotta de Leyva for the first time: they became betrothed that same month, to the great joy of the Queen Dowager, who had longed to see her son married.

Miguel de Leyva had a sister Emilia, who married a Piranha of Santa Barbara city, and lived there, after her husband's death, in a house too big for her fortune. She had been much in England with her husband, either for pleasure or the marketing of copper. She spoke English well. She caused her daughter Rosa, who had been for some years a convent friend of her cousin Carlotta, to spend a year in an English household. Rosa returned to Santa Barbara from England some months before this tale begins.

Rosa Piranha was then nearly twenty, being a few months older than Carlotta. She was slight in build and not very strong, but had a mannish spirit, with courage and dash enough for anything. She had no looks: she was very short-sighted: she always wore tinted spectacles, even when indoors. Yet she was amusing, and very attractive: several Englishmen proposed to her during her stay in England; but she would not marry into their Church.

She was brown-haired, not dark like most of her country women. In herself she had that mixture of boyish cheek with feminine grace which one loves in Viola, in "Twelfth Night."

On New Year's Day, 1887, Carlotta and Manuel planned to be married at Easter, in the cathedral church of Santa Barbara.

On that same New Year's Day, Don Lopez, the Dictator, in his palace of Plaza Verde, in Santa Barbara city, gave a lunch to some of the great of the State, the Red ministers, his son Don José, his creatures Don Livio and Don Zarzas, some merchants and English speculators and the Archbishop of Santa Barbara. At this lunch he publicly accused the prelate of using the power of the Church against the Red party. "I have my eyes everywhere, like the Almighty," he said. "Nor can there be two supreme authorities, here or in heaven."

To this the Archbishop replied: "There is but one supreme authority: Lucifer has always found that."

To this Don Lopez answered: "A greater than Lucifer prepares his wings." Having said this, in tones of threat, he rose from the banquet, told Pluma Verde to call the prelate's carriage, and invited his other guests to come within, to watch some dancers.

Roger Weycock, who was present at this lunch, has left an account of it in his history, *The Last of the Dictators*, where he says that, "It made him feel that some explosion within the State was about to occur." He wrote that evening to the English newspapers that Don Lopez had received information of a White conspiracy against him: "No names were mentioned; but all the great White families, as well as the Church, are said to be involved. It is possible that Don Lopez will be forced to take extreme measures, to end for ever the menace of White reprisals. The Whites have never forgiven and never will forgive his part in 'the Liberal struggle' and in the remaking of the land. The Church hates him for his establishment of secular schools: the great landowners hate him for his establishment of a commercial class which out-manœuvres them in Senate and out-votes them in Congress. This must not seem to suggest that either Church or hidalgos would go so far as to employ an assassin; but both parties of the White side control large numbers of violent, ignorant, passionate fanatics, to whom the killing of Lopez would be an act pleasing to God. What Don Lopez seems to expect is a *soulèvement générale* of the Whites against his government at the time of the Easter celebrations.

"Undoubtedly, with such a ruler as Don Lopez, forewarned is forearmed: we need not doubt that he has the situation well in hand."

As it happens, another Englishman, without any bias of party or interest, saw Don Lopez on this New Year's Day, and described him thus: "I watched Don Lopez, while I was with him, very carefully, because of the strange tales I had heard of his extravagance in building, in cedarwood, ivory and silver, etc. I had thought that these were lies or exaggerations, but I am now convinced that they are true. He has built or begun to build such buildings, but not finished them: he never finishes: he begins, then begins something grander, and then begins something new.

"All the time that I was with him some unseen musicians made music upon some Indian instruments, seemingly of some kind of strings and a rattle. It was irritating at first, then perplexing, then troublesome and exciting. I was told that he has this music always in his palace. He listened to what I had to say with attention, and said that what I wished should be done. Then, to my surprise, he said, 'They are seeking my life. One of them was behind the gateway this afternoon. See there, you see that man passing beyond the gates? He is a murderer, paid by those Whites to kill me.

My mission here is not accomplished. It is but begun. What did Jove do in heaven? He forged thunderbolts. He crushed them. But Jove was all-seeing. I, too, am becoming all-seeing. This palace may seem stone to your eyes, but it is not stone. It is all eyes, and this city is all eyes, and I see into their hearts, into their councils, into the pretence of their God. But a little while longer and the world will see that a ruler can be godlike, as in Rome.'

"I was made a little uneasy by his words and by the restless, queer manner in which he uttered them. I had seen him some years before, when I had been much struck by his air of overbearing masterfulness. That air was still on him. He looked masterful and overbearing, but there was something about him now which did not look well. His hair seemed thin and somewhat staring, his skin seemed dry and his eyes both dry and bright. Then his mouth, which had always shown an expression between a snarl and a sneer, seemed permanently caught up at one side, so as to show the teeth. Possibly it was some malformation, possibly some play of muscle, which had become habitual or fixed, but it gave the effect of a state of nerves, never (as I should imagine) quite human, that had become those of a tiger about to bite. I was suddenly reminded of one of the late busts of Nero.

"Seeing me looking through the window at the marble tank surrounding the palace fountain, he said to me, 'What colour is the water in the fountain?'

" 'It looks whiteish.'

" 'So has my mercy to the Whites been,' he said. 'But let them beware or I will fill that fountain with their blood and their daughters shall come to see it play. If they call too much upon God to help them, God shall reveal Himself. If you have any White friend, tell him that. I am as patient as God. But tell them that.'

"All the time that he spoke his two great negroes stood behind his throne, each holding his sword. They were naked to the waist. People mistook them sometimes for bronzes. That disgusting creature, his son, Don José, stood at another window, killing flies. He was a languid-looking youth, sickly and vicious, with a face of exquisite features, showing neither intellect nor will, nothing but depravity. He turned to me as his father ceased speaking.

" 'There will be a baptism of blood,' he said, 'to the sound of flutes.'

"It was time at that moment for the Dictator to ride abroad. His Indians entered with his riding costume, a golden head-dress and a tunic of gold chain-mail all set about with the plumes of the scarlet-crested dill-birds.

" 'See,' he said, 'this is what they force me to wear. I, who am God, the father of this land, have to wear gold mail, lest I be assassinated. Let them see to it.'

"When he had put this on, he looked, as he always did, magnificent beyond description. I understood how it was that his Indians worshipped him as God. They decked him with a scarlet serape and led him out to his horse. It was a white stallion, which he was afterwards said to have fed with human flesh. He and his bodyguard of Indians set out at a gallop. They always galloped at this time from this fear of assassination, which had become an obsession to him. I must say that I was glad when he had gone.

"One of his two negroes, the one with the knife, said, 'He ride the White horse; that show the Whites he ride them. He ride with spur, too: you see.' "

Bill Ridden was an English gentleman who comes a little into this story. In his youth he spent some years in Santa Barbara, where he made a good deal of money in the copper boom at Matoche. He was a very good friend to the Piranhas at this time (and later in the copper crisis). He was a man of strong affections; he kept in touch with his friends in Santa Barbara long after he had returned to England and settled down. He married in 1857. His wife was Sarah Ocle, a loud, fresh-coloured, robust mare of a woman, by whom, as he put it, he "sired some colts and fillies, as well as a darned pup I might have drowned." This "pup" was his youngest son, Highworth Foliat Ridden, born in 1869, who was not quite eighteen when this tale begins. It was at Bill Ridden's house that Rosa Piranha spent her year in England.

This house was the Foliats, in Berkshire, where Bill's mother's people, the Foliats, had lived. It was a small, red-brick Queen Anne house, with a racing stable at the back and the Downs behind the racing stable. Here Bill bred steeplechasers and rode much to hounds. Bill was an ugly devil, foul-mouthed and rude, something between a publican and a horse-coper in appearance, yet strangely gentle with women and horses. He had a Judge Jeffreys manner on the bench of magistrates. He loved his daughter Bell and hated his youngest son. "If he had been a pup," he used to say, "I could have drowned him; if he had been a trout, I could have put him back; but being this, by God, there is nothing that I can do, short of pitching him in at the deep end, to see if he's got guts enough not to sink."

His wife, Sarah Ridden, was fond of this son, but wished that he would be like others boys, "not always messing about with cog-wheels." Her children had gone from her into the world, with the exception of her daughter Bell, a year older than the boy. She found life easier with the boy out of the house, "not putting my old man's back up." Quiet life, the Liverpool Spring Meeting and asparagus were the things she loved best; but she was a fine rider and understood horses.

Bell Ridden, the daughter, was a lovely, shy girl, worshipped by her father and mother. As she lived at home, she helped her father in the stable: she was clever with horses; the stable boys loved her: she got more out of them than Bill could. It was her instinct that sent the Lilybud to Mandarin, by which Bill got Chinese White, the horse which won him his glory.

The five older children were scattered: Polly and Sally married, Harold in a line regiment, Chilcote and Rowton in the city, in copper.

This brings us to the youngest son, Highworth Foliat Ridden, the Hi of these pages, the lad who had not yet found what he could do. He was of the middling height and build, with brown hair, and a pleasant, freckled face, somewhat puckered at the eyes from his habit of not wearing a hat. His eyes were grey-blue, under eyebrows darker than one would expect from the eyes: his nose was a small pug nose, neatly made and set. His ears were well made and placed. His mouth was wide, pleasant, thin-lipped and firm. He was a nice-looking lad, who would have done well enough under other parents, or with none.

Being the last of the seven, he came at a time when both his parents had had enough of children, but wanted, as they said, "a filly to finish up with." As Hi turned out to be a colt, or as Bill put it, "another of these buck pups to have about," he was a disappointment to them from the first.

He went to the school where the other Riddens had been, he got his second eleven colours in his last summer term; but learned nothing; he was "always messing about with cog-wheels."

In the Christmas holidays Bill called him into his "study," where he kept two hunting horns, six long hunting-pictures by Henry Alken, seven foxes' masks (one of them almost white, killed in the winter of the great frost), eleven crops on a rack, three small oil portraits of Moonbird, Sirocco and Peter, much tobacco of all sorts, and many bottles of liqueur, made by himself.

"Now, Highworth," he said, "you've come to an age now when you've got to decide what to do. You've had a first-rate education; at least, if you haven't, it's your own fault, I know it's cost enough. Now what are you going to be? What do you want to do?"

"Well, sir, as you know, I've always wanted to be an engineer."

"I've already gone into that, boy. I thought you knew my mind on that point once for all. But it's the kind of answer I expected from this last report of yours. You waste your time at an expensive public school messing with toy engines with that young maniac you persuaded us to invite here, and then say you want to be an engineer. A nice thing it would be for your mother and sister to see you a ... mechanic doing the drains with a spanner. By God, boy, you've got a fine sense of pride, I don't think."

Hi said that engineering was a fine profession and that lots of people went in for it.

"What do you know about its being a fine profession?"

"Because it gives men all sorts of power, sir."

"Power be damned, boy. Power to stink of paraffin whenever they go out to dinner; though that must be seldom, even now, I'm glad to think."

"Sir James Russel was a fine man, sir; and so was William Horrocks, who made the Gartishan Dam."

"Sir James Russel may have been God Almighty, for all I know or care; I never heard of him; but William Horrocks I do know, or at least know of, for his uncle was old John Horrocks, the mealman down at Kill Hill, and a dirtier, old, snuffy scoundrel I never saw out of an almshouse."

"I don't know what his uncle was, sir."

"No, boy, but if you will let me say so, the point is, that I do."

"Yes, sir, but I am talking of William Horrocks."

"I think I understand as much. I am merely pointing out to you, in the teeth of a great deal of interruption, that your hero was a man whom no one here would touch with a barge-pole or have inside his house."

"Sir, a man ought not to be judged by what his uncle is, but by what he is in himself."

"A man is judged by what his uncle is. In this country, thank God, having respectable relations counts for a good deal, and so it should. You're a Ridden and a Foliat, and I'm not going to have you messing an honoured name with wheel-grease because you've read some damned subversive rag which you've neither the sense to drop nor the wit to judge. There are some things which a man can do and keep his self-respect and be asked out to dinner, but going round with a spanner isn't one of them."

"I don't ask to go round with a spanner, sir, nor to be asked out to dinner."

"What do you ask, then?"

"I would like to learn engineering, sir, because I've always enjoyed engines and the application of power, and that sort of thing."

"What do you call that but going round with a spanner? And how do you propose to learn engineering?"

"I hoped, sir, that you would let me go to an engineering works."

"Engineering works be damned."

"I don't see it, sir. It's the thing I should do best."

"Well, I do see it, sir, and it's the thing I won't have."

"But why not, sir? I should work at it. I shouldn't disgrace you."

"Your notions of disgrace aren't mine. Your notions of disgrace are the sort of damned sentiment that will wreck this country and all that's in it."

"I don't see why, sir. I don't want to argue with you, sir; but it is important to me: what I am to do all my life."

"It is equally important to me that my son should not make a mistaken choice."

"But what a man most wants to do, sir, can't be a mistaken choice."

"You're not a man; but a damned young ass. That being so, and it is so, it's for me to decide. I've got to supply the money whatever you do; I suppose you won't deny that."

"I was wondering, sir, whether you would advance to me Aunt Melloney's money, that I'm to have when I'm of age, and let me pay for myself."

"Pay what for yourself?"

"The fees or premiums, sir, for going through the shops."

"So that's what the fellow meant, was it? Now I know. 'The shops,' he said. There was a drunken engineer at Newmarket, who said, 'Let the gentleman keep clear of the shops.' He was drunk when he said it; but that's what he meant; now I know; and he showed a fine sense of the situation."

"Would you advance me the money, sir?"

"I'll do nothing of the sort. These engineers and fellows are a gang I will not tolerate. They defile God's country. They've already spoiled the hunting, and the racing's following as fast as it can go. If you'd been a boy with any guts, instead of clockwork, you'd have been glad, I should have thought, to have been at home here, and borne a hand in the stable. Breeding is about the last thing this poor country's got in these damned days. We've still got horses, thank God. We don't depend on a traction-engine gang, doing a tenth of the work for double the money. Why don't you take off your coat and come into the stable? It's a needed job; a pleasant job; and a gentleman's job, what's more. What's wrong with that?"

"Nothing, sir; but I'm not very good at horses. Besides, you've got Bell in the stables. I should only be in the way."

"Ashamed of working with your sister, are you?"

"No, sir; but Bell wouldn't want me there, and you'd always be swearing at me."

"Damme," Bill said, "there are things in you boys that would make any father swear. You go to a prep. school for three years, then to a public school for five years, then you ask to be kept for another seven while you learn a profession, and by God, when you've learnt it, you can't make a living at it. I've been talking to your mother about this, as well as to Rosa Piranha before she sailed. You'll not go back to school, that I'm resolved on, after this last report. You'll stay here a week or two to get some clothes, and then you'll do what I did. You'll go to Santa Barbara and see if you can keep your head above water by your own hands. If you can, well and good. You will have letters to people; a lot better people than I ever had; and you will have time given you to look about you. You ought to be able to make good; I don't say in copper, that is over, but in a new land there are new things and new opportunities. There are always sugar, tobacco and ranching; there should be timber, cocoa, piacaba, countless things. As I said, you ought to be able to make good. If you can't, it will be your own lookout. You've got to paddle your own canoe, like any other youngest son. Now I'm not going to have any argument about the superior beauties of cog-wheels. I've written to people and written about your ticket. Since you won't work in the stable here and have no choice of your own, except a damned dirty falallery which I won't have, you'll go to Santa Barbara. You may count yourself more than lucky to have the chance. Very few youngest sons ever get into the sun at all, but stink in a rotten town, by God, where even the horses puke at the air they breathe.

"You turn up your nose, do you? I wish I was going to Santa Barbara to have my time again. You can turn up your nose as much as you like, but that's what you'll do, so make up your mind to it. When you've seen the place you'll thank me for having sent you there. When you've been there a few days you'll thank your stars for your luck."

Hi did not answer his father, knowing that thumbs were down. His heart sank at the thought of the foreign country, yet leaped again at the thought of liberty from school and life beginning. He had still one little ray of hope, which his mother extinguished.

"Your father's got his back up," she said. "Between you and me, Hi, he has had a bad year. Newmarket was nearly a finisher. So be a good old sport and go; there's a dear. There's far more scope there than here; everybody says so. Besides, your Aunt Melloney's money went into Hicks's. I don't know that you could get it out, even if your father agreed."

There was a brief delay, in spite of Bill's speed, because the first letter from Rosa Piranha brought the news that Santa Barbara politics were somewhat unsettled. Bill had to pause to make some enquiries, through his sons in the copper business and his friends in the United Sugar Company. "It's probably nothing much," he said, when he had heard the reports. "These Reds and Whites are always at each other, in the way these foreigners always are. It won't concern the boy, if he's got the sense to keep out of it. Let him go and learn sense in the only school for it." After this, there was a second brief delay for farewell visits to relations. When Hi returned from these, his clothes, of drill and flannel, were ready in their ant-proof tin trunks. Towards the end of February, he sailed for Santa Barbara city in the *Recalde*.

During the week in which he left home, Don José, the son of the Dictator, caused his favourite, Lucas Zanja, to be beheaded in the ivory room, "so that he might enjoy," as he said, "the beauty of the blood upon the ivory." Don Lopez' papers called this a

    DASTARDLY ATTEMPT TO ASSASSINATE

    OUR PRESIDENT'S SON

and added in smaller type

    ASSASSIN PERISHES IN THE ATTEMPT.

The Whites did nothing. Zanja was infamous, even for a Red of the palace set.

CHAPTER II

Hi had planned to learn "enough Spanish to rub along with" on the voyage out, but fate disposed of this plan. He was seasick till after Lisbon; then they started cricket; then, by chance, he met the third engineer, who was as fond of cog-wheels as himself. After this, he passed most of his time either in the third engineer's cabin or in the engine-room. He learned no Spanish whatever. "You'll not need it," the third engineer said, "they're very intelligent people: they'll make out what you want."

Ten mornings later Hi was roused from sleep by his cabin steward.

"The dawn is just breaking, Mr. Ridden," he said. "We are just entering the outer harbour now."

Hi turned out on deck in his pyjamas; he saw before him the promised land of Santa Barbara about which he had thought so much. It was still dim, close in shore. A big light was near at hand to his right; a small revolving light blinked far away to the left. In between, in the arc of the bay, were the lights of the city and of the ships at anchor. The city itself was little more than a smudge against a darkness. Far beyond the city, in a line like an army, were the high Sierras of the Three Kings. Their peaks rose up out of the clouds like mountains in another world. As they were now catching the dawn they seemed made of jewels. Mount Gaspar was golden. Mount Baltazar was like a bubble of blood, and Mount Melchior a blue and evil finger glistening. As Hi watched, amazed by the beauty of the scene, colour began to come upon the bay. He saw away to his left an enormous expanse of shallow water, over which strange birds, such as he had never seen, were now passing from their night ashore.

"You see those birds?" said the fourth officer of the *Recalde* beside him. "They're bobacherry birds. You always see them working their lower jaws as though to get the cherry in. It's a pretty place, Santa Barb, of a morning like this."

He passed away to get the watch to the washing of the decks; Hi remained staring at the shore.

"I had never thought that it was to be like this," he thought. "It's like an earthly paradise. I might have been stewing in London like Rowton; or being frozen up six months of the year in British Columbia. I shall be as happy here as the day is long."

As the *Recalde* passed the dead-slow limit Hi saw some lighters bearing down upon her from both sides, urged by the sweeps of such men as he had never seen nor dreamed of. They were wild-looking men of enormous stature. All were almost naked; all shone as though the life in them made them radiant. All were of a rich red-golden colour like new pennies. Even the smallest of them looked a match for two strong Europeans. Even the most benign of them looked like the devil he was and the cannibal he could be. All wore gold, ivory or copper placques, shaped like new moons, which hung from their noses and covered their mouths. They looked curiously like the lids of letter-boxes.

"See those fellows, Mr. Ridden?" said the captain on the bridge. "They're Pitubas from up-country and they're cannibals to a man. You'd better put a coat over those pyjamas of yours, or the sight of you may be more than they can stand. They like their meat white, and they like it young."

Some of the lighters swept alongside and made fast, the winches at once began at all three hatches; baggage and mails were hove out before the *Recalde* reached her moorings. At breakfast the tables were covered with flowers and fruits, of kinds new to Hi. Clinging to the flowers were insects, coloured like jewels, shaped like sticks, or leaves or blades of grass.

"This is your first taste of the new world, Mr. Ridden," said the captain, "what d'you think of it?"

"I think it's amazing, sir," Hi said.

"Well, it's all that," said the captain, "but after a few years of it, you'll curse these blue skies and give a year's pay to be able to see your breath."

"I don't think I shall ever tire of this, sir," Hi said. "It's the kind of place I have dreamed of all my life."

"Pretty scenery," the captain said. "But give me Sefton Park."

After breakfast, Hi was rowed ashore from the *Recalde*, to begin his new life. He saw the *Recalde*, which linked him with home (for his mother had walked her deck and leaned over her rail), now drop away into the past. In front of him was a new world, to which he had at present three keys, his friendship with the Piranhas, a letter to Mr. Roger Weycock of the Sugar Company, and a letter to Mr. Allan Winter, a sugar-planter (not far from the city) whom Bill had known in the past. These were his keys, but his father had told him not to trust to them. "The thing you've got to trust to, and the only thing, is just you yourself. That's the only key that will open doors to a man, of any kind worth getting open."

With some distrust of this key and some anxiety about his boatman's fare, he drew near to the landing stairs, where pirates of five colours, in turbans and kerchiefs of every colour, showed their teeth at him and offered him all things, from brothels to the new cathedral. As the boat sidled up to the steps, he heard his name shouted: "Mr. Highworth. Mr. Ridden. Mr. Highworth." He caught sight of a little man diving down the stairs at him and crying, "Dammy, dammy, dammy, I'll get drunk to-night."

"O, Mr. Highworth, Mr. Highworth, Mr. Ridden," he cried. "Don't 'ee know me? I knew you, sir; the minute I seen 'ee." Here he turned on the other pirates who were laying hold of Hi's baggage. "Get out of this," he said, in the seaport language made up of the oaths of all civilised lands. "Get out of this, heekoes de pooters. I take all the Señor's gear. Don't 'ee know me, Mr. Highworth? I know thee, soon's I seen 'ee." He was weeping like a child and sucking his tears into his mouth with twitches of his face: he had all Hi's baggage in his hands. "Pay the boatman, sir," he said. "One of the big ones and a small one. This sort is sharks. You'd ought to have took a licensed boat, which would have been only one peseta." He led the way up the stairs and shoved through the crowd on the Mole. "O, dammy, dammy," he kept saying, "I'll break into my burial money, but I'll get drunk to-night." He was dressed in an old pair of English riding breeches, a black velvet coat, much too tight at the shoulders and elbows, a tall black sombrero, and part of a yellow serape. Hi didn't like the look of the man, nor his display of emotion.

"Look at me, Master Highworth," he said. "Don't 'ee know me?"

"No, I don't," Hi said. "Who are you?"

"Don't 'ee know 'Zekiel Rust?" the man said. "I did use to beat for Squire William Ridden, many's the time, till I had to run for it. I knowed you and your father and Mr. Rowton and Miss Mary. But you were young, Mr. Highworth. You might never have heard tell. They may have kept it from you, the deed of gore I done. I'm not an ordinary man, you understand. I had to run for it; I'm Rust, the murderer. It was I killed old Keeper Jackson. I'd a-been hung, if they'd a-took me. Now you remember me? You remember how I killed Keeper Jackson?"

"Good Lord," Hi said. "Yes; now I remember. And you have been here ever since."

"Dammy, dammy, bless you for remembering," the man said. "Now, but Master Highworth, I don't want to presume; but I've been all these years, seven years now, in this unchristian land, and I never see a word of anyone come from the old part. Anyhow I'll see to thy baggage, Master Ridden. Now you want to go to a good hotel. The Santiago is the one for you. I'll see you to there, Master Highworth, and I'll look after you, and don't you turn from me, Master Highworth, for anyone would have killed Keeper Jackson, the way he spoke.

"I was out on a moony night, and I'll tell 'ee just where I were. I were up there by the valley, where the water comes out; and it wasn't murder really. I'd gone out with my old pin-fire. It was a lovely moony night, and I got a hare. Well then, a hare's a rebel, ain't he, and game? So I got a hare and put 'un in my pocket and I was going on away along up, when I see another hare. He was on a bank just above the road. So 'I'll have 'ee, my master,' I says, and I up after him and I give him my pin-fire and he went over the bank, and I went over the bank; and he wasn't a hare, not really, he was a fox. I see him when I got up the bank. And there was Keeper Jackson and he says, 'I've got you, my man,' he says, 'you best come quiet.' And I says, 'That wasn't a hare,' I says, 'that was a fox, and a fox is a rebel and he isn't game.' And he says, 'You come quiet. I've had my eye on you a long time,' he says, and he lets fly at me with his gun. And one of the pellets went through my gaiters, and so I give him pin-fire. And when I see I killed him, I go along up the downs and there I come upon a man driving sheep. I put old pin-fire in a ditch and cover him over. I goes along with the man driving the sheep, until we come to Salisbury. But I'll tell you all about that. We'll go along to the Santiago."

Hi remembered the man very well now as a poacher, who did odd jobs for Squire Bill in the dog-breaking and ferret business. It was perfectly true that he had murdered Keeper Jackson and had been searched and advertised for as a murderer, but had escaped.

Hi had been only ten at the time; but the thing had made a stir in that quiet place.

By this time Ezekiel had hailed a carriage, partly by signs and partly by noises, which the signs explained. For a moment he showed Hi plainly that he meant to run after the carriage until it reached the hotel, but this Hi would not allow. He made him sit with him inside.

"You're the first ever I've seen from anywhere near those parts, Mr. Highworth," Ezekiel said. "You see, after I got to Salisbury, they read in a paper how the body was found and it was me, so I thought I'd best not stay there, so I out of the pub, and, as I come out of the pub, there come up thirteen policemen and they were looking for me. And they walked straight by me and never took me. So I thought the best thing I could do is to follow these men now they've passed me, so I followed them along a bit, and then they separated, and I thought, 'This won't do,' so I went along the road a bit and there was a man driving some cows, so I said to him, 'I'm going along the road a bit. Shall I help thee drive?' So I drive them along a bit, and he said to me, 'Where are you going?' And I thought, 'Well, it won't do to tell anybody where I'm going,' so I said, 'I'll just turn back and go into the town now.' And so I turned back, because I thought, 'Well, he'll notice me,' and he must have been suspicious or he wouldn't have asked where I was going to. And I thought, 'Now, I'll diddle him like I diddled the policemen. I'll go right across this town and out the other side. No one would think of looking for me there.'

"Well, I went across and, as I was going across, I passed like an inn yard, and just at that inn yard door, like a gateway, there was Black George Rylands that used to drive Mr. Hanshaw. If I'd a-took another step I'd a-been right into him, and so I thought, 'Now, Ezekiel Rust, you're doomed. They all knows that you're here. They're all on the scent.' So then I don't know what to do, and presently I see Black George turn away into the inn, so then I made one dart.

"So then I got out of Salisbury, and I come up out on a place, like it was downs, and there were some gipsy fellows there. I'd known some of them come round with baskets, but they didn't know me, and I asked them which way I'd better go to get out of England, and they said they'd set me on the road, part of the way, and so we set off next day and we come to a town. I thought I was safe when I was with them, but, coming through that town, my blood run cold."

"Why?" said Hi. "Were there more police?"

"No, Mr. Ridden, there was not more police, there was soldiers—soldiers after me, hundreds of 'em. I come into the town, and there was all they soldiers in red coats, looking for me. But I got past 'em and I come to a town, and there was a man wanting another man to help him take charge of a bull. He was coming out to these parts and there was to have been another man in charge of the bull, but the other man, if you understand me, Mr. Ridden, he didn't want, when the time come, to live up to his bargain. And I didn't want to let it be known, not at once, that I was eager to get out of the country, because that wouldn't have done. They'd all have known that I was a murderer, if I let 'em think that. Naturally that was the first thing they'd have thought. So I pretended first I was afraid of bulls, and then I said I didn't like to leave my old mother, and then I said I didn't much like these foreign parts by what I'd heard of them. I let them think the wrong thing, you see, Mr. Highworth. But in the end I said I'd help take the bull. So then they said they didn't want to run any risks, and said, 'You'd better come on board straightaway.' So they took me along and we passed through a gate where there was a lot of notices and there I read what made my blood run cold. Now I had always been against they photographs. Often people said to me, 'Now you stand there and let me take your picture.' But I knew better. 'No,' I always used to say. My golly, Mr. Highworth, I tell 'ee, there they'd got me all described and wrote out. 'Wanted, for murder, suffering from a crushed left thumbnail,' it said. It must have been Mrs. Thompson told them that.

"You may talk what you like, Mr. Ridden, about there not being a God, but there is a God. And how do I know that there is a God? Because, when I read that, there was a policeman there and I got my left thumb in my pocket at the moment, and, if I'd not had my left thumb in my pocket at that moment, why, he'd have seen it, wouldn't he?

"There, that shows you whether there's a God or not. So the other fellows that wanted me to take the bull, they didn't want me to be reading there; they wanted me to come along. But it wouldn't have done to come along, not with that policeman there. No, because he'd have thought at once, 'There's something funny,' if I'd have gone along. There was fifty pounds reward, too, for me.

"And the policeman says to one of the chaps that was with me, 'Seen anything of this chap?' he says.

" 'No,' they says, 'worse luck, because we could do with fifty pounds.'

" 'Well,' he says, 'he's pretty sure to be coming around here. Who's this you've got?'

" 'Why,' they says, 'he's a drover coming to look after the old Astounder, that big bull they've got on board.'

" 'Well, I wish him joy of his job, then,' the policeman said, 'for a bull is a fair coughdrop, when he's seasick.'

"Well then, we got on board the ship. That'll show you whether there's a God or not.

"Well, I hope your troubles were at an end then," said Hi.

"No, Mr. Highworth, they were not. And why were they not? Why, use is second nature, as we say. Soon as I got on board that old ship, they said the captain wanted to see me and so I thought, 'Well, now they've caught me; now what am I to do?' Then I thought I'd better go, I might brazen it out. And I went up to a place all shining, and there was all the chief detectives of London town come to look for me. And the captain, he says, 'Now, my man, what's your name?' Now what would you have answered? Use is second nature, isn't it? So I plumped out straightaway 'Ezekiel Rust,' I said. Then, directly I said that, I see what I done. And he said, 'Well, you put your name on that paper there.' And then I know what to do. I said, 'Please, sir, I can't write.' And so he says, 'Well, you must put your mark.' And there was a man writing on a paper and he wrote my name, only he hadn't wrote it right. He wrote it wrong, because he hadn't followed what I said. He put 'Jack Crust.' And so I put my mark and the detectives they looked at me and they didn't recognise me and I thought, 'My boys, there's the worth of fifty pounds in me and I never been worth more than eleven and a penny at one time before, and that they cheated me of, coming back from the races.' And so he said, 'Now, my man, go down to that bull and mind he don't toss you. They call him the Wrekin's Astounder,' he said, 'and he'll astound you, if you don't be careful.'

"And I went down and had a look at the bull and I thought 'This 'ere creature will be a friend to me. They won't come looking for me, not down with this old Astounder.' But they did come looking for me, and a policeman come and they come with the captain and he says, 'Who've we got here,' he says.

" 'Oh, that's the prize bull and his keeper,' they says, 'what you read about in the papers.'

" 'Well,' I thought, 'now I'm safe. There won't be any more policemen come along for me.' Then the steward come down. He calls me, 'Crust, Crust. Where's this man, Crust?' he says. It make my blood run cold to hear my name called like that. So he says, 'Come along and get your tea, man. Get your tea while you can eat it. We shall be gone in another hour and you'd best have something to be sick on, if you're going to be sick.'

"Well, I sat down to supper with a lot of others, and be darned if one of them didn't say, 'Your name Crust? You any relation of the murderer?'

" 'No,' I said, 'thank God.'

"And another said, 'What murderer's that, Bert?'

" 'Why,' he says, 'a man called Crust shot a gamekeeper and there's fifty pounds reward for him.'

"So then I saw that they suspected me and I said, 'There's only one way to deal with murderers and it's what they call the old way. They used to get a great big tin of paraffin and they put the murderer into that and then they boil him. Wherever that's been tried,' I said, 'people know enough not to do any more, because they know what they'll get.'

"And then one of them said, 'Yes, but they're not always caught. They know that.'

"And I said, 'No, they're not always caught at once, but in the end they're always caught.'

"Now you'd think that I'd run dare-devil escapes enough by that time. That very evening the ship began to go and I thought, 'Now I'm free.' And then I wake up in the night and the ship were groaning awful. She gave great creaking groans like right down and I thought, 'I know how it's going to be. There's going to be a storm, because it knows that I'm on board and there'll be a storm until they find out who it is.' And then some men came by with a lantern and I was in the stall, if you understand me, next to my bull, and I lay down in the straw and they went past. They didn't see me. And the next morning, when I got up, I thought, 'I'll see whether we're away from England or not.' So I went up, and the first thing I see you could have knocked me down. There was a lot of men-of-war's men. Some of them was here and some of them was there, if you understand what I mean. They made my blood run cold. 'I see what it is,' I said, 'They know I've come this way, but they don't know which I am and so they're stopping and watching every place. My only chance is to keep down just by the bull.' So I went down to him and he knew I had shot old Jackson, and he rammed at me with his great horns and I stayed there all day. I stayed down there two weeks. Proper lot of whiskers I grew while I was down there. At the end of that time the captain said, 'I've never had a man,' he said, 'look after a beast like you've looked after that old bull. Now I'll give you five pounds,' he said, those were his words, 'I'll give you five pounds,' that'll show you what he thought of me, 'if you'll stay and take the other bulls that we have, like you took this. He eats out of your hand just like a tame canary.'

"So I said, 'No, thank you, sir, I'm sure. I'd like to go with my bull.'

"So you'd think my troubles were at an end then. We come to the foreign place where the bull was to go ashore. It wasn't here, it was somewhere further down from here. I heard one of the men say, 'The police-boat's come alongside,' and then my blood run cold. I thought, 'They know that I'm on board here, because why, they'll have sent the description and that. It would have gone quicker by post than we could have come.' So I stayed down by my bull and presently, when we got the bull ashore, there was a policeman, at least he didn't look like what we should call a policeman. He stopped me, but luckily for me there was the captain there and he knew me and he said, 'He's come with the bull.' And so I went with that bull; oh, a matter of five hundred miles, I should think. I don't know where we didn't get to. I come to a very nice place. I never see more rabbits than were in that place, though they weren't rabbits neither, come to think of it: I thought, 'If I had got old pin-fire and my two ferrets, I'd have some of you fine chaps.'

"Well, that's seven years ago, and I've been up and down since, and I'm married to one of these foreigners now. Isabella her name is. I don't understand what she says half the time, because she don't talk any Christian language. And we live in Medinas Close, Cercado as they call it, but it means close, three floors up, number 41; where we've got a room, and, if ever you want me, Mr. Highworth, it's the middle room of three, and there's no job I can't turn my hand to; or if you want an English body-servant, it wouldn't matter my having a wife, because I knowed your father, Mr. Highworth, Squire William, and I know all about this land, in case you wish to know. There's goings on and there's goings on, but what I once say a white man is a white man, isn't he? You can't get away from that. Isn't he a white man? And why did the Lord make him a white man, do you suppose? Why, so that he shouldn't be a black man, I suppose. Very well then, there's fine goings on. I don't say a word against black men. There's very good ones here, very cheerful sort of people, the black men here. Only their feet—they don't have feet like we do. The leg-bone comes down in the middle of the boot, not at the end, like with us. But, when you get used to that, they're very nice, cheerful people; they wouldn't do you any harm. You trust the black people and they'll trust you. No, it's these yellow fellows, those are the ones, and there's queer goings on. Now, look there, look there, Master Highworth Foliat Ridden, there's what I don't like to see, those yellows."

At that moment the carriage had to draw to the pavement. There came a noise of a barbaric music of rattles, drums and gongs, to which cavalry were marching. A column in twos came slouching by the carriage. They were led by an almost naked yellow savage who wore scarlet plumes in his hair. The music followed him, swaying from side to side or giving little leaps in their seats from the excitement of the rhythm. After the music came the troop of perhaps fifty savages, carrying red pennoned lances. They wore nothing which could be called uniform, except the metal moons over their mouths. Some wore linen coats or drawers, some had ponchos or serapes. They were smoking, singing and calling out to the passers-by.

"There," Ezekiel said, "they're the yellows. Tents of Shem, I call it. They all got lids to their mouths. Government's made those yellow soldiers; and they come in, hundreds of them. Now, Government doesn't see them in the way we see them; they don't live with Government the way they live with us. But these yellow fellows, they've been brought into this here city, and they don't look Christians do they, and they aren't Christians. And why aren't they Christians? Because they're cannibals. And they've been billeted down Medina Close, and what do you think they say they've come here for? They're going to eat baked Christians, they say, baked Christians!"

He said all this in a broad English country dialect, mixed up with scraps of Spanish and emphasised by a lot of signs, which no doubt could be understood by Isabella. Hi thought that the man was as mad as a hatter as well as being a murderer.

He did not quite like being with a mad murderer, even though it was seeing life, but it smote him to the heart to see the poor old fellow weeping at the sight of him, and swearing to be drunk that night, even if it took the burial money: his heart warmed to him.

They drove through a square where a squadron of Pituba lancers, newly arrived in town, were forming a bivouac. These men looked as though they had been on a foray. Some of them had newly-slaughtered sheep slung across their horses in front of them, others had big round loaves of army bread or, in some cases, chickens, on their lance-points. They rode uncared-for, wiry, evil little horses of a pale sorrel colour. They rode with a leather thong instead of reins. Most of them had no stirrups, but knotted leather thongs, hanging from the saddles, which they clutched between their toes.

"Now, Master Highworth," 'Zeke said, "I don't expect anything from you, neither now nor any time. You're a great gentleman and you don't want to come and speak with a murderer; not that he was a murderer. And why wasn't it a murder? Because old Jackson, he was a rebel, and he fired at me, didn't he, and he'd got a better gun than me, didn't he, and he shot me through the gaiters, didn't he, and besides it wasn't a hare I was after, it was a fox, and he knew that as well as I, and I didn't know, not really, when old pin-fire would go and when he wouldn't, for the matter of that. But Number 41 Medinas Close, three floors up. Don Crust they calls me and my wife Señora Crust. Anybody knows me. I could tell you of queer goings on, very queer; things you'd want to know, so as you could watch out, Master Ridden. But there's another thing, Master Highworth; you wouldn't want to come to Medinas Close not after dark, not in your good things. It's always safer to wear a poncho—because why? Why then, if they come at you, you've got something to stop it with. It isn't like these ordinary tight things. You can't really tell where a man ends inside a blanket.

"Besides, there's another thing, Master Highworth, which I wouldn't tell to everyone; but old Keeper Jackson's forgiven me. He didn't at first, not he. In the night, he used to come to me, 'Darn 'ee,' he said, 'I'll have 'ee yet,' he said. He used to come all sideways at me with his blue teeth at first; not quite at first, you understand, Master Highworth; for he must have been a bit confused at first, from old pin-fire and being in the moon, but it was when I was with the bull he began to come. Many a shiny night he come at me. 'You come back,' he said, 'you best come quiet, or darn 'ee I'll make 'ee come.' And he done his best to make me come; there were temptations come to make me go back, but I saw through them. But he lost track of me among this new religion. He didn't know the lingo or something, or else their tiddlewinks upset him.

"Then one night he come again; be blest if he didn't come again. But he didn't come like he ever come afore. He come in sort of shiny, not what you would call an angel, Mr. Ridden and sir, but he hadn't so many teeth as the other times, if you understand what I mean. 'Darn 'ee, Rust,' he says to me, 'you've given me a bad go in Tencombe graveyard, along of all them damned and women. But I'm out of sitting there,' he said, 'and I don't mind about it now, like I did. It's a darned poor snipe,' he said, 'could sit on a grave seven years and bear malice at the end. Besides,' he said, 'I'm going; they've given me a horse, and I'm off in the morning.'

"He wouldn't tell me where he was off to. He was always one of they artful ones. 'I thought I'd tell 'ee I was going,' he said, 'there's a whole lot of us got horses.'

"But 41 Medinas Close is where you'll find me, Master Hi; it isn't a nosegay, nor anything to please the eye. It's back of the cathedral, not dead back of it, for that's the Bishop's, but keep to the right of that, and then there's a gate, but you mustn't take that, for it don't lead anywhere, but bear round, and then you'll come to a place stinks like chemicals, for it is chemicals; only you don't go in there, but more round, if you understand, till you come into Two Brothers Fountain Lane. Well, it isn't far from there. Two naked brothers in a fountain; you'd think they'd a-been ashamed; but these foreigners don't know the value of clothes the same way that we do."

"How did you know me?" Hi asked. "I was only ten or eleven when you saw me last."

"Master Highworth, I've known all your family since I don't know when. I know your blessed great-grandfather, when he wore his pigtail. But use is second nature, as we say; they all wore pigtails, come to think of it. Then I know old Mr. William and Master Rowton, not your brother Master Rowton, but your father's, the squire's, older brother that was. Lord, he was a proper one, Master Rowton. 'A horse can jump anything,' he used to say, 'if you want him to.' Well, he wouldn't take warnings; not once, nor twice, so the third time they bring him home on a door. That was jumping into that pit at Beggar's Ash. Old Mr. William didn't say much about his son, but he took on about the six-year-old, for he'd backed him in a race.

"So when I seen 'ee, I said, 'That's a Ridden out of the Foliats,' I said; 'don't tell me, because it can't be anybody else. And it won't be Mr. Chilcote, for Mr. Chilcote keeps his lip cocked up, and besides, this is too young for Mr. Chilcote. And Mr. Rowton's got a swelled mouth, like old Mr. William had the same, almost as though he'd had a smack on it, so it won't be him. It's young Mr. Highworth."

Hi promised to see him within a few days. He did not like to offer the old man money, but contrived to make him a present, partly as a wedding present, partly to celebrate his meeting with a Tencombe man. He found himself in an upper room of the hotel, looking out on an array of roofs from which washing was hanging. Somehow, the washing looked more romantic in that bright light than it had ever looked in England. He was cheered at being at last an independent man of the world. He had had a lovely voyage, and at the end of it there had been this welcome, from one who knew all his people and the land from which he came.

His room had a scarlet carpet and a red plush rocking-chair, which seemed out of place in that climate, already as hot as an English May. The walls, which had been white, were marked with dirty fingers. Somebody, who had occupied the room earlier that morning, had smoked cigars in it. Bitten ends of cigar were in a flower-pot near the window. The place seemed frowsy, untidy and feckless. The mosquito-curtains over his bed were smeared with the bloody corpses of old mosquitoes. All round the room, wherever the carpet failed to reach the wall, little pale yellow ants came and went. He sat down upon his bed, feeling suddenly homesick; then, realising that there were three electric fans in the room, he set them all going, knelt down and began to unpack. He had not knelt for thirty seconds when something bit him viciously in the leg; glancing down, he saw a small black thing flying at great speed along the floor. He looked at the place bitten, which had swollen and was itching. He scratched the place and went back to his unpacking, but was bitten again and then again. This time, having learned to be very swift, he slew his attacker, who smelt, when dead, worse than he liked. Feeling indignant at being placed in such a room, he went down to the hotel bar to see the proprietor.

"Yes, Mr. Ridden," said the proprietor, "what is it? What can I do for you?"

"Look here," Hi said, "you've put me in a room all full of bugs and things."

"I haven't got a bug in the house," the man said. "Them ain't bugs, them's bichos. What you want to take is this bottle here, called Blenkiron's

Bicho Blaster. No bicho nor skeeto will come where Blenkiron blasts. Squirt Blaster freely round in floor and bed, the skeetos will be downed, the bichos dead."

After unpacking, Hi walked out into the city to see the sights of the new world all shining in the sun. On the water-front, negroes and Caribs were loading a lighter with what looked like bunches of rusty wire: they were nearly naked: they shone and sang. Old negresses in scarlet turbans kept time for them by clinking bottles together. At the south end, were the gates of what had been the Viceroy's garden in the old days. They stood ajar, yet still bore the device of the horse and globe. In the garden were flowers, butterflies like flying flowers, and birds like jewels and flowers. Beyond the flowers was the old white Spanish fortress, from which floated a blood-red banner, with a golden star for each province.

"I am glad I've come to this place," Hi thought, "if only I can find something to do, I shall be as happy as the day is long."

In his saunterings upon the water-front, he paused to look into the window of a picture-dealer's shop, which was decked with three sketches in oil of scenes in a bull-ring. The picture-dealer, a man with a strangely broad face, was smoking a cigarette at his door. Hi asked him if the scenes had been sketched in Santa Barbara. The man replied, "You'd better inform yourself, sir." The unusual rudeness of the answer made Hi wonder if the man were sane: he noted the name over the shop, and passed on, less happy than before.

Yet in spite of this one man's rudeness, the morning proved to be a long adventure of delight.

The narrow, busy, crowded streets, so full of life, colour, strangeness and beauty, all lit as never in England, excited him. There were fruits and flowers, and costumes like fruits and flowers, men from the west, Indians from the plains and from the forest; negroes, Caribs; women in mantillas, women with roses in their ears; men in serapes, men hung with silver, like images in chapels; peones in black and silver driving ox-teams; church processions intoning Latin; all were marvellous. Yet an impression formed in his mind that all was not well; the Indian lancers and certain parties of foot soldiers, who looked as though they had been rolled in brickdust, seemed to be there for no good.

At the cathedral parvise, some workmen were sinking scarlet flag-poles into sockets in the gutters. Inside the cathedral, men were hanging scarlet draperies all round the sanctuary; Hi supposed that they were making ready for the Easter festivals. "They're beginning early," he thought.

Near the cathedral was the green in which the palace stood. "Palacio," a guide, explained to him. "This is the palace of President Lopez." He had never seen a palace before; he stopped to stare at it. The guards at the gate wore scarlet serapes; they rode white horses so bitted with heavy silver that Hi longed to protest. The palace was a big, squat, yellow building; at one end of it was a glittering pinnacle still surrounded by scaffolding. "I've heard of that," Hi thought, "that's his silver building. I'll bet it isn't silver, though; but quicksilver. I suppose the President is inside there somewhere, because the flag is flying."

It was now drawing towards noon. Men in evening dress, wearing scarlet rosettes or sashes, were driving to the gates, dismounting from their carriages, and entering the palace precincts, either for a cabinet meeting or for lunch. Some of these people were cheered by the onlookers, especially one man, who had the look of a "spoiled priest."

At noon, some gunners in red fired a noon-gun in front of the palace; instantly throughout the city there came a change in the noise of the day as though everyone had ceased suddenly from work and pattered out to dinner. Hi returned to his hotel, to lunch upon foods which were strange to him: okra, manati, water-melon and a sangaree of limes.

After lunch, he wrote to his mother and to Señora Piranha, to say that he had arrived. Having posted these letters, he set out to the offices of the Sugar Company, to present his letter to Mr. Roger Weycock, who received him very kindly and asked him to dine that night at the Club.

"Do you know any other Englishman here?" he asked.

"I've a letter to Mr. Allan Winter."

"That's lucky. He's in town. He was here a few minutes ago; we'll get him to dine with us. Oh, all the English here belong to the Club; we must see about making you a temporary member. But we'll go into that to-night, shall we, at the Club?"

At dinner at the Club that night, Mr. Weycock introduced Hi to Mr. Allan Winter, who was a grizzled and rugged soul, of long standing as a sugar-planter.

"I'll call for you at eight to-morrow," he said, "and drive you out to my place, where you will see the sort of place it is." Seeing that Hi was perplexed, he added, "But perhaps you're doing something else to-morrow."

"No, thanks, sir," Hi said, "but I've written to a friend to say that I shall be here all day to-morrow."

"Oh, have you friends in Santa Barbara?" Mr. Weycock asked.

"I know a girl," Hi said. "Miss Rosa Piranha, sir. Perhaps if you know her you can tell me if she's in town?"

"Oh, you know Miss Piranha, do you?" Mr. Weycock said. "I suppose you met her in England?"

"Yes, sir."

A change came on Mr. Weycock's face, as though the subject were unpleasant to him. "I have met her," he said, "but I do not know whether she's in town or not. You see, Ridden, my work brings me into touch with the dynamic party, the Reds, now in power here. I am not well in favour with people like the Piranhas. You can always call on the Piranhas. I would go with Winter to-morrow, if I were you."

"I'd love to," Hi said, "but I don't feel quite free."

"No, I see your point," Mr. Winter said. "You aren't quite free. So don't decide now. I'll call at eight to-morrow and you can come if you can. You may have had an answer by then. Leave it like that."

Hi asked why so many soldiers were in the city.

"Precaution," Mr. Weycock said; "the Reds, the present Government, are being threatened by the Whites. The feeling is running very high."

"I should think it ought to run high," Mr. Winter said, "when these gangs of cannibals are imported to keep order. I never saw such a set of ruffians in my life. 'I will not ask what the disease be, the cure being what it is.'"

"They are surely as civilised," Mr. Weycock said, "as some of these Whites, who would burn heretics here to-morrow if they had their will. Besides, you must know, Winter, that the Pitubas have always been allies here. They helped the Spaniards in the Conquest."

"I've nothing against that," Winter said. "But whatever my politics were, if I were a white citizen here, seeing those yellow cannibals brought in to keep me in order, would make me want to shoot someone. But I don't meddle with politics here and, I hope, never will."

"I do not meddle in them," Mr. Weycock said, "but I'm bound to watch them for the sake of the firm. I only hope that the measures taken will be sufficient. It would be a disaster to this Republic if Don Lopez were to be killed now."

"Killed," Mr. Winter said, "killed and disaster? Rats."

"Well, I'm glad you take that cheery view."

After this, they put away all thought of Red and White, but dined and were merry. Hi was introduced to several very good fellows; he was nominated for election at the next ballot and admitted to the Club privileges pending election. He passed a very pleasant evening. As he walked back to his hotel, he thought that he had never passed so wonderful a day.

"And I may spend my life here," he thought. "It may not have the charm of engineering; but it must be wonderful to pass one's days in a place so beautiful."

Yet as he walked, he saw three Pituba lancers dragging a white man to a divisional gaol, which had its entrance on the water-front. The sight angered him strangely; and again he had the feeling that things were wrong in the land. "There are strange goings on," old Rust had said; "they're going to eat baked Christians." He noticed the looks of citizens who watched the dragging, and the looks of other citizens watching for looks of disapproval. "I'll ask Rosa about all this," he thought. "There ought to be a letter from her in the morning."

There was no letter from her in the morning, but Mr. Winter called and drove him out to his plantation at Quezon.

CHAPTER III

During the drive, he asked Winter if he feared any civil trouble.

"Yes and no," he said. "The Whites and Reds always bicker a bit at Easter; they go out of their way to do it. They'll do it this year. But it will be nothing. And my advice to you is to pay no attention to politics here, unless you're naturalised. I'm not a citizen, and don't intend to be, so I keep clear of both parties. What you want to steer clear of in this country are foreigners with axes to grind, like Weycock's old uncle. I say nothing against young Weycock; he's friendly and decent, and all that, but when I hear him boosting the Reds I wonder how much his uncle's had to make him sing."

"But he said that Lopez was in fear of being murdered by the Whites."

"Rats. The Whites won't murder Lopez; they've got no one to put in his place, and they know it. Besides, they know that it isn't Lopez who is running this land, but the foreign firms who've put money into it and mean to get it back. As for Lopez being afraid of being murdered, I say, rats again. He's afraid of nothing, from hell-fire up; never has been."

Hi spent a happy day at Quezon, slept there, and was driven back to his hotel the next morning. "You go in and see your friends," Mr. Winter said, "then come out here again and spend a week or two. Everything's hard work here, like everywhere else. A lot of these young bloods come out here thinking life's going to dances and belonging to the Cocktail Club. You're too wise for that foolishness; you've got some sense.

"And now just let me say this, I stand in *loco parentis* here, mind. Don't accept a job from the United Sugar people without just coming and talking it over with me. They may have nothing for you, of course. They're in with a very queer set, who aren't out for sugar or any other kind of sweetness, but just both hands in the till. I see their workings, and I know. The matter with Lopez is not that he's afraid, but that he's too darned indolent to watch their steps a little."

When he returned to the hotel, Hi found no letter from the Piranhas. "No answer," he thought. "She's had time enough for a dozen answers. It means that she's out of town. Yet Rosa, in her last letter, said that she would be in town now."

He wandered out into the streets, where the work and beauty of a seaport filled every yard with wonder. He felt that he could never tire of a life so varied, so full of colour, passed in such light. Yet again the people gave him the impression that all was not well. He was a newcomer, who saw the game from outside, with fresh eyes. He felt that the Whites and Reds were certainly going out of their ways to bicker at this coming Easter. On his way back to the hotel, he saw some Red officials sacking (as it seemed) a little newspaper office. A young American, who seemed amused at his want of grasp of the case, explained that the cops were pulling the joint and pinching the editor.

"What for?"

"I dunno. He's one of these White guys. I guess he wrote something some big bug didn't quite stand for."

He watched the sack to its completion. He could tell from the looks on people's faces what their politics were, and his heart went out to the under dogs, the Whites, who were outnumbered there, and dared not show all that they felt. "Rosa is a White," he thought, "I'll get her to tell me what is going on."

He was just about to lunch at his hotel, when a negro waiter, who seemed impressed by something, came to tell him, chiefly by signs, that he was wanted in the foyer. Wondering what he could have done wrong, or what could cause the negro's manner, he went out to the foyer, where a footman, in a green and white livery, very politely told him, in Spanish and pantomime, that there was something very important for him, seemingly outside the doors. Looking as the footman's signs directed, he saw an old carriage, in which two ladies sat, beneath green parasols. "Rosa," he thought, "Rosa and her mother."

One of the ladies was old, with white hair; she sat upright with an absorbed look as though she were praying. The other was Rosa, but changed indeed from the Rosa of the Foliats; this creature was painted into a kind of purple mask with high lights of white powder on her nose. Over her eyes, arches of plainly false eyebrows had been put in with the brow-stick. Great gold ear-rings, enclosing green stones, hung from her ears, her mouth was scarlet. He had never seen a more raddled-looking baggage, yet this was the Rosa of four months before, who had galloped hatless astraddle before breakfast with him. Both ladies turned to him at once with an air which made him feel ashamed that he had no hat to take off to them and very thankful that he hadn't. The old lady was more subtly made up than her daughter, but even she seemed to wear a mask or glaze of enamel. "I suppose it's the fashion here," he thought.

Glaze or not, they were plainly great ladies here, conferring incredible honour upon the hotel. Half the staff was there to attend their pleasure already. The Señora held her hand for Hi to kiss (his good angel guarded him from shaking it), she bade him welcome in English. He had not seen her since he was a little child, but he remembered her clearly, as Donna Emilia, a lady who held herself very straight and was always praying. "She needed not to have made up," Hi thought. "There is something very beautiful in her face."

"Welcome," she said; "your father has been a good friend to us. You and yours have been good friends to Rosa. I hope that all your household was well when you left England. Let me see you, Highworth. You are liker your mother than your father. But my eyes are failing, I cannot be sure of this. Come now, with us, will you, to spend some hours at our house?"

"I should love to," Hi said.

"Go and get your hat, then, and put it on," Rosa said. "Never, never come out without a hat again. Put it on at once, or this sun will skin you. It doesn't come through a watery envelope as it does in England. That is your vanity, wanting to look brown. You wouldn't look brown, you'd crack, and all your poor little brains would pop."

They drove down the water-front, past the Viceroy's garden, to the gate. Several houses on the water-front were displaying the scarlet banners, starred with gold, which Lopez had declared to be the national flag.

"Is there to be some sort of celebration?" Hi asked.

"A display, I understand," Donna Emilia said.

"How wonderful the bay looks with the shipping," Rosa said quickly. "Do you see, Hi, the shallows beyond the bay? All that southern bay is only about six feet deep."

"Good bathing, I should think," Hi said. "Is one allowed to bathe there?"

"I believe that some of the Indians sometimes bathe there," Rosa said, "but there are swarms of sharks. If you go out in a boat, they'll come all round you, and rub along the side and try to tip you out."

"What do you do then?" Hi asked. "Sing them to sleep?"

"The best way is to hit them a bat with the flat of an oar-blade."

"I wonder you don't stare at them," Hi said. "No shark can resist the power of the human eye."

"Women's eyes excite them," Rosa said.

"I should have thought a haughty look would shrivel them. The books are full of it: 'She darted a freezing glance at him.'"

At this moment they were passing through the gate of the city. On their right was a park of palms, flowers and busts, on their left, beyond the fortress, was the approach to the market pier, where the boats landed fish, fruit and other produce at dawn each morning. A party of men and women were coming from this pier with donkey carts laden with fruits, eggs and vegetables. "They're the second market," Rosa said, "they buy up the leavings from the boats and hawk them through the closes."

The men of the second market recognised the liveries of the Piranhas. They stopped their carts, stood still, uncovered and cried, "Long live the Whites. Long live the Whites. Let the Reds perish." To Hi's astonishment neither woman took the slightest notice. They stared ahead as though they neither saw nor heard. Hi thought it odd that they did not bow; Rosa turned to him.

"Do you see the boats, Hi?" she asked. "Those are some of the coast boats which bring the produce. There are many market gardens along this great shallow bay, especially at La Boca, ten miles down. The gardeners send their things in the boats, which are just as fast as boats can be. They often race both ways. We can see them from our windows."

Out in the bay there was enough wind to ruffle the water. About a dozen boats of queer rigs were rushing home under all the sail they could set. Some were lateen-rigged with striped sails of blue and white; most were polacca schooners with steeved bowsprits setting a sprit beneath upon a yard. The sails of these were of a bright orange colour. All had high curved whaler's bows topped with gilt emblems. All were fast boats; even Hi was surprised at the way they travelled. A rounded white gleam at their sides showed their speed and the cleanness of their thrust.

"Aren't they like dolphins?" Rosa said. "Don't they seem to enjoy it?"

Less than half a mile from the gate of the city they entered the gates of the Piranhas' estate, which lay to the left, between the road and the sea. In the niches of the masonry of the gates were figures of painted terra-cotta, representing Friendship and Affection, one on each side. They had been labelled when new, but time had destroyed the plaster on which the labels were painted. "We can't tell t'other from which now," Rosa said. "People think they're both the Virgin, and lay little bunches of flowers before them on their way to work."

The gates were old masterpieces of wrought iron, now frail from rust, their palm leaves were snapping, some of their bars had worn through.

All within the gates showed the same marks of decay. It had once been an Italian garden, but time, poverty and the sea winds had helped to bring it to ruin. Marble busts of poets and nymphs were fallen, or overgrown with trailers. The great red clay or terra-cotta urns had been split by the roots of their flowers, so that they looked like fountains of flowers falling under the living glitter of the humming birds. The shingle of the walk, though marked with wheels and horse-hoofs, was almost overgrown with a thick green-leaved trailer, full of minute blue flowers. The house was a biggish, oblong, yellow building, with decorative panels of scarlet plaster in the recesses of the masonry. The scarlet had faded to pale red, it was scaley and mildewed; altogether, the house looked out of fashion. There had been a device between supporters over the door. The supporters were now nothing but legs, two hairy, with paws, two human, with feet. The device was wholly gone. Part of a label bore the legend:

non sufficit.

Hi wondered what it was that did not suffice.

As the carriage stopped below the perron an old negro with powdered hair, wearing the uniform of the Piranhas, white with green splashes on the shoulders, came down the steps to welcome them. He carried a long ebony cane with a gold pineapple at the end. Hi helped Donna Emilia up the steps. Outside the house, all things gave evidence of a great family coming down in the world. Inside, it was all as it had been in the time of its splendour, except that colours had faded.

"Come into my room, Highworth," Donna Emilia said.

She led him into a pleasant room hung with portraits of her own and her husband's families. She took her seat in a great brocaded chair that was like a throne. Hi was only a boy, but he was impressed by her bearing. She gave him the impression of being a work of art held together by nothing but will, and a sense of style.

Hi closed the door at her bidding. Rosa was gone.

"It is thirty years, Highworth," she said, "since your father in this room brought news to my husband and myself that our fortunes were secured in the days of the copper crisis. My husband promised then that this house should be a home to any of your race. There to your right you will see a drawing of your father as he was then. It is a pleasure to me to see you stand where your father stood."

She rang a little bell which stood on a table beside her; the negro with the ebony cane appeared. "This is my old retainer, Pablo," she said, "faithful as one of the old age. Pablo," she said, "this is Mr. Highworth, whose father you will remember. In all ways and at all times you are to consider him as one of this household."

After Pablo had gone she turned again to Hi.

"This is talking beneath the surface," she said, "which the English do not do. Now tell me. What are your plans for your life in this country? Your father says that you have letters and that we are not to help you till we see that you have helped yourself."

"I have only just landed," Hi said. "I have letters to Mr. Weycock and Mr. Winter."

"To Mr. Mordred Weycock?" she asked.

"No, his nephew."

"Did either Mr. Winter or Mr. Weycock tell you of troubles impending in this country."

"They seemed to think that things were not perfectly settled," Hi said.

"And what do you yourself think, now that you have seen them?"

"They don't seem quite happy somehow," Hi said.

"How can they be happy," she said, "with Antichrist upon the throne? I am a woman and meddle little with politics, but very much with religion, which is a force that your Mr. Weycocks do not admit to exist. He and his friends, Highworth, are rousing up in this country something which they cannot understand, the very depths of the soul of this people. But come, Highworth, take this flower. Give me your arm. Open that door for me. This is the chapel of the Piranhas; this tomb is where my husband lies. He loved your father, who was more than a friend to us in a time of calamity. Lay the flower upon his tomb. He will be glad to know that your father's son is in this house in this time of calamity."

"Surely Señora," he said, "the calamity is not so great."

She looked at him and could not answer.

"Leave me here a little, Highworth," she said. "There is a Greco over the altar. But you will not care for these things. You will find Rosa in the garden room."

It was dim in the chapel. It was built of white Otorin marble in barrel vaulting, with one piercing in the sanctuary. Hi saw a blackness with bronze gleams where he laid his flower. He knew that Donna Emilia was crying.

"O Señora," he said. He felt that he could not stay there: he went quickly back to the light.

Pablo led the way to a room full of sunlight: it opened upon the garden, but was itself more full of flowers than the garden, from a bank of white cuencas near the French windows. The light poured upon these, so that every white trumpet of the cuencas seemed to quiver with life. Little yellow butterflies poised above the flowers. A crested humming bird with a dazzling throat hovered in the light near the door.

"Well, Hi," Rosa said, "how are you liking Santa Barbara?"

"Oh, I love it."

"You came in the *Recalde*, of course. When did you write to mother; do you remember?"

"Yes, the day before yesterday; a few hours after I landed."

"I thought so," she said. "I suppose you wondered why we didn't answer."

"I thought you were out of town."

"We did not receive your letter till this morning," she said. "The censorship is on again."

"What censorship?"

"The Government's. You see, we are a White family. All our people are Whites, or Surplices even, the sort of purest of the pure. The Reds have been planning something unusual for some time. They have been talking about a conspiracy to kill Don Lopez and evidence of a White rebellion. They always talk like that before a devilry. Then they say that they were provoked to measures of safeguard.

"Latterly there has been no censorship of letters; but I was afraid that one had begun two or three days ago. Now I am sure of it."

"What do they do?"

"Take all the letters addressed to eminent Whites to some Red officer in the fortress; then he steams them, I suppose, and reads them and has them photographed or copied before they are delivered."

"I wonder they take the pains," Hi said. "If they're dirty enough skunks to read other people's letters, they're dirty enough skunks to forge false ones."

"Oh, they are; but they like to know what is going on, as well as what they imagine. Don't speak of these things to mother, or before her, Hi, if you don't mind. I'm afraid I rather shut you up when you asked about the celebrations. But mother hasn't been well for some time. She thinks that something terrible is happening; or soon going to happen. Any allusion to the Reds just now upsets her."

"Right," Hi said, "I'll be silent. But I say, Rosa; I wish you'd tell me why you didn't bow or smile or anything when those market people cheered you."

"Did it seem very bad manners?"

"It struck me as a little odd."

"We're Whites," she answered. "We're watched pretty closely. What is to stop the Reds from sending agents to cheer the Whites in our presence, and watching whether we applaud? What would stop them arresting us for fomenting party feeling or 'encouraging White excesses,' as they would call it?"

"They couldn't,"

"Why not? What is to stop them?"

"For smiling and bowing just because people cheer you?"

"Yes, Hi, and for even looking as though you wished to smile and bow. 'Gestures prejudicial to civil peace,' is the phrase they use, or 'conduct deemed to be provocative of civil disturbance,' that is another."

"Arrest you and your mother?"

"Yes, rather; like billio."

"But, good Lord, what are the Whites doing to let these Reds do these things? They must be jugginses."

"There aren't many Whites on this side of Santa Barbara: the Whites are all in the west."

"Yes; but they must know."

"It isn't so easy as it sounds. The Whites did a lot of stupid things when they were in power; trying to stop the Schools Acts and other Acts which the Reds had just passed; naturally the Reds were furious."

"Yes; but hang it all, Rosa, stopping a sort of Act of Parliament is done in a civilised way, by law; but these Reds have brought in all these yellow devils. I can't see why the Whites allow that."

"The Pitubas? We're used to them here. They're not so bad as they look. They don't eat all the babies they're credited with. They may munch a finger here and there. What I mind is the censorship and the spying, and the knowledge that all the time these Red officers are making dossiers against all whom one holds dear: false dossiers, with forged evidence, which they may use."

"Why should they use them?"

"You haven't seen the gang who governs us? They are in touch with a set of people who want to 'open up' this land, as they call it and will pay for the privilege. Naturally, they would get their money back a hundredfold. Since the Whites stand in the way, naturally the Reds want to get rid of them; and the dirty way is the way the Reds take by nature, being what they are, people without dignity and without belief."

"I don't know anything about it, of course," Hi said, "but I should have thought it would be a good thing to get opened up a bit: have a few more railways and get more of the land under cultivation."

"If a gang of scoundrels came down on England, to open England up a bit, would you like that, Hi?"

"Father always says that that is what is always happening in England, so I suppose we are used to it."

"Well, we aren't. Now I've got heaps to do. I've got to cut all this linen to pattern for our children's Easter frocks. So although you may not think it a manly job, I want you to help me at it, will you, like a brick? We'll open this linen up a bit to make little panties for our bambini."

Hi was always ready for any job. They set to work.

"By the way, Hi," Rosa said, "my cousin, Carlotta de Leyva, will be here at lunch. She talks English, so you needn't be scared."

"I shan't be scared, if she's anything like you," he said.

"Well, she isn't, worse luck," Rosa said. "But I thought I'd have you alone to warn you. Carlotta is a very special person. She's not like anybody else; but it's no good your falling in love with her."

"All right," he said; "I shan't fall in love."

"It won't be any good if you do," she said. "Carlotta is to be married from here in less than a month. By the way, you'll have to come to the wedding, heretic or no."

"Who is she marrying?" he asked; not that he cared.

"Don Manuel."

"A sort of local buck?"

"You would call him that."

"Has he a surname?"

"Yes. Encinitas."

"I thought that was a province."

"So it is: he owns most of it."

"And she owns most of the province next to it?"

"Her brother does."

"So when the two marry, they will control about half of Santa Barbara between them?"

"Why shouldn't they, if they are wise and good?"

"It seems rather a lot for two; what sort of a man is Don Manuel; a good sort?" Rosa made a grimace.

"He hasn't done much good yet. Even if he had, he wouldn't be good enough for her."

"That is what women always say before a wedding," he said, " '. . . of course he isn't good enough for her.' "

"Any man before his wedding will say it's true."

"Men in love will agree to anything. I say, Rosa, is there anything I ought not to do at lunch?"

"Any local custom?" she said. "Yes, we don't eat with our knives and we always cluck as we swallow to show how much we are enjoying it."

"No; I say Rosa, you're always ragging. What ought I not to do? You might tell a fellow."

"I've warned you, Hi: not to fall in love with my cousin."

"Fall in love: rats," he said.

"That's the spirit," she said. "Rats."

Someone in the hall outside was moving to and fro, arranging flowers in the bowls on the tables. At first, Hi thought that this was Donna Emilia; then the unseen woman began to sing in a low voice, as though thinking of something else. It was not Donna Emilia. Hi could not make out the words, but thought the voice and tune pretty.

"What's the song, Rosa?" he asked.

"That? An old lullaby. It's about roses going to bed because it's late."

"It's pretty."

"My dear boy, you're cutting that thing so that it'll have neither cut nor hang."

"Oh, dash it, so I am."

"You pay attention to what you're doing and never mind about lullabies."

Presently, after the song had stopped, something bumped upon the door; the voice of the singer called to them in English to "open the door, please." Hi opened the door. A woman stood on the threshold, holding a jar full of sprays of white stellas.

"I've brought these for you, Rosa," she said.

"That's sweet of you," Rosa said. "You two haven't met yet. Carlotta, this is Mr. Highworth Ridden, an old flame of mine. He's helping me to cut panties; men do these things in England. Hi, this is my cousin, Señorita de Leyva."

"How do you do, Mr. Ridden?" Carlotta said. "Will you take these flowers for me?"

He said something in broken Spanish and took the jar to the table; the stellas were the sweetest flowers he had ever known. In a gush of memory he saw a hedge of honeysuckle at home in June. At the table, he turned to look at Carlotta, who was unlike anyone he had ever seen. "She's an angel of Paradise," he thought.

He had not thought of women; until that moment he had never bothered his head about them. He had considered them as a race apart, with ways of their own which, on the whole, he resented. From time to time he had met a girl who had been a jolly good sport: Rosa was rather a good sport; anyhow, they were the exceptions. The rest were in a world of their own, with nerves and standards of their own which he disliked but respected. Now suddenly there stood before him a woman who realised all his dreams of what a woman should be. Yet she was not like any other woman. She was as little like a woman as a humming bird is like a bird. She was a small, perfect, spiritual shape, glowing like a humming bird. He had once heard somebody say that "you only get perfection in small things"; he had thought the man an ass at the time, but remembered it now. This woman was perfect. Her hair was of a most deep, dark brown, very abundant, but caught close to her head by a narrow fillet of gold. This gave her something the look of a boy, enough, perhaps, to establish a sympathy with a boy like Hi. The eyes were darker than the hair. They shone as though the brain behind them were one glow of light. They were not only kind, good eyes, but so very merry. The eyebrows were remarkable. As in most clever faces, the base of her nose, at the brow, was broad, and the space between the eyes not small. The unusual beauty of the eyebrows was their length; they continued the demarcation of the brow to the right and left; they were straight in line over the eyes, and lifted a little at the right and left sides, in a way impossible to describe, though it made the face most vivid and unusual. The nose was straight. The ears, which are seldom beautiful, even in the beautiful, were perfect in her. The cheeks were of a rich colour as though the life within were very intense. The mouth was the great distinction: it was of a faultless beauty. All fun, all thoughtfulness, all generosity, were in those gentle, sensitive, proud curves. She wore white, with a green jacket. Her voice seemed to Hi to be the quality of voice he had always most longed to hear. She spoke English faultlessly.

"So Rosa has put you to cutting out Easter dresses?" she asked.

"Women are always making men slaves," he said.

"Well, after lunch, you shall be free. Manuel will be here to lunch, Rosa, so if it's cool enough we might play tennis afterwards. Would you play, Mr. Ridden?"

"I'd love some tennis."

She picked up some pattern-paper, turned it, folded it, snipped it with scissors, refolded it, snipped it again, and then shook it out as a sort of cape or shawl of lace.

"That is what the negresses wear in San Jacinto," she said. "They cut the linen and wear it over scarlet; it looks just like lace at a little distance."

"You are clever," Hi said, "to cut it all out like that. I wish you'd show me how you did it."

"Like this," she said, picking up another piece of paper.

"The English are always wanting to do things," Rosa said. "They never say, 'Here's a perfect day, let's think about perfection.' They say, 'Here, it's stopped raining, let's do something.'"

"You did your share when you were in England," he said, "so you needn't talk."

"She seems to have been busy this morning," Carlotta said. "We'll talk about perfection, if you like."

"I don't want to talk, but to listen," Rosa said. "Suppose you sing."

Carlotta went to the piano and sang a couple of Spanish songs, one strange, the other grim, both haunting. Hi thought them the most beautiful things he had ever heard, sung by the most marvellous voice. He could not turn his eyes from her face and throat. She was the most exquisite thing he had ever seen. He felt himself to be vile and a boor, and unfit to walk the same planet. He wondered whether he could possibly take the pattern-papers which she had cut, or the scissors she had used. He stared and stared. He knew it to be rude, but could not help it. "My God, she is beautiful," he thought. "She is lovely, lovely. O God, I wish I could fight for her or do something for her."

He noticed her hands. They were not the thin, pale, very knuckly bundles of skewers which ladies' hands usually seemed to him, but perfections of form and marks of capacities. There was a ring on one finger. "There it is," he thought; "she's engaged to be married, to this devil Manuel, who isn't good enough for her. This devil Manuel can kiss her. I'd like to call him out." Glancing suddenly away from the lovely face he saw Rosa watching him with a certain malice tinged just a little, unselfish as she was, with envy. No one had stared at her in quite that way before she had taken any pains to secure it.

Rosa smiled somewhat bitterly; a gong was beaten to call them to lunch.

"Manuel is late," Carlotta said; "he said he might be."

Hi hated Manuel for being late, and for being called "Manuel," and for being at all. He wanted to shine before her, but could think of nothing to say; he seemed to be spurting orange-juice everywhere. Then he was ashamed that three women, living in this lovely room, should all speak good English, in compliment to himself, while he could hardly say, "Thank you" in Spanish.

CHAPTER IV

"Rosa, my daughter," Donna Emilia said, "I have had such a strange message from Señora Artigas. Her son, Estifanio, has disappeared."

"We passed him in the cathedral last night, mother, at about six or half-past, as we left the service."

"He was at home after that. At nearly midnight two young men, in evening dress, called for him to say that Porfirio Rivera, his great friend, had been hurt in a duel, was dying, and had asked for him. Estifanio did not know the young men; but, of course, he went with them, and he has not returned."

"If his friend were dying, mother, he would stay with him."

"But the story was false, my dear. Porfirio called for Estifanio this morning; he had fought no duel, is in perfect health, and has sent no message. Estifanio has disappeared. Imagine his mother's anxiety."

Hi saw Rosa and Carlotta look at each other with a glance which he could not interpret. He felt that there was trouble and that he had better say something.

"We had a fellow at school," he said, "who disappeared one summer holidays. He went out in a boat with another fellow. The boat upset, but they were picked up by a steamer. However, the steamer was carrying the mails and could not stop, so these two fellows had to go all the way to New York before they could send a message home. They'd both been buried, or at least had the burial-service read over them by that time."

"Estifanio will turn up, in the same way, mother," Rosa said.

"I trust so," the old lady said. "Suddenness of death is ever a thing I pray God to spare my friends."

"Estifanio is a great hunter," Carlotta said. "He rides out to this 'drag,' do you call it? which the English have started. Are you fond of hunting, Mr. Ridden?" He thought her an angel of tact to have changed the conversation a little.

"I love riding," he said, "but of course, my father only lets me ride the old crocks. Still, sometimes he lets me be his second horseman, and then I have had some wonderful times."

"Rosa said that you are fond of engines."

"Yes, I love engines."

"So do I," she said. "I'm racing my brother with one. He is having an irrigation canal dug by men, and I am doing a little bit of it with machines; but the nature of the ground doesn't make it quite a fair match. What engines interest you most?"

"No particular engine," he said, "but more the nature of engines. I'm always thinking of all sorts of little engines which everybody could have. For instance, a little engine to sweep the floor of a room, or dust walls, or clean big glass panes like the windows of shops. Then, I expect you'll think it very silly, but don't you think one could have a little engine on a boat?"

"Oh, the engine on a boat," Rosa said. "Hi is a lovely character, Carlotta. He would die for me or for you at a moment's notice; but the engine on a boat is his mad streak. Of course it's nice to have a mad streak; it shows the oldness of your family; but there it is."

"Why should there not be an engine on a boat?" Carlotta asked. "What sort of little engine do you mean, Mr. Ridden?"

"Oh, call him Hi, Carlotta," Rosa said. "This is his home here, remember; call him Hi."

"I don't know whether he will let me," Carlotta said.

"I'll be frightfully proud if you will," Hi said, and blushed scarlet, and knew that Rosa watched the blush.

"What sort of engine . . . Hi?" Carlotta asked.

"Thank you," he said, wondering whether he would ever be able to save her life and in reward be asked to call her Carlotta.

"You see," he said, "Rosa is always ragging. She worked at this engine when she was in England. You see, we live in a part of England which is mostly rolling grass hills. We call them downs, but they are really a sort of ups. Well, we are a good long way from the Thames; too far to go for a day's boating. Now I'm not much good at rowing, but I do love messing about in a boat. I mean, being in a boat."

"I do, too," Carlotta said; "there is a sort of lake at home. I go out in a boat to watch the flamingoes."

"We've not got any lake, alas," Hi said, "but there is a little sort of brook, or chalk-stream. It's got plenty of water always, but it isn't broad enough for oars. So what I've always wanted to do is to make a little engine to go in a boat. I don't mean a steam-engine, but a hand engine, so that one could have the exercise of rowing. A man would sit on the thwart and turn a crank, or pull it to and fro, and that would turn a paddle-wheel; only I don't want the paddle-wheel to be at the side, but either in front or let into the boat in a sort of well, so as not to take up room. They all say that it couldn't go, but I say it must go."

"Of course it would go," Carlotta said.

"How could it go?" Rosa asked. "It could no more go than if you were to stand in the boat and pull the boat-rope."

"You've not even got enough mechanical sense, Rosa," Hi said, "to make you keep quiet when mechanics are being talked. If I'd had an old boat or punt to experiment on, instead of a clothes-basket covered with rick-cloth, I'd have proved that my thing would go."

"If it would go, why hasn't it been done? All the English are always messing about in boats."

"My engine is not for ordinary rivers, but for the brooks at home, or even the canals, where you cannot always row, nor even paddle in comfort."

"There wasn't much comfort in your clothes-basket, if I remember rightly," Rosa said.

"There isn't much comfort in any good thing."

"I should have thought religion," Rosa said.

"You try it and see."

"Manuel is very late," Donna Emilia said. "We're almost at an end here. Do you think that he will come, 'Lotta?"

"Yes, I think I hear him." A horse came at a quick canter up the drive. Carlotta turned to Hi.

"After my marriage," she said, "you must come out to stay with us, if you will. There are rivers there not unlike what I should imagine yours to be, and rolling hills of grass."

"I would love that," he said. He looked at her, and was at once shot through with anguish to think that she was to be married to a man not good enough for her. "He has frightened her," he thought, "or got some hold upon her, in the way these beasts do."

Suddenly he realised that Don Manuel was there, kissing Donna Emilia's hand; he must have come in like a panther.

"I say," he thought, "what a man."

All manly strength, beauty and grace moved in that figure; but the face was the extraordinary thing; it won Hi at once, partly by its power, partly by its resemblance to the bust of the young Napoleon on the landing at the Foliats. The man turned to Hi, with eyes most strange, masterful, unbearable and bright as flames. "This is an extraordinary man," Hi thought. "Either splendid or very queer, perhaps both." The extraordinary man greeted him in English; then burst out with:

"Ah, I am glad to see you, Mr. Ridden. Your father sixteen years ago sent me two English hunting saddles, because I rode his stallion, what? And how is your father? And how do you like Santa Barbara? Ah, your father; I was proud of those saddles; no gift have I liked so. You shall come to me at Encinitas and ride and ride. That is the life, what?"

He took Hi's hands in both his own, in his impulsive way, and looked into his eyes, in a way that was both frightening and winning; it entirely won Hi.

"You're not a bit like your father," he said, "not a little bit. Your father likes being top-dog; sometimes bully, sometimes blarney. You want to make things. I know your sort.

"Where are you staying?" he continued. "At the Santiago? That's a vile hole, the Santiago. Yet all our visitors form their first impressions there. Whereabouts have they put you?"

"On the third floor," Hi said, "Room 67."

"Looking out on the back, what? Well, looking out on the front wouldn't have been much more cheerful. The palace, the Santiago and the cathedral. I'd like to raze them all three and start afresh.

"By the way, about your Santiago. I am a night bird. I pass the back of that hotel at night at two in the morning. You can get in at the back through the cellar-grating. The negro waiters run a gambling hell there; fan-tan, what? They also do a private trade in the hotel liquor. And now forgive me everybody for being so late."

"You are scandalously late, Manuel," Rosa said. "You deserve no lunch."

"I want no lunch," he said, "but coffee and some bread. I am late, because I have been tracking a crime. Estifanio Artigas was murdered in this city last night."

"Then it was murder?"

"We were talking of him a moment since."

"That will be death to the poor mother; her only child."

"There is more than this," Carlotta said. "The murder was planned. By whom?"

"The Murder Gang of the Palace. A club of young criminals headed by Don José, the son of our Dictator, Mr. Ridden. They murdered the lad in that tunnel or passage where the windmills used to be. I have been with the murderer. Here's a copy of his confession, made before Chacon, the notary. I've sent copies of it to Chavez and Hermengildo, as well as to your brother, Carlotta. Who could want food after this? Now the Whites move again; we have a cause and a case.

"This Murder Club was founded by Don José at the end of last year as a new excitement; he and eight young men are the members; all very select. They have now murdered five men; one a month is their rule, each in a different way.

"Pablo Hinestrosa was chosen to kill Estifanio. Two of the others came to help him; four were posted, to keep guard during the murder; the other two brought Estifanio to the place.

"I learned all this from Pablo's own lips this morning."

"Pablo Hinestrosa was always as weak as water," Rosa said. "Cruel, too; I remember him putting worms under his rocking horse as a little child."

"I found Pablo in the street, as I came back from my ride this morning," Don Manuel continued. "He was crying and quaking; so I brought him to my rooms. Bit by bit, I got the story out of him."

"One moment, Manuel," Carlotta said; "this Hinestrosa man, who is plainly of weak intelligence, may have imagined all this."

"Ah, no, alas," Don Manuel said, "I have proved it to be true. One decoyed the victim to the carriage, one drove the carriage to the tunnel. Then the decoy led him into the tunnel, where Pablo killed him. Don José helped in the killing. There were the tracks and the body, everything corresponded exactly.

"You will think this next a strange thing:

"Don José is very clever as well as very vicious. He and Spallo took Pablo home after the murder, and, as they saw that he was shaken, they feared that he would betray them.

"Now Pablo feared that they feared this, so he contrived to leave them where he could hear them talking. He heard Don José say: 'I knew that he would be sentimental. He will confess the whole thing to the first priest he can find. Shall we finish him? It would be rather a neat end to the night.' It must have been an anxious moment for Pablo, waiting for the answer; but Spallo said, 'Better not. . . . He'll be all right after a sleep.'

"After that, Spallo and José went away, but now another strange thing happened. When they had gone (so Pablo says) the ghost of Estifanio's father came in and sat beside him. He never spoke, but whenever Pablo tried to run from the room, this ghost slid in front of him."

"What happened then?"

"Pablo said that he 'burned the ghost away, with matches and texts of Scripture.' When the ghost was gone he ran into the street; but it was worse there, he said, because Estifanio kept looking through the windows at him.

"I got a doctor to give him an opiate; now he's asleep in Chacon's house."

"God give us mercy," Donna Emilia said. "Is there to be no measure to the wickedness of this time?"

"When will General Chavez know of this?" Carlotta asked.

"Now. He'll be in town by six. Congress meets at eight. We will arraign the palace on this question."

"God help this unhappy land," Donna Emilia said.

"God is helping this land," Don Manuel said. "He gives us this sword against the Lopez gang; now we shall end them."

"I am not so sure, Manuel," Carlotta said. "There is much shrewdness in the men about Lopez. They would be only too glad to get rid of Don José. This case may rid the land of Don José; but I do not think that Lopez will be involved. His hands may even be strengthened."

Manuel listened to her with much attention.

"Not as ours are strengthened," he said. "Chavez and Bazan must stir at this. I have the confession and all the evidence. The Reds suspect nothing. We shall have a *coup de théâtre* in only five hours. This magazine shall explode under their feet."

"I wonder," Carlotta said. "General Chavez may think the time inopportune."

"Inopportune? When the Reds are declaiming about a White conspiracy?"

"If not inopportune, he may find some other excuse for not acting."

"He must act upon this."

"He is a very indolent man."

"If he will not act, we will find who will. I see three here to start with; no, four, for I am sure that Mr. Ridden will be with us."

"Rather, if you'll have me, sir," Hi said.

"It will begin your stay here well, to help in the downfall of a Dictator."

"Manuel," Rosa said, "you are not to drag Hi into our party politics."

"Manuel," Carlotta said, "I think that you are going beyond the present issue, which is, to denounce the Murder Club. Lopez has sufficient readiness, and bigness, to banish, or even to prosecute, his son; and then face you in a stronger position than ever."

"I believe that Lopez is mad," Manuel said. "To-night, when this begins, I shall declare him to be unfit to govern."

As he spoke, the major-domo entered with a telegram upon a salver.

"For Don Manuel," he said.

When Don Manuel had read the telegram, he changed countenance; it was plain that he had received a blow.

"Is it ill news from Encarnacion?" Donna Emilia asked.

"Is your mother worse, Manuel?" Carlotta asked.

"Yes," he said, "my beloved mother is dangerously ill at Encarnacion. I must go at once."

"There will be no train to San Jacinto till noon to-morrow."

"No," he said, "but I can go by the mountain train at four; and ride from Melchior, it is only sixty-seven miles. If I telegraph for horses, I can be at home by dusk to-morrow night. That will save five hours."

"You must go at once, if you are to catch the four train," Carlotta said. "I'll drive you to the station."

"We will go, then," Manuel said. "While they bring the chaise, I'll order horses; you shall send the telegrams when I am gone."

As Don Manuel made his farewells, he took Hi's hand in both his own hands. "My greetings to your father," he said. "Tell him I remember the saddles. I shall expect you presently at my home."

"You will stay with us, will you not?" Carlotta said.

"I would love to," Hi said. "I would love it more than anything."

They all went out of doors to see them start. Carlotta was driving two marvellous little horses, full of fire. Hi looking at her as she sat watching her horses, felt that the only possible happiness on earth would be to live and die for her; since everything about her was beautiful and came not from this world. He saw that all there thought as he thought and felt as he felt about her. "You beautiful and gracious and glorious thing," he thought. "I wish I could die for you."

The peones stepped from the horses' heads, the gates opened, the horses strained to the collars and the marvellous girl was gone. Often, afterwards, he thought of that scene.

"I trust that he may find his mother alive," Donna Emilia said.

"I must be going, too," Hi said.

"Going! nonsense," Rosa said. "You've come for the day. You've had neither tennis nor a swim. Come in."

When he had come in, Rosa looked at him with malice.

"Isn't he handsome, Hi?" she asked.

"Handsome? I should think he is," Hi said. "He is everything and has everything."

"No; he hasn't everything," Rosa said. "I know several things that he has not. But even if he had everything, he wouldn't be good enough for her."

Hi did not answer, for the thought of Manuel having the beautiful Carlotta went through him with a pang.

"He wouldn't be good enough for her; would he?" Rosa repeated.

"I hope so."

"No, you don't," Rosa said. "You know that he wouldn't. Confess, Hi, he wouldn't."

Hi looked at her with a look of pain.

"Isn't she wonderful?" she said.

"I understand your being fond of her."

"Fond of her? People aren't fond of her. They worship her and would die for her. Wouldn't you?"

"Yes, I would," he said, after a pause. "You know I would. And you would, too."

"I told you not to," Rosa said. "I gave you fair warning. You'd better put her out of your mind. Besides," she added with malice, "he's frightfully jealous."

"He'll have some cause, I should say."

"Well, come on into the garden. I'll play you tennis."

"No, be square, Rosa. You don't really want me. I must clear out."

"I'll tell you when to clear out," she said. "But stay a little. Carlotta will be back in half an hour. Stay to see her. It will be the last time you'll see her before she marries."

"I thought you said that they wouldn't be married till Easter."

"Not now," she said. "She'll go to him by the noon train to-morrow; you will see. I shall have to go with her. She'll be married by the Bishop to-morrow midnight, so that the mother may see the son married. Then she'll be with that man all her life."

"She chose him, out of all the men in the world," he said. "And I don't wonder; he's a fine fellow."

"A fine fellow? Only a few years ago he was the friend of this Don José of the Murder Gang."

"I don't know about that," Hi said. "He's a fine fellow now; and she thinks so."

"She thinks so now, but in a week, in a month . . . with that man all the time."

"Here's Pablo, with a message for you," Hi said.

"There is someone to see you, Señorita," Pablo said, "Tomás Chacon, the notary from Santa Barbara."

"Strange," Rosa said to Hi. "This is the notary whom Manuel left in charge of the murderer. If you will stay by these roses, to watch the humming birds for a moment, I will speak to him."

He watched the humming birds for ten minutes, while Rosa spoke with the man. He did not think of the humming birds; the love of Carlotta was eating him up, in an agony that was yet sweet.

> I did but see her passing by,
> But I shall love her till I die.

"She will be married to-morrow midnight," he thought, "and he will have her till she dies. If she could be chained to a rock by a dragon we could prove who loves her best."

When the visitor had gone, Rosa returned to him. "I knew that there would be trouble," she said. "Chacon has let the murderer escape. The Reds are warned now and all Manuel's plan will miscarry. He'll be furious."

"How did he let him escape?"

"Somebody betrayed it, and the Reds rescued him. I've sent Chacon to tell General Chavez; but nothing will be done now that Manuel is away: Chavez is an idler.

"Of course," she added, "he may act because Manuel is away. These soldiers and politicians are as jealous of each other as prime donne."

"Surely," Hi said, "this isn't a matter for politicians, but for the police? Surely the police will take the murderer?"

"The police?" she said. "Why, Hi, they're married men, with families, most of them. Do you think they'd risk their pensions by arresting a Red on a White warrant? They're not philanthropists."

"What are they, then?"

"Paid partisans."

"Golly."

"Well may you say golly. However, that is a little thing, compared with this marriage. I'm used to the police. I'm not used to the thought of that man with . . ."

She had paused at the little fountain, where she gazed down into the basin and let the fingers of one hand open and close in the water.

"But I'm not going to talk in this beastly way," she said. "Forget what I said, will you?

"Of course, Hi, you'll come here whenever you like. Mother told me to tell you that a place will be here for you at lunch on every Tuesday, Thursday and Sunday; when you can come, we'll be glad, and when you can't you needn't write or send word. You needn't think it's decent of us. We're only too glad. You were all lovely to me at your home, and your father simply saved us from beggary. Besides, it will be a charity to two lorn females."

"Thank you," Hi said, "you're a jolly good friend."

"There's my hand on that," she said. "And when you're settled out here, we can always put you up. Now would you care to swim? We have a bathing pond here. It was made in the days of our glory, but, being made, it is easy to keep up."

She led the way through a gap in a rose-hedge to a terrace of white marble, in the midst of which was a swimming pool, full of clear water.

"There you are," she said, "if ever you want a swim. A plunge now would do us both good; but before we plunge, shall we just walk back to the house, to see if Carlotta has returned?"

"Yes, certainly," Hi said; "but I haven't heard her horses."

"Nor I," she said. "But she ought to be back. She is the swimmer amongst us. She does all things well, but she swims like a sea-bird."

They found that Carlotta had not returned.

"She ought to be back by this time," Rosa said. "But in this country trains are sometimes late in starting, as you will find. Let us walk to the gates, to see if she be on the road."

They saw no one on the road, save three men with a handcart who were coming slowly from the direction of the city and pausing at intervals to paste handbills on walls and palings. They paused to paste a bill upon a ruinous wall opposite the Piranhas' gate; Rosa and Hi watched them.

"Bill-stickers," Hi said. "I did not know that you had them here."

"Oh, yes," Rosa said. "We are civilised here; bills, drains and only one wife, just like Europe. But we keep them for great occasions like bull-fights, these bills, I mean."

"Bull-fights," Hi said. "Do you still have them?"

"This is the season for them; probably this is an announcement of them."

"I'd love to see a bull-fight; it must be frightfully exciting. Do let us wait to see what it is."

The bill-sticker, with a few deft thrusts of his brush, set the poster in its place. It was a yellow poster, printed in blunt black type with a tall red heading:

"Proclamation of the Government."

"It is only a pronunciamento," Rosa said; "not bulls after all. Can you read it from here? I cannot see anything without my glasses."

"Something about religion, as far as I can make it out," Hi said. "Dios is God, isn't it?"

"Yes."

"That's what it is, then; all about religion."

"There are rather a lot of Dioses," Hi said after a pause; "but then I suppose it's Lent."

"Yes," Rosa said, a little snappily. "In my Church it is the season for Dioses."

Donna Emilia met them on their way back through the house to the pond. "Carlotta not yet back?" she said. "She has probably driven to one of the stores. Come in, then, to drink maté. Tea here is never good, Highworth; we drink maté amargo, a bitter drink; not unlike your camomile tea, they tell me; we think it refreshing."

Hi did not find it refreshing, but drank one little silver pipkin for the experience and a second for politeness.

CHAPTER V

"Is anyone coming here this afternoon?" Rosa asked. "No one, so far as I can tell," her mother answered. "I am not asking people, because I want you to see Carlotta while you can. Besides, it is Lent; one should be quiet in Lent."

"They are putting placards in the road," Rosa said. "We could not read them; but they seemed to be about quiet at Easter."

"I am glad," Donna Emilia said. "The last exhibition of disorder disgraced our country."

The old butler entered. "Señora," he said, "Don Inocencio desires to speak with you, if it be your pleasure."

"Let him come in," she answered. "Don Inocencio, Highworth, is one of the Senators of the White party, to which we belong. He was an old friend of my husband's."

"Shall I not go?" Hi asked.

"No, stay, it's very good for you," Rosa said.

Don Inocencio was a little pale man with a habit of inflating his cheeks; when he did this, he looked more important than at other times. He held a roll of paper in his left hand; he had very nice manners and spoke in English on finding Hi there. He was in a state of some agitation.

"My dear lady," he said, "I have come all this way, in a great hurry, because of the importance of the occasion. The man has been permitted and permitted till he has presumed and presumed; but now he has outstepped all bounds; he has, if I may say so, without inelegance, burst, like the frog in the fable."

"Who has burst without inelegance?" Rosa asked. "Do tell us. Could he do it again, publicly?"

"He has done it publicly," Don Inocencio said, "It cannot be done twice in a civilised country."

"Who is this?" Donna Emilia asked. "I do not quite understand? Has there been some accident?"

"I thought that at first," Don Inocencio answered. "I thought at first, this is not genuine; this is a ruse or trick, designed by an enemy. It would be a skilled thrust, though that of a devil, to lead people to suppose that this came from our enemy. Then I thought, no, this thing is too mad to be anything but genuine; no counterfeit would be so crazy."

"But what is it, Don Inocencio?"

"Have you not read the proclamation?"

"A proclamation; which; what proclamation?"

"There is at present only one, which will be historical. This is it, this scroll. They started to put this upon the walls at the time of the siesta; it is now everywhere; can it be that you have not seen it?"

"No; no, indeed."

"Then I am a bringer of news. When I read it, I thought, this, if genuine, will be a landmark in our story. I must have copies of this; so must Donna Emilia; therefore I procured copies from the bill-stickers.

"You know that I am a collector of documents, which will go to my nephew; all things, especially documents, if old enough, have romance; this will have much more than romance, being the cause, if I am not much mistaken, of great events in the near future. We live in stirring times, Miss Rosa. You, Mr. Ridden, will see great events, really great events, as the Blanco party reasserts its ideals. Wait, now; for this big document; I will display my wares upon this chair."

He pulled a chair towards him so that he could spread the paper upon the back: it was a yellow paper, printed in blunt, black type with a tall red heading:

"PROCLAMATION OF THE GOVERNMENT."

He glanced at the faces of his audience for some expression, which he did not find.

"What," he said, "no comment?"

"None," Rosa said. "Mother and I cannot read well without our glasses."

"And I," Hi said, "cannot read Spanish very fluently yet. In fact, I can only get as far as 'Government.'"

"Perhaps, Inocencio," Donna Emilia said, "you will be so kind as to read it for us."

"Certainly," he said, "I will read it aloud: only I must warn you, that its contents are not such as are usual, I will not say in a proclamation, but in print of any kind. To begin with, it is, I must warn you, from first to last a print of the last blasphemy of madness."

The listeners did not answer this, but looked and felt uncomfortable.

"Will you not read, then?" Donna Emilia said at last. Don Inocencio began to read aloud. He bent a little over the paper, so that he might read; he beat time with his left hand, in a pumping stroke, to mark his cadence. He began as follows:—

"This," he said, "is his preludium or exordium.

> PROCLAMATION OF THE GOVERNMENT.
>
> Forasmuch as I, Don Lopez de Meruel, King, Emperor and Dictator of Santa Barbara, am convinced of my divinity and of my oneness with God. Know all men, that henceforth, throughout this my heaven of Santa Barbara, I assume the style and name of God, with the titles of Thrice Holy, Thrice Blessed, Thrice Glorious.

"What do you make of that?" he said, "for a beginning?"

"The man is mad," Rosa said.

"It is blasphemy unspeakable," Donna Emilia said. "I tremble lest fire descend on us."

"This is nothing to what follows," Don Inocencio said. "I will read on. The rest is incredibly much worse. But the rest, I, for one, rejoice at. It continues thus:

> I therefore, thy God, decree, that henceforth my mortals worship and sacrifice to me in all churches, chapels and places of worship whatsoever; that all prayer, praise, worship and adoration, with all hymns, psalms and spiritual ejaculations of whatever kind, be henceforth addressed to me, whether in public or in private, I, thy God Lopez, decree it.
>
> Likewise thy God decrees (and in reading this, Donna Emilia, I ask pardon of my Maker) thy God decrees, that all other Gods, saints and suchlike, hitherto worshipped in this my Heaven, such as (here he writes in a way that cannot be quoted) shall be cast aside, their images defaced, their altars denied and their rituals omitted, upon pain of death.

Furthermore, thy God decrees that my image be placed in all churches and in all chapels of churches, wheresoever there be an altar; and that instead of the services hitherto used at such places, a service to me only shall be used, with the title the Red Mass to God Lopez, the Thrice Holy.

And thy God decrees, that at the mention of thy God, at His passing, at His coming, upon His feast days, as at the passing of His priests and in the presence of His decrees, all My people, without exception, shall cry, Blessed be God Lopez, and shall sign the mark of thy God, a circle and a dot, upon breast and head.

Lopez, Thrice Glorious, Thrice Blessed, Thrice Holy.

All who infringe This My Decree, in Thought or Word or Deed, shall suffer Death.

From My Heaven in Plaza Verde,

⊙ LOPEZ GOD LOPEZ. ⊙

"That," Don Inocencio said, "is our ruler's proclamation in this year of grace. What do you think of it?"

Rosa went to the paper to read some printing at the foot.

"It is genuine," she said. "It is printed at the palace press."

"I believe it to be genuine," Don Inocencio said.

Donna Emilia crossed herself for the third time: she spoke with some difficulty.

"Did you say, Inocencio, that you rejoice at this proclamation?"

"I do," he said, "sincerely, Emilia, I do. We have been for far too long apathetic: now this outrage will rouse us from sleep: it may be our salvation as a nation. We ourselves are in some measure responsible for this madness. We have connived at madness in the palace too long: he takes advantage of our supineness to seize us by the throats. Now there can be but one answer."

"Surely," Donna Emilia said, "a vengeance of Heaven will fall upon a man like that."

"Our Caligula will not long survive his decree," Don Inocencio said. "Our old days of the Blancos will begin again."

"What will people do?" Hi asked.

"They will do much," Don Inocencio said. "For a beginning, the priests are already leading their young men to tear down these placards. In the

New Town, a priest known to me was gathering the fraternity of his parish as I passed by on my way here. The week will see Don Lopez out of his palace."

"I wonder," Rosa said.

"Wonder what, dear?" her mother asked.

"Whether this follows on what Chacon told me half an hour ago. The Hinestrosa creature escaped in some way. The Reds must know by this time that the Whites are planning something. This is their counter-stroke."

"Let us at least be thankful that General Chavez must be in the city by this time."

"I think he must be," Don Inocencio said. "Perhaps it is too early for General Chavez to be here, or indeed to be already on his way, but preparing to be on his way, that, yes, we might declare with confidence. Undoubtedly, he is preparing to be on his way, to, how shall we put it? to draw the sword of outraged religion."

"Thank God that we may think that," Donna Emilia said. "We know, that however indolent Luis may be, he is great enough to overcome his indolence when his country calls."

"I don't think so, mother," Rosa said. "I don't think he is. His country has called ever since the last election. What has he done? He has been at home distilling liqueurs and trying to grow Pommard grapes."

"And why not?" Don Inocencio said. "Thus the great Roman patriots were employed when their country cried to them. They were on their farms, pruning their vines, or 'binding faggots,' as I think Horace puts it, 'at the bidding of a Sabine grandmother.' But when their country called, they arose; exchanging, as someone says, the service of the rustic god, whose name I forget, for that of Mars. Besides, Luis Chavez is a soldier. He needs the opportunities of the soldier, attack or defence, rather than those of the debater and intriguer."

"I do not think that he is a soldier any more than he is a statesman," Rosa said. "He is a self-indulgent, indolent country gentleman, who loves his garden and his book."

"I have known Luis Chavez for a great many years, Rosa," her mother said. "You are not just to him. He is a good man. If he be not hasty, it is because he is wise. He weighs situations before he decides. He asks God's direction before he acts. I think that we ought all now to pray that he may be directed to act wisely now."

"Before we do that, mother," Rosa said, "we really ought to send into the town for Carlotta. She has not yet returned. There is a good deal of noise in the town; listen to that. There may be rioting or shooting."

"Let me go," Hi said.

"I thought I heard the horses," Donna Emilia said.

"There are no horses."

"There is a noise though," Hi said. "There is shouting. Someone is shouting and coming along the road."

Rosa was sitting beside Hi. She clutched his arm as though she wished to crush it. He felt her tremble or thrill like a taut guy suddenly stricken.

"Hi," she whispered, "is it rioters in the road, mobbing her?"

"No, no," Hi said, "it sounds like a man crying news."

"Listen," Don Inocencio said.

"It is only one voice," Hi said.

"Yes, it is only one voice."

"Have you town-criers here?" Hi asked.

"It is a newspaper seller crying some special edition," Don Inocencio said. Pablo, the major domo appeared, with maté for Don Inocencio.

"Pablo, is this shouter in the road a newspaper seller?" Donna Emilia asked.

"Yes, Señora. He announces some murder."

"Cause Felipe to procure a copy of the paper for me, will you, Pablo?" Don Inocencio asked.

"I will, Señor."

When Pablo had gone, Don Inocencio rose, with a look of great importance.

"It is quite clear to me," he said. "Judgment has overtaken the blasphemer already. Some deliverer has stricken Lopez in the moment of his blasphemy. I knew that our nation did but sleep."

"I trust that no such thing as that has happened," Donna Emilia said. "Of all the terrible things, to be flung suddenly into death is the most terrible; and for one to die in the very utterance of blasphemy is what no enemy could wish."

"One cannot think of him as a blasphemer, mother," Rosa said, "but as a poor madman. And if some other poor madman has mak'd him siccar, I don't think one should examine the ways of Providence too critically."

"It would be like the slaying of the Philistine," Don Inocencio said. "Another David has arisen."

"Carlotta has not returned, mother," Rosa said. "I think Felipe ought to go to enquire what is happening."

"May I go?" Hi asked.

"She has Manuel with her," Donna Emilia said. "It may well be that the trains are stopped. In these crises they often put embargo on the trains. Manuel will have taken her to her brother's at Medinas."

"Well, won't you let me go, to make sure for you?" Hi asked.

Pablo entered with the newspaper, which he gave to Don Inocencio. Hi noticed that Pablo looked much shaken and that he said something in a very low voice as he gave the paper. Plainly something terrible had happened. Don Inocencio opened the paper, with a trembling pair of hands; he looked suddenly deflated. Pablo left the room softly closing the door. Don Inocencio turned very white, sat down hurriedly and dropped the paper.

"What is it, Inocencio?" Emilia said.

"Not Carlotta?"

"No, no, no, no," Inocencio said. "Chavez. General Chavez has been murdered."

"My God. Luis? But how?"

"It tells little. 'We grieve to announce the terrible news, that General Luis Chavez was assassinated by a ruffian, at the station of Aguas Dulces, at half-past two this afternoon, while waiting for the train to Santa Barbara, where he was expected to speak in Congress to-night. The murderer has been arrested.'"

"My God."

"And where is Carlotta?" Rosa cried. "She is in the city all this while. Is she, too, in the hands of the Red murderers?"

"God in Heaven forbid, child."

"There are her horses," Hi said. "That is the jingle of their silver; they are almost at the door."

"Let us come down, then, to meet her."

They found her chaise and horses at the door: Carlotta was not there.

"Were you in time for the Meruel train?" Donna Emilia asked the driver.

"Yes, Señora, in good time," the man said. "Afterwards, the train being gone, on hearing of rumours, the Señorita drove to Medinas, whence she sends this letter."

"Thank you," Donna Emilia said. "You had better stable your horses, then." As the man drove to the stables. Donna Emilia opened the letter, and dropped the envelope, which Hi picked up (and kept). "She has gone to Miguel's," Donna Emilia said. "Miguel is her brother, Highworth. Miguel thinks she had better stay there for the present."

"Wisely decided," Don Inocencio said. "And I will now take my leave, since I must go to the Circle, to see Hermengildo before the House to-night. Let me drive you, Mr. Ridden, since I pass your hotel."

While they waited in the drive for the caleche a party of Pitubas, under a negro who wore a green feather in his hat, rode up to them. He saluted Rosa, and presented a warrant. Rosa read it, called Pablo, and gave him some directions. Pablo led the troops to the stables, from which they removed all the horses, including Carlotta's team. The Senator's horse, being old, they left. When they had secured these horses, they rode off with them to another White house further down the bay.

"They're taking the horses," Rosa explained. "They always begin by taking our horses. That's the first danger sign."

"But good heaven," Hi said. "Why?"

" 'Military reasons,' they say in their warrant; but they really mean, so that the Whites shall not communicate with each other."

"Will you get them back?"

"No, probably not. You see, they've only gone to the White house down the bay; not to those two Red houses. This may make you understand our local politics a little. It shows you Santa Barbara as she is. It isn't the Paradise it looks, is it?"

"It's got angels in it," he said.

"Hi," she said, "I'm so anxious about her."

"She is safe at her brother's, surely?"

"She ought not to have gone there."

"Why ever not?"

"I don't know, but she ought not. I knew it when I saw the chaise had not brought her. She has done the wrong thing."

"I will take a note to her if you like," Hi said, "and bring her back here, too, if she wishes."

"She won't come back here," Rosa said. "Nor could she, after dark, with these patrols in the streets; but if you will take a letter for me, I shall be grateful. The de Leyvas live outside the West Gate, off the Anselmo Road, in a part called Medinas."

"Medinas Close is where my old murderer lives," Hi said.

"There are fearful rookeries close to the palace," Rosa said. "They are all owned by the de Leyvas."

She wrote a letter, which she gave to Hi to take.

"If she wants to send any message," Hi said, "of course, I will bring it back at once."

"Hi," she said, "you really are a dear." She caught him by the neck and kissed his forehead.

"Somewhat rougey," Hi thought, as he mopped his brow, while he drove with Don Inocencio. "But an awfully good-hearted sort, Rosa."

The drive to the hotel was interesting; Hi had never before seen a city in a state of excitement. The newsboys were crying special editions; parties of men and boys were marching to drums and fifes under Red banners; certain shops, which did not display Red colours, were having their windows broken. On the water-front a guardia warned Don Inocencio and his driver that the Martial Law was proclaimed, and that all carriages were to be off the streets by eight o'clock. "Bad, bad," Don Inocencio muttered. "I know not which of us will escape such nets." He left Hi at his hotel.

Here Hi found two envelopes waiting for him. The first contained a printed card from Roger Weycock, asking him to attend a special meeting of the English in Santa Barbara, at the Club, at seven o'clock that evening; the second contained a similar card, with a few words written in pencil by Allan Winter: "Don't go to this. Keep clear of politics here.—A. W." The cards had been hurriedly printed, probably as soon as the proclamation had appeared, the ink on them was still moist.

"Winter was right," Hi thought. "Weycock is in with the Reds, trying to turn English opinion that way, He's organising this meeting for that end. But Winter's right; we ought to keep clear of politics here; I won't go. But all the same, I am jolly well a White in this business, and I'll help the Whites all I can. By George, I suppose those devils, the Reds, could arrest me for carrying letters."

The sun was setting when he drove off in a caleche for the de Leyva house at Medinas. On his way, he saw scenes between parties of Reds and Whites which made him wonder at the strength of the feelings between them. "Killing Chavez and claiming to be God did not rouse this," he thought. "This hate has been simmering for years; this is only the boiling over."

At the West Gate, a Red patrol was stopping the traffic for examination before permitting it to pass; its officer turned back a carriage which had been trundling in front of Hi for some minutes. He then came forward to question Hi, found that he was English and allowed him to proceed. He did this, as Hi thought, grudgingly, in a way which made him wonder, whether the English were as much loved as his father had always said.

Beyond the gate, the Anselmo road was a narrow street from which narrow courts opened. Street and courts swarmed with people, all talking at the tops of their voices, but above all the talking the harsh bellow of public orators in praise of violence sounded. The place stank of mice, sweat, fried fish and damp washing. Hi called to the driver: "Is this Medinas?"

"Medinas, si," the driver said.

Little boys clambered on to the caleche, asking for "Frencha penny. Ingles penny." A fat, pale-faced young man hopped on to the step and poised there while he made his proposals.

"You want to see the sights?" he said. "I be your guide. I show you very funny sights. I show you not the usual sort of thing. You like a nice cock-fight, no? You like a quail-fight, no? See now, I take you to a special thing, not many knows about, a good dog-fight. There now, only three dollar. Well, I take you to a special thing to-night; something you never see, perhaps ever again. No? Well, you go to dam prayer-meeting, see? dam prayer-meeting."

He swung off to seek for a client elsewhere. The caleche passed from the narrows into a broader space, went under an old archway of withering red and yellow plaster and came out into an avenue of palms lit by electric light. Turning from this through an ilex grove it stopped at the de Leyva palace.

Hi was admitted into a great cool hall built of white Otorin marble. All round it and against its columns were the stands of the de Leyva armour, some of which had marched in the Conquest. Carlotta joined him almost at once; he gave her the letter.

"I thought that perhaps you would bring a letter," she said. "I suppose Rosa wants me to go back to her? My brother is against that."

"I hope," Hi said, "I do hope that Don Manuel will not be attacked by these Reds."

"He is far away by this time."

Hi felt that he had said a tactless thing, even to suggest that Don Manuel might be attacked, so he added:

"I should pity the man who attacked Don Manuel."

"It is nice of you to say that, Hi," she said.

"Did he see the proclamation, or hear of the murder, before he started?" Hi asked.

"No. Rosa tells me that his captive, the Hinestrosa, has been rescued."

"Yes."

"What do you think of my country?"

"It's produced you and Don Manuel and Donna Emilia," he said. "I think it's a marvellous country."

"It may be marvellous, if it turn now."

"It will turn," he said. "No nation will stand that proclamation."

"If a nation be only mad enough, it will stand anything," she said.

"I hope," Hi said, "that Don Manuel will find his mother better, when he gets there."

"I fear that there is little hope of that," she said. "A telegram came here . . . he can hardly see his mother alive again."

"I am sorry to hear that."

"Others are not so sorry," she said, in a strange voice. He looked at her with a rush of understanding that she was standing alone, through her love of Don Manuel.

"Oh, but they must be," he said.

"Sorry?" she said. "Alas, they are thanking God that my lover is out of the way at this time. You do not know the Whites: how broken we are into cliques. My brother, a great man in so many ways, dreads and hates my lover: he thinks him too dangerous: he wants Bazan to lead the party. If Manuel were here now, Bazan would not stand for five minutes. Then, I suppose, my brother would challenge Manuel to a duel. So, if I bring Manuel back, I break with all I have loved in the past."

"But you will bring him back," Hi said.

She looked at him in a way which he never forgot; but she did not answer.

"Let me go and bring him back for you," Hi pleaded. "Of course, I'm only a boy, but I'll go like a shot. I'll take any message you like. Do let me. I'll never be anything again all my life, probably, except just a planter. But just this once let me ride for you. I only saw you for the first time this morning; but you don't know what you are to me . . . in my life, I mean . . . you I mean, just there being such a person. Of course, you're sick of men saying this to you. Miss de Leyva, will you let me go?"

"Carlotta will not let you go," she said, "I'm sure Miss de Leyva won't. But I cannot bring Manuel here, against my brother's prayers, even if I would, from his mother's death-bed. But there is one thing which I wish you would do for me: take a note from me to Rosa."

"Of course, I'll gladly take a note," he said, "and bring back an answer."

"There will be no answer. You will just have time to leave the note and get back to your hotel before the streets are cleared."

While she wrote the note, Hi thought of a suggestion.

"I say," he said. "Quite apart from calling Don Manuel here, there is some point in letting him know the news and telling him not to come. Couldn't you let me do that for you?"

"You're very determined, Hi," she said. "But you must stay in Santa Barbara and keep out of our politics."

"But why? You will have to send someone."

"I will not send you, Hi."

"Why not? Have you anybody better?"

"There could not be anybody better, nor as good; but this is not a thing I could let you attempt. Do you know, that if the Reds were to find you doing this you might be expelled the country, or even shot."

"For taking a message?"

"That counts as spying in time of war."

"Who would know that I was taking a message? I should just be an English tourist. That settles it. I'll go off and get a horse and start at once and find him and tell him."

"No, no," she said. "It is impossible."

"Because I'm a boy and don't know Spanish?"

"No, no, indeed," she said, "but because we want you to settle here. Become a citizen later, if you wish, but, until then, you must avoid our troubles. Now here is my note to Rosa, if you will deliver it."

It was very dim in the hall away from the tapers on the writing table. There were amphoræ full of sweet-smelling shrubs. He could see her face and hands against the darkness of the leaves: her head seemed crowned by white flowers. She switched on some lights so that the hall seemed suddenly full of armed men.

"Will you give me a sprig of those flowers?" he asked.

"Willingly." She broke a spray for him.

"What is the flower?"

"Hermosita."

"May I ever see you again?"

"Of course. Come to-morrow to lunch: you must meet my brother."

"Oh, thank you. I'll bring back an answer from Rosa, if she sends one. Anything that I can ever do for you will always be absolute happiness; you know that, don't you?"

"Thank you, Hi."

She gave him her hand, in the foreign fashion, to kiss: he was grateful for this. A clock chimed for half-past seven. "You must go," she said, "you haven't much time."

His caleche jolted him back through Medinas, which was now lit for the night from its many windows. He saw it as a darting of children and a slinking of men, amid a noise of babies squalling, men singing and women screaming. A gas-lamp at a corner of a lane lit the words on a wooden direction post, To Medinas Close; he could just see a lit space surrounded by decaying old black houses, seven or nine storeys high. "So that is where 'Zeke lives," he thought. "I'll go to see the old man as I come back to-morrow."

There was delay in getting through the gates, in spite of his pleading that he was English. He delivered his letter to Rosa, learned that there was to be no answer, and then drove off (his driver in a hurry) to reach the hotel before eight o'clock. On coming to the gate on his way back, he had some trouble with the guard. Unfortunately it was not the guard which had passed him through ten minutes before. The sergeant of this guard was a mulatto (with an Irish accent), who was very rude and smelt of aniseed.

"You damned English," he said. "What's stopping ye staying in your homes? I suppose ye're ate up by your lice, and think ye can scrape them off on us. Well, get through and be damned to ye and obey the proclamation another time."

The hotel people opened their doors grudgingly to him. They gave him a tasteless supper in the ill-lit, frowsy dining-room, from which all the life had gone; everybody seemed to have gone to bed. He hurried through the meal and then went up to his bedroom.

Here, in bed, he went over the events of the day with a great deal of relish.

"I have had a day," he thought. "I have never enjoyed a day so much. She is beautiful, she is marvellous, and to-morrow I shall see her again. Oh, my God, she is beautiful."

He kept repeating this as he thought of her image with praise and blessing: he could not sleep at first because of her. At a little before midnight some rifles were fired in the streets.

"By George, rifles," he thought. "I say, this is the heart of life." The firing, whatever it was, stopped after a couple of minutes. In the quiet which followed, perhaps not long after twelve, he fell asleep.

CHAPTER VI

When he had slept for nearly a watch, he was wakened by a ticking as though the wind were shaking a slat in a Venetian blind. As the noise continued, he sat up, thinking, "Here is the breeze. I'll have to shut my window."

He realised, then, that the noise was from the door. It was a little light ticking noise, not unlike the gnawing of a mouse, except that it never varied nor grated.

"It's only a death-watch," he said. "No, it's the breeze, rattling the door. I'll jam it up with a piece of paper." He turned out of bed and groped in the dark for the cover of his paper-backed novel. "I'll wedge it up with this," he thought. He tore off the cover and folded it into a wedge.

"By George," he thought, suddenly, with a leaping heart. "It isn't the door rattling, it's somebody knocking."

It was no doubt somebody knocking, but with a special secret midnight knock which might awaken him but alarm no other person on the corridor.

"By George," he thought, "somebody's tapping with finger-nails. This is romance, by George. I'll have to be jolly careful now, or very likely I'll have my throat cut. Who can be knocking?"

He could not think who would be knocking, but he did not for one moment think that it was a woman come for love of him. He was not frightened. The knocking was of a piece with the romance of the day before. It gave him a thrill of delight to think that the knocker might be in peril and the knock a warning to himself.

"Why not?" he thought. "I'm a foreigner here, as well as a heretic. Why shouldn't there be a sort of Bartholomew massacre beginning?"

He crept to the door. The key was in the keyhole; he could see nothing there but darkness. By the fanlight, he could tell that the corridor beyond was almost pitch dark. The knocker paused, as though he had heard the creak of his approach.

"Who is there?" Hi whispered. "Who is there?"

To his amazement, Rosa answered him.

"It is I, Rosa. Rosa Piranha. Open, Hi; open quick."

He opened the door swiftly yet silently; Rosa glided in.

"It's only me, Hi," she whispered. "I thought I'd never make you hear. Lock the door, lock it, but don't make a sound. Oh, my God, my God."

"I'll strike a light," he said. "Whatever is the matter? I'll have a light in a minute."

"No light," she said. "Don't strike a light. We might be seen from outside."

"I must get you a light," he whispered, "or you'll be falling over things, and rousing the house."

He struck a match: he had a glimpse of Rosa dressed as a peon with a sombrero jammed over her eyes.

"I'll sit on the bed," she whispered. "Put the match out, Hi."

He put out the match; she sat on the bed and began to shudder till the bed quaked. As he did not know what to do, he did nothing. He stood well away from Rosa, waiting for her to speak.

"Good old Rosa," he said at last.

"Yes, good old Rosa," she said with a giggle; then she trembled until she began to sob.

"Good Lord, Rosa," he said, "pull yourself together. Good Lord, what is it? What has happened?"

"Those devils, Hi. They've got Carlotta."

"What devils? The Pitubas?"

"Yes. At least, I don't know if they were Pitubas. Anyhow the Reds have got her."

"But I saw her after seven o'clock."

"They arrested her at ten. They got her brother, too. They're rounding up all the Whites. A peon of the de Leyvas came to us to tell us. They shot at him, but he got away. Hi, they've put her into prison. The Reds have put Carlotta into prison."

"Good Lord. But, hang it, Rosa, they've got no case against her. They'll certainly let her out in the morning."

"But Lopez has gone mad, Hi. We don't know what is happening."

"But... good Lord. It's four o'clock in the morning; more. How on earth did you get in? Look here, is there anything that I can do?"

"They've got her in their prison on a charge of resisting authority, or being deemed to be the associate of those planning to resist authority. The peon heard her deny the first charge. The officer said that he should arrest her on the other. And they may shoot her, Hi."

"Shoot Carlotta? Never."

"They may."

"Oh, hang it, Rosa."

"This isn't England, Hi, but a place where we hate; you don't know how we hate. Mother cannot stand these shocks, but I had to wake her and tell her. She said at once, 'We must get word through to Manuel.'"

Here she stopped at a horrible memory.

"Go ahead," Hi said.

"This isn't like England, Hi," she said. "Twice, even in my life-time, Whites and Reds have made it dangerous for each other. So we make arrangements and codes for messages. We had one of our boys, Estevan Osmeña, sworn to take a message in case of need. We roused him up. Our horses were gone, as you saw; the horses are always the first thing they take, but we sent him off to where he could get a horse. I thought nobody saw him go."

Here she stopped to tremble till the bed seemed to giggle at her.

"Go on," Hi said, "cheer up and go on."

"About two hours ago," she said, "when we had all gone back to bed, a patrol rode up to the house and summoned mother to open the door. I said that she was too ill, but that I would open. So I lit up and opened. There was the mulatto, Zarzas, with some Pitubas. He said, 'This is for you.' He gave me Estevan's hand, cut off at the wrist, with mother's letter pinned to it. He said, 'This is the Dead Letter Post; the White letter comes back Red. I would recommend you send no more.'

"Then I had to serve him and his men with drinks, of course; he called it 'postage for midnight delivery.'"

"Then they had killed your groom?"

"Yes."

"I say," Hi said. "But hold on a minute, I'll just dress, if you'll excuse me. But tell me, how did you pass the patrols and the gates?"

"Market people can always pass in the early mornings. I brought in a basket of flowers like a gardener's peon. You remember Manuel said at lunch that there was a way into this hotel at the back. I came in by that. I knew your floor and room. But I nearly died of terror when I heard the negroes at their gambling."

"I don't wonder. But I say you have got some pluck."

"Oh, Hi, forgive me," she said, "but you're the only person I can think of. Will you take the news to Manuel?"

"Why, of course I will, Rosa. I wanted to last night but Carlotta wouldn't let me. I'll go like a shot."

She fell upon her knees and kissed his hands, calling upon God and the saints to bless him.

"That's all right, Rosa," he said. "That's all right. We'll save her."

"This devil, Lopez, is going to wipe out the Whites," she said.

"Not he," Hi said. "Don't you think it, Rosa."

"What is to stop him? We're all in his power."

"Not you," Hi said. "He's done something wicked and stupid, which won't prosper; you'll see it won't. Now about getting to Manuel. I don't know a word of Spanish, except Dios and si and the oaths those sailors told me. Where can I get a horse, to begin with? I suppose all the livery stables will be closed?"

"You'll get no horse here."

"Even though I'm English?"

"No. This city is isolated. No trains, no horses. You'll have to walk to a place called Anselmo, about fifteen miles from here."

"You mean, out past the de Leyvas' place? That Anselmo?"

"Yes. There are two White brothers there, the Elenas, George and William, horse-breeders. They will give you horses and put you in the way to get relays further west. There are two ways of getting to Anselmo; one, by the road, past the de Leyvas' place, which you'd have to walk; the other is, to take a boat down the bay, nine or ten miles, to the place La Boca, where you could probably hire a horse or trap and ride or drive there."

"How would I take a boat?"

"At the pier there are scores of market-boats. Ask for Pedro Ruiz and ask him to take you to La Boca. If Pedro isn't there, dozens of others will be; they're mostly Italians."

"I'll make them understand," Hi said. "Will they let me down the pier?"

"Yes, if you aren't stopped beforehand."

"The boat way seems the quicker," he said. "I'll try the boat way. But look here, Rosa, they'll surely watch the boats for people trying to get away."

"They may, but that and the road are the only ways to Anselmo."

"Well, we'd better try both. Why not send my old English murderer from Medinas? He'd go like a shot and you could trust him absolutely."

"That is an idea, Hi. I suppose he can ride?"

"He was a stable-lad in his youth. He was even a jockey once, of sorts, I think they said, but he was warned off for something or other. I know he sounds awful; so he is, as well as a little mad, but I know that you could trust him."

"You say that he is mad? Could he remember a message?"

"Yes."

"All he'll have to remember is, 'Reds have seized Carlotta: come at once'; that and the address, 'Don Manuel, Encinitas.' "

"He'll have to know more than that," Hi said. "He'll have to get the horses out of these Elena people, at Anselmo."

"Our code word, *Dorothea*, will do that."

"And suppose the Elenas aren't there?"

"George or William must be there."

"Right, then; between us we'll fix it. I say, this is exciting. You are a brick to come to me for this."

"If you knew what I think of you for taking it as you do."

"I suppose," Hi said, "I suppose there's no means of telegraphing from Anselmo to Don Manuel."

"None. We've no telegraphs here, except along the railways, and no railway at all across the central provinces. You'll have to ride."

"No means of telegraphing to anyone, in code, or something of that sort? It would save so much time."

"The telegraphs are all under censorship, no message would be sent. There's no telegraph within seventy miles of Encinitas, anyway."

"It'll be a long ride," Hi said. "I wish I were more in trim for a long ride. It will take three days."

"Oh, Hi."

"I might do it in two, with luck."

"Oh, if you only can," she said.

"Now how about you."

"I'll be all right."

"I'm blest if you will be. I'll see you home."

"Oh, Hi; no."

"Yes, I will."

"No, no, Hi. I shan't be stopped with my market basket and in this dress. And by the Farola there is a short cut through the waste to our garden."

"I'll see you there, then. I must. I've got to ask you scores of things which I must know. When you're reasonably safe, I'll get to Medinas, see my murderer off, and then come back to the pier and yell for Pedro Ruiz."

"Please God, the boats will be late this morning," she said.

"Why?"

"If they come early, they go early; there may be no boat for you."

"Golly."

"There's a lot to say 'Golly' about in this Republic."

"There's more in it than meets the eye," he said. "I suppose you've got no map of this city?"

"No. Why?"

"Can I get to Medinas from the pier without going back through the city?"

"Yes, easily. There's a road from the Farola to Medinas, on the line of the old city ditch."

"All right, then; that's a weight off my chest. Our main task is to get out of this hotel to the pier: if we can do that, we shall be fairly clear. Will there be patrols on the roads outside the walls, or people on the watch at La Boca and Anselmo?"

"Probably."

"All right," he said, to cheer her. "We'll fix them. I suppose the Elenas will know some English?"

"Not much; but if you say *Dorothea* to them, they'll make your next course clear, even if they have to send a guide with you."

"Good. I think I've got it all pretty straight. All right. I'm ready. We'll start, then. Oh, but wait one minute. I must get something out of my trunk."

Some hours before, when he had returned from Carlotta, he had pressed her spray of hermosita between two sheets of the hotel blotting-paper, which he had then laid away in the trunk. He now opened this precious packet, broke off a leaf from the spray, and placed it in his pocket-book; the rest he put back into the trunk. He then wrote a few words to the hotel proprietor.

"I'm ready now," he said. "I'll leave this note to say that I'm coming back, and want my room kept."

"Oh, Hi," she said, "I've brought no money."

"I have got money enough," Hi said, "but I have not got a revolver. Father wouldn't let me take one. I knew he knew nothing about it. Now we had better have a story in case we're stopped. We had better say that your mother wanted me and that you had come to fetch me. They couldn't object to that. Where is your market basket? In the cellar?"

"No, in the hall."

"We had better go out by the hall," he said. "And I had better take no baggage. Then they would ask no questions. If I were caught going out with a bag, they would think I was shooting the moon. I have got some handkerchiefs. That's enough."

"What will they think of my market basket?" she said. "They will think I have come to steal the linen."

"Leave it here," Hi said.

"But I must have it to pass the gates."

"Well, you can show that it's empty," he said. "We must chance it. Come on."

They crept out into the deserted corridor, where all was silent save for a snorer in one of the near-by rooms. They crept to the stairs. All seemed silent on the landing below. On the next floor they heard a child wake up with a whimper. The coarse voice of a nurse from one of the French-speaking islands called "Chocolat" to quiet it. As this failed she made a testy reproof and turned grunting out of bed.

All seemed silent on the floor below. Rosa touched Hi's arm at the stairs.

"There's a night porter asleep there," she said, "on that sofa on the landing."

"He's sound asleep," Hi said. "Come on."

On the third step from the bottom the porter had left a small tray with glasses and a soda-water bottle. Hi trod upon this, so that both he and it fell. The glasses broke, the soda-water bottle rolled on to the broad uncarpeted steps which led to the ground floor. It fell on to the first step, then on to the second, then on, step by step, making a noise like "Keblonk, Keblonk" at each step. Hi sat on the mat at the stair-foot in fits of laughter. Rosa stood beside him, giggling hysterically.

"Hark at the beastly thing going 'Keblonk,' " he said.

With a little tinkle the bottle rolled itself still. The porter on the sofa sneezed suddenly and sat up.

"Oh, for de Lord," he said.

"For de Lord," Hi said.

He and Rosa clutched each other, shaking with laughter.

"Oh, you lovely angels, keep away the flies," said the porter and settled himself to sleep again.

"Come along," Hi whispered. "He's asleep. We must slide down the banisters of this flight. Don't kick old Keblonk as you pass."

All was dark on the ground floor, but far away some servant was already sweeping. This was the only sound save the occasional crackle in the wicker chairs, as though some ghost had sat down or arisen. In front of them was the main entrance of the hotel, a glass barrier, broad steps with deserted offices at each side, then the front doors. A light was burning in the office to the left. Hi stole forward upon tip-toe.

"The night porter's asleep in the office," he whispered.

He stole through the glass doors and tried the front doors, which were locked and the key not there.

"The key's gone," he whispered.

"It's in the office, I expect," she said.

He looked, but could not see it on the key hooks nor on the table.

"It must be somewhere here," she said.

"I expect he's got it in his pocket," he whispered.

There came a little flop upon the floor. Rosa had knocked off a timetable from the edge of the table. The man stirred in his sleep but did not wake.

"If he's got it in his trouser pocket," Hi whispered, "or even in his side pocket, we're done."

"Well, Hi," she whispered, "come on down the back way through the cellar. Besides, I have got to get my flower basket."

"Oh, dash, I had forgotten the flower basket."

"Hi," Rosa said, "there's someone coming."

They edged out into the hall as some of the hall lights went up. A woman with a broom came along the corridor. She took a good look at them, and Hi said, "It's all right, thanks. I'm English."

She seemed to think that it was not quite all right. She made a gesture to show Hi that he could rouse the porter.

"Si, si," Hi said, "but it's absolutely all right, thanks."

"Are you looking for the key?" she asked in English. "The key is here on this palm."

She unhooked a key from one of the stubs of the palm tree, fitted it to the lock and opened the door. She gave a searching glance at Rosa. She closed the door behind them on the instant.

The breeze was coming in from the sea bitterly cold. They looked up and down the deserted street. They saw no sign of life except a cat on the other side of the road.

"Come on," Hi said, "down to the water-front."

In the darkness of the cross roads a mounted policeman, drawn into the shadows, watched them approach without making a sign. When they were within a few yards of him he put his horse suddenly across their path.

"It's all right. I'm English," Hi said.

The man seemed to have orders not to molest foreigners. He drew his horse back and jerked with his hand for them to pass. Perhaps it was a guilty conscience which made them think that he stared hard at Rosa. Anyhow he let them pass.

On the water-front the tide of life had begun to flow to the quays. Men and women were going to work that had to be done, whatever rebellion came. They saw the bright light at the pier end.

"It's there," Rosa whispered, "that the market-boats come."

Two men who were slouching in front of them paused to light cigarettes. They watched Hi and Rosa as they passed and made remarks evidently very offensive, which made Rosa catch her breath.

"Come on. Don't stop," Rosa whispered.

Colour was all over the eastern heaven and touching the upper roofs and spires.

"Hi," Rosa said, when they had gone a little distance, "we shall never be able to do it. I am seen to be a woman and there is a patrol in the streets stopping people."

"Where?"

"There in front."

About a hundred yards in front of them there was an interruption in the flow of people. They could see the gleam of helmets beyond the blackness of the crowd, which grew greater as men and women flocked up to it. Plainly the police or troops were examining all who were going that way.

"Hi," Rosa said, "I can't face the police in this dress. It's very silly, but I shall faint."

"Hold up," Hi said. "It will be perfectly all right. We will get down to that barge on the beach there and you can pin your cloak round you for a skirt."

Within a stone's throw from the water-front was a green barge, which Hi had noticed on the day of his landing. She was lying on her bilge with the butts of her timbers sticking out like bones. In the shelter of this wreck Rosa pinned her cloak as a skirt and made her hat look less manly. After this they marched into the crowd, which closed up behind them as others arrived. It was a silent crowd of men and women not fully awake. One or two voices asked, "What are they stopping us for?" Some said, "Dogana," or "Search of suspects," or "Search of the accursed Whites, the murderers."

The light grew upon the faces at each instant, the crowd gathered and the delay continued.

"What are they stopping us for?"

"Close up, brothers."

"Who are you shoving?"

"It's not me that's shoving."

"This way for the harem. Get your money ready."

"The whistle will be gone. We shall be fined half a peseta."

"What are they stopping us for?"

No one could answer that question.

Hi could make out that several times a minute one or two people in front were allowed to pass on. At every such passing the crowd surged forward till they were all jammed up together, feeling breathless and inclined to faint. They could hear a kind of catechism going on at the barrier, voices bullying and voices submissive.

"Why can't they let us pass? What are they asking?"

The crowd was not to know why they were stopped. After they had annoyed some hundreds of people with it, the police suddenly removed the barrier and told the people that they might get along out of it. The crowd slowly surged forward among growls of "Keeping us waiting all this time and in the end they didn't want us. Now we shall be fined a peseta for being late."

They passed through the city gates, to the open space where the market folk had cheered the Piranhas the day before.

"There is the pier, Hi," Rosa said. "I can get home through that waste piece, the old graveyard. You go up that gully to the right, to Medinas."

"All right. Good luck. I'll fetch Manuel."

"God bless you, Hi."

"You, too. My love to your mother. And good luck. And cheer up."

She nodded, not having more words; she turned out of the stream of workers into the old graveyard of the town and did not look back.

As Hi set off for Medinas, he looked back several times after her, till she had disappeared.

"She's got some pluck," he thought. "I don't think she'll be stopped now, going that way."

His own way led through a road which having once been the city ditch, was still a city dump and refuse pit under the walls. On the left hand of the refuse were shacks and sties of wood, for pigs, cows, horses and fowls; though men lived in them, too. The road was an unpaven track in a kind of gulley between the dump and the sheds. It was in a mucky state at that time from the recent rains and the habits of the market people. It stank, it was littered with tins and stalks, rats were rummaging among the garbage, and pariah dogs with the mange were scraping against the sides of the sties. However, no men were abroad in it nor any sign of a patrol. In about twelve minutes he was in Medinas.

For some minutes he had noticed a glow upon the city buildings, which he had thought to be the dawn. He now found that it came from the red-hot shell of what had been the de Leyva palace, which had been burnt since midnight. A good many Medinas people were grubbing in the embers for what they could find. Others were carrying away what they had already found. A heap of things of all sorts, armour, pictures, marbles, bronzes, furniture, porcelain, curtains, clothes, cushions, musical instruments, antiques, books, and portfolios, which had been looted before the fire took hold, were being sold to all comers by a ruffian with a big voice, who bellowed aloud his bargains, joked, tossed the money received to a guard of Reds, and often gave away what he could not readily sell. He was in the act of selling a bronze female torso when Hi came up. Hi noticed among the crowd the broad-faced picture-dealer who had been rude two days before on the water-front. This man winked at the auctioneer that the bronze should be set aside for him. The auctioneer stopped his obscene remarks and laid it aside.

Medinas Close looked marvellous in that light of nearly dawn, helped out by dying lamps. Its well of tall, mean, narrow tenements, built on a slope, about a triangle of grassless earth, needed some murderous half-light to give it its quality. At the entrance to the Close an imbecile woman, with the face of a corpse, held her hand for alms. At the entrance of No. 41, black as the mouth of a cave, two little boys, who talked through their noses as though their throats were rotted away, were sharing what they had stolen from the burning. Most of the Medinas tenants had been picking plums from that same snapdragon. In the well of the Close were some chairs and other furniture which had been pitched down and smashed, because they would not readily go through the narrow doors.

"On the third floor," Hi said to himself, "the middle room of the three, if I don't have my throat cut on the way." He went into that black cave, which stank of rat and mouse; he struck himself a light so that he might see the stairs, and came at once on a woman and a man clasped at the stair-foot. He saw the woman's eyes, like the eyes in a skull. The man detached himself from her; he stank of wine, she of musk. "You like to see my sister?" he said, thickly to Hi.

"No."

"Three pesetas."

"No."

"Two pesetas."

"No."

"You like to buy a nice watch, very cheap, very good?" The woman, who had caught some glimpse of Hi, said something in a low voice, which made the man stand aside to let Hi pass to the next floor, where a man was beating his wife in the intervals of a sermon. The morning light gleamed a little on to this landing from a room which had no door. Up above was the third floor, much darker, being lit only with a taper.

Some weeks before this a man had been murdered at the head of the stairs there. The dwellers of 41, having scruples about the murder, had placed upon the wall a coloured print of the Virgin, to whom they lit a taper each night. This taper now showed Hi the three doors of the landing; he knocked gently on the middle door.

After knocking a second time, he was aware of a tenseness in the room within, though no one answered. At a third knock, he felt, rather than heard, other doors in the tenement softly opened, while unseen eyes took stock of him. Someone inside the room was moving something: "putting something under the bed," he thought. A board dropped with a clatter, then a chair (so it seemed) was jammed against the door from within, then a woman's cautious voice asked, "Who is it?"

"Señor Rust," Hi said, in a low voice, "Señor Rust."

She did not let him in. He heard her moving about inside, with queer little clicking noises as though she were snapping on some pairs of stays (which indeed she was).

"Señor Rust," he repeated, "Señor Rust."

The lamp in the room, which had been turned down, now turned up; the door opened a little; a short, sharp, elderly dwarf of a woman stared at him, and motioned him to come in. He went into a hot little lamp-lit room, where 'Zeke stood stock still, fumbling with his hat, beside the bed. The woman bolted the door carefully behind him. She had a skin like parchment, coloured like old ivory. She looked at him out of sharp, black, beady eyes which missed nothing. Her head trembled a little; her long green ear-rings waggled and clicked. She looked like a gimlet about to pierce. Hi knew, without any telling, that he had come at a ticklish time, when the two were appraising loot from the burning. His knock had been mistaken for the knock of the police. Something had been stuffed under the floor and a mat drawn over the place: 'Zeke was now standing on the mat.

The woman asked him in Spanish about his health, adding that for her own part she asked nothing better from God, since she was ever better after the rains, which, as it was well known, drew away from the air we breathe many most pestilential vapours. Hi replied in English that he was afraid that he came at a very inconvenient time.

"Rust," he said, "could you take a message for me, and be away, perhaps, for some days?"

"Yes, Master Highworth," 'Zeke said, "I daresay."

"Starting at once?"

"Where would it be to, Master Highworth?"

"Could we speak out of doors somewhere?"

"It's a bit unsettled out of doors, sir. We could slip into the church for a bit."

"Let us go there, then."

'Zeke said something with gestures to Isabella, who seemed suspicious and not well pleased. She questioned 'Zeke several times before she let them out. She then followed him to the stair-head with questions, which 'Zeke put from him with gestures and ejaculations. She was not satisfied with these replies, because she went back to the room, growling. Glancing upwards as he entered the Close, Hi saw her head and shoulders craned from the window to see where they were going.

In the almost complete darkness of the church, Hi told 'Zeke what was wanted.

"I been to 'Carnacion," he said. "It was there I went with my bull, where the rabbits were. It was this Don Manuel owned my bull; only I didn't go so much by land, as by sea, to Port 'Toche. I know the way to Anselmo; it's by the Foxes Inn. And I know the Mr. Elenas at Anselmo, Mr. George and Mr. William, only they don't pronounce it like that. They breed horses, the Mr. Elenas.

"I did a job of work for the Misters Elenas one time. You see, Mr. Highworth, they got a stallion one time; my word, he were a horse, only he wasn't what we would call a stallion, you understand, being for draught. Not a shire horse, neither, but one of they French sort, really. 'Whicker,' he went, and 'Whicker,' he went, oh, it was a treat to hear him: down he would go and up he come; and all in play, really: only he hate his grooms, Mr. Highworth, one after the other. It was all in play, really, only they didn't understand him, that was what it was, really. You know he couldn't abide velvet, this velvet stuff the grooms wear. You've heard of the red rag to a bull? Well, it was the same with him, only velvet. That was all it was. When I showed 'em, they left off this velvet, then he didn't eat them, except, maybe, now and then a pinch and that. And is that all I'm to say to the Misters Elenas and to Mr. Manuel, just *Dorothea,* and he's to come at once?"

"Yes, that's all. How soon could you reach Anselmo?"

"Three hours and that. But I'll get a horse out along the road, maybe."

"It's a long way to Encarnacion," Hi said.

"I like a bit of sport, when I get a horse like these country ones that's got meat on the ribs."

"You'll hurry all you can, won't you? People's lives depend on it."

"Dammy, Mr. Highworth, I'll go like your old grandfather, and like what the old gentleman, old Mr. Ridden done."

"Thank you."

"I suppose it's all right, Master Highworth?"

"Yes, it's all right."

"These foreigners aren't like us, most of the time. They got this devil-worship and all sorts. Now a man likes to know what's what and that. That's only fair. But it's these yellow devils makes them not go above board. They brought in the yellows to rule the whites; it's that causes all the trouble."

"That's the cause of the trouble."

"Well, I'll do my best, Mr. Highworth."

"Thank you. I can't thank you enough."

"Nothing I like better, really, than a bit of sport. I was having difficulty, if you understand me, Master Highworth; but then first I met you and now comes this other job. I never had so much luck at one time before, except that once at the races; and then I was cheated of it."

Hi gave him some money for expenses, thanked him and urged him to go.

"Not by the door we came in by, Mr. Highworth," he said. "That would never do. Them that see you go in may watch for you out."

They were near the High Altar as he spoke. The door by which they had entered the church was opened: someone crept into the church. Hi saw the snub-nosed profile of Isabella motionless for an instant, while she sought in the darkness for her prey. 'Zeke on the instant plucked him through a curtain to a swing-door and thence to a lane.

"We dodge the Close this way," he said, "and I'll be back in a week or a bit better. And that will be all right, Mr. Highworth; and I thank you, sir, I'm sure, very kindly. And I wish you a happy Christmas, sir, though I know it's a long time to wait."

He set off as he finished speaking, in the shambling run with much bending of the leg which old Bill Ridden called "the poachers' trot." Hi had often seen old men of the 'Zeke kind running in that way on winter mornings when the hounds moved off to covert. He himself set off at once by the old city ditch to the pier: it was almost full morning. He wondered whether there would be any boat for him.

He also wondered, with some misgivings, about poor old Ezekiel. The phrase, "He never had so much luck at one time before," smote him to the heart. It might not be much luck; it might be deadly; it certainly would be dangerous, to go off on this errand when the Reds were out. "I've taken him from his wife, too," he thought. "However, she's no chicken." As he went on, he wondered whether Isabella might not have seen, chased and caught her husband: in which case the message would not go. Or suppose the Foxes Inn proved too much for him? "I must chance all that," he thought. "He's as likely to get through as I am."

Thinking these things, he came out of the ditch into the colour and life of the racing of the carts to market from the Farola, with fish and fruit. These carts were light, open lorries, each drawn by two horses, driven by natives, who stood bare-armed, cloaked with coloured serapes, singeing their lips with the sucked stubs of cigarettes across which they cursed their horses. The workers scattered from before them as they raced. The horses' hooves struck fire, the drivers leaned on the reins, beat with their sticks, and screamed:—

"Ar-re. Ar-re, sons of malediction."

"Accursed be thy fool mare of a mother."

"Dog of a Pablo, give room."

"Ay, ay, ay, we bring fish into the city."

All the carts swayed into each other yet did not touch. They swerved together as the road narrowed for the gate and so disappeared. Hi turned from the open plaza on to the pier. It was then a few minutes after six o'clock.

CHAPTER VII

On the pier, Hi found a scene of confusion and shouting, men and boys staggering with boxes and baskets to carts; women urging them to hurry, or screaming at their children, or cursing at the mules and horses: carts were being backed and baskets dropped: everybody was violent and abusive, not from ill-temper but excitement, for this race to market was the event of the day.

Hi thrust into the midst of the crowd, treading on a litter of leaves, upon which the beasts had browsed. All that part of the pier was heaped with things for the market, bundles of living fowls tied five and five by the legs, baskets of pigeons, geese from the sea marsh, musk melons, water melons, pumpkins, gourds and vegetables of every sort and shape, oranges, limes, bananas in crates and gaily painted earthenware jars packed in the paper-like streamers of corn sheathes. Hi came upon an Englishman, who was superintending the lading of some big red clay jars into a lorry.

"Where shall I find the fish boats?" he asked.

"At the upper end of the pier," the man said. "That's where they auction the fish. You may find the fish boats gone by this, though."

At the end of the pier was a wooden building, above which was a pharos or pier light, which made a big, rosy star against the dawn. Underneath this light the fish market was being held. Hi heard a jabber and chatter of bargaining.

"Look you, I will tell you what I will do. I will do it for you, because I like you. I would not do it for anyone else on earth, may St. James be my witness. I will give you 3.75 the tierce."

"By God, I had rather fling them back into the sea. By God, I will fling them back into the sea. Here go some back into the sea. The rest shall follow. 4.30 the tierce or back they go."

"Now look here, I will tell you what I will do. I will do it for you because I like you. I wouldn't do it for anyone else on earth," etc., etc.

Beside the bidders lay heaps of fish, many of them still gasping. Small, black, slimy things, which looked like pickles, crawled over their bodies. The fish lay in heaps of shining paleness with odd jags of fins and prickles, vacuous eyes, and mouths which bulged out and then collapsed in.

Hi stopped a fisherman with the question:

"Are you Pedro Ruiz?"

"How?"

"Are you Pedro Ruiz?"

"Who knows?"

"Pedro Ruiz?"

"Ruiz?"

"Yes, Pedro Ruiz?"

"Not know," the man answered.

"Pedro Ruiz of La Boca?"

"How?"

"Of La Boca."

"Ayla Poca?"

"Yes. Si."

"Not know Ayla Poca."

"No; not Ayla Poca," Hi explained, "but of La Boca. Of, that is, de, La Boca, a place, a sort of a ciudad, sabe? in the bay par la; La Boca."

"I do not know at all," the man answered.

"What does the Englishman want?" another man asked.

"Pedro Ruiz of La Boca," Hi said.

"Ayla Poca?"

"No, not Ayla Poca. Of La Boca. De la Boca."

"Boca?"

"Yes. Si."

"La Boca?"

"Yes."

"Oh, La Boca?"

"Yes, yes. La Boca."

"The poblacion beside the bay, La Boca?"

"Yes, that is it."

"Oh, La Boca. Hear you, Enrique, the gentleman wants La Boca."

"Oh, La Boca. Ah, yes, indeed. Truly, it is that. Oh, yes, La Boca," Enrique repeated.

"It is there, La Boca," the man said, pointing south along the bay. "La Boca is there."

"I want Pedro Ruiz of La Boca."

"How?"

"Pedro Ruiz."

"Pedro?"

"Si. Yes. Pedro Ruiz," Hi said. "R-u-i-z." The men looked at him in bewilderment yet with courtesy. They smiled and shook their heads. Hi thanked them and turned from them. He did not much relish shouting aloud in that crowd of foreigners; but he shouted:

"Pedro Ruiz. Pedro Ruiz."

A couple of lads mimicked his method with some success. He repeated his cry.

"Ah, ha," Enrique said to him full of pride. "You want Pedro Ruiz?"

"Yes, si."

"Ah, yes, indeed, Pedro Ruiz."

"Is he here?" Hi asked.

"No," Enrique said.

Enrique began a long harangue in Spanish, of which Hi understood not one word. Hi could not make out from the gestures whether Pedro Ruiz had been disembowelled or had been drinking soda water.

"See you," he said, "can I get a boat to La Boca? A boat to La Boca by the sea?"

He made signs of going by boat in the direction of La Boca. Three other men had gathered about them to give counsel. Some of them suggested Giordano.

Hi turned to these men and asked, "Is Pedro Ruiz here? Pedro Ruiz?"

They did not understand what he meant. They repeated the syllables. All were courteous and eager to help, but they were puzzled by the words.

Enrique asked, "You want go La Boca?"

"Yes please, si," Hi answered.

"Giordano," the men repeated. "Giordano."

Hi had a suspicion that "Giordano" meant to-morrow. There was, he knew, some foreign word like "Giordano" which meant either yesterday or to-morrow. It was "oggi" or "aujourd'hui" or some other word with "jour" in it. What would he do if there were to be no boat till to-morrow?

"This way Giordano," Enrique said.

He led him to the end of the pier. Some birds were wheeling about the rosy light. From time to time they swerved down with exquisite white grace, which glowed into rose colour in the beam of the lamp, to snatch some fish from the pile. Enrique looked over the rail at the edge of the pier.

"Giordano," he called.

"Si," a voice answered.

Enrique explained that here was a gentleman eager to go to La Boca; he displayed Hi. Giordano was a very tall, thin, melancholy man, dark and distinguished.

"Can you take me to La Boca, please?" Hi asked.

"La Boca? Si."

"It is so," Enrique exclaimed. "Giordano can take you to La Boca."

"There," another man said. "Giordano will convey you."

Giordano spread a boat rug for Hi. When Hi was seated in the boat, he bent over a job of fitting two pieces of wood together. He explained what he was doing, but Hi could not understand. He sat in the boat, which bobbed and rocked at the side of the steps. Giordano went on with his work, whittling a piece of wood with his knife and trying if the pieces would fit, then whittling some more. Presently a boat shoved off from the pier beside them and stood away for La Boca. Then another boat pushed off and presently a third. But Giordano still went on with his carpentry with no apparent thought of starting. Hi thought that perhaps there had been some mistake.

"I say," he said, "you are going to La Boca, aren't you? You go La Boca?"

"Si," Giordano answered.

He went on trying to fit the pieces of wood. After some time, with a gesture of triumph, he showed that at last they fitted.

"Bueno," he said.

Yet even now he made no effort to start. He rummaged in the after locker and presently produced some nails, which were bent, and a hammer with a broken handle. Then he set himself to repair the hammer handle by lashing another piece of wood to it. Next he rummaged among the bottom boards of the boat for a pig of ballast. He placed this on the stern sheets thwart as an anvil. Then with great deliberation he began to straighten his nails. Time seemed to have no meaning for him.

"You go La Boca soon?" Hi asked. "La Boca pronto?"

"Si, si."

But he made no attempt to start. He hammered his nails straight with great skill, then very neatly he straightened the heads, which had been bent. Then he rummaged for a file and touched up the points with it. Another boat stood away from the pier towards La Boca. Her helmsman called out something to Giordano, which Giordano answered reflectively. After the boat had gone he fitted the two pieces of wood together and with great care drove his nails so as to clinch them.

"You start La Boca?" Hi asked.

"Si, si. La Boca."

"I believe the brute isn't going to La Boca at all," Hi thought. "There, they've put out the pier light now. I might have been at La Boca an hour ago. If there's another boat going, I would go in that."

He clambered up the stairs of the pier to look for someone who could speak English. The rush of the market was now over. He found Enrique and his friends in a corner among the baskets.

"I want to go at once, pronto, to La Boca," he said.

"Giordano go pronto," they said.

"But I want to go now."

"Si, si," they said, "La Boca."

"Yes, but now."

"Si, si."

He took off his hat to them and hurried along the pier to the Englishman, who was still there, superintending the packing of the jars.

"You want to go to La Boca?" he asked. "Oh well, I wish I'd known. I thought you wanted one of the fish hands. I could have sent you to La Boca an hour ago. What do you want at La Boca?"

"I have an appointment there."

"Oh, who is your appointment with?"

"A friend," Hi said.

The man paused to say something to one of the packers, then turned again to Hi.

"Who was your appointment with, did you say?"

"A friend."

"Ah," said the man, "what's your friend's name? I only ask because I know La Boca, and it might be a question of putting you ashore either to the north or to the south."

"He will be at the inn," Hi said.

"Which inn?" the man said.

"Is there more than one?" Hi asked.

"Is your friend an Englishman? What's his name?"

"Excuse me," Hi said, "but can you get me to La Boca?"

"Let me see," the man said, "did you mention your name and your friend's name?"

"Jones," Hi said in desperation.

"Well, Mr. Jones," the man said, "if you'll step along with me, I'll see if that boat's gone that was here. Is it your brother that you're going to see in La Boca?"

"No."

"Oh, I see. Not a brother, only a friend. I don't remember the name of Jones in La Boca. What's he doing there?"

"He's only just gone there," Hi said.

"Oh, a newcomer, like yourself. Well, this is the La Boca boat."

He spoke to the master of the boat, who was putting what is called a fish in the yard of his sail.

"That man will take you to La Boca," the man said. "He's just going to start. If you had come to me on your way, I could have sent you off in one of the vegetable boats hours ago. Don't give him more than two pesetas. By the way, where will you be staying at La Boca, Mr. Jones? If you or your friend should want any of these earthenware jars, I am in a position to get them as cheap as anybody. What initial did you say yours was?"

"H," Hi said.

"And your friend's?"

"R," Hi answered.

"Mr. H. and Mr. R. Jones," the man said. "Where are you stopping, did you say? Because I can get you nice rooms in a boarding-house, which would be cheaper for you than any hotel."

Here the boatman invited Hi into the boat.

"Where are you stopping?" the man called. "Where did you say you were stopping? I should like to call round in the evening and see you, if you're not doing anything. They always say that Englishmen ought to stick together."

Hi was about to answer, but the boom gybed at that instant and knocked his hat into the well. The boat had shoved off.

"Inquisitive beast," Hi thought. "I never knew a man ask questions like that before. I shouldn't wonder if he's a detective put there to stop passengers leaving the city. If that's the case, I'll very likely be stopped at La Boca. If that devil telegraphs, I shall very likely be met at the pier and shadowed. However, for the moment I am off. That's the main thing. But I've wasted simply hours."

His boat passed close beside Giordano. He was bent over his carpentry in deep attention, putting a whipping over the join.

"He doesn't mean to start for another hour," Hi thought. "I am glad I tried to find someone starting sooner."

The master of the boat, Chigo, the boatman, and Luigi, the boy, ran up their new striped sails, so that the boat leaned down and sheered the water. Then they brought out bread, onions, wine and water and some little transparent fish, which were meant to be eaten raw. They invited Hi to their feast and all breakfasted together. After breakfast, while the boat was still moving swiftly to the south, Hi amused himself by looking into the shallow water at the fish and the weeds of all the colours of the rainbow. Presently something, which seemed like a piece of the bottom of the bay, blundered up alongside, turned over and seethed out of the water into a whiteish blunt thing, which had a kind of cat's mouth that clicked. The click missed by at least two feet, as the thing did not aim very well. It blundered over, rubbed against the side of the boat with a slow rasping movement and disappeared.

"A shark, by George," Hi said.

The boatman laughed at his scare and the master signed to him not to lean over the side. Soon after this Hi noticed that La Boca did not seem to be getting any nearer. The wind, before falling, had drawn ahead, so that they had to make a short board out to sea.

"This is a bore," he thought. "I may not be at La Boca till mid-day, if this goes on. But I'll do it yet."

The wind, which had drawn ahead, now chopped round a few points to the west and failed altogether.

"What's the matter?" Hi asked.

"Wait for de breeze," the master said.

"Shall we have to wait long?"

"Sometimes half hour, sometimes hour."

"Would it be possible to row in to the shore?" Hi asked.

"Not got oars," the boatman said. "Only one oar and a boat hook."

There was nothing for it but to wait while the sun climbed up out of the sea and became hotter. Hi tried to judge the distance from La Boca. It seemed so near across that fore-shortened glitter of sea. Three miles, possibly four miles, he thought. The sea and the boat seemed to settle down to sleep.

"We shall be hours at it like this," Hi thought. And they were.

What was hardest to bear came an hour later, as they lay becalmed. Hi saw a boat further inshore creeping down to La Boca under sweeps. Something in her helmsman's figure seemed familiar to Hi, who was watching her with envy.

"Is that Giordano?" he asked.

"Giordano, si," they answered.

She was helped by more than the sweeps. She was a better boat in light airs and, being much further inshore, she missed the northward current then moving across the outward bay.

"Why, we are further from La Boca than we were before," he thought. "We are drifting back. She will be in hours before us and I might have been in her, if I had had a little patience. I was an ass," he thought. "If I had only stuck to Giordano, I might have been almost there now."

There was no remedy but patience, which is no remedy but a substitute. Hi watched Giordano's boat edge on and on. After what seemed to be hours he noticed that the men in Giordano's boat laid in their sweeps and tended sails. Chigo, who had been watching for something of the sort, laid aside his fender making.

"Here is the breeze," he said.

The breeze came down to them with a darkening of the water. Very gently the boat began to steal southward again. At a little after ten o'clock they began to draw in to the settlement of fishermen and market gardeners at the mouth of the Miamia river. It was an array of little lime-washed houses, roofed with red tiles. It had a mission church of three bells. At the mouth of the river there was a harbour made by baulks of green-heart timber, which had been steeped in a red enamel as a defence against the worm. Hi had been intent upon his thoughts, planning his ride. Looking up, he saw that Giordano's boat had not entered the harbour, but had stood on down the coast towards the south. Looking up at the dock in front of him, he saw some Pituba soldiers watching the approach of the boat. Among them was a white man, who seemed to be an officer.

"Just as I thought," Hi said to himself. "That man on the pier in the city was a detective. Now here I am being shadowed and am going to be questioned."

He looked at this officer. He didn't like his looks at all. He looked too snappish and ill-tempered.

"A bite from that lipless mouth would be worse than its bark," he thought, "though the bark has a curse in it."

This man called out something to the master of the boat, who stood up and answered with a question, which Hi thought civilly put. It brought down a storm of oaths from the officer, who repeated his original remark in the tone of an order. Very politely the master again objected, pointing to Hi.

"What is it?" Hi whispered to Chigo.

"He tells us not to land," Chigo whispered. "The padron ask if you may land."

"Sir," Hi called to him, "I am English. May I not land here?"

"What you say?" the officer asked.

"I am English. May I land here?"

"You are Inglays?"

"Si."

"Inglays?"

"Si."

"Inglays with cat's tripes?"

"No."

"But I say, yes. Meester Inglays with cat's tripes, I say, yes. Take your baboon-face hence lest I mistake it for your stern and kick it. And tell your Inglays brothers that this is not their land, but a land of men. It is not for Inglays Miss, no tank you, nor for Meester Aow and Pipe Tooth. You come here you be shot."

"You'd get into pretty hot water, if you shot me," Hi said.

"You say?"

"You'd get into pretty hot water, if you shot me."

"What the pretty mouth say? I no catch?"

"You'll get into pretty hot water, if you shoot me."

"Oh, dear, the Inglays Meester threaten me." He came a step or two nearer to the edge of the pier, so as to read the number on the boat's bows. "Padron," he said, "your boat, number B 71, is suspect. You will take your boat down to Carpinche and report to the commandant there. If you try to land anywhere nearer, you shall be arrest, you and cat's tripes; yes, and shot. To Carpinche: go."

The padron civilly asked whether there were any warrant upon which he could be ordered to Carpinche.

"Yes," the officer said, "a very good warrant. The proclamation of martial law." Here he drew out a revolver. "I command here for the Republic, which now scrapes off the foreign lice that cling to her. You rebel, I shoot. To Carpinche."

"One moment, please," Hi said. "I want to see the English Consul here."

"No, no," the padron said. "No consul here."

"Well, anyway, I've a right to land."

"No, no," Chigo whispered. "You get into trouble."

"What does Miss tank you, the Inglays, say?" the officer asked.

"I want to see the English Consul," Hi said.

"Oh, he wants to see the Inglays Consul?"

"Yes, sir."

"The Inglays Consul, you say?"

"Yes, please."

"Tank you, but I not please. I tell you to go to Carpinche. You know your Consul live in Santa Barbara, where you just come from. Why you lie to me you want him here? To Carpinche, or I send you back to your Consul, on my ordnance mule, by phê, with your feet tied under his belly."

The boat had by this time drifted across the mouth of the harbour, where she caught a gust which drove her a few yards out. The padron, who was in that land only to make a living, shook his head, as he let the sails fill on the new course. "We must to Carpinche," he said. When the boat was some lengths from the pier, he took a stiletto from his boot and snicked it to and fro, passionately, on his boot-leg.

"Ise kill-a that man," he said.

Hi hesitated. If he tried to land there, he might be shot: if he did land, he might be sent back to Santa Barbara.

"Where is this Carpinche?" he asked.

"South, ten miles."

"Could I get a horse there?"

"Si."

"Is it far from Anselmo? A place called San Anselmo? San An-selm-o?"

"San Anselmo?" Chigo suddenly said. "Si, si. There." He pointed inland to the west.

"Can I get there from Carpinche?"

"To San Anselmo from Carpinche?"

"Yes," he said. "Can I get there?"

"Si, si."

"How far is it?"

"How far?"

"Yes, how far?"

Chigo debated with the padron; the boy made some suggestions. They thought it might be forty kilometres, thirty kilometres; perhaps not so much.

"Twenty kilometres, we going there," the padron said.

Twenty kilometres was about eleven miles, Hi thought. He tried to figure it out, how it could be so little, but thought that these men might know. All the time the boat was moving away from the pierhead.

"Say that it is twenty miles," Hi thought, "and this ten miles more sailing added on to it, I shall not be there till the afternoon."

"See," the padron said, to Hi, with reproach, "you should not have angered the commandant."

"No," Chigo added. "If you not speak at all, if you leave it to the padron, he let you land all right."

"I'm blest if he would," Hi said.

"Si, si."

"He would not have: he had refused."

"No, see," Chigo explained, "the padron he explain: he say what, that man not go any sense, he let you land all right."

"Then you ask, then he stop you."

Hi could not see it as they saw it; but their point of view, however, imperfectly grasped by him, added to his trouble. What if they were right? What if he had been hasty? What if he might have landed at the pier, had he left it all to the padron?

"Won't you turn back, then, and let me try him again?" he asked. The padron shook his head.

"Not turn back," he said.

"He angry now," Chigo said. "He shoot you now."

"Well, can you put me ashore somewhere near here, at one of the little landing places?"

"Ashore here?"

"Si."

"Not now," they said. "The commandant angry now."

"But he would never know. He is not following the boat, and cannot see."

The padron shook his head with a gesture which meant that it would be well not to think of any such thing.

"Besides," he said, "look, we are past the landing places. We cannot take the boat in to the shore here."

This was true; a short way to the south from La Boca the beach changed character from sandy to boulder-strewn. The boulders were packed together almost like a paving of cobbles, and as it were cemented with the broken shell of the beach. It looked a bad beach to beach on.

"The boat is made only of very thin wood," the patron said, mainly by signs; "she bump and bump and bump and knock herself all to pieces."

"When we get to Carpinche," Chigo said, "another officer will say, 'Back to La Boca.' Then, when we come back, Yellow Face will say, 'Back to Carpinche.' Thus we shall pass our day."

"Such are soldiers," the padron said.

It was not a cheerful prospect to Hi, but it seemed possible and likely. "I may not be started before dark," he thought.

"If we have another commandant at Carpinche," he thought, "I'll say nothing."

Carpinche lay in the south-west angle of the bay, among wooded foothills. A dark, romantic glen of trees, marking a water course, sloped inland from it in the easy places of the hill. Great trees grew about Carpinche. The hill to the south of the bay lay like a lioness crouched to drink with her head between her paws. As they drew nearer to this hill the wind failed them. "See," Chigo said, "we too near the shore: see? The shore stop the wind."

"Blanketed," Hi said.

"How?"

"The shore stops the wind."

Gusts of it came in a baffling way; then these, too, ceased. They drifted rather than sailed into a place of shelter, where the trees looked down into a water like glass. The blackness of the rock near the shore made the water seem deep as the pit. Chigo and the boy helped the boat forward by paddling with her bottom boards. Hi also took a bottom board and paddled, with thoughts of that machine of which he had talked to Carlotta only the day before. All four of them stared ahead for some sign of soldiers: they could see none.

"No commandant here," Hi said.

"Siesta," the padron said.

The boat edged slowly into the Carpinche river towards a village among the trees, which towered up there to a vast height. The forest made the place dark, though glaring light fell beyond. Giordano's boat lay tied to the pier in front of them. She had lain there for perhaps a couple of hours. "Oh, if I had only stayed in her," Hi thought, "I might have been in Anselmo by this time."

They edged alongside the pier and made fast.

"No commandant here to report to," Hi said.

"Ah, the commandant," the padron answered. "That man a bad man. He know there no commandant."

"Is there an inn here where I could get a horse?"

"Si, si, in the village."

"Perhaps," Hi said, "since you have all been kind and are here partly through me, you will all come with me to the inn for some refreshment?"

They all accepted this: they set out along a track of red earth which had recently been mud. The raised wooden ways on each side of the track had lately been washed out of position, so that they lay all poked up, like stretchers on a battlefield. The village seemed dead save for a yellow dog, who came out and howled at them.

"The people here get up very early," the boatman explained, "so they have siesta early."

In the inn, half a dozen men, including Giordano, were lying asleep on the benches or leaning over the table. The boat-master called out to the hostess that here was a gentleman who wished to hire a horse.

"Alas," the hostess said, "the horses are all gone with the men to the fiesta. There will be no horses till to-morrow."

"What then can the gentleman do?"

"Who knows?" she said.

One of the sleepers at the table roused.

"There are horses at the house at the cross roads," he said. "If he will ask there, he might have a horse."

"How far are the cross roads?"

"Four miles."

"Are there no horses nearer?"

"Not here. All went early this morning to the fiesta. At five or even at six you might have had your pick of horses, but now there are none."

It occurred to Hi that, when he had paid for some drinks, the hostess might be more helpful.

"Ask her to serve some wine," Hi said. "You deserve the best wine after your morning."

The hostess was pleased to serve wine, but the order did not make her more forthcoming about horses. Plainly there were none.

"I must go on to the cross roads then," Hi said, "if you will point out the road. I will try for a horse there."

By his watch it was a quarter to two when he stepped across the bridge, which led out of the village.

"Nearly ten hours," he thought, "since Rosa called me."

His track led uphill into the forest. "Now best foot foremost," he said to himself. "Never mind the heat or anything else. You've got to save Carlotta and every minute is precious."

Very soon the trees closed over the road, so that he walked in the cool twilight of a tunnel. He saw nothing remarkable for the first couple of miles. Then he came upon a hare sitting upon its hind legs, seeming to be praying, while a big snake sat opposite, swaying a little, making up its mind to strike. Hi flung some stones at the snake, which ducked its head and turned towards him with an ugly raising of the crest. With a few more stones he drove it away. He then walked to the hare and stroked it and spoke to it. Its fur was sick and staring. Presently it fell over on one side, recovered and went shambling away.

"What an ass my father is," Hi thought. "He knew that I might meet things like this, yet said that I should never need a revolver. I shall need one twenty times a day. If I came on one of these snakes asleep, I should never see it until I trod on it. I had better have a stick."

Unfortunately there was no stick nearer than forty feet from the ground. He was in a place which grew nothing but feathery thorn and gigantic timber in a solitude which might have been thousands of miles from men. Giving up the stick, he went on for half an hour without seeing a soul. The only living things he saw, apart from the flies, were deer, moving like shadows among the trees, and very bright things, which he supposed to be parrots against the sky, when the sky showed. After he had walked for an hour he saw a gleam of water below him; soon he came to a wooden bridge at which some tracks converged. There had been a ford or drinking place for cattle above the bridge. This was now a collection of pockets of red mud full of little snakes: beyond the bridge were houses; a farm, somewhat old and untidy, built of wood in need of paint, with stabling beside and behind it. Nearer to the river were two very ramshackle sheds or cottages of wood, which had once been tarred but were now rust-coloured. Dirty bedding hung from the windows of these sheds. Over the door of one of them was a tiling shingle on which someone had drawn in tar, with his forefinger, the word

CAMAS

(with the final S reversed). To the left of these, well away from the river, and on the other side of the road, was a trim, white, prosperous looking house, with a tiled stable. A cornfield of red earth strewn with the shocks of young maize, stretched uphill behind this house. A fair-haired, blue-eyed white man was hoeing among these maize shocks, although it was the heat of the day. He was a South German, who spoke a little English. He said that it was fine vetter and that Hi might tank Gott for such fine vetter. As for a horse, his brother had gone with the horse to the fiesta, but the old frau in the house opposite might lend her colt.

He was a friendly, helpful young man. He took Hi across the tracks to the old untidy farm where everybody seemed to be asleep. Here, after they had both knocked and called for some minutes, a negress appeared, rubbing her eyes with her skirt. This girl took them through a darkness, which stank, into a hot shuttered room, where she called several times by whistling like a kite. When something between a snarl and a gurgle answered to her call, she opened the southward shutters so that Hi could see.

He found himself near the door of a bare room, the floor of which was trodden earth. A table, with fragments of fruit upon it, stood against one wall. Against the end wall, opposite the window, was a tall-backed red chair or throne, in which an enormously fat old woman, swathed in folds of black, sat blinking as she roused from sleep. She was mopping her brow with the handkerchief which had kept the flies from her face while she slept. Hi had the feeling that she lived and slept in the chair. She had a book of hours upon her lap; its marker, hanging from a red ribbon, dangled from her knee. She soon checked her gurglings: she woke up with great completeness. A pair of sharp and very cold grey eyes shone out of her vast pale face with that narrowed glimmer which made Hi think of the snake.

"You want a horse?" she said, in fair English, in a guttural voice that was half a cough.

"Yes, please, Señora."

"Where will you go with the horse?"

"To Anselmo?"

"Where to in Anselmo?"

"George Elena's house."

"When you bring him back?"

"How far is it?"

"Thirty kilometre: twenty kilometre. When you bring my horse back?"

"I'll send him back to-morrow."

"Send? Eh?"

"Yes."

"Why not bring him back yourself?"

"I may not be coming back."

"Who will bring him back?"

"One of Elena's men will bring him."

"Which one?"

"I don't know."

"What you do?" she asked after a pause. "Why you go this way to Anselmo? Where you from?"

"Santa Barbara."

"Which way you come from there?"

"Carpinche."

"You know the road to Anselmo?"

"No; but I can find it."

"How you know you can?"

"I have found you, Señora."

She sat staring at him, fanning her face with her handkerchief; her face was without more expression than a large uncut ham.

"What you going to do in Anselmo?"

"I've business with George Elena."

"What business?"

"Horses."

"Why you come this way, if you go on business? This ain't the way. Why you not go the proper road?"

Hi wavered at the question, but said:

"I thought it might be quicker to sail down the bay and come this way."

"How long you been here?"

"Three or four days."

"Horses," she grunted in a tone of great disgust. She fanned herself, looking over Hi's head at the wall. There was no expression on her face, but her big jaw worked a little: she was solving the problem of what brought Hi there.

"I got no horse," she said at last.

This, besides being ungracious, was false. Hi felt that she spoke thus because she was cross from being wakened and did not want to be bothered.

"I tell him, maybe you lend your colt," the German said.

"I got no horse to lend."

"No, of course, Señora," Hi said. "I don't ask you to lend him. I want to hire him."

"How much you pay?"

"How much do you want, for the two days?"

"What you pay?"

"What do you usually charge?"

"How much you pay? I can't be buyer and seller, too."

"I don't know how much these things cost in this country," Hi said.

"Well, what you give, see?"

Hi produced his peseta notes and small change, to which the woman made an emphatic gesture that this was child's play.

"Well, how much, then?" Hi asked.

A tall, lean man had come silently into the room behind Hi; he had taken up his position facing Hi, with his back against the table. He was picking his teeth with a sprig of macilente, which he chewed. Hi did not like the fellow's looks. He had almost no brow; his hair and eyebrows merged into each other. Under this shag, the man's eyes were very black; his face was hungry-looking, with pale, sunken cheeks. The mouth was greedy-looking or wolfish, although it split into a smile over the toothpick. The teeth glittered; they looked evil, being pointed and inclined inward, something like snakes' fangs. His ear-rings glittered at each bite upon the sprig. There was a glittering about the man's person, apart from ear-rings and teeth, because his waistcoat was buttoned up to the throat with some thirty small globular silver buttons.

"All is not gold that glitters," Hi thought. "Mr. Bright Tooth, you look like a wolf who would scratch up a grave."

"Well, how much, do you think, would be fair for a horse for two days?" Hi asked.

The woman fanned herself for a moment, then she said:

"You see, we not know you. You may be very fine gentleman, but we not know you. My horse, all the horse I got. You want to go to Anselmo? That fifty kilometre, forty kilometre from here through the forest; pumas in the forest; eat horses; then you go over the fords; the fords all out with rain. Very like you get my horse drowned. Then you not know how to look out. You get the horse bitten by snakes, or else you lose your way. Then suppose you reach Anselmo. You say, that old woman, pah, she not want her horse. I got to Anselmo, what the hell, see? How I to know you send the horse back?"

"I promise you I will."

"Promise. Look. I'm a woman: see? I don't believe any promise any man ever make. When a man want a thing, he promise anything. Does he pay? Nit, I don't think; with the fore sheet, what? So don't promise me nothing, Albert; it's pretty to hear you, but it don't lead to nothing."

Bright Tooth entered the conversation with the question:

"You got English sovereign?"

Hi had three English sovereigns; he offered one of them, which at that time, in that country, would have bought two horses, with their harness, outright. After some more haggling, backed by Bright Tooth, the old woman agreed to lend a horse, saddled and bridled, for two days, for one English sovereign and all the small change Hi had. It was, however, agreed that this small change, amounting to seventeen Santa Barbara pesetas, should be returned to the man who brought back the horse. Hi thought that they drove a very hard bargain with him; but to have a horse and to be away upon his journey were the desires of his heart at the moment. Even so, he knew enough not to pay for a horse till he had a little knowledge of it. He asked to see the horse.

Bright Tooth led him out to the yard at the back of the house, with the remark that he was a very nice horse, a horse for a king or queen, being tireless and good spirited, as well as so beautifully boned. Hi had heard horses sold in England, by his father. He waited till they were in the stable, where two horses were in stalls. The one nearer to the door was a nice dark chestnut mare, which seemed somehow, even at a first glance, a little too good for such a stall.

"Is this the horse?" Hi asked.

"No," Bright Tooth said, "the other."

The other was a sour-coloured pony engaged at that minute in gnawing off the top of the partition between the stalls. He was doing this with an ugly chucklehead screwed sideways, so that his yellow hooked teeth might get a purchase on the splinter. He was rough-haired, having been out in the rains (apparently in a hog wallow). The hair, stuck to patches of mud, was scaling off him. He had not been shod nor had his feet been pared. They stuck forward in long, splitting growths of horn almost like slippers. A sort of gaiter of hard red mud coated his legs to his hocks. He was straight-shouldered, and what old Bill always called "a bit goosey in the rump." His head, when he ceased from gnawing the barrier, was loutish and ill set on. "Stunsail ears and a Roman nose," Hi thought. "Worth six bob a corner."

"This is a horse," Bright Tooth said.

"Ay, in the catalogue ye go for horse," Hi quoted to himself, from the Macbeth his form had "done" the term before. "Good Lord," he said aloud, "I can't take a beast like that."

"There, a lovely horse," Bright Tooth said. "Never fail. He never, never fail. There come soldiers here for horses, one time. They say, he too small, not allowed to take so small a horse; but that the horse for a soldier; he got the good guts."

"Guts. Good Lord," Hi said. "He's got no more guts than a herring. I never saw such a beast in all my born days. Let me have the other, the mare."

"No, not," Bright Tooth said. "The other one not belong here. She not our horse."

"Whose is she? Perhaps I could hire her."

"No, no," Bright Tooth said, "she wait here till after the fiesta; then the man come to ride her home. He be here in a few minutes now."

"In a few minutes?" Hi said. "I could wait a few minutes."

"He not be here in a few minutes. I make mistake, see. This yellow horse the only horse. He go like the wind."

"With those feet?"

"I tell you about those feet. The rains make it very slippy. With those feet he never, never fail: any kind of mud, any kind of stick, he stand fast."

"I'll bet he will stand fast," Hi said. "Is there no other horse?"

"No other horse anywhere, except the mare. And the man who owns the mare, he very proud man; he not let anyone ride the mare."

"Well, all right, then," Hi said, "I suppose I must take the pony. Let me see the saddle and bridle."

The old woman had hobbled to the stable, the German had gone back to his work.

"I like to see the colour of your money," the old woman said. "I not know you, see, so you make me a little present."

Hi paid over the money, which mother and son (if that was, as he supposed, the relationship between the pair) watched with eyes that burned with voracity. The old woman bit the sovereign, to test its goodness, as though she were going to eat it.

"You go armed, in case of robbers?" the old woman asked.

"Yes." Hi said. "Rather."

He was feeling at the moment uneasy about this couple, lest they should go back upon their bargain and deny the horse, after taking the money. But the man Bright Tooth saddled and bridled the horse and led him out. Hi noticed that the pony was an arm-snapper.

"I'll borrow this stick of yours," he said, picking up a crooked stick which rested against the wall. "Your beast is too free with his nippers."

"Where you keep your gun?" the old woman asked.

"In my pocket, all ready," Hi said. He noticed that she had a sharp eye upon his pockets as he mounted. "Now, which way to Anselmo?" he asked.

She swung her hand round to the west, to point to the track leading past the German's house.

"Straight on," she said, "past the ford and out of the wood."

"Thank you, and how far is it?"

"Seventy kilometre: sixty kilometre."

"Oh, rats, Señora," Hi said, "it can't be. You said it was twenty a little while ago."

"Quien sabe?"

Bright Tooth stepped down the yard from them to open the gate.

"Adios, Señora," Hi said, moving off. It was twenty-seven minutes to four; but he felt that he was now really started. A kind of gleam came upon the Señora's face: the horse with the slippered feet clacked slowly down the slope to the track. Hi saw the German leaning on his hoe, watching him as he drew near.

CHAPTER VIII

The German came slowly towards him, waving with his left arm towards the left.

"Dot der way to Anselmo," he said. "You mind out at der ford."

"Thank you for your help," Hi said.

"Very welcome."

The German turned back to his hoeing and Hi set out upon his path. When he was out of sight of that settlement, really on his way to Anselmo, he thought of those warning words, "You mind out at the ford."

"You meet highwaymen at the fords," his father had said, "or did in my day, but I expect it's all altered since then."

"I wonder what that German meant," he thought. "Perhaps that devil Bright Tooth may be playing some trick, but probably what he meant was that the floods are out. It will be rotten if I can't get across."

Then the question rose in his mind how far Anselmo was. "Twelve or fifteen miles," he thought. "I can be there by 5 or 5.30 and I will be."

He whacked up the horse into a solitude of rocky barren, densely grown with small thorn and prickly pear. The strangeness of the landscape, the blueness of the sky where the eagles were cruising for their prey and the glory of the adventure on which he rode made his ride a dream of delight for some miles, till the rocks on both sides of him grew in towards him, so that he rode in a kind of gully, where the hooves made more echo than he liked. The gloom of the place was made greater by the prevalence of the pudding-cactus, which exuded over his path like jellyfish flecked with blood or snakes which had been pressed to death. Multitudes of flies feasting on the stickiness of the plant gave it the appearance of corruption. In nearly all the puddles there were snakes. The noise of the echoes of the horse's hooves became louder and louder. Hi, looking back, saw that a horse and man were coming after him.

The man was bent down in his seat with his sombrero jammed down over his eyes. He had a look of Bright Tooth. His horse looked like the dark chestnut mare which Hi had seen in the stable. She had seemed a beauty then, if a little small. She showed like a beauty now in the grace of her going.

"It's Bright Tooth all right," Hi thought. "I'll bet he comes for no good."

Seeing that he was seen, the man sat up and called to Hi to stop. He was certainly Bright Tooth.

"Why should I stop?" Hi thought. "I am not going to stop for a swine like that. Let him jolly well catch me up and explain."

As he saw that Bright Tooth was not carrying a gun, he rode on, though Bright Tooth called repeatedly something about stopping or returning, to which Hi answered, "Si," or "Bueno" or "That's the ticket." Bright Tooth pressed his horse up to Hi's off quarter with the cry, "You Englishman return." He motioned back towards the cross roads.

"I am not going to return," Hi said.

"Then you give back the horse, see?" Bright Tooth cried.

"I don't see," Hi said. "Why should I?"

They were now riding side by side at a good speed, because both horses thought that it was a race.

"You turn back, see," Bright Tooth cried. He motioned backwards, shaking his head.

"All right, old sport," Hi said. He did not turn, nor did he mean to turn; he kept on, with an eye for the road and the next move. He shoved his stick into his bridle hand, so as to have his right hand free.

"Give up the horse, see?" Bright Tooth cried again. "Your money bad. Bad English money." He gave a violent imitation of biting a coin and being sick. "You come back," he cried, "or pay good money."

"Rats," Hi said.

"Your money bad."

"The money was good," Hi said.

"You pay more money. Another sovereign, see?"

"I won't pay a red cent more."

Bright Tooth shot forward, stooped and made a clutch at Hi's rein. The yellow horse shied away from him, so that he missed his clutch and nearly fell. Hi, too, was nearly off. He recovered first. He dropped his right hand to the pocket where he kept his knife. He poked the end of the knife from within the pocket towards Bright Tooth, as though it were a revolver muzzle. He had read somewhere of men shooting through the pocket. He called out, "All right, old sport, I've got you covered. Cuidado." He did not know what cuidado meant; but he had heard the third officer in the *Recalde* use the word as an alarm note. He saw Bright Tooth whip out a knife with a blade a foot long, sharp on two edges and spear-pointed.

They looked at each other a few feet apart. Hi enjoyed it, because Bright Tooth did not attack.

"You pay another sovereign," Bright Tooth said. There was about Bright Tooth a sort of suggestion of a rush preparing.

"Clear out," Hi said, "clear right out of it. Get back where you belong."

"You give the bad money," Bright Tooth said; there was a whine in his voice. Hi edged towards him; he edged away.

"Clear out."

Bright Tooth cleared out. He turned, in an anxious manner, to a point ten yards away. As Hi turned after him, he retreated hurriedly for fifty or sixty yards; then, as Hi still slowly followed, he retreated further.

"You keep where you are. Don't you try to follow me," Hi called. He tapped his pocket, and added, "This is what you'll get, if you try any monkey-tricks with me, my son."

He watched Bright Tooth for half a minute; then, as he seemed not disposed to try any monkey-tricks, he turned again upon his way through the woodland across the puddings of the cactus. Whenever he looked back he saw Bright Tooth following. If he paused, Bright Tooth paused. If he turned back, Bright Tooth turned back. When he went on, Bright Tooth followed.

"I haven't done with him yet," Hi thought. "He knows of some place ahead where he can get me."

After some time he passed a turning to the right. Looking back, he saw Bright Tooth turn down this track at a quickened pace.

"He's riding to head me off," Hi thought. "I wish I had at least a club."

There was, however, no chance of getting a club in that wood. He rode on into a meaner country and from this to a forest darker than the last, where he could hear nothing except a murmur or steady beat like the noise of water somewhere ahead. "That's the ford," Hi thought, "and the river's in spate. Well, the longer I think of it, the less I shall like it."

Almost at once the forest became sparser. He rode out on to a hill of moist red soil, at the foot of which was a violent little river, blood-red and bank high. Tracks led to what had been a ford there, but the water was romping over the ford in a way terrible to see. Not far below the ford the water went down a rapid. Near the ford, where the tracks ceased to be boggy, Bright Tooth and a friend sat on horses waiting for him. Bright Tooth had his knife, the friend had a revolver. "Here we are," Hi said.

They signed to him to come forward and moved towards him. Hi had not any time for thought; he moved on the impulse of the moment. He banged his horse forwards down the slope towards the water in such a way that he could not stop, even had he wished. He yelled as he went. His horse went scattering down the slope. The man struck at him and someone shot at him. The water went up suddenly in a bright sheet over him and then he was in the hands of the river. In the first rush of the fall he lost his horse, and nearly choked with the filthy water in his mouth. Catching a gulp of air, he saw his horse again as the banks of the stream ran away from him. Then he saw Bright Tooth on a jibbing mare gathering the coils of a lasso for a swing. Then he was tumbled headlong and endlong down into a roaring pit that banged him and wouldn't let him get his breath. He felt that he had tumbled down all the stairs in Christendom. The tumbling and banging seemed to last through this life into eternity. In another few seconds, when he had leisure to open his eyes, he was in a round, filthy, surging pool, where boughs, shrubs, trees and drowned beasts were milling and churning amid enormous bubbles of red yeast.

Striking out to the side of this, he came to a steep bank covered with trailers of bindweed dripping down upon him. Putting down his feet, he touched rock and stood. He caught the trailing plants, waded to the bank and then felt suddenly faint. Holding on to the trailers, he saw that they were not the bank, but a screen to it. Behind them was a cave, into which the sun shone. He clambered into this and lay down upon a water-smoothed rock, closed his eyes and wished that the world would stop spinning.

After he had lain there for some minutes he heard voices. Through the creepers he could see Bright Tooth and his friend on the other bank of the river, peering for his body. Presently he saw them lie down upon the bank in an effort to see under the creepers which hid him. They went up the stream for a little, then went down it, then came back to point, jabber and explain their theories over the pool. He could see what was in their minds. Bright Tooth thought that he had been washed underneath the bank. His friend thought that he had been jammed under water in the pool. They were there, watching the water, for a full quarter of an hour. Suddenly he saw them exclaim and point at something. The body of the sour colt, which had jammed in a snag in the rapids, came blindly down. The current shot it over to Bright Tooth's side on the way down-stream. He saw them watch for the rider, but no rider followed. After some more searching and consulting, the two seemed to be agreeing to return later, when the water had fallen. They mounted and surveyed the water from their saddles and then slowly rode away with many glances back.

"They won't be gone for long," Hi said to himself. "They will come back separately soon, each hoping to find me before the other has a chance."

As soon as they were hidden from him by the forest, Hi ventured out of his cover. By a little scrambling among slippery rocks he found a way out of the river-bed to the dry land. He saw the sour colt's body drifting across a rock in mid-stream. The rage and rush of the filthy falls down which he had come made him marvel that he was not jammed there with the horse. He went on into the scrub away from the river till he came to a pool in the hollow of a rock. Here he stripped, washed, dried his clothes in the hot sun and took stock of his position. His nose was swollen and uncomfortable; he had an after-football feeling that he would be very stiff in the morning. "But that's nothing," he thought, "I ought to be thankful to be still alive." His horse and hat were gone; his watch had stopped at seven minutes to five. His money was safe; among the coins were two crumpled, soaked ten peseta notes, which he had forgotten; he dried these carefully. He had a pocket-book, a knife, two handkerchiefs, a box of matches, which he dried one by one, a pair of pocket-scissors, some string, two pencils and a small shield-shaped silver locket containing camphor. His sister Bell had given this to him at Christmas; he had carried it with him ever since.

All his clothes looked as though they had been dipped in old blood, but they soon dried in the sun on that hot rock. He made his second handkerchief into a sunbonnet. His tie, which had been black with green spots, had spread a greenish black tinge all over his collar; the tie itself looked like a snake which had been run over. He judged that he would look more like a tramp with these two things than without them, so he left tie and collar under a bush, with a qualm, that he was leaving bits of England there. "The Elenas," he thought, "will fit me out with a tie and collar when I reach Anselmo. After all, everybody has a collar.

"And now," he added, "I will be off for Anselmo, as hard as I can put foot to ground. It can't be more than eight miles."

Away from the river the ground was desert-like and hard, growing scrub, mezquite, cactus and prickly pear in the spaces clear of rock. He picked up the trail for Anselmo, and went on at a good pace till he came out into the sage in the open country. He had often heard his father speak of the Santa Barbara landscape, now he saw it in its sweep, with the mountains near at his left, Gaspar thrusting out in front of them, above a rolling plain over which the wind exulted. Santa Barbara made a smudge against the paleness of the lower sky far behind him to his right. In front was this infinity of swaying sage, which ran on into grass for hours and hours of going. The forest lay dark to the left, all over the foothills of the Sierras; but one could not look at the darkness with all that light to choose. Straight in front of him, how far away he could not tell, in that clear light, which had so often deceived him already, was a round hill topped by a tower. It seemed to be not much more than a mile away in that clearness. The tower was foursquare and tall. One of its angles was topped by the figure of an angel clasping a banner.

"That is it," Hi said, "there it is. That is Anselmo tower; the village must be beyond the hill; I shall be at the Elenas in half an hour. Oh, cheers; come on, now, for the last lap."

He was so much cheered by the sight of his landmark that he began to run towards it. Soon he drew clear of a patch of scrub into sight of the great south road from Santa Barbara to Meruel. It went straight from the city across his path through a copse or woodland half a mile in front of him. On the road, coming from the city towards this wood, were four ox-waggons each with teams of eight oxen. He could see the slow, stately lurch of each swaying ox and hear the songs and cries of the negro teamsters. They were going with heavy loads. The whips cracked like rifle shots; the soft tenor voices adjured the oxen to pull in the names of countless saints. Hi saw a waggon enter the cover of the copse, then a second, then a third, then the last, but as he went on he did not see them emerge on the other side. "They can't have stopped for siesta at this time," he thought. "I suppose they are taking a halt."

He went on towards the copse or little wood, watching idly, as one will, for the teams to emerge on the other side. They did not appear, so that he thought suddenly, "I know what it is; there is a turning in the wood towards Anselmo. They have turned off to Anselmo, and so of course the wood hides them. Yet that can't be, either; for they aren't singing nor cracking their whips. I suppose they have pulled up for maté or a cigarette."

It took him longer than he had expected to reach the copse. When he was close to its edge, he heard from within it a sudden scream of pain followed by the laughter of men.

"What on earth is that?" he thought.

He broke into the covert, past a water; he heard voices and horses, and smelt woodsmoke and tobacco; soon he came out into the open upon a curious scene.

For three hundred years, carters and horsemen using that road had turned into that copse to camp or siesta. A wide space on both sides of the road had been browsed and trampled clear; the cleared ground was black with old camp-fire marks. In the road, in the midst of this cleared and trampled space, the four teams of oxen stood with straying bent heads in front of their waggons. All about them was a troop of Pituba lancers, perhaps fifty strong, who had been halted there boiling maté at little reed fires when the waggons had come in upon them. Now the lancers were standing guard over the teamsters, who were being questioned by their captain.

Hi recognised the captain at once. He was the little, short, fierce, bullet-headed snappy man who had forbidden him to land at La Boca. His yellow eyes were still bloodshot with rage. He was barking at one of the teamsters, who had perhaps made some rash or unfortunate reply. After he had sworn at this man, he gave an order to some of his men, who threw the teamster to the ground and bent his head down to his knees. Two Indians then pressed a piece of wood across the back of his neck and lashed it there with strips of hide. Hi knew at once that they were going to make the man what is called a broody hen; his father had told him of this torture. But before the order could be given to complete the trussing of the victim, the officer looked up, and recognised Hi.

"Ah," he said, "the Inglays from La Boca; the Inglays with the too much talk."

"Si," Hi said.

"Then you did not land at Carpinche as I bade?"

"Yes, I did."

"Yes," the officer said. "But what does Mr. Inglays do here, on the Meruel Road, after being told to stay in Carpinche?"

"I'm going to Anselmo."

"To Anselmo? And where is your permit to go to Anselmo?"

"Surely I do not need a permit. I am English."

"So? He does not need a permit: he is Inglays. To whom is the Inglays going in Anselmo?"

"I'm not going to anybody. I want to see that angel on the tower."

"Ah, to see the angel on the tower? A holy Inglays. You will come to Ribote, where your angel of the tower shall be a little searched into. You are under arrest."

"I'm English," Hi said. "I have not broken any of your laws. You had better let me go."

"It is for me to judge whether to let you go," the officer said, "and whether you have broken the laws. You are walking without a permit on a forbidden road. You will come with me to Ribote."

"But I can prove that I am doing no harm," Hi said.

"If you can prove it, you can prove it at Ribote," the officer answered. "But to Ribote you will certainly come."

He turned his back upon Hi. He left him in charge of two troopers, while he strolled away to drink his maté. When he had finished his maté, he gave orders that Hi should mount a spare horse. When the troop had formed up, with Hi in the midst of them, they set off at a quick pace along the great road to the south. It was half-past five, as Hi judged, when they set out. The mountains were stretching their shadows like fingers along the plain. Glancing back, he saw the angel of the tower of Anselmo growing smaller and smaller. "We are miles from Anselmo now," he thought. "It will be midnight now before I can get there." He had no fears for himself. "They won't really dare to harm me," he thought, but he did bother acutely about the delay of the message. "Here's the whole day gone," he thought, "and I haven't started yet and these beasts may jail me for a week."

He was going, as far as he could judge, south or south with a little east in it. Presently they were riding in the dark, except for a flaring lower sky behind them and the young moon westering over the plain. "This is ten miles," he thought, "or fifteen miles from Anselmo. I am no nearer than I was in Santa Barbara."

At about seven or later he saw lights in front of him running up a slope. They came into a town of some size built on the side of a hill, which was crowned with pine trees. "Here is Ribote," he thought. The town, though it was mainly a collection of wooden houses, was lit with electric light. Near the entrance of the town there was a big enclosure containing a mansion. The troop rode past this, up the hill to an important stone building, which looked like a large public-house partially converted into a Greek temple. As it had a flagstaff with two small guns in front of it, Hi judged it to be the city hall. The troop halted outside this hall. The officer with about a dozen men dismounted, drew their revolvers and entered. Perhaps thirty seconds later there came a cry from within and shots were fired. A few minutes later, three men, the better sort of citizen, were brought out from the hall. As the officer brought these men into the open, he caught sight of Hi, whom he seemed to have forgotten.

"Here is this Inglays again," he said. "You shall rest from your horse ride."

He said something to a native in a ragged blue uniform, who looked like a sweeper or a porter of the building.

"Yes, it is so," he said. "You shall rest awhile to consider the angel on the tower and other matters. You shall have your hands free, so that you can catch your lice. You will find some brother Inglays where you are going."

Hi realised that he was going to be jailed.

"Sir," Hi said, "will you please let me go? I am not a subject of this State."

"Sir, we will please let him go," the officer said. "He is not a subject of this State."

The man in the blue rags led the way into the house. The officer ordered the Indians to take Hi in after him. Hi was thrust along a hall into a corridor, then across a yard, paved with concrete, to a low building or shed, where the ragged man unlocked a door. When the door was opened, Hi was flung through it. He went staggering for a couple of steps, stumbled over a body which grunted, staggered on and trod upon a second body, which roused up, cursed in English and subsided.

The door clicked to and the lock turned. The key was withdrawn and the footsteps of the jailer passed away across the yard. A door closed behind them. It seemed to Hi to shut him into an "everlasting prison, remediless." He apologised to the two bodies, on which he had trodden, but had no answer, except drunken muttering.

"I am jailed," he thought, "locked up in a jail and can't get out. And I can't tell when I shall get out. I may be here for days."

After a little time the room seemed less dark. He began to have glimmerings of its shape. There was a grated opening high up which let in air. A little grating in the door let him peer into the yard. It was a biggish, long prison room about twenty-four feet by eight. There were three people in it, a dead drunk man, a less drunk man and himself. The dead drunk man was out of all knowledge of the world. The second, from words uttered when trodden on, Hi judged to be a deserter from the Navy.

Peering through the grating, he could see little beyond except the four concreted sides of the yard sloping to a central drain. An evergreen stood in a tub at each corner of the yard. The slopes of the pent-houses surrounding the yard kept him from sight of the heavens, but a glimmer in the water of the drain showed that the stars were shining. He shook at the door, which rattled a little. It was an iron slab. He was a prisoner. "And Carlotta is a prisoner," he thought. "And how on earth is Don Manuel to be warned?" He saw no way. "They've diddled us between them," he thought.

While he stood at the little grating, rattling at the door, a great tumult broke out at the lower end of the town where Hi had seen the mansion. After twenty minutes of this he noticed that the pent-house on his right began to take colour. A glow came upon the tiles. The racket continued for half an hour. "They're having a good old racket of destruction," he thought. When he looked again through the grating, he noticed that the glare upon the tiles of the pent-house had changed to a glittering intermittence. "I believe they're burning the town," he thought. "If they are, we shall be burned like rats in a trap."

"What say?" a voice asked.

Hi looked round startled. He saw the second of the two drunkards sitting up and looking at him. He was a littleish man with a flushed hatchet face which shone in the light.

"The town's on fire," Hi said; "we may be burnt if they don't let us out."

"What say?"

"The town's on fire: we may be burnt."

" 'Ere, let me come on deck."

He came on deck, a little unsteady on his legs and smelling very strong of aniseed. "Damn to hell," he said, when he had come on deck and looked through the grating.

"A bit of fair old, rare old," he said.

He turned on Hi suddenly to ask:

"What you in for, mate?"

"Nothing. They shoved me in."

"That's me, to rights," he answered. "Nothing: same 'ere. Burning's pineful, too. Let's 'ave a look at that door. Say, mate, got a bit of wire?"

"No." Hi said, "I haven't."

The man took hold of the door, struck a match and examined the lock. He lit a cigarette before the match burned out. He had a packet of cigarettes. Hi thought him rather scurvy not to offer him one.

"You've not got a bit of wire?" the man said.

Hi said he hadn't.

"What are you doing here?" the man said.

"Come to learn sugar-planting," Hi said. "What are you doing?"

"None of your damned business," the man said. "If I'd got a bit of wire," he said, "I'd soon have this door open. But you haven't got a bit of wire?"

"No."

"That's a proper barracker. Coo lummy, she ain't half caught fire. The skylight's no cop, neither. It's a bit of all Sir Garnet, if you ask me. You ain't got a bit of wire?"

"No."

Here the other drunkard gurgled in his sleep.

"Cor blimey," the little man said, "what was that?"

"The other man."

"What other man? I didn't know there was another bloke; that's straight. Lummy, 'e's been in luck. 'E's enjoyed 'is lunch. I'll 'ave a look, see, if 'e's got a bit of wire."

He was down on his knees on the instant, rummaging in the drunkard's clothes; for more than wire, Hi thought. He sucked his cigarette to a glow till his face shewed sharp as a wolf's over the body.

"Not a bleeding bit," he said at last. "The grating's out of reach too, unless I stood on your back."

"Come on," Hi said. "Stand on it, and try."

"Right," the man said. "Tuck in your tuppeny."

Hi tucked in his tuppeny beneath the window, the little man made a run and leap and fell over.

"Mizzled the bleeding dick," he said. "I'll do it next time."

The next time he did do it; he leaped on to Hi's back and poised there; he was a horrid weight, but Hi was struck by the ease and certainty of the jump, and also by the silence of his tread: he was wearing old white deck shoes with rubber soles. He felt the man try the gratings by heaving all his weight on them.

"Not a give in the whole bleeding barrow," the man said, leaping lightly down. "Now if old Alf was along, what got out of Princetown, it would be all right, wouldn't it? You ain't got a bit of wire?"

"No."

" 'Alf a mo'; go easy," the man said. "You ain't seen my cap since you come in?"

"No."

"It ought to be somewheres, unless they pincht it. It's a fair barracker when they pinch kit as well as quod a bloke. You ain't got a cap: did they pinch yours?"

"No: I had none."

"Cor blimey, I'd a sweet jag; coo. This sweet shumpine, the sime the toffs; coo. But you feel it in the sweetbreads; that's where it is; next day's the day; that's straight. Say, mate, would you mind looking for me cap. This grilling's a steak's game."

They groped on the floor for the cap; the glare without increased so that they could see a little.

"We'll be as nice as mother makes it, no bleeding error," the man said. "If we don't get out of here, we'll be bleeding pancakes; that's straight. Cor blimey, I seen men burned. Coo, kid; it's a barracker, being burned; a fair barracker. You can always tell when a man's dead, when you see him being burned; yes, you can, because. . . . Cor blimey, here's me cap. Nar then."

He struck another match, lit another cigarette, and rummaged swiftly at his cap in the glow at the door grating.

"Got a bit 'a wire," he said. "Nar then, to be or not to be."

He had taken the piece of wire which made the frame for the top of his cheese-cutter cap. With this, when he had bent it in a certain way, he began to fish within the lock, using a niceness of touch which Hi had not expected from a drunkard. He took some little time. The lock rattled and clicked under his fishing: often he swore a little and readjusted his wire. Once he stopped to look at the glare upon the tiles.

"It won't 'alf be a bit of real life," he said, "if the fire reaches Matiro's. 'E's got seventy tons of blasting powder under where 'e keeps 'is chickens. Cor, mate, that'll mike them think the bleeding post's come: seventy ton. Now, you bleeder, I've got you."

Very delicately, he brought pressure to bear on the tough twisted wire: the lock turned: the door opened.

"There's the bleeding door," the man said. "We'd best hop it, mate. What's the way out is the barracker for me."

"Across the yard and then through the house," Hi said.

They set out across the yard; some rats in the drain sat up to look at them. Hi saw their eyes glisten. All was still in the municipio. The door into the building was shut but not locked; Hi opened it and peered into a dark passage droning with mosquitoes.

"It's through here, then to the right," Hi whispered.

"Lummy," the man said, "I ain't half got the sours in my sweetbreads."

"We must get the other man out," Hi whispered.

"What other man?"

"The drunk man."

"Garn."

"We can't leave him to be burned."

"Burned. Blimey, you can see the fire ain't anyways near. Besides, 'e's bin lunching; 'e's necked all what come in the waggon."

"Well, I'll get him out of the cell anyway. Will you give me a hand?"

"No bleeding fear." The man passed into the passage and closed the door noiselessly behind him. Hi stole back to the cell to rouse the drunkard. It was strange how differently the glare of the fire seemed from the yard. It was not near at hand, but at the far end of the town. All the same, it was burning fiercely and perhaps drawing near to Matiro's. Hi shook the drunkard's arm.

CHAPTER IX

"Come along," Hi said, "wake up. Come on out of this."

"What's that?" the man said.

"Wake up, man," Hi said, "we've got the door open; we can get away."

The man sat up, pulled out a sheath-knife, spat, and said:

"I'll cut your guts out."

"Never mind my guts," Hi said, "they'll keep; but we may be spotted, if we don't hurry."

"Garrrr," the man screamed, "Garrrr and guts. See? Garrrr and guts. Harrar." He rose upon his feet, with a brandish of his knife. "Come on the lot of you," he yelled, "you don't daunt me. I'm Henery Peach Kezia and my blood's vitriol. I'll seal you for your tombstone. Harrar you planets, I'll put some of your lights out, once I get a hold of you." Here he lifted up his voice into a yell.

"Ayayayayay," he yelled, "I'm the frog who would a-wooing go. See me hop."

"Hop out of the door," Hi said. He held the door so that the frog might hop. He was frightened not only of the madman, but of his noise, which might bring the guards.

"Where's the door?" the man asked.

"Here."

"Where's here?" the man asked. "How am I to know where *here* is?"

"Are you blind?" Hi asked. "I didn't know you were blind."

"I been blind since I was a poor little orphan child," the man said. "I only smell things. There's a smell of roses here, or maybe it's lavender. You guide me to the door, my dear young Bible friend. Just reach me your hand and the blessings of the poor blind man will follow you. Oh, Heaven bless you, my sweet young gentleman angel, Heaven will bless you for this."

Hi had taken the man by the left arm, while he kept the door open with his body. The man came unsteadily through the opening into the yard.

"There," he said, "there." He drew a deep breath, suddenly wheeled upon Hi, stabbed at him with his knife, and screamed:

"And now I'll cut your guts out, like I said."

Hi had half expected something of the kind. By a twist of his body he shook himself clear, so that the door, at once swinging-to, struck Henery Peach Kezia and made him miss his stab.

"Don't you think to dodge me like that, when my blood's up," Kezia said, "you young swine. I'll cut you double for that. I'll cut you crossways, so's your own mother will deny you." He began to laugh with a deep down, joyless chuckle, which made Hi's blood run cold. He was not very steady on his feet, but he had a horrid danger about him, because of his sideways lurches. Hi dodged him in his rush, but not by much, for they were on the concrete slopes of the yard and Hi wore English walking-shoes, the man stockings. It was as bright as bright moonlight from the fire.

"Now, then," Kezia said. "Now we'll see. Some would have took pity on you; but not me. Do you see jouncer? This knife's jouncer. And as soon as I've breathed on the blade he's going into you."

He panted on to the blade like a hound getting breath, then he made a sudden dart, missed by about a foot, and then followed with dreadful speed and certainty round and round the yard. The fire, wherever it was, burned up with a brighter blaze to light him. Hi aimed to reach the door into the municipal building, but the man was too close behind him for him to try to open it. He slipped on the concrete, caught one of the pillars which held the pent-house roof, and swung round it with such force that he struck Kezia from behind. The rush and excitement seemed to steady Kezia.

"Ha," he said, "ain't this fun? Ain't this nice hide and seek? And I'll bleed you into veal in the drain; white meat; eightpence a pound, prime cuts."

Here there came a crash. Perhaps the brightness of the fire had been fed for the past twenty minutes by the timbers and rafters of the roof. These now suddenly gave way and launched the blaze into the pit of the wreck; the glare of the burning died at once from about them. Hi was in the dark, poised behind a pillar, trying to see the drunkard, who was near the desired door. There was silence for about thirty seconds, each was trying to see the other; at last the drunkard spoke.

"Say, brother," he said, "will you shake hands and let's be friends?"

"I can't shake hands," Hi said, "when you've got a knife in your hand."

"The knife's nothing. I took the knife out to cut you a nice nosegay from all these pretty little bloody roses."

"That was kind of you," Hi said.

"I love you," the man said; "you are like a lovely little angel."

"I am, rather," Hi said. The darkness of the man seemed to edge a shade nearer.

"I love angels," the man said.

"That's right," Hi said.

"I always loved angels," the man said, "since a boy."

"Stick to them," Hi said; "you can't do better."

"You blasted young swine," the man screamed, making a rush. "I'll cut your gall and your milt and your pancridge."

Hi had expected the rush; he slipped to the left as it surged out at him. The man had expected this movement; he slashed out sideways with his knife, but missed. He was after Hi on the instant, roaring, as he rushed, his war cry of "Harrar." Hi twisted sharp to his right; the man followed, he seemed horribly near. Hi heard a splash, followed by an oath, and a fall; the man had put a foot into the drain and fallen.

Hi fled to the door into the hall, where he paused; the man had not risen; he was lying in a heap in the well or drain, muttering oaths. The fall may have hurt him: it had certainly knocked the fight out of him.

"Will you come and give me a hand up?" he said.

"No."

"Oh, Lord, my leg's broke, man; I can't hurt you."

"Rats."

"God, man; I'd not leave you, if you'd got a broken leg."

"Wouldn't you?"

"The bone's coming through the calf of me leg; I'm just bleeding away."

Hi did not answer this; the man went on:

"It's pretty poor goods," he said, "when an Englishman will leave another Englishman to rot in agony. Oh, the torment, it's awful. I feel it corrupting the blood."

Hi was touched by the man's moans, but did not answer. The man groaned some more.

"Young fellow," he said, "if I die, and I am dying, you'll take my love to my poor mother? Mrs. Jones, her name is. She lives at No. 27, Cowpop Street, Sale, Cheshire. It's the only house in the street with a brass knocker. Say my last thought was of her. And I want you to sing "Rock of Ages" over my tomb. It's cruel to die in a foreign land, but I'd rest better after "Rock of Ages". Won't you come and just hold my head up; I can't breathe; there's darkness coming. Lift me; won't you lift me?"

"No, I won't," Hi said.

"You young swine," the man said; "it's lucky for you you didn't, for if you had, I'd have settled you."

Hi went through the door and bolted it behind him. He tiptoed swiftly along the passage to the corridor down which the Indians had dragged him. The corridor stretched right and left along the length of the house. Hi could make out a staircase, the blackness of doors, and light in one place from a half-opened door. Hi listened.

All was silent at first. Then from somewhere upstairs he heard the noise of stealthy footsteps, moving slowly. To his right, from time to time, there was a little light fluttering noise, as though the wind were stirring an ill-fitting shutter or loosened jalousie. The man in the prison yard was quiet. The smell of tobacco smoke shewed that the other prisoner had passed that way.

Hi went quietly to the half-opened door, listened there, heard nothing suspicious, and peeped in.

The room was lit by an oil-lamp which had been turned so low that it stank. He could not see far into the room. From within there came again the fluttering noise, which was now not quite that of a shutter, but liker the yielding of paper under pressure, as though someone were opening a book and pressing the pages down so that it should remain open at the place. It gave Hi the sense that some industrious old man was working there in the half darkness gumming papers together.

He pushed the door very gently till he could see that the room was a kind of board-room, with shuttered windows. The table, from which the chairs had been flung back, was littered with papers. A big picture, partly out of its frame, was hanging askew on the wall to the right. Nobody was to be seen; but the noise of the pressed papers came from somewhere on the floor beyond the table.

Hi thought, "It is rats gnawing papers," but on coming into the room he saw that it was a dead man beset by myriads of cockroaches. The man's pockets had been turned inside out.

Hi suddenly whirled about in terror: someone was at his elbow.

He saw at once that he had no need to be terrified; it was the little man who had opened the prison door. He had stolen up in his silent way. He grinned at having scared Hi.

"Didn't 'ear me, did yer, cocky?" he said. "Seen the stiff? They done him in and gone through him; grizzled party; one of these Digos. We'd better 'op it arter 'ere."

Hi noticed that the man was carrying a long heavy ebony ruler which had been a part of the office equipment. He had the feeling that this was the man who had turned out the dead man's pockets.

"Bleedin' old beano goin' on down the boulevard," the man said; "kind of a Brock's benefit. If they come on 'ere agine, the goin' won't 'elp us; we shan't 'alf 'ave all right."

He led the way out of the room and so away towards the front door, from which fresh air was blowing into the house. On the top step a great yellow pariah dog stood, longing to enter, but scared by their approach. He snarled and slunk away from them as they came out into the open. Moved by the thought that the dog might eat the body, Hi closed the door behind him.

That part of the town was empty of life, except for the moths about the globe of the electric light. The houses were shuttered and seemed to be deserted; but Hi saw that a great disorder had raged there since he had been thrust into the prison. Household gear of many kinds had been dragged into the street and left. Far away down the hill was the glow of the shell of the mansion, each window red as a furnace mouth. All the inhabitants, as well as the lancers, seemed to be at the fire, except a few who came thence quietly with sidelong glances, having pickings from the wreck under their cloaks.

"I'm goin' to 'op it arter 'ere," the man said. "No 'ot potitoes in mine. Coo lummy, what's that?"

From the back of the city hall, from the direction of the prison yard, there came a sound of song, mixed with the tolling of a cuckoo. Henery Peach Kezia was lapping himself in soft Lydian airs:

> O the cuckoo bird sings in the merry May morn.
> Singing cuckoo, O cuckoo, how happy am I.
> O cuckoo, O cuckoo, O cuckoo.
> Cuckoo.

"It's the drunkard," Hi said.

"The stiff? You woke him?"

"Yes."

Hi noticed that the man's eyes were fixed upon him somewhat strangely.

"Which way you goin', cocky?" he asked.

"Anselmo," Hi said. "Do you know it?"

"I know it well," the man said. "I don't mind setting you there, or on the way there."

"That's very kind of you," Hi said. "But are you going that way?"

"Never you mind where I'm going," the man said. "You're a damn sight too nosy."

"No more nosy, as you call it, than you," Hi answered. "I know the way to Anselmo; if it's out of your own way, I can find it myself. But we'd better not go straight past the fire; we might be recognised."

"Come along 'ere, cocky," the man said. "If we go along this road a piece, we can easy cut across later."

They turned up a road which opened to the north not far from the city hall. The houses near it were small adobe bungalows, with roofs of red tiles. The stars in the heaven shone like lamps.

"I say, look at the stars," Hi said.

"Are you being pleasant?" the man asked. "You're doing 'Oh, the starlight'; but they're cocky little bleeders, stars."

They walked on together for a minute, till they were in the midst of a grove, where a night singing bird was making a plaintive, exquisite haunting call. The man paused.

"What was the nime of the plice you was goin' to?" he asked.

"Anselmo."

"Anselmo, that was it; Anselmo." He seemed to think for an instant. "Well, there's no plice of that nime anywheres abaht 'ere."

"But you said you knew it," Hi said.

"What was the nime agine?"

"Anselmo."

"Oh, Anselmo," the man said, "the plice you see over there?"

"No; over there," Hi said, turning to point. Some instinct told him to look out, but it came a fraction of a second too late. He never knew certainly what happened next, because he was knocked unconscious by a blow on the point of his jaw, which ended the world for him for four minutes.

When he came to himself, with a dizzy head full of confusion, he tried to stand, but found that his feet hurt. Groping down to find out why, he found that his shoes were gone. Instead of them, a pair of old white deck shoes, with rubber soles, lay beside him in the track. Then a certain slackness at his waist seemed unaccustomed. He put his hand to his waist and found that his money belt was gone; then he found that his pockets had been searched: he had been robbed. He called aloud at this. Then he looked about for his companion, whom he at once judged to be the thief. There was neither sight nor sound of him. He had vanished into the night where he belonged. There was no sound of anyone running, no noise of steps, nor of bushes being thrust aside. The bird was still making a plaintive call in the tree.

"I can't think what has happened," Hi said. He sat down to try to compose himself. When he began to know that he had been knocked out, he wondered, "for how long?" The stars had not changed position much, so far as he could see, and there was still some warmth or so he thought in the toes of the shoes.

"He knocked me out and robbed me," he thought. "I'd gladly have gone halves with him. I don't know what the deuce to do now. Well, I must get to Anselmo, that's the first thing. And it must be nearly midnight by this time and I'm further from Anselmo than I was when I started."

He put on the deck shoes. There was a meanness in the theft of his shoes which hurt him more even than the loss of his precious pocket-book with the sprig of hermosita. When he had put on the shoes and felt their discomforts, as well as their kind, which was specially loathsome to him, he walked back to the town, he could not afterwards tell why. He had no very clear thought of what he was doing nor of what he ought to do, for the brains were still shaky in his head from the knock upon his jaw.

When he turned into the street in front of the city hall, he saw some of the lancers, followed by a mob, riding uphill towards him. He turned uphill away from them, till he was out of the town, in a rocky path near a pine wood. The lancers paused at the city hall, as though to bivouac. Hi felt a deadly weariness overcoming the need of reaching Anselmo.

"I am done," he thought. "I have done nothing, but I have been through a good deal to-day. I must rest for a bit before I go on." He was cold as well as weary, for the cold sea breeze was blowing. "It must be midnight," he thought. "I will rest for just an hour among those rocks. If I had only not spoken to that officer at La Boca, I would have been fifty miles on beyond Anselmo by this."

He was so stupid from fatigue and the blow that he paid little heed to his going, as he pushed through the scrub towards what looked like shelter. Suddenly he caught a whiff of scent, a rustle of movement and a gleam of something: he was aware that people were hiding there. A startled somebody, speaking intensely, in a hiss of anxiety, said "Padre? . . . padre mio?"

"I'm not the man," Hi said.

Immediately somebody surged out of the darkness, flung him down and got him by the throat. He realised at once that he was in the hands of someone much stronger than himself, who could break his neck at will, if he made a noise. Some years before, at the Old Berks Steeplechases, he had seen a welsher caught by the crowd. When overtaken, the man had fallen and lain perfectly still, as though dead; this came back to Hi on the instant as wise.

The man who had grappled him got him well by the throat with one hand, while he reached back for his knife with the other. Hi saw a darkness of face staring into his, and beyond it pine boughs and stars. Other people were there: he smelt the scent of verbena: a woman's voice gave a caution. A woman seemed to be trying to open a box of matches and to take out a match: her fingers fumbled on the matches and people whispered. A man who came hurriedly from among the rocks struck a match upon his trouser leg, screened and held it down. Hi saw a lot of faces staring with surprise at him. He counted four persons: an old woman with white hair, a girl with great black eyes, a man with a somewhat finicky pale face, like the Aztec in the waxworks (he was the one who held the match), and a swarthy, fierce, very splendid-looking young man who had him by the throat. Hi noticed the muscles in the clear brown flesh of the arms which held him. "Golly," he thought, "this man could tear a pack of cards across." At this instant the match went out.

"It's all right," Hi said. "I'm English."

"Inglis," they repeated. The younger of the two women asked him in halting English: "What you doing here?"

Hi felt inclined to ask them what they were doing there, four civilised people, with jewels and scents, in the wilderness at midnight, garrotting strangers. He said that he was going to Anselmo and that he had been robbed. They seemed to understand a part of what he said, but they were puzzled by it.

The man, who was holding him, allowed him to sit up and said something in apology for having been so rough.

"What are they doing in the city?" the young woman asked.

"They are plundering and robbing, Señorita," Hi said.

At this instant some horses were heard trotting near to the pine clump. The man, who had held Hi, signed to him to remain still, while he stole away through the scrub to see who came. In a few minutes he returned with the riders of the horses, one of whom carried a lantern. This man was a swarthy, bearded, elderly don, more than sixty years of age, but still lean and alert. His face was both hard and melancholy, with something of watchfulness stamped on it by a life passed upon a frontier. He held up the lantern to examine Hi, while the others repeated to him Hi's story of Anselmo, which he did not seem altogether to accept. "Allan Winter said there was a feeling against us," Hi thought. "Now here it is." He debated whether he should tell them that he was a White, going on a White errand. "It might be all right," he thought. "But supposing it were all wrong. Supposing these people were really Reds. Then I should be in a fine mess."

The family drew aside to debate what should be done. Presently the daughter left the group and explained to Hi that they had to ride to safety, that they did not doubt his good faith, but that their lives depended on leaving no witness of their going and that, in short, Hi must come with them.

"We are most sad to ask it," she said, "but it is for our mother and sister. You see, this is war. They might kill us."

"We not take you far," the young man said. "We set you on your journey, when we get to friends."

There was something good-natured and well-bred about the young man which won Hi, who was, in any case, too utterly weary to protest. He said he understood and would gladly do as they asked. The girl and the young man said that it was very nice of him to take it like that. They mounted him on one of their spare horses, and set off together, through a woodland track, which set, for a while, to the south, and then curved west. Hi watched the direction as well as he could by the stars, so as to keep his bearings clear. About north-north-west was his course, he judged. "Now here I am going south," he thought. "The Lord alone knows when I shall get to Anselmo." He fell asleep on his horse and knew nothing more of his journey till he was wakened by the horses stopping.

He saw that they had reached a point in the hill from which, looking down a ravine, they could see far below them the lights of the town and the glowing of the burnt house. The night wind had roused up the flames on the last of the wreck so that it made a beacon still. The riders were staring at this, all strangely moved. The two women were sobbing: the men were muttering curses, or prayers that were of the nature of curses.

"Ah, the accursed, the accursed."

"For all this they shall pay sevenfold."

"You saints that bear the sword grant me the sword that I may smite these accursed ones."

"It is their home," Hi thought, "where all their past lies burnt. They were chased out of it and then it was fired."

The father interrupted the scene by saying, "It suffices. To-morrow is a new day: let us get to-morrow." He took his wife's rein and led the way on, the others followed him. Hi heard the nice young man say something to him, but he was too heavy with sleep to know what it was or to answer. He fell asleep again upon his horse. The high southern saddle kept him in his seat; sometimes he joggled forwards, sometimes backwards, while the horse went quietly on with the others.

At about two o'clock in the morning they came to a ranch which was guarded by mounted men. Here they all dismounted and went indoors (Hi with them) to what seemed to be a gathering of the clan.

There was a long room, lit by electric light, like all the houses in those hills even at that early age. There was a fire at one end of the room, for the night was cold enough. A maid of enormous strength, with a fine, square, good-humoured face, was making or dispensing maté among the gathering. There were perhaps forty men there, most of them talking at once, yet the room was so big that they did not crowd it.

As the party entered the room, the girl with the verbena scent noticed how weary Hi was.

"You are tired," she said. "Enrique, this gentleman is weary. Anton, get him a maté." (Enrique was the Aztec; Anton the nice one.)

"Sit down," she said, showing a seat which ran round the wall. "Anton will bring you a maté."

"You sit," he said. "Let me bring you a maté." Anton shoved him down on to his seat.

"Our guests do not wait, they are waited on," he said. "You are not a Red, I am sure, to rob us of the last of all our pleasures."

"I am a White," Hi said.

"You are a White?" the girl said. "But we thought all you English were Reds."

"I'm a heretic, of course," Hi said, "but a White."

Anton brought him a maté, which revived him. He saw the Aztec step into the midst of the gathering call for silence, and begin a long harangue, with many gestures. The babble of his voice, the heat of the room and more than twenty-four hours of strain together made him fall asleep with the bombilla in his hand.

This falling asleep may be said to mark the end of the first day of Hi's going to warn Don Manuel. His going had not prospered, mainly because one of Don Lopez' chief supporters, the half-breed Don Livio, a man of vengeful temper, had detached some lancers to burn the mansion of the Ribotes, who had had the misfortune to be the lords in the village in which he had passed his youth.

This act of private vengeance brought the lancers across Hi's path at the wrong time.

While Hi was being checked by event after event, on this first day, Ezekiel Rust was riding to the west with his message. At the very moment, when Hi was falling asleep, Ezekiel Rust was rousing from his rest eighty miles away to begin his second day's ride.

CHAPTER X

Hi may have slept for half an hour, when he was wakened by the tinkle of his bombilla falling on the floor. He roused up as a big, elderly rogue-bull of a man, with bloodshot eyes and a heavy ruminating mouth, which seemed to be chewing the cud of fifty different plans, came in, to take charge of the gathering. Plainly all there looked up to him as a leader. A flock of talkers surged up to him with a gabble of explanation and persuasion: some of it very hot, Hi thought.

Presently, Hi found this man staring at him, though as yet without comprehension. His eyes were fixed on Hi while his lower lip moved in and out under the strain of thought. After a time, his bull-like brain began to notice that Hi was a stranger in the camp: he turned to a man, indicated Hi by a jerk of the head, and asked, "Who is that?" Then, turning to Hi, whom of course he knew to be English, he jerked with his head, saying, "Come here, you. What are you?"

Anton explained as Hi came forward; Hi heard the words "caballero ingles": then Anton, after asking his name, introduced him to Don Pablo something of Meruel. Hi was refreshed by his sleep and eager to be doing. He made up his mind that as these were Whites he would tell his tale, so he did. He said that he was going on urgent White business to Don Manuel at Encinitas; he asked for a horse that he might proceed.

When he had said his say, he knew that he had said something wrong. "I believe they are Reds, after all," he thought. "Now I've put my foot in it." Anton drew him aside a moment and explained: "All the Whites here are anti-clerical, they hate Don Manuel like poison. You have said, 'I take nice Luteran message to the Pope.'" Anton seemed to think it very funny, but Hi was appalled. "I've done for myself now," he thought, "they'll probably jail me for a week."

"Business with Don Manuel at Encinitas?" Don Pablo repeated. "And what business?"

"To tell him that the Reds have put Señorita de Leyva into prison."

This was news to the assembly, but on the whole pleasant news: the de Leyvas were blamed for most of the troubles which had fallen on the Whites.

"At least," Don Pablo said, "you cannot reach Don Manuel from here."

"I don't want to," Hi said. "I want to reach Anselmo from here, and from there go on to Don Manuel."

"Very pretty," Don Pablo said. "There are telegraphs in Anselmo. You could warn Santa Barbara of all that has been said here."

"No, sir," Hi said, "unfortunately, I know no Spanish, and have not understood what has been said here: besides, I am not a spy."

"You are the first to mention the word," Don Pablo answered. "You are here, we are here, the trouble exists, the telegraph exists, Santa Barbara exists. I consider the situation."

"Yes, sir," Hi said, "but I have been only four nights in this land, I know nothing of your politics."

"How comes it then," Don Pablo interrupted, "that you go at all upon this errand? Why are you sent? Who sent you?"

"I must not tell you that, sir," Hi answered, "but I was sent because the need was great, and because an Englishman will not be suspected by the Reds."

"Very true," Don Pablo answered, "but he may be suspected by the Whites. See you," he added, turning to address the assembly in Spanish, "this boy may justly be suspected by us, when he comes from we know not where and says that he wishes to reach Anselmo."

As most of those there were like water, ready to flow in any direction opened to it, as long as it were downhill, this turned the company against Hi. They agreed that he might justly be suspected. Why should he be there, they asked, if he wished to reach Anselmo? This was now war; Anselmo was a place of the Reds undoubtedly; this was an English boy; that he should be sent on a message was a farce. Undoubtedly he was a spy or might be used as a spy. Hi did not know their words, but their meanings were plain.

"You may be this or you may be that," Don Pablo said, in English, "but you cannot go to Anselmo."

"But, sir, I must go."

"What say you?"

"Sir, I must go."

Don Pablo pretended to be deaf, he held one of his ears with his hand, so as to catch the sound: the company tittered.

"What say you?"

"Sir, I must go to Anselmo."

"Ah," Don Pablo said with a smile, turning to the men, "He says that he must go to Anselmo. *Must go*; this very important English word. No, sir," he said, turning to Hi, "you may go to your Reds in Carpinteria, or you may go home to your English in England; no one shall stop you; it is a healthy walk, for you English are accustomed to walk; but you shall not go to Anselmo. You shall not go to Anselmo, because it is a special place, which I am determined that you shall not see."

His face, as he spoke, became gorged with blood like the wattles of a turkey cock. Having settled Hi, as he judged, he turned to the assembled men and made them a long harangue in Spanish. Long afterwards Hi learned that the purpose of the meeting was to keep the Pituba raiders out of that part of Meruel. The men there were Whites, but anti-clerical and, on the whole, in favour of Lopez, because he was a Meruel man. Pablo's purpose, at that moment, was to get the party to ride to a well-known ranch to get from it the reinforcement of its company.

All there seemed pleased at his suggestion, except those whose mansion had been burned in Ribote. These retired in a group in some indignation when the others left the room. Hi was left alone in the great room, save for the broad, good-humoured maid, who was gathering up the bombillas. She was a friendly soul; she made remarks in Spanish to Hi, so that he might feel at ease.

"Many bombillas."

"Si," Hi answered.

"Better many guests than many locusts."

This was beyond Hi, who grinned. After a little time, she added, with a sigh:

"There are more guests than lovers."

Hi did not know what she said, but he answered, in English, "Such is life."

After some twenty minutes of talking outside the house the assembled men mounted their horses, which had been kicking and snapping at each other, from anger at the cold, through all the hours of the discussion. Even when they had mounted they made no effort to start. They continued to discuss till it was broad daylight, when they all set off together.

Anton entered with his sister. He came up to Hi to apologise for Don Pablo.

"It is absurd," he said, "that that man should have stopped your going to Anselmo. There is no reason why you shouldn't go to Anselmo. Of course you may go there."

"I have no horse," Hi said. "Would you lend me a horse so that I could go there?"

"Do you know the way?" the girl asked.

"No."

"It must be forty kilometres and a difficult way except through Ribote."

"I could find it," Hi said.

The brother and sister looked at each other with some hesitation. Hi was afraid that they were wondering whether to trust a tramp, who came at midnight, with neither collar nor tie, from God knows where.

"I am sorry to say," he said, "that I have got no money with me, but Mr. Winter, of Quezon, beyond Santa Barbara, knows me, and Señora Piranha and her daughter know me."

"Rosa Piranha?" the girl said. "You know her?"

"Very well. Do you?"

"We were at the convent together," the girl said. "Of course we will lend you a horse. What is your name?"

"Ridden. Will you tell me yours?"

"We are Ribotes," she said. "But what makes us consider is, the road to Anselmo. It is no road, my brother says."

"It is a bad road," Anton said.

"I don't mind how bad it is as long as it is a road," he said. "And I'll not let your horse down or give him a sore back or anything; I swear I won't. And I don't know how to thank you for saying you will lend me one. The point is, getting him back to you. I'm going to the Elenas, the horse-breeders, of Anselmo; I am sure they would send him back or I would bring him back myself, if you would not mind waiting a few days."

"Bring him back yourself," Anton said.

"Yes, yes," the girl said.

"The horse will be all right," Anton said, "but how about the rider? First you must have food."

They gave him sausage, bread, coffee and figs. Then they filled saddle-bags with these things and with corn for him to take with him. Anton brought him a silk scarf.

"You will want this for your neck," he said. "There will be ticks or mosquitoes in the forest."

No doubt they would have given him money, had they not feared to hurt his feelings.

"I don't know how to thank you two," he said. "You have been most frightfully kind."

"The least we could do," Anton said, "after nearly murdering you in the dark, as I did."

They brought him out to the stables, where they saddled a horse for him.

"He will take you to Anselmo all right," Anton said. "The question is, will you be able to find your way there?"

"I will try," Hi said.

"Not so easy," Anton said. "Look there."

From where he stood Hi could see nothing but great swathes of rolling forest, amid a mist that was lifting and falling as though it were alive.

"You see that it is not easy," Anton said, "even when you get out of the forest."

"I think I'll find it all right," Hi said. "I'm good at finding my way."

Anton pursed up his lips and shook his head. "I hope," he said, "I hope. You got good remembrance?"

"Yes."

"Good. Then I tell you all the way."

"Right. I'll remember."

"It is difficult," Anton said. "You follow this track here for three kilometres, through the scrub. Then you come to a place very big as a saucer; big, big. Then north-west across it to a hole, snap, cut off, like so, in the hills, a long way, fifteen kilometres. Out there you will see peones who ride. One will show you. You must not go so, no; but so, because, so, there is no ground; all is gone. But this not for twenty kilometres. Till then, you look for the place big as a pan, very big; and the hill that has like so; high, yet so, snap, see; no, more like so."

This was not clear as a course should be, but his gestures made it clearer. Anton knew the dangers of losing a trail; he turned to his sister for an English rendering of what he wished to explain. Unfortunately she had not seen the place which he strove to describe, nor was her English much better than his, but she added a few words.

"After this track," she said, "there is a . . . very big."

"A lake?" Hi suggested.

"A what?"

"A water?"

"No, no, no; very big dry."

"I understand. A dry valley?"

"Si, si. Then you cross this; oh, it is long. Then you look a way out. There is a hole in the hill, like so."

"A pass?" Hi said. "A gap? A way to go through?"

"Si, si."

"But," Anton said, "you must not go to this side, right side, because no ground; go to left side. Ask peones."

"Will there be peones?"

"Always peones."

"And if I cannot find a peon to ask?" Hi said.

"Bad, bad," Anton said. "A difficult way. Not for some kilometres. But keep north through the path through the forest; see?"

"Anselmo is north from the pass," the girl said.

"I'll find it," Hi said.

"Si, si, you will find it. It is narrow road in the forest; but to the left. Then you get out of the forest you will see."

Hi was well used to finding his way on the downs; he had plenty of confidence in himself. "I'll find it," he repeated. "But one thing more; if any people stop me, may I say that I come from you?"

"They will see that you come from us."

"How?"

"The brand," Anton said, pointing to two wavy marks, one above the other, on the horse's quarter.

"Thank you again," Hi said, "for all that you have done for me."

"Good luck," the girl said.

"Come tell us how you got on," Anton said.

"I will, indeed, if I may. Thank you."

His horse was one of the rather small, sturdy, savannah ranch horses, bred in the uplands from the descendants of the conquerors' mares by the stallions imported from England. He was dark, wise and full of go.

"Will he buck?" Hi asked.

"If you meet a tiger."

"If a pig, he kick; so you know," the girl said.

"Right. Thanks. Good-bye."

"Con Dios."

The horse was as eager to be gone as Hi to go. He sailed sideways down the avenue. Just as he turned into the thicket, Hi looked back to wave to his friends; they waved back to him. In two seconds more they were out of sight; he was riding through forest that was all dropping dew and trailing mist.

"I am really off at last," he thought. "Twenty-four hours late in starting and twice as far from Anselmo as I was."

The mist strayed itself out into clearness and the tops of the trees began to glitter as the sun rose higher. Little birds came flying just in front of him, as though to show their speed. Their cries, as they flew, sounded as though each bird were calling to "go it." "I'll go it fast enough," he said.

For a long time he heard no other noise than the cries of these birds and the drumming of the feet of the horse. As he went on, he caught another noise, which at first he thought must be the wind in the tree-tops. Then, as it grew louder, he recognised it as the noise of water. He came round a curve upon a scene so beautiful that it made him pull up.

He came unexpectedly upon a ravine or gash in the hill. Close to him, on his left side, the hill, which had always been steep, changed suddenly to crag, over which a brook was falling in white, delaying mists, for some seven hundred feet. At the foot of the fall some long distant collapse had made an undercliff, nearly flat, across which the water loitered in a broad shallow rock basin, till it reached another fall. What he had been hearing was the noise of the falls.

As the ravine and pool made a wide open space, all the hillside in front of him was in such light that he could see, for the first time, what colour can be. The timber grew to great heights beyond the pool, but all the timber down the glade was heaped and piled with a pouring fire of creeper in blossom. A white flowered creeper had piled itself like snow even to the tops of the green-hearts, and fell thence in streamers and banners.

All the crags, as well as the rocks of the pool, were of a pale blue colour, like lapis lazuli. Mists from the falling water made rainbows all down the cliff. White birds cruised among the rainbows and changed colour in them.

He saw all this in a few seconds of admiration. Then he saw that the broad shallow pool was peopled by a priesthood, in rosy mantles, moving with an exquisite peace along the water. The leading priest rose into the air silently and gracefully; the others followed, till all the flight were moving away, more like flowers or thoughts or dreams than birds. He watched them till their effortless wings drooped them to some lower pool out of sight. "Those are the rosy ibises," he thought.

"Damned pretty birds," his father had said, "only you don't often get a shot at them."

He rode through the pool to the rising trail beyond; soon he was in the gloom again, winding up into the hills among forest. "I must be near the big dry pan or valley," he thought. "I hope I haven't gone wrong."

Almost as he uttered the thought the thickets thinned to an undergrowth in blossom noisy with bees. A few yards more brought him out to the "very big dry" of the savannah, which was unlike anything ever seen by him.

His first thought was that it was the crater of a volcano or the bed of a lake, perhaps twenty miles long by seven broad. It may well have been both, in turn. Now it was an expanse of grass ringed by hills. Some eagles were cruising over it; their majesty suited the vastness of the expanse. The emptiness and the freedom of the vastness made Hi catch his breath. He was the king of that space; there was nothing there but wind and grass, with clumps of tussock-grass standing out here and there.

He did not take it all in at once; then he thought, "I was to meet peones here, who will set me on my way. I see no peones."

A searching of the distance showed him, far off, some specks, some white, some dark. "Those are the herds," he thought. "And the peones are with them. How those white cattle shine in the sun. But they are all miles away from here. There is none near me.

"But what was it that they said I was to look for? I was to go 'north-west across it to a hole, snap, so,' ten miles away. Well, let's have a look. That will be north-west, roughly. And there, by George, is a sort of snap in the hills, as though they were cut or broken. That is the pass he means; that is my way. So let us forward for there. But what a place, what a land, what a life."

It was a good enough life for a man, to ride that expanse on a horse worthy of such going. The horse felt the stir of that freedom. Hi felt him kindle beneath him into the tireless stride of the horse of the savannah. As he went, his hoofs drummed up myriads of glittering green beetles which whirled about them and flew with them, sometimes settling on horse or man, then whirling on again, now with shrillness, now with droning, till the noise they made was the ride itself set to music. "I shall save her," he sang to the music, "I shall save Carlotta. And she will marry her man, of course, but all the same I shall have done that; and we shall be friends of a special sort all our lives. It will be something that nobody else will have."

He kept headed for the pass, but his eyes roved the land for a peon. Soon he was startled by the light on the distance to his left; he had seen nothing like it. All the things in that southern distance became so distinct that he felt that he was looking at them through a telescope. At the same time, the calls of the peones, the beating of their horses' hoofs, and the movings of the cattle came to him from across the miles of the savannah. "It is odd that things should be so clear," he thought. "I should say it means rain." The tops of the southern hills brightened till they seemed to spout flames into the sky. These flames soon changed into streamers of cirrus, less fiery than copper-coloured, with rose half-way up the heavens. "It is just as though the sky were feeling bilious," he thought. With this change in the heavens, a change came into the air and into the horse; all the delight of the going went; the beetles gave up their play. Presently the copper-colour darkened along the hilltops to something like the smoke of a burning.

"It's going to be a storm," Hi thought. "I'd be just as well in the cover of the pass before it breaks. Come up, horse."

The horse made it clear that he was uneasy about something, or was in some way feeling Hi's uneasiness. He had become nervy and on edge in a way which Hi could not explain. He himself felt nervy, but the restlessness of his horse frightened him. "I believe he smells some wild beast or snakes," Hi thought; but he could see neither; there seemed to be no creatures on that llano save some beasts like tailless rats and a few birds which piped and fled. The edge of the clouds tattered out into rags which soon laid hold of the sun so that all the joy died from the scene.

"We're in for a storm and a half," Hi thought, "one of those electrical storms my father was always gassing about." He took a look to his left, where now the darkness had blotted out the line of the hills, then he took a look to his right, where the hills stood in a glow which made them look like hills in hell. Straight ahead was the gash or pass by which he was to descend. He could see no cattle nor peones there. "Perhaps they are in the pass," he thought, "in some ranch or corral there. But I hope they are, for then I may find some shelter."

The air had long since lost its zest. It was flat yet heavy, though both Hi and the horse were sweating, there was a feeling of death being present, which suggested cold; all kinds of evil seemed about to happen. Waifs and strays of thought came into Hi's mind and went out of it; he felt that he could not concentrate upon any one of them. A few drops of rain splashed down, like florins and half-crowns, with a rattle on the tough grass.

He had made an effort to be in the pass before the storm broke. He reached it in time but, being there, he found it grim enough. It was a gash, between two cliffs of rotten rock, which curved round into a grimmer gash, all black with a grove of vast trees. "Better under the trees than in the open," he thought, so he turned towards the cover. The noise of the hoofs upon the stones made echoes like the smacking of nails into a coffin. "That's got you, that's got you," the smacking seemed to say, "that's got you." He stopped the horse, so that the echoes might stop. Looking back at the crater over which he had ridden, he found that he could see little save a greyness out of which came a sighing. All the place seemed to moan at him with a moan of despair, that sounded like, "Oh, it's got us at last." Out of the greyness a coldness came suddenly from the icefields on the mountain. Then the great grassy expanse disappeared from view. The storm, sweeping up, shut out the world. "Very little more," he thought, "and I should have been caught in the open." Suddenly streaks of greyness ran like men along the ground and struck flashes with their feet. "By George, it's rain," he said; "it's all rain. This is rain indeed."

On the instant, the greyness sighed into a hissing, hissed into a rushing, and rushed into a roaring. It sucked up all the last of the savannah, surged over the mouth of the pass, beat Hi breathless and engulfed him, in a roaring of pouring, as though a river were falling. Hi felt that he was freezing and that everything else had turned to water: he was in water and under water, the air he breathed was water: the earth his horse stood on was running water. Thunder sounded not far off: he could not see the lightning, but remembered his father's stories of iron outcrops in the rocks near the Meruel border, which seemed to "attract" any lightning there might be. He did not know whether iron outcrops could "attract" lightning; probably it was one of his father's insane theories, but it might be the fact, in which case he was near the Meruel border, and might be standing on the magazine waiting for the spark. The thought of trying to push on, through the rain, did not enter his head: he could not see twenty yards in any direction.

The violence of the rain lasted for some two hours, after which it relented to a downpour not worse than that of steady rain in England. When once it had relented thus, it steadied, as though it would never cease: it was this steadiness which daunted Hi. "It's raining like an eight-day clock," Hi thought. "It might keep on at this pace for days." He sought to the thickest cover that he could find and hoped for the best. In another hour, the heavens descended on him, so that while water streamed from heaven and forest, the air was a greyness of melting and moving cloud. All the forest was alive with the rushings, the laughters and the forebodings of rain falling or being shaken: sometimes it came at him like the footsteps of enemies, sometimes like lamentings, anon with a crackle as though a pack were afoot. "The horse would take me out of this," he thought, "but he would take me straight back to the estancia, so that I should have to start again. I'd better wait here. After all, if it rains like this it must rain itself out before long: no clouds could stand it. I wonder where all the cloud can come from. As soon as this mist or cloud or fog goes, I'll push on."

Having made his plan, he stuck to it: the cloud seemed to do the same; it did not go: it even increased till the earth seemed melting and the air liquid. "Golly," Hi thought, "this cloud isn't going to go. I may be here for days." He reckoned that he had been there already for some hours. "I must find some browsing for the horse."

This the horse found without going far from where they were: he led the way to some shrubs, which he ate with relish. "I hope he knows what is good for him," Hi thought, "for I don't."

He secured the horse from straying: then he sought about for a shelter from this never-ceasing drip: there was no shelter in sight. "Probably there isn't one anywhere," he thought, shuddering. "I shall be here for the day and night, and goodness knows how much longer besides."

He had come back to his horse, partly from fear of losing him, partly for his company, when the greyness dimmed to a greater density, so that he could not see his outstretched hand. In this dimness an eternity passed. The rain continued unabated. He contrived to tend the horse, and to give him some of the corn which Anton had provided; later, when he had watered him, he contrived to tether him securely near the bushes where he could browse. After this he himself ate, very sparingly, of the food which Anton had given. When he had supped, it was dark: the night had fallen. Hi made himself a nest of unease in the edible bush, which smelt like his mother's tooth-powder. Lying on a mess of trampled boughs, which kept him off the mud, he crouched himself into a ball till something like warmth came into him; then he even slept a little, in starts and nightmares, from which he would leap up, terrified that the horse had gone.

This was his second night upon the road to fetch Don Manuel. At about the time when he lay down upon his boughs Ezekiel Rust, dead beat, pulled up somewhere in sight of the lights of San Jacinto city, at the other end of the Central Province. Out there in the barrens, the old man was comforting his horse, before lying down in the sage with a rope round him to keep off the snakes. He had had such a ride as he had never dreamed of; but being soft to the saddle, after some years in a town, he could go no further without a rest.

CHAPTER XI

Some hours after midnight, Hi woke aching with cramps and dripping with sweat: it was oppressively hot and still: all the forest was holding its breath, as though about to do something dreadful. There was a deliberation, even about the droppings from the trees. "Golly," Hi thought, "it feels as though the earth were going to open." It was pitch dark in the forest: the mist had gone from the trees, yet there was no glimmer of any star: the moon, being young, was long since gone. The stew of air gave Hi the feeling that a heaven of cast-iron was descending bodily upon the tree-tops to squeeze the earth flat.

The suspense of waiting for the heaven to fall was broken suddenly by thunder, rain and wind, all rising in violence until, at about an hour after dawn, they reached a pitch such as Hi had not believed to be possible. Then, while the forest was crashing with falling boughs and trees, and the air all vehement water and flying fragments, the heart suddenly went out of the storm; the darkness from above rolled away to leeward, showing the sun. The wind, which had been a thing of death, at once became a thing of healing: the storm was over: nature was freed from prison: Hi could go on.

He could go on; but he had lost another complete day and the going was changed. He was in a world of mud like the first chaos. All the wood was littered with thousands of young leaves, twigs and caterpillars. The millioned life, which had thrust at the first rains, had been washed to a smalm by these last. The ground of the wood had been so worked by the rain that it looked and trod like a ploughed field in a wet November. He rode out of the wood, all streaming as he was, towards the gulley of the pass. For one glorious minute, he saw all things glitter in the sun: the warmth beat upon him like life itself; then the rain began again: not heavy rain, but a steady trickle.

By this time, he was in the ravine of the pass into which every gulley, meuse and cranny, as well as the gashes cut by the storm, had been draining for many hours. A mess as of a dozen ploughed fields, of different colours of clay, had been washed into the pass, plastered there and sprinkled with boulders. Here and there boulders too big to shift had stood as obstructions to the floods. Near these, small boulders and ridges of rotten stone had been washed or flung so as to form moraines or dams across the hollow of the valley. Sometimes these dams held pools of water many feet in depth. All the pass rang with the noise of falling water.

He went on, cold and soaked; on foot in the mud, leading a miserable horse through pools, morasses and over stones. The rain fell steadily, and there was no road nor signpost, nothing but the direction of the gulley down the hill, the noise of water, sometimes birds, but never beast nor man.

"And the worse of it is," he thought, "that I must be coming to that place where I was to turn off, if I was to turn off. That was what he meant, I think: that I had to go to the left of a crossing. I only hope that it will clear before I reach the place."

It did not clear: it went on raining.

"This is what father meant," he thought, "when he said, 'You'll thank me before the year's out for sending you to a land of the sun.' "

He wondered much into what kind of country he had come, for he could see so little, except the faces of rocks all streaming, then mist, then folds of hill, from which streamers of rain came out and passed. Presently he came to trees which had hard leaves that clacked: his teeth clacked in sympathy. Not long after this, he came to a bridge, not over but in a torrent; and here he had to blindfold his horse to get him across. On the other side of the bridge, at a little distance above the waters, was a stone with an inscription in Latin:

> Pray for the souls
> Of Espinar, Gamarro, Velarde.
> Drowned here.

He wondered as he looked back at the bridge, with the water swirling across it between the balusters of the parapets, how he had ever crossed. He patted his horse "for being such a sport." He judged that this river must be the upper waters of the river at La Boca; but any sense of direction was long since gone from him: he did not know where he was.

Memory of his friend's direction, that there was no road to the right, made him edge to his left, whenever there was an opening. He was not on any track or trail now, but in mud or scrub among the clouds; sometimes rocks loomed out at him, sometimes trees. When he halted, as he sometimes did, to shout, in the hope of an answer, he had no answer, save the noise of the rain that wept as though all hope were gone. "Well, if I go on, I must reach somewhere," he said. "I can't go back, even if I wanted to, because the river's rising, and nothing would take me over that bridge again, with the water worse than it was. One good thing about this rain is, that there won't be any forest fever yet, since the rains aren't at an end."

It was consolation of a kind; but he was as sick and shaking from cold and misery as most fevers could have made him. He noticed after a time that he was going uphill again. After some hours of this he came into a forest of giant trees. There was no undergrowth and little light in this forest. He rode in a gloom full of sighing like voices and full of dropping like footsteps. The rain seeped in films and streaks through this wood: mists of it paused in places, like ghosts looking at him from behind trees. Sudden gusts sent rushes of water to the ground with the noise of the steps of beasts. It was in this wood that the rain began to slacken.

At first, he thought that this was only a seeming, due to the shelter of the trees; but soon the mists of the rain cleared from the boles, which at once became like gods for bulk and silence. Soon the birds and insects reappeared; ants came to forage among what the rain had brought to earth; ticks fell from the trees; the big red and yellow fungi at the tree roots unrolled themselves into enormous spiders which waved their front legs at Hi in a terrifying rhythm, as though they were trying to hypnotise him. They did it slowly, with their eyes fixed upon him. They seemed to be repeating:

Fee, Fi, Fo, Fum,
I smell the blood of an Englishman.

Hi could see no tracks anywhere on that wet earth, but he realised that his horse was leading him somewhere.

"Good old boy," he said, "you know more about these parts than I do. If you can bring me to any comfort I'll be grateful."

A long time passed before comfort appeared. It came with the brightening of the light in the gaps among the tree-tops: the very sight of this was warmth to him. "The sun," he said, "I'll do it yet, if I can only find someone to direct me." The horse went straight ahead till at about two in the afternoon, as Hi guessed, he paused and whinnied, and horses whinnied in reply.

There, at a little distance in front of him, on a level patch, where the trees, being small, had been easily cleared, was a hut or shack with smoke rising from the chimney. It was a white man's, not an Indian's hut, because it was sided and ended with unbarked planks and roofed with shingles. It was old and falling to pieces. It must have been deserted for years, Hi thought, yet smoke was rising from it. Beside it was a long, ruinous pent-house or shed, with a torn canvas crib or manger running along its wall. "I suppose it is an outlying camp," Hi thought, "or some old winter house for the timber cutters; anyhow, thank Heaven, there are people there." He could see two pale faces peering round the half-opened door at him. When he lifted his eyes from the house, he saw, at a little distance, two tethered horses pausing from their grass to stare at him. As he advanced from his halting place, the faces at the door moved forward, so that he could make out a man and a woman. The man advanced to a pace beyond the door. He was a short, fresh-coloured man, with fair hair, and a small sandy moustache. What Hi noticed more particularly was that the man looked guilty, as though he had been caught in the act of something. "He's scared at something," Hi thought. When the man saw that Hi was only a boy, a relief came over his face, a relief so great that it made him laugh unpleasantly.

The woman had drawn back out of sight inside the shed, where (from the sound) she seemed to be doing something with bedclothes, making a bed or packing something in blankets. Hi thought: "There's something fishy here. I've caught them in the act at something. And it must be pretty bad or he wouldn't be in such a funk."

"Is this the way to Anselmo?" Hi asked. The man looked blank. Hi repeated the question, more than once; after a while the woman came to the door.

"Anselmo?" she asked.

"Si, si, Anselmo."

"Por aqui, Anselmo."

She was a willowy woman, all slink and gleam, with a speck in one eye and something swollen in lip and nose.

"This is, then, the way to Anselmo," Hi said. "La via a Anselmo? The calle or route a l'Anselmo?"

"Si, si," the woman said, nodding.

The first wish of the couple, to get the stranger away from the hut, without letting him peep inside, now changed to another wish: a strange look passed between them, which made Hi uneasy. The man had enormous fore-arm muscles: his right fore-arm had been bruised or scraped quite recently. In his trousers he had a gun pocket which plainly had been used for a gun, though no gun was there at the moment.

"Por aqui, Anselmo," the man said, taking Hi's bridle and turning the horse away from the shack.

"He show you," the woman said in English.

"Is it far to Anselmo?" Hi asked.

The man said he could not understand.

"I don't understand, either," Hi thought, "what you two have been up to, here in the forest. You aren't living here; you only came here an hour ago; because there are no tracks to the door, except brand new ones. Why do you two come here in the rains to pack something in blankets? What were you packing in blankets?" What indeed?

The man led him past the two tethered horses into the forest on the trail by which the horses had come there an hour or so before. Hi had noticed horse tracks ever since he was a child: he noticed suddenly the tracks of a third horse in the soft earth. Three horses had come towards the shack that morning: the third had gone off suddenly into the forest. Why?

The man led on, saying nothing, but thinking the more. Glancing back, Hi saw the woman moving from the shack into the forest. "I wonder if I'm going to be led round to meet her," he thought. "And if so, why?" Glancing forward, Hi saw that the man was looking at him with a strange expression.

"I believe they're up to no good," he thought. "I'll get out of it."

For a moment, he did not know how to get out of it, nor how he could manage without a guide if he did. Then the certainty that this couple were wicked urged him to act. Something said in his brain, "Behind that door they had a lad like you, whom they had murdered." A picture formed in his brain of the woman behind the door, rolling a body in a blanket. Whenever she rolled the body face up, the face which showed was his own. "It may be all imagination," he thought, "but I'll go on alone."

He checked the horse, with a sign to the man: he did not know what on earth he was to do next.

"Dis donc," he said in a mixed speech. "Esta Anselmo loin d'ici? Anselmo . . . sabe? Anselmo, est il bien loin? La ville d'Anselmo, est il far?"

The man nodded his head and grinned, as though to reassure him. Something in the man's face, the pouchy look under the eyes, reminded Hi of one of the portraits of Henry VIII: it looked evil from evil done and evil planning. The man turned to his path and seemed about to lead the horse off the trail. "I daresay," Hi thought, "the woman is the shot: she has the revolver. He'll lead me round to her and she'll pot me from behind a bush. Yet he's as strong as an ox. I can't hit him or break from him without getting the worst of it. What can I do?"

The voice in his brain said, "Scare him"; but he did not seem to be an easy man to scare. "I could make the horse shy," he thought, "though if I do that, I may be bucked off myself."

"Dis donc," he said again, "sont ils beaucoup de guardias civiles in Anselmo? Moi, je ne veux pas le police. Sabe? Comprende Usted? Police? Muchas guardias me muchas afraido."

The man said something in his sullen way that all would be well, better than well: again he turned to his task, leading the horse off the trail.

"Things are getting to be critical," Hi thought. "I must try a scare."

He was about to try some sudden startling of the horse, when the woman called out something. The man stopped and shouted in reply: from the woman's answer Hi made out that she wanted the man for some reason, to do something which she could not do. "Wants him to load the revolver, probably," he thought. The man seemed vexed at the request: he seemed to ask if she could not manage as she was: she answered "No."

The man growled in his throat. "Bah. Las mujeres." He let go the rein, with a look of threat and misgiving. He said something to Hi, which seemed to mean: "You stay here a minute: I'll be back directly." He strode off in the direction from which the woman had called. Hi let him go about ten yards, then he turned his horse, and urged him up. The man turned and called out to him to stop. Glancing back, as the horse got into his stride, Hi saw the man running back to where the horses were tethered.

"The brute's going to chase me," he thought. "And he'll track me, even if I dodge him. The worst of it is, that I don't know whether I am headed for Anselmo or the new Jerusalem; but I must come out somewhere if I keep on. This forest can't go on for ever."

This was true; but he had a memory of his father saying, "The forest goes all the way to Cualimaçu on the Matulingas, 1,500 miles if its an inch." If he happened to be heading for Cualimaçu, his journey to Anselmo was likely to be protracted. For the moment, however, his thought was to get away from these people.

Almost at once, his horse shied from a pool of blood where men had trodden within the hour. It was surrounded by big blue butterflies as greedy for salt as English butterflies for honey. "That's where the murder was," he thought, "and those two will follow me because they know that I know."

After an hour, however, when he halted for the third time to listen for the sound of pursuit, he felt sure that he was not pursued. He rode on slowly through the forest, leaving the direction to the horse, who now seemed to know where he was going. As far as he could tell, in the gloom of under the trees, he went westwards but not directly, for the thorn thickets forced him now in one direction, now in another.

Presently the horse cocked his ears at something and challenged. Hi halted, expecting and fearing to see some wild beast, but in a few seconds he saw that there was a horse in front of him, standing still among the tree trunks, watching him, some fifty yards ahead. He was almost invisible at first, for a horse will fade into any background or dimness; as he became distinct, Hi saw that he was saddled and bridled, though not mounted.

"That is it," he thought, "the brute has headed me off. This is the murderer. He has slipped off his horse there, and is somewhere among the trees waiting to pot me. Even if I dodge him, there'll still be Mrs. Now my only chance is to dodge."

He was about to dodge, knowing the futility of dodging, when the horse strode out of his covert into view. He was a darker horse than the two big sorrels tethered near the shack. He had a running cut on his side and a saddle twisted underneath him. He came ramping from his place, full of power and alarm. "By George, it's the dead man's horse," Hi cried, "and what a beauty. I'll have him." However, the horse had been terrified once that day; Hi's coming set him off again full tilt into the wilderness, with his stirrups flying from flank to foreleg or swinging back to clank under his belly. Presently, the girth buckle broke, the saddle fell and made him stumble, but he recovered, shook it clear and strode off into the woods.

Soon after his stridings had ceased to beat in the ears, the air above began to sigh with the homings of countless birds which settled on the trees with cryings and shriekings. Then suddenly there came a darkening all over the forest, as though the light had been turned off at a tap. Hi knew what this meant. His father had often told him that when the sun went behind Mount Melchior the light went off, so that you couldn't see to shoot. "Now here I am with the day gone," he thought. "It will soon be dark, and I have not yet started for Anselmo. Buck up, old horse, and get me out of the forest."

The horse seemed to be bound for somewhere; but after another hour of going, when it was beginning to be dark, he was still in the forest. He could see no gleam of open country nor hear anywhere any noise of men. When he halted to shout, he had no answer, except the sudden silence of birds and beasts. He was there in the depths, out of the reach of his kind, as alone as a man can be.

Perhaps in the past the horse had had some happiness in that part of the forest, which led him thither now. When it was almost too dark to go further, he bore his rider into a space where Indians had made a cassava patch by burning off the trees. Indians and cassava shrubs were long since gone, but the space was still clear of forest. In that patch of ground, some eighty by fifty yards across, there was tall grass of a bright yellow colour between two and three feet high. About this, the trees grew to less than their usual size, being (as it seemed) bowed down by the weight of the creepers. Over the patch was the dome or depth of violet sky in which there were already stars.

The horse thrust into the patch and fell to eating greedily. Hi dismounted to look about him; he found that there was water at one edge of the patch.

"I'd better stay here for the night," he thought, "because I'm lost. In the morning perhaps I may be able to find a way out. If I could only see the sun or Polaris I would be out in no time."

He unsaddled his horse, rubbed him well down with grass, and having haltered him, hitched him to a tree. He gathered him some armsfull of the grass, and talked to him, as he ate, for comfort.

All through his ride he had not tasted food, because of something he had said to himself at breakfast, "I hope my next meal may be at Anselmo." Now, when he saw plainly that he could not reach Anselmo for many hours to come, he drew his food from his bags. The rain had made a paste of the bread, but he scraped some of the paste together and ate it with some sausage; he drank of the water of the pan, which smacked of the marsh. He reckoned that he still had one tolerable meal of paste left in his bag, and one good feed of oats for the horse. These things he resolved to keep in reserve. Under the paste of the bread he found five silver pesetas, which Anton or the girl had hidden for him.

He was much touched by this.

But his main feeling was one of overwhelming anxiety for his friends who were depending on him. "Oh, they must feel that I have failed them," he thought. "They must have sent someone else. If this has happened to 'Zeke as well, God help Carlotta. God help her."

A strange whiteness of light glimmered high up in the trees: in a few moments it died, leaving all things strangely dark.

"Here is the night," he thought. "Oh, it is lonely. This is my third night away and I haven't even started yet. But I'll get my bearings and start at dawn. I'll get through somehow."

The stars deepened overhead: the birds lapsed into silence: what noises there had been in the wood became suddenly stealthier. Little bright burnings came and went in the air as the fireflies began. Hi gathered more grass for the horse, tried his tether, and then made himself a nest of grass in which he could not sleep, because of the cold.

During the morning of this, the third day, of Hi's journey, Ezekiel Rust came at a gallop to the house at Encarnacion, where Don Manuel watched beside the dead body of his mother. Being admitted to Don Manuel, he delivered his message, with what news he could add from the underworld of Medinas. Don Manuel waited for half an hour, while his mother's body was buried; then he rode to San Jacinto city, to intercept any other messenger coming from the capital. By the early afternoon he was summoning all his friends and adherents in the Western Provinces to come with arms, fodder and horses to a rendezvous east of the river. At about the time when Hi was settling to his nest, Don Manuel's first supporter, Pascual Mestas, came in to the rendezvous with twenty men from Santiago. Ezekiel Rust was given a bed in the inn at San Jacinto, with the promise that he should not want again in life.

CHAPTER XII

After some hours, by crouching knee to chin, covered by his saddle, a kind of warmth crept over Hi, so that he slept an uneasy sleep, full of cramps and nightmares.

Uneasy as it was, it was deep. Eternity seemed to go over him like a sea. Down at the bottom of its pit, he became conscious that the universe was vast, and that in the depth of it, one little ache, which went from his back into his stomach, from the cold, was himself. All kinds of vast things watched this ache with indifference; but the ache was all-important to himself. It kept urging him to rise. "That is the point," he muttered, "I've got to rise. I've got to rise."

Something from the heart of things was calling him to rise. With an effort he shook himself out of the cramps and nightmares into the coolness and stillness of reality. He thrust aside the saddle and sat up, aching. There were the stars overhead, in all those odds and ends of constellations of the southern heaven which have no easy guides for the wanderer like King Charles's Wain. The grass was all pale about him, the trees were all black, tree-tops and grass-tops seemed to waver a little: something near the water pan made a ticking noise, as though some mouse were snouting there under fallen twigs.

From all these things, he came suddenly to focus on the thing which mattered. His horse was staring intently, rigidly and silently at something which Hi could not see. This was why he had been called upon to rise. The sleeping partner in his horse had called him up to face the enemy. A wave of fear passed from the horse into the master; Hi sat up to stare as the horse stared; he rose to his knees and stared.

He could see nothing but the film of the grass against the black of the forest, yet somewhere in that space was something at which the horse was staring with all his nature. In that dimness and indistinctness before the darkness something was abroad, not stirring, but staring at them. What was it? Was it a snake waiting to strike, or a puma, or a ghost out of the grave? There was nothing to show, nothing to see; but both knew that there was something, deadly unspeakable. Hi felt the hair rise on his brow: he heard the sweat drip from himself and his horse.

How long this lasted he never knew, but at last, from that indistinctness in front, there came the faintest of sounds, that marked the ending of the tension. Something dark seemed on the instant to merge back into the darkness behind it. There was no noise of step or tread, no motion in the grass, nothing that one could swear to seeing, only the suggestion of a scent, like the ghost of the flavour of musk, and then the knowledge that the thing was no longer there. He believed that his horse sighed with relief, as he himself did.

He could see nothing, but the horse saw. Hi saw the horse's eyes follow the thing slowly round. What thing was it that could move so slowly? What thing of precaution was moving, pausing and deliberating? When it deliberated, its will hardened against them, the horse knew it, and Hi knew it from the horse. The fear came again, that the thing might strike, had almost made up its mind to strike: it had some kind of a mind.

Yet again the tension snapped suddenly, with a sigh of relief from horse and man: the evil seemed to withdraw, so that the horse felt free to change his position. Then the night, which for some minutes had seemed to hold her breath, began again to speak with her myriad voices out of the darkness of her cruelty. The whisper and the droning of the forest sharpened into the rustlings of snakes, the wails of victims, the cry of the bats after the moths, and the moan of the million insects seeking blood.

For some two hours Hi stayed by his horse, waiting and watching, till at last he felt free to lie down to rest. The insects took toll of him, but he contrived some shelter, and being young, as well as weary, he slept again. He may perhaps have slept for as much as an hour.

He was wakened suddenly by that inner messenger who told him that the danger, whatever it was, had returned. He heard the horse wheel round with a little cry to face in a new direction. Hi faced it, but again could see nothing but a blackness of trees, now like steel at the tops from the false dawn. Hi stood beside the horse, with an arm on his neck, staring. There was tenseness and silence, with fear passing from beast to man and back again. What was there, Hi could not see, but the horse saw. All that Hi thought that he could distinguish was a blotch of blackness which wavered against the blackness that was steadfast. It seemed to him to be some snake swollen to the size of an upright at Stonehenge. When the waiting became unbearable he challenged.

"I see you," he said. "What do you want?"

There came no answer, nor any sound from the thing; the only result of the challenge seemed to be that the tenseness became more tense and the silence more still. Staring forward more intently, Hi felt that the blotch of blackness was not there, but that something was there, but what thing? Ah, what thing could it be that was slow, silent as the coming of a fever, and deadlier than pestilence? It was there making up its mind for half an hour.

Then, as before, in one instant it was not: it was gone. Hi looked up at the heaven suddenly, to find that the steel of the tree-tops was now burnished with colour. Some birds in those tree-tops right over where the danger had been now woke all together with ejaculations and the clapping of wings, which spread from tree to tree, till all the forest was awake. High, shrill cacklings and screamings, full of good spirits and energy rang aloud all over the wood. With a clattering of the quills of wing-feathers, some big birds shook themselves loose from sleep. After a time, flocks of little birds passed overhead with thin, sweet cries. The false dawn, which had made the sky warm with colour, died away into dimness; then, almost at once, the darkness thinned and dispersed: colour surged into mid-heaven in flames of scarlet, which made the tree-tops glow. Within a few minutes it was dawn. Hi was cold, miserable, swollen and itching from bites, but safe from the powers of darkness; the night was gone; he had never understood what night was, now he knew.

In the glow of the warmth with all things so full of colour he looked at the place where the danger had threatened. The danger had now gone, the horse was eating at peace. There was no trace nor track that Hi could read, nor any mark that he could find, that might not have been made by himself or the horse. Yet about the places where the danger had been a flavour or sickliness of musk still lingered, so faintly that it could hardly be noted. "It is not musk, either," Hi said to himself. "It has a sort of edge to it. It is the smell of some stuff that kills, it has to do with death. This is a deadly place; we'll be gone from it."

Having groomed and fed his horse and himself, he set out from that clearing. "I have got my bearings now," he said. "I am facing north, probably straight towards Anselmo. Any going to the right will bring me out towards La Boca; any going to the left will put me too far to the west. As I am headed now, I ought to be clear of the forest by noon. I don't know what Rosa will think of me, losing all this time, but I'll get there somehow, so that she shan't be too much ashamed of me."

He had not ridden for two minutes before he felt a change in his horse; all the gallantry was gone from his going, there was no spark nor stir passing from horse to rider. "Poor old boy," he thought, "he has been awake all night, from that thing in the clearing, he is feeling a bit tucked up." He went gently through the forest for rather more than an hour. It was good going, more open than it had been the day before, with patches of savannah where the trend of the shadows gave him his directions. He was thankful for these savannahs, because of their warmth and colour, which restored him like draughts of wine. But his horse went on like a log beneath him, with no life nor spirit, and his own heart was troubled enough at all the delays. "At least, I am started now," he thought.

He came to a green expanse, broken up with pools of water, where reeds of delicate stems, topped by pale blue tufts of flowers, attracted multitudes of golden-throats, which poised at each tuft and glittered as they fluttered. The patch was perhaps three hundred yards across and of an intense glittering greenness. "Soft going," Hi muttered; "this is bog."

The horse knew something about earth of that greenness. He would have none of it. Hi dismounted to look at it; it looked like bottomless bog leading to deep water, with bog on the further side. In the midst of the green expanse there was a sort of bubbling wriggle of small snakes. Sometimes a red turtle crawled out of a pool, wallowed along the mud and sank into another. "Here's a lively place," Hi thought. "I'll have to get round it. I'll work round here to the right and go round the end of it."

He set off in good spirits, but after two miles or more of exploration he found no end of it. Instead of an end, the bog seemed to have a growth in that direction into a lake or pool edged with bottomless mud. Something in the water, whether tincture or germ, had killed the trees which it had touched. Three or four hundred dead trees stood in a pool the colour of stagnant blood, each tree was leafless and barkless: they stood as bones, silent save for the beetles clicking on them. "Here's a nice place," Hi thought. "It would be first rate as a shrubbery to a morgue."

There was no sign of any way across or round that bog. The blood-pool stretched on to what looked like an oil-pool, black and rancid, with prismatic gleams oozing outwards from it. Beyond this, there was swamp, with enormous plants with branches like water-lily roots, or like knots of snakes intertwisted, rising from the pools. The bark of these twigless branches had been gashed, perhaps in some act of growth, so that it hung in weepers, showing the red or yellow flesh beneath; "beggars with sores," Hi called them.

"Since I can't get round here," he said, "I must go back and try the other end." The mosquitoes were eating him alive here, so that when he clapped his neck suddenly his hand was covered with blood. As he had heard that oil will drive away mosquitoes, he smeared his hands, face and neck with the skimmings of one of the pools; this relieved him for a time.

At the other end, he found a tongue of dry land which seemed to thrust right across the bog. "Here is a way," he thought, "this will take me over." He set out upon it with good hope.

After a mile of open going, the reeds closed in on both sides of him, so that he rode in a narrow space between ranks of stems, grey-green and golden, topped by plumes of blue. The horse needed continual urging forward, until he came to a patch of a plant like rest-harrow, which attracted him; he seemed eager to crop it.

"Well, if it's going to do you good, old boy," Hi said, "you'd better eat some." He slipped the bit from his mouth to let him eat, but it proved to be a sick beast's fancy; he would not eat. He plucked two or three croppings, but dropped them from his mouth. Hi didn't like the look of his eyes nor the feel of his skin. "What is it, old son?" he asked. "What is turning you up? Was it the rain yesterday, or what?"

The horse drooped his head and trembled a little. "This is bad," Hi thought, "but I must get on, cruelty or no. He may be better presently."

He led the horse forward till he reached a place where the reeds grew across the causeway. He thrust into the reeds for a minute, when he found that he was treading in water over his shoes. Four or five inches down, the roots of the reeds, the surface of the earth, or both things together, made a hard bed on which he could walk. "I think it will be all right," he said; "it seems fairly safe: anyway, this is my direction; this bog can't last much longer: I must be almost across, and I simply won't waste time by trying for another way."

He slopped on slowly for another hundred yards, leading the horse. The reeds grew thicker as he proceeded. They were hard in the leaf like cactus and tough in the stem like bamboo. He had to back into them, dragging the horse, who came unwillingly; sometimes he could not break through, but had to edge round a clump. It was hot work paddling backward thus. After the first hundred yards the water began to deepen. Birds which had never before seen a man moved away at his coming; a deep, intense droning of insects sounded about him: insects got into his eyes and seemed to like being there. Many midges, with tiny black spots upon their wings, thrust under the wrist-bands of his shirt and below his collar, where they bit like sparks of fire. Suddenly the reeds let in a great deal more light: he had backed through into the open. He found himself standing almost knee deep in a lake of water two or three miles long by a mile broad. There was no way across from there: he had come the wrong way.

Perhaps, in his disappointment, had his horse been fit, he might have tried to swim across, holding to his horse's tail. The temptation to try was strong in him; the water, though deep, looked so beautiful, and the distance, in that light, so small. What made him hesitate was a patch of weed near the further shore. "I might get snarled up in that," he thought, "or come to a mud patch and not be able to land."

At the instant, something gave a sharp and savage pluck at his leg; he kicked the thing from him and at once splashed back among the reeds. "One of those snappers that father was always gassing about," he thought, as he recovered from his start; "he always said that the fresh-water fish would eat a man. I must give up swimming it, that's all."

He turned back in depression through the reeds. "Just as I thought I'd crossed it," he muttered. His horse seemed to share his depression. He came back through the reeds in a way which seemed to say, "I could have told you that you couldn't cross here. Now you'll have to fag all the way back again, and you know that I have not any strength to waste." Going back made him realise how much further he had come than he had supposed. It seemed to be miles to the starting place, but he reached it at last.

"Dash it all," he said, while he halted to consider, "I believe that this is the place which Anton mentioned: the place he meant when he said I couldn't go so, because there was no ground. Well, if I'd only thought of that sooner, I might have spared myself some pain. Now he said that there was some sort of a track hereabouts, which would take me clean out of the forest. Puzzle, find the track. I see no trace of any track. I'll take a cast, to see if I can hit it off."

He took two casts, one in each direction, but could see nothing like a track. "If there was one," he thought, "it was very likely washed out by the rain yesterday. Anyhow, I have tried the east and the middle: they are both wrong. If there's any way at all to the north from here, it must be to the west. Here it is mid-day pretty nearly, and I have not started yet."

He set out to the west, through a forest of vast trees, which stood over him like gods watching a beetle. When he had ridden for an hour, he turned into a valley, down which suddenly a mist of rain came sweeping. It came less violently than the rain of the day before, but settled in as though it would last for ever. In a few minutes the forest had changed to a dimness full of footsteps and sighings, across which shapes of cloud faded and formed and faded.

"I must keep on, and then bear to the right," Hi said. "This won't last as long as it did yesterday."

He kept on for some hours at a walk, till he was stopped by a bog. A river or large stream which perhaps ran into the lake at its western end here had silted up its mouth over some acres of forest. A rotting mush barred the way; there was no passing. As moving to the right brought him to reeds growing in water, he moved to the left, uphill, until his horse stopped.

He had saved a feed of corn against an emergency: the horse nosed at it, but would not eat. "Poor beast," Hi thought, "he's in a pretty bad way. I'll rub him down and give him a rest. If we both rest for a little it will do no harm." After grooming the horse, he contrived what shelter he could, and fell asleep. He woke once, to find the rain streaming on his face, woke a second time, to find that the rain had stopped; then sleep took hold of him body and soul and held him as one dead.

He slept all through the afternoon and would have slept longer far into the night, but that he was suddenly startled by the shattering of a volley of shots from some place far away. "There it is," he cried, starting up, "that is Don Manuel coming to the rescue." Other shots followed, some, at first, close together in volleys, the later ones singly. After the shots, listening intently as he was, he thought that he heard the sound of many horses going together at a fast trot. Some such noise there was, it rang out, died down, clopped and clinked and then clattered. "Of course, it can't be Don Manuel," he said, coming to himself. "But it may be the Whites driving away the Reds. Anyhow, people are there: the forest ends. It may even be Anselmo. Come on, horse, here's the world again. 'They must be men, because they're fighting, and they must be civilised because they're doing it with guns.' "

The horse seemed the better either for the rest or the sound of his fellows; when Hi mounted, he set off with some kind of spirit. In a quarter of an hour he came to something which made the horse whinny; it was a trail.

"Here it is," Hi cried, "the very little trail which Anton spoke of. Now I shall be out of it in no time. Just as well, too, because I've slept a lot longer than I thought: it is almost night."

The sun was indeed behind Melchior; the birds had homed and were now screaming before falling silent. The patches of sky over the forest turned slowly scarlet, paled yellow, then changed to a green in which stars were bright. The sparks of the fireflies began to pass upon the air: cold silence and darkness came with them into the forest, so that Hi shivered. His heart, none the less, was beating with hope, because the horse was going with confidence. Then from somewhere ahead came the distant lowing of cattle, which brought tears to Hi's eyes. It was the noise made by the cows of home coming into the barton at Tencombe: now here, in this strange place, it told of the homes of men, where life was lived wisely, away from towns, and far from the madness of rulers like Don Lopez.

Suddenly, from somewhere ahead, a single shot rang out: it may have been far away, but in that still air it sounded near by. It was followed almost at once by the sound of the gallop of a horse, which was either running away or being ridden by a man in fear for his life. It stretched at a full gallop across his front and so away into the west: one horse only, mad with fear, or with his rider's fear, going at his utmost: from what?

"I wish I knew from what," Hi thought. "Listen."

He listened: many men were talking and shouting. Then there came the noise of many horses together: seventy or a hundred; "as many as in a hunt at home," moving along a paven place at a walk, then rising to a fast trot together. "And they are within two miles of me," Hi thought, "going from me." He shouted, but had no answer save the sound of the horses dying away into the west. The cattle lowed again. "There must be a ranch there," Hi said. "I'll go to where those cows are." He hailed again and was answered by little white owls which followed him on both sides, perhaps for grubs or beetles kicked up by the horse in his going.

Presently he came out of the forest into a little plantation of trees made as a wind-screen, possibly for cocoa. Beyond this, he saw a cleared space in which, less than half a mile away, were the long, low white buildings of a ranch lit up as for a festival. To his right, there seemed to be ordered plantations of fruit trees in blossom: he saw long streaks of paleness which he judged to be peach trees. To the left, rather further from him, were high corrales, where pale cattle moved and lowed; he heard them stamp and push: often they rattled their horns upon the bars.

He rode nearer to the buildings, then paused to hail, crying out that he was English, and that they were not to shoot. He had no answer to any of his hails. The place was still, save for the cattle: there was not even a dog. "The men must be all at supper," he thought, "or milking, if they milk in these parts. But it is odd that they have no dog."

The moon, now some three or four nights old, was low down over the house, near the tops of Sierras, which glittered. "I don't know what sort of a course I've been riding," he thought, "I seem to have been going due west: or is the moon different down here? It seems to slop about all over the place."

Leaving the moon for the moment, he rode on towards the house, calling out that he was a friend. Some shrubs, newly planted, on both sides of his track, gave out a strong sweet scent: beetles and fireflies were swarming over them with a droning of wings which made the silence the more apparent.

"Is anybody there?" he cried. "Hullo there. Don't shoot: I am a friend. House ahoy, I'm a friend."

By this time he was at a long white gate which had been thrust and propped open far back to its supporting posts and rails. He entered the gate, riding cautiously, still calling that he was a friend, but having no answer, and hearing no sound, save the moving of the cattle in the corrales and the buzz of insects in the shrubs.

"Not even a dog," he repeated, "and there must be fifty men in a ranch like this. What if they are all in ambush, waiting for me to come on?"

"It's not likely," he thought, after a moment, "but it is possible. They may be waiting at those windows to plug me like a nutmeg grater. But if they are, they'll wait to see who is coming with me. It feels to me as if the house were deserted."

Beyond the gate, the way had been paven, the horse's hoofs struck on a road; the house cast back the echoes, clink, clink, at each step. As he advanced, the young moon bobbed lower down towards the house-roof: no sound came from the house.

"Hey," Hi called, "I am a friend, an amigo; un ami. Je suis Anglais. Ingles."

Something in the ominousness of the silence brought his calling to an end. There was something dreadful at work here. Something had stricken the heart of that house so that its life had ceased. Yet not quite ceased, for as Hi dismounted he saw a breath of smoke blow from one of the chimneys across the curve of the moon. "What in the wide earth is happening here?" he asked himself.

At a little distance from the house, to the left of the entrance, were tethering posts from which iron rings hung. He had thought at first that they were the posts at which the slaves were flogged; but he now knew better. He hitched his horse to one of the rings, and then went slowly towards the door. The house seemed to grow bigger as he approached it: he felt himself shrink. He wished that his footsteps did not make such a noise upon the road. "It is deserted," he told himself, "it is all deserted. But it is all lit up, so that it can only have been deserted within the hour, after that shot was fired here."

Six steps from the door a thought came to him which made his heart leap for joy. "Of course, this is Anselmo," he said. "I've come to Anselmo. This is the Elena's ranch, and the Elenas and all their men have either gone to Don Manuel or joined the other Whites. That is it of course. Well, here I am. And they've moved all their horses with them; those were the horses which I heard. I'm late enough, but word has reached them. 'Zeke must have got through."

Thinking thus he crossed the two broad stone steps of the perron to the estancia door.

An electric light burned over the door: some moths were butting at it. The door itself was of black maruca, bound with steel. A big bronze pipkin, such as the country people all over Meruel use for milking, hung beside the door. "I suppose this is the bell," he thought. "It's just like a castle in the Morte d'Arthur. Here goes for a bang."

He struck the bronze, which clanged aloud, spinning round upon its cord and thrilling: then he struck again more loudly, twice. The clang died down into a trembling of the air, but all within the house was silent, there was neither voice nor footstep. There came a rustling of wind from the madre de cacao trees; nobody came, nobody spoke. "Is anyone inside there?" Hi cried. There was no answer.

"I don't believe that there is anybody here," he said. Then the thought came: "Suppose the people have all been rounded up or killed by the Reds?"

"But, no," he thought, "the Reds would have sacked and burned the place. It is not that. I don't know what it is: it must be something queer." He struck the bronze for a last time.

CHAPTER XIII

"Well, if they won't answer, I'll see if I can go in," he said. He lifted the latch by plucking the plaited leather bobbin: the door was not locked, it opened before him into a long lit corridor or hall where an English clock was ticking. As he opened the door, the wind blowing in shook the pictures on the wall: they swayed and clacked for an instant, then steadied. There were lighted rooms opening from each side of the corridor, but no sound of any living being.

"Hullo, you inside here," Hi called. "I am a friend. Is anyone there? Señor Elena. Señor George, Señor William. Hey, hey, heya. Is anyone here at all?"

His voice rang along the corridor and died away: no one was there. "Very well, I'll go in," Hi said. He stepped in, and closed the door against the wind. As he did so a letter and envelope, which had been lying on the edge of a table near him, fell to the stone flags with a clatter. He replaced them on the table; then paused to look about him.

He had heard that men of the great ranches lived like princes. The hall in which he stood was bare, big and white, lit by electric lights. There were two stiff black chairs, two black pictures of yellow nymphs, a table heaped with silver horse-trappings, and the English grandfather's clock, gravely telling the time. He walked up to the clock and read the words on the dial:

Edward Hendred.

1807

Abingdon.

These two little things of old Berkshire met thus in this strange house so many miles from Thames and Down. "Hendred of Abingdon," he repeated. "There may be a Berkshire man here who may know father." He glanced at the pictures of the yellow nymphs in their clothes blown out in the grand manner. "Religious pictures," he thought and glanced away. The house was so still that he hardly dared to go further.

"What can have happened?" he asked. "Some fight or some show or what?"

He walked to the nearest door, on his left. The door was ajar, shewing a lit room: he knocked at the door, had no answer, and therefore looked in. It was a big, long room, in use as the messroom of the household, for whom thirty places had been laid on the table. Food in abundance had been set there for a meal, which had been begun. Baskets of small Meruel loaves were on a sideboard near the door: he felt these by accident as he put out his hand: the under loaves were still warm from the oven. There was warmth in the vast silver cazuela tureen, which stood, more than half empty at the head of the table. The table was littered with the mess of the meal: broken loaves, bowls which had been used for cazuela, halves of oranges, skins of bananas, and the bones of big birds like turkeys. Yet from the look of the plates Hi felt that the meal had never been finished: something had interrupted it before they had reached the coffee and cigarettes. Somebody with some news had come there soon after they were half way through, then chairs had been thrust back and food left, half eaten and the eaters and talkers had gone. Why had they gone, and where? Hi did not like the feeling of this house.

He went again to the hall and cried: "Is there anybody here?" But there was no answer. "There must be someone somewhere in all this barrack," he said. "Surely in the kitchen or outhouses there will be a woman or a negro or a peon. There must be at least a caretaker or night-watchman. The kitchens will be along the corridor somewhere at the back."

He went down the corridor, where he found the kitchen. It was a vast room, bare, clean, and empty of people. The fire, which had done the work of cooking, had been allowed to die down; but the castle-kettle, once full of water for coffee and the washing-up of the dishes, was still boiling and half full. A black cat with its paw round its face was curled up asleep on a mat on a chair. "I'm glad that there is something alive here," he said.

Doors opened from the kitchen into outhouses, sculleries and larders: Hi felt a dread of looking into these rooms, but he overcame it: no one was there.

"Well," he said, "if there's no one to ask, I will make a mash for my poor horse. No one could object to that."

He took one of the big round-up stew cauldrons which lay against a wall. In this he made a hot mash of bread for his horse, adding some salt. He carried it out to the horse, who seemed glad of the warm food for a few instants; but it was not all that he had hoped; in a few instants his muzzle dropped from it. "Poor old boy," Hi said, "I wish I knew what I could give you, that you would like."

He lingered by the horse for a few minutes, to pull his ears, and rub him down. The breeze which had set in struck cold, so Hi moved the horse to a more sheltered place behind the immense rain vats a few yards from the tethering posts. He had hoped that somebody would come there while he was outside with the horse, but there came neither sight nor sound of anybody.

"I'll go in to explore," Hi said. "There must be someone, and if there's someone there may be something I can do."

It was harder to enter the house for this second time than it had been before. The uncanniness was greater now. The clock still ticked, the light still burned, the table still stood uncleared. "I don't want to be caught bagging things in a strange house," Hi thought, "but I'm jolly well going to bag some food and leave some money for it."

He ate and drank of what was on the table, to the amount (as he judged) of a peseta, reckoning in the bread for the horse. He left one of his five pesetas on the table for this. "What am I to do, and where am I to go?" he wondered. "If I leave this? This may be Anselmo; almost must be: yet where are all the Elenas gone? Perhaps I'll find something in the other rooms."

There were three more rooms in the corridor of the hall: two on the opposite side, one on his side, nearer the kitchens. The rooms further down the corridor had the look of being offices or studies. "I'll go into those, first," he said. "Very likely I'll come upon somebody dead in one, or on the old mad doctor who runs this private madhouse." He knocked at the door beside him, which was shut: for one instant he was shocked by thinking that at the sound of his knocking someone within the room had turned the pages of a book. He opened the door upon a dark room, into which the breeze blew from an open ventilator high up in the wall. He saw the light switches and switched the lights fully on. The room was the estancia office, as he had supposed. There was a safe, built into the wall. There were two long tables heaped with papers; but another thing impressed Hi: chairs had been lifted from the floor on to these tables, so that the floor might be swept. Two brooms had begun to sweep the floor: there was the tide mark of dust, earth, torn paper, cigarette ends and cigar butts half way across the room. There were the two brooms resting against the table, just as the unknown sweepers had left them when their task had been interrupted by what? On a third table was a row of flat, square, white china dishes, each containing about a pint of brown or reddish liquid. Hi judged that the liquid was a chemical of some sort, perhaps a parasite mixture.

He crossed the corridor to the room opposite. This was plainly a room for the women. It contained a long settle which faced a row of spinning wheels. On a table there were heaps of palm-blades partly unravelled into the white bast from which the Meruel women plaited their hats. At the further end of the room were two hand-looms on which some weavers had already woven parts of saints for the back cloth of an altar. Someone had spilled a little bottle of scent upon the palm-blades. It was oozing from its cork into a rivulet which had dripped into a pool upon the floor. "There has been a hurry, even here," Hi said. "Oh, I wish to goodness I had come here an hour ago. If only I had not taken that wrong turn, or slept quite so long, I might have found the people here: and they are good people, doing good things."

He went again into the corridor to listen: no one had entered the house. "There are all the outhouses to search through presently," he said. "I must find someone before I can leave here. I'll try this other room, opposite the dining-room."

This proved to be the main living-room of a company of men. One side of it was slung with Indian hammocks, loosely woven of dyed fibres: the rest was in the confusion in which undisciplined men will live. It was littered with clothes, shot-guns, cartridges, belts, knives, books, papers, watches, money, cigars, broken cigarettes, pipes, spurs, quirts, matches, plugs of tobacco, photographs of girls, prints of horses, shoes, laces, straps and twitches. Tobacco had been smoked there not more than an hour before, but another smell also struck Hi's nostrils. It was a familiar smell, yet for an instant in that smell of tobacco he could not say what it was. Then the sight of an empty brass revolver shell upon the floor reminded him that what he smelt was the smell of gunpowder. Somebody had burned a cartridge in that room not more than an hour before: there was the shell of the cartridge.

He picked it up, with the thought that it was the heaviest revolver cartridge he had ever seen. "Why," he thought, "a thing like this would stop a bison. This is a Jack the Giant Killer. Whoever has fired a thing like this in here?" He put the brass shell to his nose and instantly the pungent smell brought scenes into his mind of two months before. The first scene was of the wood on the down above Tencombe, on a sunny January afternoon, when he had shot a pheasant, and had stood to jerk out the shell. A red squirrel had appeared on one of the leafless oaks there: it had run along the branch to jabber at him, to within six feet of him. This scene floated by into another of the Blowbury Woods at sunset, when he had waited in the cold for wood-pigeons. The orange sky to the west had been netted black by the elm twigs, and the woods had stood still in the cold. He had had a shot at last, but had missed with both barrels, had jerked out the cartridges, and had smelt just this smell, from fumes curling up at him out of the breech.

He dropped the shell: it fell with a tinkle and rolled from him. He was standing, at that moment, some four feet from the door, within the room; he had not much more than entered to take his survey. Fear, anxiety, homesickness, and the torment of failing his friends were all preying upon him. Then he looked up, suddenly, towards one of the windows, where something made his heart stand still. A man with a white face and blazing eyes was watching him through the window with a look of rage which made his blood run cold. The man's brow was pressed on the pane, while his right hand reached back for a gun. That man was no dweller in the house, but a spy and an enemy.

He did not stay for the hand to come round with the gun, but slipped sideways into the hall, closed the door behind him and drew the bolt with which each of those doors was fitted. He slipped sideways along the hall to the front door, which he bolted likewise. Then he stood for a minute with his heart thumping, listening to hear whether the man were breaking through the window or coming to the door for him.

After a minute, during which nothing happened, his eye caught the letter that had been blown to the floor when he entered the house. The letter was on the table within a few feet of him. "It must have been the last thing read in this house," he thought. "What if it were the cause of all the people leaving here? It may have brought the deciding news, probably did. At least, it may be addressed to one of the Elenas, or will tell me if this be Anselmo."

He looked at the envelope, which was addressed in a bold hand

— — J. G.

He had a horror of looking at a private letter, even when made public in a book or newspaper. "It's a skunk's trick," he said, "but I do want to know where I am. I'll apologise if I ever have the chance." He pulled the enclosure from the envelope to read it. It proved not to be the letter (that had gone), but a piece of paper which had been sent with the letter. The paper was a half-sheet of coarse bluish notepaper on which the same hand had pencilled the words, "Si, Anselmo."

"Now what on earth does that mean?" Hi asked himself. "Yes, Anselmo? I would give something to know what is happening in this place." All was silent about him, save for that ticking of the clock.

With a little chirrupping cry, the black cat, which had been sleeping in the chair in the kitchen, came running along the passage. It was a slim, small-headed, short-coated cat, not yet of full growth; it rubbed against Hi's legs and purred; Hi leaned down to stroke it, but watched the passage to the kitchen.

"That man has come in by way of the kitchen," Hi thought. "He has scared the cat, or let in a draught upon him. I'll be out of this."

The office window seemed to be the exit most likely to bring him out beside his horse: he slipped into the office and closed the door behind him. Then he listened, with a beating heart, for some swift, stealthy footstep in the corridor or outside the window. "Perhaps," he thought, "I shan't hear any footsteps, only the brute's hand on the latch. He's a spy and a Red, that devil. Listen."

In that silence, the beating of the clock clanged like the tolling of a bell. The cat, left to preen his fur in the hall, padded back towards the kitchen. Hi was on the point of turning to open the inner shutter of the window, when a little shrill whirring bell began to scream like an alarm-clock upon some metal hooks on a stand at the table end. The shock of the sound made his hair stand stiff upon his head. He saw the instrument shaking on its hooks with the vehemence of the bell. He had read and heard of these things, but had never before seen one. It rang for ten seconds, then paused, then rang for five seconds and paused again. Then it rang again with determination for half a minute on end, as though bent on having an answer. Someone was telephoning to that house of the dead.

His courage came back in a few seconds. Someone was telephoning: why should he not answer? Possibly an English voice would speak to him or someone who knew English. Even if there were a Red outside the door, he owed it to Carlotta to run the risk, if by running it he could learn where he was and where he should go next. He did not know how to take the call. He lifted the instrument from its hooks and listened, now at one end, now at the other, to silence. "The thing is stopped," he said. "I don't know how to work the beastly thing. Yes?" he called. "Yes? Who is there? What is it?"

No answer come to him, not even the murmur of other voices which sometimes comes over the telephone. Then suddenly the thought came to him that perhaps the wire had been cut, or the unseen speaker shot down somewhere far away. He put down the instrument, moved to the window and opened the shutter. As he pulled it aside, the bell tinkled a little, whimpered again, as though about to ring again, and then stopped. "The wires are cut," he muttered, "that devil the spy has done it."

Peering out of the window, he could see nothing but a darkness which gradually took shapes to itself of trees swaying in the wind, palms clicking and clacking, and stars which became brighter as he gazed. "Here goes," Hi thought, "I cannot see that devil; I'll risk it." So he scrambled out, landed on his feet, and then stood for an instant lest someone should spring upon him. No one sprang; there was neither sight nor sound of anyone, only his horse nosing at the earth, and the wind shuffling and clicking. He unhitched his rein, mounted and cautiously rode forward.

At the space near the door he halted to listen and to try to see. No one was there.

"They'll be where the spy was," he thought, "crouched out of this cold wind. I'll see and make sure." He edged his horse a little and a little to the corner of the house, where he held him ready for a dash. Very cautiously he craned forward along his horse's neck, till he could see round the corner. Then he stared with all his might at the space lit by the windows of the living-room. No horsemen were gathered there out of the wind, but at the lit window the figure of the spy still stood with his hand reached back for his gun and his brow pressed upon the pane. He was staring into the window: Hi could not see his face.

"Golly," Hi thought, "he's still there. He's come here again." He did not move a muscle for fully fifteen seconds; the spy did not move. Hi waited for that right hand to flash up suddenly with the gun, but it did not come.

Then Hi thought, "But what's he up to? He saw me in the room five minutes ago; then probably he went after me in the kitchen. What brings him here again? What is he staring at there? Can there be another man in the room? He must know that I cleared out: he saw me do it. Is he waiting to plug me when I come back, or what?"

He waited for another fifteen seconds, but the man never stirred a muscle. He stood at the window, pressed to it, intently staring. Hi had seen cats and foxes waiting intently thus before springing; but the cats and foxes had at least trembled with the intensity of their control, this man was motionless.

"But who in the wide earth is he staring at?" Hi asked himself. "There must be someone in that room whom I never saw, but who was there when I was there." Then he thought, "Whatever is in the room, there is something wrong with that man. He is not quite of this world."

That was an opinion which the horse seemed to share, and the presence of it in the horse made Hi's terror stronger. Yet the intentness of that watching figure "not quite of this world," was fascinating. All purpose will arrest the purposeless, but this deadly purpose was absorbing. It made Hi forget that looking at a person will draw that person's eyes towards the looker. For the moment, he did not care; he longed to see what the man saw. He stared: his horse also stared.

Suddenly a gust of the wind, now blowing at its height, caught the window by which Hi had escaped. Hi heard it crash to, with a tinkle of glass. The draught inside the house flung some door open, and blew ajar the unhasped casement by which the watcher stood. The result was something which Hi had not expected. The man slithered sideways, scraping along the wall, and collapsed, with his head towards Hi, and his gun arm twisted askew as no living arm could ever twist. The light, shining now from the unobstructed window pane, showed Hi the bullet-hole through which the body's death had come.

The horse had swerved aside when the body fell. The knowledge that the man was dead, and had been dead from the first, came to Hi in a flash, at his first movement. The smell of powder in the room suddenly became significant. "That explains the big revolver shell," he thought. "Oh, golly, let's get out of this."

The horse was out of sorts, but the cold had touched him up, and something of his rider's terror was afflicting him. He swerved away from the house and galloped ahead across a peach plantation. Hi heard horses whinny and a man's voice hailing him from behind him as he entered the plantation. The dreadful fear that it was the dead man mounted on the nightmare made him crouch on his horse's neck and urge him forward. He heard shouts, calling to him to stop, or so it seemed.

At any other time, he might have stopped; but he could not now, after the corpse flopping down towards him. In a few moments, he was certain that men were shouting at him, several men, in earnest, shouting no Christian tongue. By this time he had crossed the plantation fence at a place where the bars were down, he was heading across a patch of savannah towards the forest. He heard horses coming after him. He called out that he was English and a friend. The man who was nearest to him, perhaps mistaking this for an insult, fired a shot in the direction of the voice, but missed. Hi crackled through some hard-leaved scrub into the darkness of the covert, leaving the direction to the horse. Many horses crackled into the scrub behind him. He called out again that he was English and a friend, but his bailers cursed him, called to him to stop and opened fire at him. As he rode, he heard the piping drone of birds; then, suddenly, some of the birds spat and hissed close to his ears, twigs fell from the trees about him; he knew suddenly that the birds were bullets.

The pursuers, with one exception, soon pulled up, the firing ceased, only one man still followed, calling to him to stop. Suddenly this one pursuer pulled up, and Hi at the same instant felt a coldness of fear all over him. There came a shot and shock, his horse swerved violently, staggered, recovered, and bolted into the forest. "He hit the horse," Hi said, "but not badly, or he wouldn't go like this." For the rest of the ride his task was to keep on.

How long he rode the forest he never knew: the horse went on in his terror till he could go no more, then he halted, full of the ends of terror, nervy, starting at a shadow and trembling.

The moon was long since down. Hi could make out that he was in a kind of pan or crater in the forest, with wavy indistinctness everywhere, smelling of balm. He dismounted, tried to examine his horse, who would not let himself be examined, but had certainly been cut on the crupper. He tried to comfort the poor beast. Coming to a patch of grass near a brook, he offered him grazing and a drink, both of which he refused. "Poor old Bingo," Hi said, "you're dead beat, you shall rest."

He tethered, unsaddled and spread his coat upon him. The beast stood where he was left without attempting to roll; he drooped his head as though he had come to the end.

"Now I am pretty nearly done," Hi thought. "I don't know where I am. I've been gone four days. I've killed one horse and cooked a second. Now I'm lost in the forest again."

He listened for some noise of men or the creatures of men, but heard nothing save the noises of the forest. Terrors began to take hold of him, the dread of such a terror as had come the night before, the terror of the man at the window. Yet at last sleep took him from the terror of being awake: he fell into a pit of sleep and slept for hours.

During this, the fourth day of Hi's journey, young Chacon the notary, reached Don Manuel with all the terrible news still to be told. By this time, men and horses had begun to arrive at the rendezvous. Some copies of the blasphemous proclamation, which had arrived in the west from Port Matoche, had roused intense feeling throughout the west: men answered Don Manuel's call from all over San Jacinto. While Hi was lying down to sleep, Don Manuel, with an advanced guard of about a hundred men, pushed eastward from the river to begin his march.

CHAPTER XIV

Hi woke up suddenly into terror, for the forest was filled with a crying as of creatures gone mad. A pack of things was giving tongue with voices madder than a fox's bark.

"Wild dogs gone mad," he thought. The noise of the yap seemed to strike between the skull and the coats of the brain, as the idea of the weasel strikes into the brain of the rabbit. Hi jumped to the horse, who was already trembling. He cast loose the tethering rope and swung himself on to the beast's bare back, gripping the headstall, and in an instant the horse was away with him, in a panic which Rosas himself could not have controlled. Horse and man fled like the bird knocked from roost in the night. What did the bags and the saddle matter while that crying filled the darkness?

"Oh, golly, what are those things?" he thought. "Oh, golly, if they are after us." All the night seemed full of flaming eyes, but these were only fireflies, not a pack: the crying seemed to die away. The horse floundered through mud in a cane-brake, which crashed under his trampling. Hi dug his head into the horse's neck and shut his eyes: it was like running the gauntlet for what seemed a long time. After it, he went through tall grass, which drenched him with dew. Hi felt him weakening beneath him as he came out of the grass: then suddenly water appeared before him as a lake or broad river, where the wind roused reflections of stars. Hi saw a fish leap and splash, shaking up a glittering; in an instant the horse was swimming, with the gleams all round him.

Hi knew that a very little thing would drown the horse in his present condition; he slipped off his back, slid sideways, caught his tail and swam with him. After about fifty yards, the horse put his feet down, stumbled on to his knees, but recovered and came to the bank. Hi with some trouble scrambled up in front of him, got a purchase on the reins, and helped him on to dry land. They stood there gasping together for a while, being both out of breath as well as very cold.

"O Lord," Hi thought, "what on earth were those things? I've never heard anything so awful. Thank God, we got away when we did. A very little more, and they would have been on us. I think I should go mad if they were coming after me. Listen."

There was no sound of any pack in cry coming after them. They had come to a part of the wilderness which was silent, save for the rustle of the reeds and the splash of the leaping fish. "I suppose it's going to rain again," Hi muttered with chattering teeth; "that is why the fish are leaping. I wish I'd brought my coat and the saddle."

But they were left behind with the bags in a place which Hi was little likely to find again. "Lord, I do feel wretched," he said, shivering. "I'll get away from this water. There may be alligators in it. I never thought of them before. Come up, old Bingo; we'll find a place for you."

They moved away through a thicket into a space which had been burnt the year before. From the cold and from the colour of the sky, Hi judged that it was about an hour from the dawn. The horse stopped from exhaustion. "You're sicker than I am," Hi said. "I'll do my best to warm you."

He pulled grass: the horse would not touch it, but it served to rub him: he was trembling, his coat was staring, and his head was down. "I'd give something for a bucket of warm beer for him," Hi said. "It's hateful having nothing: even the bread is gone. Well, I must hope for the sun to come soon to warm him."

The cold was so painful that he had to move away, to dance and flog his arms. The dawn seemed to take hours to bring any colour to the sky, yet it came at last.

"Thank God, here it comes at last," he said. "If only I could hear a bell with it: even a cow-bell."

It came with no sound of bells, but with a clapping of wings from all the near-by trees, as the multitudes of the birds awoke. Their cries were not sweet like the cries of so many English birds: only one seemed to have a sweetness in his voice. This was a biggish bird with black wings and orange breast. He had a sweet droning note which said, "Woe," then, after an interval, "Woe" again. All the other birds seemed to be saying, "Damn it": or so Hi thought.

As the light grew, the clamour of the birds rose to a roaring, for many of them, after trying their wings, took flight, wheeled, and sped away in their companies, to seek for food. Some of those who cried "Woe" settled on a tree which was covered with great white waxy flowers, intolerably sweet. Wafts of the sweetness came to Hi on the gusts of the wind. He saw them tear at the flowers and eat the petals. Hi, going to the tree, tasted a petal, thinking that what fed the birds could not harm himself. It was like sweetened church candle or much what he had imagined manna to have been. He ate of this manna with the knowledge that he, too, had been fed in the wilderness. When he returned to his horse, he found him stretched out dead.

It was the first time that he had lost a friend by death: he sat down beside him and wept. He was not a lad given to weeping: he had not wept for years, but he was shaken by the last four days, and in an extreme of loneliness, which made him know what a friend the horse had been in hours of danger and beastliness. Now that he was gone, Hi was alone indeed. The horse lay dead on his off side: his near crupper was scored with a bullet-mark. "So he was hit after all," Hi said, "I thought he was. And the poor old Bingo saved me twice last night, and now he is dead."

He remembered the last lines of a well-known song:

> Could I think we'd meet again,
> It would lighten half my pain,
> At the place where the old horse died.

"Golly," he thought, "I'll never be unkind to a horse as long as I live, after this."

After the stunned half hour, he picked himself up, to look round at where he was. He stood in a space of grass, ringed by trees, up which the creepers climbed in a fire of flowers. To his right were the reeds and the water, with the sun climbing above them; to his left was the dimness of the forest.

"I'm facing north," he said. "Almost due north. I'm facing the plain as I stand. I've got about a day's go in me. I must get to the plain this day, or I shall never get to it at all."

The thought of Carlotta depending on him and Rosa thinking that he was on his way to fetch help came back in force. Again and again he went over in his mind the events which had delayed him. "It is just as if I were walking on a road which moves away from where I want to get to," he said. "If I were to try to avoid Anselmo, I might get there. I've been four days and a bit. Or is it five days and a bit? If I get there now, I may be too late."

As he went on into the north, he began to hear voices which spoke in his ears, bidding him to do this or that. So many voices spoke, that he began to feel that he was attended by a flock of things like birds, which had human voices and flew invisibly beside him. The going lay over miles of dead reed and broken brush which had been laid in a tornado of the August before. The dead reed having been laid in its prime, had not decayed, but had hardened to something like bamboo: the young reed growing through the old had then matted it into a cloth too high to trample down and too tough to thrust through. Much of this reed grew (at that season) in some inches of water. At the end of two hours of it Hi came to a growth of trees which had been uprooted in a line. For three hundred yards the line stretched like a wall in a succession of the shields of black, intertangled roots standing upright over the hollows whence they had been plucked. It looked like a wall of black snakes barring his way. When he had scrambled up the wall, he saw beyond it the lake amid her reeds, cruised over by white hawks. The beauty of the water in that light, reflecting so much other beauty of forest, flower and bird, each like an angel, could not be told. To Hi, it did not come like beauty; but as a shock. It stretched away, seemingly for miles, right across his path, to left and to right. He could see the sun in heaven, in this clear space; this gave him his compass points. He had come fairly truly to the north: now the lake stretched half a mile breadth of water in front of him. There was neither ford nor boat.

"I must just edge along to the west," he thought. "This must be the water that stopped me yesterday when I was further to the east."

After letting his clothes dry in the sun, he turned westwards along the lake, not far from its shore, in a mood of anxiety tempered by hunger. After a couple of hours of going, a black bog, with seepings of oil in it which killed plants, turned him away from the lake: he had to turn to the south to get round it. When he had turned, he began to think that he never would get round it. It turned him more and more to the south, for more than an hour. When he sat down to rest, more than half way through the morning, he felt that he was perhaps further from Anselmo than he had ever been.

As usually happens in the first days of starvation, with young people, his hunger was checked by weariness and weakness from becoming tyrannous. While he rested, he saw a scuffling among birds in a sunlit path about a hundred yards away. Going thither, he found some thorny shrubs, which even at that early season were covered with yellow plums the size of sloes. Birds, butterflies and many other insects were gorging themselves with these plums; he, too gorged, thinking that no better plums had ever grown. Being schooled now to think of the next meal whenever he had food, he contrived a sort of basket or frail of the leaves of the spade-palm into which he packed a couple of pounds of plums, which he took with him.

He judged that the sun had southed when at last he was able to cross the bog and turn again to the north. The going proved to be much better beyond the swamp. He set out in good spirits, walked hard for half an hour to the west, but then was stopped by another southward trending of the lake: he had to trudge southward again.

It was after a couple of hours of this trudging, when he was most tired and dispirited at having met no living soul nor any sign of man, that he heard far off, somewhere to the south, a single rifle shot. He shouted, hoping that the shooter might reply: he had no reply to his hail, but the thought, that someone was there, who might help him in his need, and in no case could make him much worse than he was, made him turn in that direction, shouting at intervals as he went. Perhaps two minutes after he had set out towards the place of the shot, he judged that he smelt smoke. He had but one whiff of it and could not catch it again: he was, however, sure that it was woodsmoke. "There is some sort of a fire there," he thought. "I shall find somebody."

Half an hour later, while he was hallooing, in the certainty that he must be near where the shooter had been, he saw a footmark in some soft earth close to a red-heart. The red-heart had been split by age, wind or lightning: it was exuding a bright blue fungus from the split. This brought him to a halt with a start, for the footmark was his own. He had halted just beside that tree when the smell of the smoke had come to him. There could be no doubt of it; he had noticed tree and fungus too nicely to be mistaken. There was besides, the footmark, unmistakably his. He was too wise to have false hope about it: he had been walking in a circle: he was bushed.

"There it is," he said, "I am bushed."

As the words were spoken, there came into his mind the memory of Tencombe at teatime during the last summer holidays. There was his mother with the sun upon her hair and her alert, decisive way: there was old Bill standing near the mantelpiece, holding his tea-cup, while with one foot he rolled over the retriever pup. There at the table beside the rest of them was a little frail, pale-faced, red-bearded man, with a whispering voice, who had been bushed in East Africa.

His words came back into Hi's mind. "If you lose your head when you're bushed, you're done."

"I'll bet that that is true," Hi said. "If I lose my head, I shall be done."

He sat still for some minutes, trying to keep control of himself by repeating the things in his favour. "I have had food to-day: and still have some plums: it isn't raining: I can't be far from a camp or at least a place where hunters come, because of that shot: whatever wrong tracks I've taken, I can't be far from the edge of this forest: whatever happens I must not give up hope, because 'hope brings healing.' I shall get out of this mess if I believe I shall. I do believe I shall. I believe that if I climb one of these trees, I may be able to see out of this forest."

The thought fell like light into his mind, that he might see out of the forest; but it was not easy to find a tree which would both yield a view and be possible to climb. After some search he came to one that seemed perfect. It had the look of a red-heart, but was so swathed with tough creeper, which gave good hand-and-foot hold, that the bark was almost hidden. Hi set himself to climb. He discovered, before he had gone far, that the creeper stalks were bristly, like ivy or nettle stalks at home, and that the climb was hard work. "I'm weaker than I was," he thought. The dust, dead twigs and fragments of bark fell over his face and down his neck, but he persevered, even when he roused up a gang of black tree ants. He came out through the dimness of the roof into a sea of flowers of every colour in a blaze of light, beset by birds and butterflies. All that he could see was a sea of flowers, running up into crests of greenness, topped here and there by spikes, pinnacles and fountains of strange leaves. There seemed no end to it in any direction, nor any break, for even the water was hidden by the trees. It glittered and glowed: it hummed with life: it exulted with an ecstasy of life: it lived thus in the sun all day, and at night the moon and the stars gave it the shadow of a life and the peace which man never has. It was all marvellous, but it had nothing to do with man: men did not come there.

After he had clambered down, he turned away towards the west, taking sighting marks, from tree to tree, to stop any more going in a circle. His hands were tingling from the creeper bristles, as though he had been pulling nettles with them. His face was tingling in a somewhat different way. It smarted as it had smarted years before at school when somebody had kicked a wet Rugby football hard against his cheek. The smarting spread down his neck to his chest and along his backbone. He rubbed the smarting skin, but the rubbing did it no good: it made it slightly different and worse. In about an hour, he felt a puffiness about his eyes: his lips and fingers had a tight feeling. "I'm swelling," he said. "I must have been on one of those poison trees. If this gets much worse, I shan't be able to see: I shall be all puffed up."

In another hour, his eyes had become so swollen that he could not see clearly; all his face had swollen till it no longer felt like flesh: it drummed within with a drumming which seemed to beat upon his brain. His hands were so puffed that he could not bend his fingers. When he came to a puddle in the wood, he peered down to look at himself in the water. He could not see all, but he made out a bladdery appearance which frightened him. "I've gone just like the bladders we used to suck to make elastic," he thought. "If one of these blisters bursts, I shall be done." He sat down, trying not to be frightened. "I'm going to be blind," he thought. "It will probably pass off in a few hours, but I shall be blind while it lasts. I shall be blind to-night: all to-night and perhaps to-morrow: and I don't know where I am, nor how I am to get out of here. I've been a pretty rotten messenger, so far. Oh, I wish that this beating in my brain would stop."

It did not stop: it grew louder, with a rhythm which did not vary for an hour together: it beat like a heart-beat: after a while there was something almost pleasant in its recurrence. Then, suddenly, it changed to another rhythm, which was not like a heart-beat, but much more exciting. Hi was afraid to hope: he stood still, listening. "I know what it is," he said at last, "it is a kind of a mine-stamp, or engine of some sort: not far away. There is probably a mine here. I've wandered into Meruel, where the mines are: this is one of them. And I am going towards it."

Hope came back into him as soon as he was certain that the noise came from men. Even Reds would be better than the forest. He went on towards the beating noise, which presently died away so that he scarcely heard it. He went forward, praying that it might not cease. The light was fast going from the forest (from sunset, not from his blindness); he longed to be with his fellow men before the night set in. He shouted from time to time. Presently the multitudes of the homing birds drowned the beating with the noise of their wings.

When the wings were at last quiet, the noise of the beating reappeared above the lesser noises of night. It was beating now in a different rhythm, with a louder volume. "It is not an engine," Hi said. "I know what it is now. It is one of these tom-toms or native drums, like the one at home, which father used to let us play. I was an ass not to recognise it before. It must be near at hand, too. I'll shout again."

No answer came to his shouting: the drummer, if it were a drummer, was intent upon his rhythm, which was taking his soul up great spirals of recurrence into the ellipses of escape: what were night, nature and a lost human being to him?

At last, amid much that was indistinct, Hi saw a light among the trees. A little fire was burning there, though often obscured by things moving in front of it. "It is a camp fire," Hi thought. "And it must be an Indian camp, because white men would never permit this drumming."

Some little fear was in his mind lest the Indians should be hostile. He had heard that the forest-Indians were sometimes made dangerous by white criminals who found refuge among them. Still, even cannibals would hesitate, he thought, before killing meat suffering from poisonweed. "I believe that they will give me a square deal," he said. In bursts, amid the constant noise of the drumming, he heard the voices and the movements of the people of the poblacion.

He called several times more. Now he was heard, for the dogs of the camp began to bark.

In a few minutes he came into a compound, or cleared space surrounded on three sides by Indian huts of the kind familiar to him from his father's tales. Fires were burning upon stones in all the huts: by their light he could make out men in white and things like white cloths inside the huts. Some little dogs were at the doors barking. There was a splashing noise not far away. Men were talking, women were crooning to their babies, the drummer went on drumming. Somebody was thudding at something: it sounded like the beating of a wad of wet linen with a mallet. Strange things like minute devils came out of the huts, mocked at him and sidled softly away: he could not imagine what they were. The linen-thudder began to intone a thudding song of a melancholy kind, such as a dog in despair or affected by the moon will sing. The air was full of the smell of food, burning gums and sweet oils.

"I am English. I am a friend," Hi called. "Don't shoot. I am English." He called this several times before anyone paid any attention to him. Then an Indian man, dressed in white, came from one of the huts towards him. He was a chubby little smiling man, grey-haired, cheerful and kind. He spoke to Hi, in words of one syllable in a tongue which Hi had not heard. He stared at Hi's face, raised his hands and said, "Mar, Mar," which Hi took to be Indian for "You have a swollen face." "Yes," Hi answered, in English, "I have indeed: trés Mar." The Indian surveyed Hi from head to foot, which seemed to convince him that Hi was pretty Mar over all.

A coarse voice, from one of the huts facing Hi, called out an order to the Indian, who ceased in his pantomime of sympathy as though he had been stung. He seemed to invite Hi forward to enter the hut from which the voice had called. Hi went forward, with the Indian at his side, towards the hut.

The hut, like the other huts of the poblacion, was, at a guess, thirty feet long by fifteen broad. The end, which faced Hi, was open to the night: at the sides the roofs came down almost to the ground, with a tiling of palm leaves stitched with bast. The end of the hut was lit by a fire arranged among stones, which Hi could not help noticing were hewn stones. Someone was moving about beyond the fire: he called to the Indian some order, that Hi was not to come any nearer till the Indian had reported. When this had been done, the guide led Hi into the hut.

Hi could see across the fire a biggish white man, dressed in a shirt and riding breeches, with a bandolier cartridge belt. This man at the moment was bent at the fire lighting a twig, with which he soon lit a clay lamp.

"There, that's lit," he said. "Now, let's have a look at you?"

He held up the lamp and surveyed Hi with a strange expression, which Hi could not read. He was a strongly-made, rather tall, robust man, with yellowish dead coloured hair, like brass-work smeared with oil. He was clean-shaven, even in that wild place. His eyes were grey-blue in colour. His nose was small and straight save for a defiant tip. His mouth had about it a look of defiance, scorn, contempt and utter fearlessness. He was without doubt an Englishman of about twenty-five years of age who had at one time lived among people of refinement.

"So," the man said. "And where the hell do you come from?" Hi told him his tale, that he was lost while making for Anselmo.

"Anselmo?" the man said. "Anselmo? I never heard of Anselmo. Where is that?"

"I don't know," Hi said. "In the plain: not twenty miles from Santa Barbara. Isn't this near the plain?"

"This is the Melchior forest, chum," the man said. "What the hell have you done to your face?"

"I got it poisoned by poison ivy."

"That's a proper new chum's trick. You'll be blind to-morrow. What do you propose to do?"

"Perhaps you could let me stay here till my eyes are better and then give me a guide to the plain."

"I've got no guide."

"Or put me on my way then. I can't be far."

"Did anyone tell you of me, or put you up to coming here?"

"No."

"Did you come out alone into this forest?"

"Yes."

"God."

There was a pause at this point, while the man put down his lamp. Hi had become used to scurvy welcomes from the natives of Santa Barbara, but this man was a fellow-countryman with some traces of breeding in him. The man sat on the edge of his hammock, with his feet upon a low wooden stool. He swung himself to and fro while he seemed to consider.

"Got any oof?" he asked at last.

"None here. I have some in Santa Barbara."

"And I suppose you've got some in the savings bank at home?"

"Yes."

"God," the man said. "My God, my Father, while I stray."

"Very well," Hi said. "If this is all the welcome you can give me, I can go on. I am sorry if I have intruded."

"Have you got a pack of cards?" the man asked.

"No. I'll wish you good-night," Hi said.

"As you please about that."

Hi turned away, flaming with rage and self-pity at being treated thus, in his misery, there in the wilderness, by this fellow-countryman. He did not know where he was to go, nor how, in that darkness and pain, but he was not going to stop with this fellow. He moved back into the space in front of the houses, with a sense of the comfort of them. Each house seemed full of sheltered and fed men and women, who had fire, rest for the night, and certainty for the morrow, as well as companionship. He had none of all these things: he was miles from any of them: he was beside full of sickness.

"Here, chum," the man called, "where are you going?"

"Out of this."

"I don't want your carcase poisoning the bush, and putting the game off, which is what will happen if you try it," the man said. He raised his voice suddenly with a call for his Indian, who appeared on the instant, without noise of any kind. He spoke rapidly to the Indian for a moment, giving him orders. "See," the man said at last to Hi, "you can't go with your eyes in that state. I've told Chug-chug here to put you into a hut by yourself. He'll give you stuff for your blisters as well as some chow. Go along with him: he'll look after you."

"Thank you," Hi said.

"You'd better go with him, hadn't you?" the man asked.

"Right," Hi said. The Indian motioned to him to follow him to one of the huts on the right of the enclosed space. When Hi had entered the hut, which was dark, the Indian disappeared, leaving him alone there. It was like the other huts, closed at the sides by the roofs coming down to the ground, and open to the air at the ends. Hi felt utterly alone there. The tom-tom was still beating and beating: all his blood seemed to have gone thin and bitter from the poison in his skin. In the next hut many people were talking together: some were singing. Then at the door of the hut the little tiny devils appeared again: they mocked at him and sidled softly away.

Presently the Indian reappeared with wood for a fire and some burning embers. With these, he made a fire upon a hearth of hewn stones: the fire burned up so as to light the place a little. Hi noticed a couple of tin travelling trunks, much battered with service, against one of the walls. The Indian motioned to Hi to sit in a white cotton hammock, with fringes of coloured bast, which had been slung from the posts. He sat as he was bid, with his feet upon a long footstool of some hard wood. The Indians brought him a mush or stew in a calabash, which he ate with thankfulness. It was hot and seasoned with peppers: it brought the essence of life right into his being. While he ate of this dish, an Indian examined his feet for jiggers. When he had finished his meal, the Indians smeared his face and hands with a soft wet mess, which (unknown to Hi) they had been chewing while he ate. It had a rancid smell to it, but it soothed the pain at once. An Indian brought him a cotton quilt for his hammock. Wrapping himself in this, he turned in for the night: full of anxiety for his friends, wild with disappointment at having failed them, sick in body, and "perplexed in the extreme."

He could not sleep, all weary as he was, because of the discomforts of his body. He lay twisting in his hammock, while the tom-tom beat in the hut beside him, changing its rhythm once in the hour. No one seemed to want to sleep in that village. Men and women were moving about, talking, telling endless stories, or singing like melancholy dogs, for hours together. Sometimes he dozed away for a few minutes till the touch of the hammock upon his face or hands roused him again. Always, when he woke, the tom-tom was beating and someone was telling a story. Little dogs, with sharp noses, enormous pointed ears and mangy skins, came snapping into the hut from time to time, after beetles, it seemed. The sidelong devils did not come again: he thought of them often enough.

On this, the fifth day of his journey to fetch Don Manuel, the Whites of the Western Provinces mustered 437 men at San Jacinto. They moved out to Don Manuel's advanced post beyond the river, having left word that the final rendezvous would be at San Pablo, only thirty miles from Santa Barbara city. They brought with them many spare horses: this was the only excellence in their force, their weapons being mainly machetes, revolvers, rook rifles and shot-guns of all sorts and bores with whatever cartridges they had. There was no hesitation in any of them at the thought of marching upon Santa Barbara. They were all religious men, who felt that their faith was threatened. The parish priest at San Luis, where Don Manuel was camped, blessed them at their setting out: certainly no man among them doubted that his going was in the service of God.

CHAPTER XV

Towards three in the morning Hi fell into a deeper sleep, from which he was roused by the cold: his fire was out and his quilt had slipped from him. In groping for it, he found that his head had so swollen that he could hardly see. The pain was gone, but he was puffed like a prize pig.

"O Lord," he moaned, "I shan't be able to see. I can't see across this hut. I shan't be able to reach Anselmo even to-day. Now I am bound to be too late, and Carlotta may be killed because of me." He turned out of his hammock to prove himself: it was only too true, he was nearly blind: he could not hope to go on without a guide. "Horses," he thought. "These people have no horses. My only hope is a river. I may be near some tributary of the San Jacinto. If I could take a canoe down that, or if some Indian would take me, I might even find Don Manuel during to-day. There must be rivers which run into the San Jacinto. If that fellow told the truth, if this is the Melchior forest, I must be near the San Jacinto, or its eastern tributaries. I must speak to that fellow and beg him to help me. After all, he is an Englishman, though he is as ross as a mule."

As it was dark and cold, he turned back to his hammock to try for warmth and sleep. He slept a little, by starts, always broken by nightmares. The cold struck him from underneath: it got into all his bones. "Aha, you English boy," voices said to him in his dreams. "Now you've come into our power you shall be searched. You've got the cramps, you've got the aches, you've got the forest fever, you are going to go blind; you've got the poison in your entrails and we're going to wring you with it."

When he next awoke it was daylight, though still early. The village had come again to the life it had hardly laid down during the darkness. The thudding noise, of wet linen being banged on stones with a mallet, had begun again: women were singing and little brown children were playing in the *patio*. The sharp-eared dogs had tucked their noses into their flanks for sleep in sunny places. The tiny devils were sidling about, mocking at people. He recognised them now as dove-grey parrots with rosy breasts. Their bright eyes and compact bent beaks gave them the knowing look of men about town: they looked like devilled-bone-and-biscuit men. They looked at him, with their heads cocked aside, considering his offers of friendship, and then sheered off from him as something not to be trusted.

He turned out of his hammock to peer from his puffy eyes at the new world about him. His body felt as though it did not belong to him: pains and aches had taken it over. His face and hands felt dead: his mouth was full of fur. He wandered out into the morning.

He could see well enough to take a track which led past the side of his hut to a river some twenty feet broad where naked men and women were sitting in the water immersed to their chins. Some women were pounding bunches of wet cotton on the stones near the river; their tiny children, tying minute fragments of stone to strips of bast, were making bolases with which they entangled the dragon-flies.

After washing in the river, and bathing his puffy eyes, Hi returned to the huts, hoping to see the white man, who was not in his hut. Early as it was, most of the men of the community had gone to whatever work they had to do. Women were pounding and straining cassava, or baking it into loaves. They laughed at Hi in a friendly way: one of them gave him bread and a gourd full of broth. While he ate this, sitting in a hammock, an Indian, dressed in three tobacco-tin lids, took station before him, grinned, pointed to his chest and said: "Me Johnny God-dam." Unfortunately, this was all the English known to him. Hi tried by signs to find out where the white man was, where one would come out if one were to follow the river, and where the white settlements were. His performance roused great interest, but nobody understood it: he had the general impression that they thought that he was praying for dry weather.

He went back to the hut where he had passed the night; he was full of anxiety and helplessness. Chug-chug, if that were his name, appeared with some aromatic leaves, which he rubbed gently on Hi's blistered skin, with a soothing effect. He was a cheerful man, who talked all the time. Hi questioned him in English and by signs: this increased Chug-chug's flow of talk, without bringing any enlightenment.

"Oh, I ought to go on," Hi said. "I ought to go on. Yet what is the sense of going on, blind as I am, when I don't know where to make for? See here, Chug-chug," he said, with signs to represent the white man, "when will the Señor, the chief, come back into the camp?" Chug-chug knew that an important question was asked, but he could not understand it; he made a speech about the new cassava patch, which Hi could not understand. Having thus made the honours even he disappeared.

"I'll wait till mid-day," Hi thought. "The white man will be back at mid-day. Father always said that the forest practice is to eat at mid-day and then take siesta. After siesta, I shall be able to go on. The man's a regular rossy tick: yet even a rossy tick will tell a fellow the way. And the more I think of it, the more sure I am that I shall be able to reach the San Jacinto River from here. I may even reach Don Manuel to-night."

He stood at the hut door for a few minutes gazing at the scene of primitive life before him. The sun, blazing down into the compound, put new life into him: he felt both warmed and comforted. He was beginning to see a little better out of both eyes, and found that he could now bend his fingers. One of the best of his symptoms was the feeling that if he were to lie down he would sleep.

He went into the hut, with a sudden curious sensation that somebody had been in the hut, behind him, until the instant of his turning to come in. "Strange," he thought. "It is this puffiness of my eyes. Or I know what it was, coming into the gloom out of the glare, made me think that the posts were a man." He turned back to make sure of this. "I suppose that that is what it must have been," he thought. "It did look rather like a man."

He sat in his hammock, trying to think how much he was to blame for going astray. Then his thoughts turned to the Englishman. "What is he and what is he doing here, and why is he so sour? He must be a prospector of sorts: he is not an engineer, for he hasn't any engine. He won't be only a hunter or explorer: he's too much of a swine for that. I wouldn't mind betting that he is a gold or mineral prospector, who has come on a good thing out here and is afraid of some other person cutting in on him. That is it, I'll bet any money. That would explain his being so crusty and giving me so poor a welcome. I wonder what the man is. I suppose that those are his trunks, over there against the wall."

The trunks were the usual, small, flat, tin, traveller's trunks, made low, so as to fit under bunks at sea, or lie snugly along the side of a mule. They had once been japanned black. Hard service had worn away much of the japan: some of the tin shewed bright, the rest was battered and discoloured. On the top of the lid of one of them was the letter D in what had once been white paint: on the top of the lid of the other was most of the letter W. Both trunks had been neglected for some time. Sprays of creepers, which had thrust under the roof there, had grown right over them. "D and W," Hi repeated. "A letter has been blotted out on both boxes. I suppose the man's name is D ... W ... Dirty White, or Dingy Welcome, or Doubtful Wanderer: the initials might stand for any of them. They look like the sort of box a prospector would take. Meanwhile, I should be the better for some sleep."

He turned into his hammock, hoping that a rest would help to heal his eyes; he saw the dog at the hut door nuzzle further into his flank; then his overwhelming weariness pressed down upon him so that he slept unheeding.

He woke some hours later with the feeling that someone was in the hut wanting to speak to him. It was not easy to thrust aside such folds of sleep; while he struggled with them, the someone, whoever he was, had gone; there was no one there when he awoke. "Strange," he said. "It seemed as though someone were there. I thought that I saw someone, a tallish chap, who had something to say. I suppose I dreamed it. I wish that sleeping in this land didn't give one this thick sort of brown taste in the mouth whenever one wakes."

He turned out to stretch, feeling stunned and stupid, but the better for his rest. "I'll see if the D. W. fellow has come back," he thought.

He found that the village was taking the siesta; he had slept into the afternoon; the village was more silent than it had been at any hour of the night. He called at the door of the white man's hut. "Are you there, sir? May I speak with you?" As he had no answer, he peeped in; the white man had not returned. "Still away," Hi thought. "What a nuisance."

He had the feeling that he must not enter the hut while the owner was away. None the less, he looked curiously at the contents of the hut. Some clothes of a yellowish drill were hanging from one of the posts, with a leather belt on which the initial D was marked in black. At the back of the hut, beyond the hammock, was a table, made of two planks supported upon the taller sort of Indian stools, of the kind cut by them for their god-houses. This table was heaped with objects, which seemed to be mostly stones or lumps of ore; he could not make out what they were. Under the table was another tin box marked D W upon the side; this box was open and contained boots. The hammock had a good brown camel-hair blanket rolled up across its foot. Hi had just such another in his kit at Santa Barbara: his mother had chosen it for him, "For your father says the nights can be very cold, even a month after the rains."

There seemed to be nothing else worth notice in the hut, except the usual canvas water bottle, holding a gallon, a canvas bucket with a laniard spliced into its rim, and a canvas basin in which D. W. had soaped himself that morning. Hi had experience of the things bought for outfits; he noticed that all these things were very good of their kind but the worse for wear. "No tools," Hi thought. "He has a working or a claim somewhere near; the tools will be there."

"Well," Hi said to himself, "I must not spy upon this man. I wish that he would come back, so that I could have it out with him."

He walked into the compound, where he passed an hour trying to make friends with the parrots and the little dogs. Both were gentle yet suspicious; he had no success with them. The day dragged heavily over him, while he waited for D. W. to return. The village was interesting and the forest beautiful. He longed to be out of both, going fast upon his mission, while there was still hope.

After a while, he felt within himself the suggestion that there might be something of interest in the hut where he had slept. He had not examined it thoroughly; now that his eyes were so much less swollen, he felt that that would be something to do; there might even be some book tossed aside somewhere. He had seen no trace of a book in D. W.'s hut.

In the furthest corner of his hut was a small rubbish heap. He pulled a half-burnt piece of wood from his fireplace. With this, he began to poke aside the rubbish, to see what he could find. The rubbish was of all sorts, much the worse for having been in a corner of the hut into which the rain had blown. He found these things:

Part of a canvas sack, into which the ants had worked.

A briar pipe, much used, which had a bleached look from exposure.

Part of a leather strop that had been cut through.

Three small twists of tough galvanised wire.

Four bits of old bootlace.

A broken strap.

A screw eye.

A paper, containing a mouldy empty cardboard box for Marcham's Patent Trouser Buttons, with the legend, "No more sewing."

Most of a pair of drill riding breeks made in Taunton. The ants had been in these. Two envelopes, or parts of envelopes.

A sodden little fat book, rather like a newly-drowned puppy.

He brought this book into the light, so that he might examine it. It proved to be a dumpy volume of Milton's poems, complete in itself, "printed 1828 for J. Smith, Bookseller, 193, High Holborn," and bound in green cloth boards. It opened at the frontispiece, of Milton "from an Impression of a Seal," opposite a vignette of Eve among some dahlias beside a very wriggly snake. On the flyleaf of the book was an inscription in faint ink in the handwriting of a woman:

To Dudley Wigmore,
from his Mother. August 12th, 1881.

"Dudley Wigmore," Hi said. "D. W. . . . So that is the fellow's name, is it? It is an odd book for him to have. And he might have been a little more careful of a gift from his mother, one would think."

The book was swollen and stuck together from being soaked; Hi opened it in the sun, with great care. He knew little, certainly, about Milton, except that he had written a poem called L'Allegro, which Hi had had to learn by heart some years before at his prep. school. "I daresay I'll like it better now," he said. "Anyhow this is a book, and a very famous book: there must be something in it. And it will be something to do to try to dry it without pulling out the leaves."

After he had opened the book to dry, he went back to look at the rubbish heap for more treasures. He found nothing more in that heap, except some rags which the ants and grubs had riddled to pieces. He looked at the two bits of envelope, both of which bore English stamps. On one of the stamps part of the postmark could be made out when the paper was held to the light. Hi read the name "allet." He tried to think of some English place with a name which ended in "allet": he could think of none. "It sounds liker a French name," he thought. One of the pieces had been addressed to

D. Wigm— —
C/o Messrs. W— —
Sant— —

The rest was torn off. The other, which was smaller, had only a bit of the flap, the stamp, and the ends of an address, in a different hand, thus:

— — Esq.,
— — et Cie.

Hi dropped the bits of paper on to the heap. Some of the leaves of the Milton were now dry: he turned them, so that others might dry. Having nothing else to do, he brought out the stools from his hut, rested the book on one, sat on the other, and passed some hours, reading bits of the poem as the leaves dried. The Indians looked at him with curiosity and fear, thinking that he was practising magic. His mood and that place gave the poetry a value which it had not held (for Hi) in the prep. school. "When my eyes are better," he thought, "I will read this all through. It is a wonderful thing."

The day passed thus hour by hour with no sign of the white man. Some Indians who had come to the poblacion with cassava, brought out some stew for Hi with a piece of hot bread, which he ate. Having eaten, he brought the stools and the book into the hut where he had slept.

"It is strange," Hi said. "Whenever I come into this hut I have the feeling that there is somebody here. It is the way that this hammock-post catches the light."

The sun was now fast dropping behind Melchior, so that it lit up the end of the hut where the rubbish had been thrown. Something sparkled on the floor beyond the rubbish. Hi picked it up. It was a little gold locket clipped to a rusty steel watch-chain. After wiping the locket, he opened it, with some trouble. It contained a tiny photograph, not so big as his thumbnail, of a young woman's face. She was a handsome young woman, of the hawk brunette type.

"I suppose that this is his girl," Hi thought, closing the locket. "He must have dropped this somehow in the dark; he'll be glad to have it again."

He dropped the locket on to one of the wooden stools, so that he might have it at hand when D. W. returned; then he sat in his hammock, thinking of Carlotta. "Early to-morrow," he thought. "Early to-morrow, whatever happens, I shall get away from here. Even now, with luck, I might not be too late. But I simply must not be too late. I must be in time."

As the light suddenly passed from the world at the dropping of the sun behind Melchior, he wondered whether after all he would be in time. It was hard to say what might have happened under a madman like Don Lopez. Supposing that the worst had happened? Supposing that he were not in time?

He was weary from the hardships of the journey, all his body was crying out for rest. He edged himself into his hammock, for the comfort of lying prone, and there fell asleep. He slept heavily, having still some arrears to make up, and yet, for all its soundness, his sleep was troubled with the sense that all was not well. Gradually, as his sleep weakened, he began to feel that there was an unhappiness, or something worse, close to him: someone in distress was there. "Ah," he answered in his sleep, "it is you, Carlotta. All right, I'll do my best to warn him and bring him. I'll do my best, though I do seem to have muddled things." Then, as his sleep weakened still more, he knew that it was not Carlotta who was there, but a man who had been there before.

"Yes," he said, in his sleep, "there was a man in the hut this afternoon: so he is here again; well, what can I do for him? Where are you? Let's have a look at you."

He struggled out of his sleep to a knowledge of the waking world, which came upon him slowly, as another world, that had taken its place, moved away in fiery mist. He saw, or thought that he saw, the man standing near the hut entrance, looking at him, with sad eyes. "All right," Hi cried.

"Is it supper-time? I've been asleep, but I'm awake. I'll be up in one moment." As he blinked and sat up, the figure faded away into the darkness behind it, which was now a blackness of leaves moving against stars. "It was only a dream, after all," Hi said. "But it is odd how there always seems to be a man here. I suppose one gets to imagine these things."

He came back fully to the world of the village, where now lamps and fires were burning, women singing and the tom-tom drumming. "I'll see if D. W. has come back," he said.

He was prevented by the entrance of Chug-chug, who came to ask him by signs to come to the other hut. "D. W. is back, then," he thought. "Now for it."

He followed Chug-chug to the other hut, which was lit by three lamps. A trestle-table had been rigged up, food was set upon it. The man sat on his camp-chair at the table-head, facing Hi. He had a much worn cartridge belt slung over his shoulder: one of the pouches of it was stamped D. W. He had been cleaning a light sporting rifle with a pull-through and an oily feather: he now held the rifle across his knees, and kept opening the breech and snapping it to. Hi could see him more clearly than had been possible to him the night before. In the main, he felt his impression confirmed, that he did not like the man: there was more force in him than wisdom or goodness.

"You'd better have some chow, chum," the man said.

The chow was the oily, peppery meat stew, served with cassava bread, of which Hi had already eaten twice that day.

"Find yourself a pew there," the man said. He was not a gracious host: he seemed to resent Hi's presence there, yet this was a kind of invitation from him to sit down and dine. Hi pulled a stool to the table and sat down.

"I suppose I'd better introduce myself," the man said, "like the ladies do at these receptions. Did you ever hear of Brocket Letcombe-Bassett, the hundred yards Blue?"

"No," Hi said.

"Well, he is my father's second cousin. My father's a clergyman, or was. I don't know whether he's still alive; I don't much care."

"Then are you Mr. Letcombe-Bassett?"

"Yes."

"Then is there another Englishman here; a Mr. Wigmore?"

"Wigmore? Did you know him?" the man asked.

"No," Hi said. "But I found a book of his and this little gold locket. Did you know him?"

"Yes, he was a prospector here," the man said. "He died of forest fever here a couple of years ago."

"Poor chap," Hi said. It seemed a lonely death for a man with a mother and a lover.

"Yes," the man said. "He died of forest fever a couple of years ago. There's a lot of forest fever here as soon as the rains call off."

"Were you with him when he died?" Hi asked.

"Not actually with him, no; but in at the death, yes. I was as near as I wanted to be. Forest fever's an easily caught complaint."

"Is he buried here?"

"Yes; or not far from here. I had the Indians to bury him. Indian fashion, in a hole in the hut."

"In the hut where I am?"

"The hut where you are? No. In the hut in the bush where he kicked the bucket."

"Were you able to let his people know that he was dead?" Hi asked.

"No; I didn't know that he had any people."

"Hadn't he letters?" Hi asked. "There are scraps of letters in the hut; torn up. Perhaps we could piece them together."

"There weren't any letters," the man said. "Wigmore had no letters. I expect you saw bits of some of mine, from my loving father: blast him."

"No, these were to Wigmore."

"Oh," the man said. "Well, I saw none. I looked through his things. Of course, out here, an Englishman with another Englishman, that was the least one could do."

"He had a girl and a mother."

"How the hell do you know? I knew Wigmore well, my damned young cub. As well, that is, as anyone could know a fellow of that stamp."

"I don't know about damned and cub," Hi said. "I'm not your father."

The man stared at him for an instant with a look of fury, which died on the instant into contempt.

"I was talking about Wigmore," he said. "If you think that this is a Sunday school, you'll learn it isn't."

"I think no such thing," Hi said. "But I won't take 'damned young cub' from a hundred yards Blue, let alone his second cousin."

"The hell you won't," the man said. "Well, I always liked guts, so we'll reckon it not said."

"All right," Hi said. "As we were. I really thought that you were Wigmore. The book was from his mother, and the locket has a picture of his girl inside it. That was what made me think that he must have people alive."

"He was a very odd fish, Wigmore," the man said. "He was a man under a cloud. When you come to one of these solitary men, prospecting in a place like this, you may always be sure that there's something wrong. He never talked about his past; but he let you see he had one. He drank like a fish, too."

"Did he ever find any gold?" Hi asked.

"He was one of these pleasure-miners. They always get enough to pay their Indios and keep themselves in cartridges. They go brown after a bit; that is, they turn Indian."

By this time, he had slung his rifle by its bandolier to the crutch in the post. Hi could see the initials D. W. burned upon the stock: it had been Wigmore's rifle in the past. Hi was uneasy at the way the man spoke about Wigmore: he wished to know more.

"It's a pretty awful end," Hi said, "to die out here in the wilderness, all those thousands of miles from home."

"Damned sight better end than being poisoned by doctors in a frowsy hospital."

"I wish we could make out enough bits of letters to find out where his people are," Hi said.

"There aren't any letters, I told you."

"There are bits of letters, because I saw them. Do you know, there is one way we could find out about him?"

"How?" the man asked, with a sudden close attention.

"From people in Santa Barbara. He had a letter addressed to him in the care of a French firm in Santa Barbara. I expect that they were his agents. There can't be more than two or three French houses in Santa Barbara. I could enquire at them all, and through them we could easily find out where he came from."

"Agents? A French firm?" the man said. "You mean Chardenal? It is a general stores in Santa Barb'. He used to get his stores there. They weren't his agents: he was a customer there. As a matter of fact, I sent an Indio in with a chit to them when Wigmore died to cancel his last order. They know that he is dead."

"Wouldn't they know where he came from?"

"He was a very dark horse, Wigmore. He never told that to me, in all the months we were together. I don't see why he should have told his grocers."

"I suppose you don't know any English town with a name ending in 'allet,' do you?" Hi asked.

"Allet?" the man said, suspiciously. "No, I don't know any bally 'allet.' If you'd ask my opinion, I should say you were getting Wigmore on the brain. Are you sure you've not got a touch of forest fever? It often begins like that: getting excited about somebody's bally corpse and that."

"I'm not excited about him," Hi said. "Only it is rather rough on his mother and girl, if they are wondering about him, and hoping to hear from him all this time."

"As I said before," the man said, "I don't believe for one moment that he had a mother and girl. In all the months I knew him I never knew him mention them nor have any letter from them. Put him out of your mind. He was a dark horse and a tank. It's my believe that he was wanted for something: anyway he was under a cloud. Now about yourself: you say you want to get to Anselmo? Is that near Santa Barbara? Well, if it is, it's seventy miles from here; and here is twenty miles from any road there."

"Could you let one of your Indios guide me to the road there, early to-morrow?" Hi asked. "My eyes are well enough. The swelling will probably be quite gone by to-morrow."

"I couldn't, to-morrow," the man said.

"Why not? I'd be ever so much obliged if you would."

"I couldn't send an Indio to-morrow: he wouldn't go if I did: it will be one of their moon-feasts."

"Well, then; why not to-night?"

"You're not fit to go to-night: besides, these Aracuis won't move a step at night. I don't blame them. The snakes are abroad. Then there are tigers. Besides, there are too many ghosts for them."

"I would chance the ghosts," Hi said, "if you would direct me on my way."

"You would never find your way," the man said. "I couldn't hope to show it to you in a first quarter moon."

"Will you show it to me to-morrow?"

"Yes, I'll show it to you to-morrow."

"Early; first thing? Would you mind starting early, so that I may reach the road before dark?"

"I'll start fairly early."

"Will you tell me what you are?" Hi said. "I mean, what you do out here in the wilderness?"

"I?" the man said. "I'm one of the damned lost souls, who like my own way and mind my own business."

"Certainly," Hi said. "I didn't mean to be inquisitive."

"You say you haven't any money?"

"No."

"Do you play cribbage?"

"Yes."

"It's not much fun playing anything without having something on the game. Haven't you got a ticker?"

"Yes, but the water's got into it. It's stopped."

"Then you haven't got a tosser?"

"No."

"Damn well on your uppers?"

"Yes."

"My God, My Father, while I stray. You'd better go and turn in, then, if you want this early start. I can't play beggar-my-neighbour with you, like a damned kid. Next time you look in, you'd better bring some ooftish to cover your cards with: your mess-bills, too, if you don't mind."

"I'm sorry that I've no money," Hi said. "But as for mess-bills, if you'll tell me your name and agents, I'll pay what you think fair for what I have had here. Or you can take my watch. It is a good one and nearly new: it will go well when cleaned."

"We'll talk about bills to-morrow," the man said. "You'd better go and turn in."

"Very well. Good-night."

The man did not answer. He stood staring at Hi out of his cold, hard blue eyes: his lip was lifted in a sneer. Hi felt that he had never yet met a man so hateful. "He is a loathsome swine," he thought. "A vile, taunting, silver-ring tick."

He came to his hut and again had the sensation that someone was there: this time so strongly that he called out. "Yes, who is it, there?" before he saw that there was no one. "It is odd," he said, "I keep thinking that there's a man here. I've got to be all jumpy from being in the forest; and then, this hammock-post is like a man, and gives me the illusion every time. I wish there were a man here, Dudley Wigmore or another; then I might not be so dependent on this sneering devil."

Still raging against the man, he turned into his hammock to think of things which did not bear thought; Carlotta and Rosa depending on him; Carlotta's marvellous grace, beauty and goodness; now in gaol among blackguards at the whim of a madman; then, himself, who was to have saved her, all astray in a forest, all those miles from even beginning to send word about her. There was no sleep for one with thoughts like that.

Sleep would not have been easy in any case, for the village was celebrating something, a hunt or a moon-feast: he could not tell what. Half a dozen drums were beating. Presently the boys of the tribe lit a bonfire in the midst of the *patio* or space in the midst of the village. They piled it high with wood which the women had collected during the day. As soon as it burned well, they began to march round it, blowing into horns of one note and flutes of two notes: some of them clacked discs of hard wood or rattled beans in goobies: those who could not make music, sang. The little, sharp-eared dogs sitting on their haunches at the hut doors put back their heads, till they seemed all throat, and sang likewise. The babies wakened from their sleep wailed upon high notes. The men of the tribe sang or told stories: the women and little girls dragged wood for the fire.

"I might be a thousand miles from anywhere," Hi thought. "It may take me days to get to Anselmo or anywhere else."

The bonfire lit up the inside of his hut so as to shew the tin boxes marked D and W. Since he could not sleep, his mind turned to these boxes. "There is something queer about this man," Hi said to himself. "There is something odd about his relations with Wigmore. He said something about these solitary prospectors being always bad eggs; well, he doesn't strike one as being a very lofty egg. He says he went through Wigmore's things and found no letters. I know that there were letters, which he pitched on to the rubbish pile only a little while ago. He made no effort to find Wigmore's friends. It's true that he says he sent in an account of his death; yet he wears Wigmore's belt and uses his rifle. And then, to keep away from the poor chap while he was ill: good Lord."

There rose in his mind suddenly the image of the forest fever, as a grey thing without a head, a thing like a worm, which said: "It is just after the rains now: very likely I have put a touch upon you, so that people will leave you in a hut till you are dead. It is a very catching complaint, the forest fever."

"Very likely," he said, "very likely I have caught the fever: in which case they'll never know at home what became of me: no one will ever know, except the Indians who will bury me here."

"I'm going to look in those boxes," he said, turning out of his hammock. "Perhaps there is some map or chart, if Wigmore was a prospector. With a map I might be able to find out where I am and how to get away from here."

He pulled out the nearer of the two tin boxes from its covering of creeper. It felt and proved to be empty save for two small studs and a trouser button. He tipped the box on its side, to make sure that there was no label or address. "No further help there," he said. "Now for the other."

The second box had been used to block a hole which the dogs had routed in the hut wall. It had been weighted inside with a biggish hewn stone, so that the dogs should not thrust it aside. Beside the stone were some scraps of rubbish which Hi brought out to the light to examine. The things were:

A buckle of a strap.

Two halves of a lead pencil which had fallen apart.

The lead of the pencil.

A mouldy piece of knotted ribbon, which looked as if it had once gone round a packet of letters.

Two sodden letters in envelopes, both post-marked Shepton Mallet, the one on February 1st, the other February 8th, 1886, and addressed, "Dudley Wigmore, Esq., c/o The United Sugar Company, Santa Barbara." One of these letters was signed "from mother": the other was from "your loving May."

Last of all was a much-weathered, ant-eaten pocket-book, sodden with damp and so clutched together by a rubber band as to be liker a piece of mouldy wood than a book.

"This is queer," Hi said. "These letters have been opened and carried about in a man's pocket. They are dated only about thirteen months ago. Yet that fellow said that Wigmore died a couple of years ago." Either Wigmore was alive a year ago, or that tick opened his letters a year after he was dead. It isn't likely that that fellow could have made a mistake about Wigmore's death. He said 'a couple of years.' One could hardly go wrong on a point of that sort. One would remember when the only white man within twenty miles died.

"Then that fellow said, that Wigmore was a prospector, a pleasure-miner, and drank like a fish. Now it's odd that there are none of the prospector's things here: no pans and sieves for washing, no scales nor any stuff for making assays. Then if he drank like a fish, it is odd that there are no bottles left. It wouldn't have been easy to drink like a fish out here; but if he drank at all he drank from bottles, and there are no bottles nor parts of bottles. Now father said that any forest Indian would work for a week for a bottle, which is a very valuable possession here. They make bottles into lamps, canteens, jewels, knives, scrapers and arrow-heads. There isn't a trace of a bottle in this settlement, that I can see. So probably Wigmore didn't drink like a fish. Probably also he wasn't a prospector. Probably also he didn't die a couple of years ago, but a year at most. This man has been lying about him. If he lied about his life, probably he has lied about his death. There has been a Wigmore here; that Wigmore is probably dead. The man who knows about his death has his gun and cartridges, and perhaps also his gold-claim and his mining things. The man who lies about him has profited by his disappearance. Supposing this man, whoever he is, this hundred yards Blue man, should have murdered Wigmore, in order to take his things?

"Who is this hundred yards Blue man? I'll bet that name isn't his real name, but a false name given to make me think that he is related to decent people. He is not a gentleman nor a man of ordinary decent feeling: he is a tick or criminal. I wouldn't be a bit surprised if he has murdered Wigmore. If he thinks that I think that, he'll probably murder me. I don't think he'd think twice about murdering a chap. I'll have to be jolly careful to-morrow. But, first, I'll look at this book, to see if it will help at all."

The book proved to be little better than pulp. It had been at one time a neat oblong pocket-book with a cover of black leather: now the dye in the cover and the endpapers had soaked through into the leaves, which were stuck together and stained like crushed blackberries. In the centre were two leaves which contained some legible jottings in pencil in a neat handwriting. They were seemingly columns of names. Closer examination shewed Hi that they were lists of words in different tongues. The left hand columns contained English words, the other columns were the Indian words in different dialects.

"It's a vocabulary or dictionary. A polyglot Indian dictionary," Hi said. "That explains what the man was. He was one of these men who write books about the Indians, and Indian grammars. This isn't the hand of a man who goes pleasure-mining. This chap was a scholar. The only prospecting this fellow did was finding a new tribe with a different dialect."

He had been standing bent over the book close to the door of the hut, where the glow of the bonfire lit his examination. Something told him suddenly that he was being observed. Looking up, to his left, to the point prompted to him, he saw Letcombe-Bassett standing at the mouth of another hut, three parts hidden, watching him. "The beast has been spying on me," Hi thought, turning away. "He knows that I think things are a little fishy: he has been watching to see what I have been doing."

The thought of being spied upon made him at first uneasy, then gay. "If it comes to spying," he thought, "I'll see if I cannot lead you a dance."

He put the book on the shelf of the post for the night: then he turned into his hammock, thinking uneasy thoughts till he was almost asleep.

He was lying high up in his hammock, with his head propped by what sailors would have called the nettles. A faint noise at the mouth of his hut made him instantly alert: someone had crept stealthily thither, breathing anxiously.

"Yes? Who is there?" Hi called.

"Oh, are you awake?" Letcombe-Bassett answered. "I was going quietly so as not to wake you. I was afraid you might be asleep. I only wanted to say that we'll start in good time to-morrow, if you feel up to moving."

"To Anselmo? I'm up to moving."

"I know nothing about Anselmo. I can start to set you on a road which will take you to Santa Barbara."

"That will do. Thank you."

"Right. We'll start then after an early chow. Sleep easy."

He moved across the hut entrance towards his own hut; Hi wished him good-night. "He's a pretty bad egg," Hi thought. "He is here for no good and he means me no good."

These thoughts in his brain slowly merged into the noises of the village, which in turn grew into a night that covered him: he fell asleep in his hammock half covered by a quilt of cotton.

On this the sixth day of Hi's journey, the five hundred odd men of Don Manuel's army made their first march of fifty miles to the eastward, so as to camp at the water-holes at Amarga. At the water-holes, they were joined by some seventy more men, who had either followed them, or ridden in from the north or south. When they left Amarga they were more than six hundred strong.

CHAPTER XVI

It may have been the cold working upon a body worn by anxieties and hardships: it may have been confusion in a brain nine-tenths asleep; or it may have been another thing. As he slept, Hi became aware that Dudley Wigmore was in the hut, sitting on a box, waiting for him to wake. He could see him distinctly; a sad-looking man, of the middle build, fair-haired, blue-eyed, gentle and thoughtful, yet with a clench of resolution, in mouth and chin, which made the face memorable.

"I'm an ethnologist," Wigmore was saying. "You want to escape from here without fail. This is Murder Poblacion."

"Is it?" Hi answered. "By George, did that tick murder you? Wait a minute: I'll be awake in a minute: then, I'll ask you something." He struggled with his sleep as he spoke, beating aside the quilt. He sat up to see Wigmore beside him, sad-eyed, resolute, yet in some way remote from this world. Wigmore was looking at him with a look so sad that he could hardly bear it; he was plainly there, in a suit of old drill, real and touchable. Yet in an instant Hi saw the thatch of the hut wall through the man's body: the body was and then was not, like mist in a change of wind: Dudley Wigmore was gone.

"By George," Hi said. "This is Murder Poblacion. I want to escape from here. That was pretty real. By George, if that wasn't a dream, I've seen a ghost. I believe that that was Wigmore's ghost."

He was not scared by the ghost, if it were a ghost; it had come with too serious a warning for that. He was thrilled through with excitement; he was pitted against a murderer in a place twenty miles from friend or weapon.

"Golly," he said. "That proves it to my mind. I've no further doubt that that man murdered Wigmore: he did."

As he turned out of his hammock, he saw that it was almost dawn: the young men were mustering to a hunt. One of them began to make a melancholy noise upon a flute, to which the others answered by tapping upon their blow-pipes. Women were already at work at the cassava presses or at splitting away the twigs from the branches brought for firing. The young men moved off into the forest: the young women in a group moved off to bathe: the babies, dogs, pigeons and parrots came all to life at once: none but the grown men remained in their hammocks, even they were smoking.

"I'll go through that pocket-book by daylight," Hi said. "Perhaps I shall be able to make out rather more of it, when I have the light." He put his hand to the shelf for the book, and found it gone: it had not fallen to the floor nor into his hammock: it was gone.

"I say," Hi thought. "That fellow must have been watching me last night, to some purpose. That was why he crept to the door, that first time. When I was asleep, he must have crept in again and bagged it from where I put it. All right. It's just as well to know that he is roused. I am roused, too. But, by Jove, he'll never let me get to Anselmo, now that it has come to this."

He was standing, thinking these thoughts, with a daunted heart, near the door of his hut, when a sentence floated into his mind as clearly as though a voice had spoken in his ear. "He will never let you get to Anselmo," the sentence came. "Look out for him."

It came with the distinctness of personality from the depths of his being to voice the thought matured there. "It is true," he repeated, "he will never let me go. I must look out for him. But what am I to do?"

He had no time to think of what he was to do, because at that moment Letcombe-Bassett appeared: he seemed to be in a much better temper than hitherto.

"So you're up," he said. "Good. There's nothing like the bally dawn in these bally tropics: one soon gets into forest habits here: they are the only ways that keep one alive here. As soon as Chug-chug brings our chow, we'll pasea."

"It's jolly good of you," Hi said, "to see me off upon my road."

"Not a bit," the man answered. "Out here, an Englishman with another Englishman, that is the least one could do."

Hi thought that to see a man off the premises is perhaps the least that one can do: he also thought that the man's mood had strangely changed for the better since the night before. Then he had been savage at the thought of showing the way: now he was eager to show it. It occurred to him that there might be a reason for this change, and that this reason, coming from an unpleasant nature, might be an unpleasant one.

"I suppose I might reach the road before to-night?" Hi said.

"Reach what road?"

"The road to Santa Barbara?"

"Oh, that road," the man said. "I'm not so sure."

"But you said it was only twenty miles."

"Did I? Hell. Well, it's more than that. But I suppose you might reach it. Yes, if you're not lamed or crocked or ill you ought to reach it."

"And can you let me take some food and water?"

"You'd better not take those here: you'll only have to lug them along. No. We'll stop at another settlement, some miles from here, and get a swag and a gooby for you there. Then you won't have so much to carry. But here is Chug-chug with the chow. I always have chocolate, Spanish-fashion here, for breakfast. A man has to be pretty hard up to drink maté in cold blood. I'd as soon drink swipes at a wedding."

After breakfast, the man suggested that they should start. He had his sporting rifle under his arm and his bandolier buckled to him. Hi kept his eyes from resting on the letters D. W. so plainly stamped upon them. He had taken pains to avoid any reference to D. W. He wondered, as they set out, whether he would not come to know the contents of that rifle during the course of the morning. He wondered whether that was why the man had dissuaded him from taking food and drink. "Naturally, if I'm going to be shot," he thought, "he won't want to waste food and drink as well as a cartridge. But am I going to be shot? Does he intend to kill me? How am I to dodge it, if he does? I can't refuse to go with him. That would bring things to a crisis at once. I must go with him, and look alive and trust to my luck. The worse I expect, the better I shall find."

The man led the way out of the village, across the river, where the Indians were bathing, to a narrow path through a cane-brake. The set of the path was to the south and west, which Hi knew could not be the course for Santa Barbara.

"This can't be the way," Hi said. "Santa Barbara must be north and east of this."

"Of course it is," the man said. "But this is the way. It swings north after a bit, but anyway you have to go west first of all, to clear the marshes. All the mountain water which isn't soaked up by the trees seeps out at the foothills and makes marsh. You'd better let me lead you."

"Lead the way, then," said Hi. "It's jolly good of you to trouble." He thought that at any rate it was jolly good to have the man with the gun in front of him. The path was a well-trodden, very narrow Indian track, running irregularly between walls of high growing canes, which glittered and rattled. They had hard golden shafts from which pale sheaths, like corn-husks, peeled. High up, seven feet above his head, their shoots were bluish or seemed bluish from the sky above; while the sky in the narrow gash above was greenish from their yellowness. The path curved in and out, exactly as the leader of the tribe had swerved from snag or snake long years before, when the Indians had first gone that way. It was impossible to keep direction after the first few minutes. The most that Hi could say was that he never headed to the east, because he never had the sun in his eyes.

"We'll keep forest habits, going," the man said. "We'll not speak on the trail."

Hi was much relieved at not having to talk. He watched the man's back in front of him, going on and on with the head down. "What is the brute thinking?" Hi wondered. "How soon he shall turn round and bowl me over? Or what a neat job he made of Wigmore and how it can be bettered? Or is he debating whether I'm too much of a kid to bother about? As to that, I wouldn't mind betting that he's made up his mind to do for me. The question is, when?"

That was the main question; but the other questions were not answered, they recurred continually, the question, "Will he?" and the other question, "What can I do to stop him?"

There seemed to be no likely way of stopping him. Hi's mind was working very clearly and weighing all likely chances. The man was armed; he was carrying his rifle at the ready. He was a quick man, probably trained by years in the forest to wheel and make snapshots suddenly. He was a strong man, much stronger certainly than Hi. If Hi were to dart in upon him, to seize the gun, he would certainly settle Hi without trouble; being stronger, quite as active, much more dangerous, and in better condition. If Hi were to lag behind a little and then turn and run back, he would only run to this man's village, where no one could direct him to safety, and all would tell which way he had taken. If he were to leap to the side into the cane-brake, he might be lucky; he might by some miracle leap into cover which would hide him: far more probably he would at the first spring land in some thicket which would hold him, like another Absalom, till his enemy could deal with him. Even if he were not shot in the first minutes he would still be alone in the bush, lost, not knowing his whereabouts nor his course. He might wander for days there without finding a way out.

"What I must do," he thought, "is to wait, if he'll let me, till I can see some real chance of escaping, and then take my chance: the first that comes: any way of getting away: there's none at present.

"But why does he lead me all this way? We must be three miles from the village. If he had only wanted to get rid of me, he could have potted me long ago and put me on an ant's nest. Perhaps, after all, he is setting me on my way to Anselmo or to the road. By Jove, if he is running straight, I'll apologise to him. But I'll bet he isn't. He's got something in his mind and the time for our settlement hasn't come yet."

They went on in Indian file through the cane-brake, neither speaking, with strange thoughts and threats passing from one to the other, till the cane-brake gave way to a jungle, which arched over the path, shutting out the sky. They walked in a tunnel of greenness, pierced with slats of glare, down which flakes of living glitter and colour floated and soared, or sometimes paused as butterflies. Hi looked for some place to his right side into which he could dart for safety: no place shewed there. The man led on without uttering a word.

After half a mile of the tunnel of the jungle, Hi saw in front of him the glare of a clearing, and at the same moment felt or heard a call within his mind, to look to his right side. Afterwards he decided that he heard the call as sound and at the same time felt it within him as warning. He looked, as the call bade, to his right side, with the sense that that part of the wood was evil. It looked more than usually black and joyless, being a thick cover of trees made like stage Druids with lichens. Yet at the point where he looked there was a space of mournfulness, in the midst of which, upon a mound from which a foot protruded, he saw the figure of Dudley Wigmore, as he had appeared at the hut the night before. The face was sad as it had been the night before: it had a look of hopeless brooding.

Hi was quite certain that he had seen it: he looked for one second: it was certainly there: he looked again: it certainly was not there; though the foot was there, a white man's foot, in a boot. He looked to his front instantly, just in time to catch the look of Letcombe-Bassett, who glanced back at that moment to see what he was looking at.

"We're nearly there now," he said.

Hi felt that they were, but answered: "Surely not at the road?"

"No," the man said, "not at the road, but what we're coming to."

"How far have we come?" Hi asked. "Four miles?"

"Call it two and a bit."

"It seems more, in this forest," Hi said.

"I'm used to this forest," the man said. "Do you find it gloomy at all?"

"No," Hi said. "Not when I can see the sunlight."

"The last bit is a bit gloomy," the man said. "It would be a good place for putting anyone away, if anyone were inclined that way."

"I suppose it would," Hi said, becoming very watchful. "I didn't consider it in that light. I suppose you always run some risk from Indians in a forest like this? Or are you too much feared by the Indians?"

"You never know where you stand with Indians," the man answered. "But this is the sort of place they would choose, if they wanted me to pass over Jordan. And no one would be any the wiser. One would be bones in a week and green plantation in two: undiscoverable; just like part of the world."

He led the way into a space which had been cleared not very long before by many men working together. Hi knew that Dudley Wigmore had been murdered by this man at the spot over which they had just passed. That was Wigmore's foot sticking from the grave; that was Wigmore's wraith dreeing his weird there. How soon was he to be added to Wigmore's grave by those hands now playing upon the rifle?

"There now, what do you think of that?" the man asked, nodding ahead.

That was a stone temple carven with gods by some race long since forgotten. It had been covered by jungle until a few months before: now by many burnings, hackings and tearings its face had been cleared and its doorway laid open.

"What do you think of that?" the man repeated.

"I suppose it is one of these Indian temples," Hi said.

"Yes," the man said, "one that hasn't been touched. Do you know anything about these places?"

"No," Hi said, "I'm afraid I don't."

"What do you think of it?"

"It's very grand." Indeed it was very grand, being in two orders of colossal architecture, carven to the cornice with grotesques of gods. It seemed to Hi to be five cricket pitches long. It was built with a tough stone facing over brick. Wherever trees had broken the facing, the brick core was laid bare: they were small bricks laid in a mortar like melted flint spread very thin. The bricks were rose-red and seemingly as tough as stone. All the roof of this temple was covered with trees, shrubs, plants and flowers, beautiful exceedingly. It occurred to Hi that this was the sort of place for which Dudley Wigmore may have come prospecting.

"I've had the men at work at this one for some time now," the man said. "I'm getting it a bit clear now. Where do you suppose the treasure would be?"

"I suppose the Spaniards got all the treasure at the conquest."

"Not from this one: they never came near this one."

"I'll bet they did," Hi said.

"Well, I know they didn't," the man said. "This place was lost in the jungle centuries before the Spaniards came. I can prove it: look here."

He led Hi to the temple door, in front of which a great heart tree had once grown. This tree had been sawn through and removed: the near-by ground was all burnt and scattered with its wreck.

"There's the proof," the man said, "that tree was blocking the main door long before the Spaniards landed. Count the rings in the stump."

"That's true," Hi said, glancing at the countless rings. "But don't these tropical trees put on more than one ring in a year?"

"No, they don't," the man said. "Whereabouts inside do you suppose the treasure is?"

"I suppose under the altar, wherever that would be. But the people would have taken it with them when they went from here."

"They didn't go from here."

Hi waited: he knew that the man wanted his help in some way in this treasure-hunt. He would not ask any question which might bring in or suggest Wigmore. He was certain that Wigmore had discovered this place and had been murdered because of it. Any knowledge which the man had was Wigmore's.

"It will be hard work," Hi said, "to get inside this place."

"Nothing like the work of getting to it. The roof hasn't fallen."

"I'll be surprised if it hasn't," Hi said, "with the weight of the trees growing on it."

"The roof can't fall," the man said. "These builders couldn't vault a roof. That is why this place is so narrow. The roof is of slabs of stone laid upon balks of stone. It's as strong as a hill. It is all enormous walls, with narrow rooms inside them. There's a certain amount of mess inside, of course: these tropics sprout like sewage, but it can be easily cleared: that is, fairly easily."

"It would be interesting work," Hi said, "to get inside and see what it's like."

"Interesting? I believe you," the man said. "This place was built by the Quetzals, whoever they may have been. They had a picture writing of sorts and kept a history in it. They've got rolls of their history in Santa Barb'; people have been deciphering it. Nothing much is known of them yet, for they were gone before the Spaniards came. Now I've reason to believe that this place is the great temple of the Quetzals; the Temple of the sun, or the Temple of Gold. It was a legend when the Spaniards came, as I expect you know: they heard of it: they often looked for it, but they never found it; the forest fever saw to that. Except by a sort of miracle no one could have found it. The Quetzals were a great race: you'll see their cities up in Melchior; but the fever came in and wiped them out. I believe that this old god-shop is bung full of gold."

"What gold?" Hi asked.

"Gold of offerings."

"That would be exciting."

"The Sacramento would be a fool to it."

"Do you know that they offered gold?"

"They offered all the gold they found, so the histories say: thousands of pounds for hundreds of years: believe some of what you see and a tenth of what you hear: it is still likely that they brought a lot of gold here, and here it is still."

"That will be a find."

"Well, what do you say to giving me a hand to get it? I've cleared this space by the help of the Indians, but I'm not going to have these Indians looking for the gold: not likely. That is the white man's perk: none of my brown brothers in this for me: no fear: the hunting parties would go wearing gold till the Barboes learned of it: news soon spreads in this forest. Then we should have the Government in. As you can see, it's more than a one man's job in there, but I reckon that two could shift the stuff and find the altar. And we'd need two to get the gold melted down and into Santa Barb'. They buy it there, pesos for weight, at the Assay Office. I tell you, the Ballarat field is just footle to it. This is Tom Tiddler's ground, that the kids play."

"It sounds pretty thrilling," Hi said.

"Thrilling? I guess it is thrilling: p.d. thrilling."

"I'm awfully keen on getting to Anselmo first," Hi said.

"I know you are," the man said, "I know you are. But what is Anselmo beside what I offer you here? We should shift our traps to here for a couple of weeks, and after that what would Anselmo be? Why, you would be able to buy Anselmo: buy it ten times over and all that's in it: miss and mister. And I'd be a lord at home and have a bloody deer-park."

"Yes, I know," Hi said. "I say, it sounds exciting. But have you any picks and crow-bars?"

"Yes, in a stone trough there: out of the way of the ants."

"I suppose we could get done in a couple of weeks?"

"We'll have to, for the sooner we lift it the better. Not that anyone will come."

"You mean that the fever will come down?"

"No, but these Aracuis go talking: and news spreads. Shall we start, then? What do you say? Off saddle and at it?"

"I'd like to, frightfully," Hi said.

"Well, here you are then," the man said. "I'll give you a third share in anything we find: very likely a million pounds."

"I say, that's generous. But before we start work," Hi said, "I'd like frightfully just to walk along the building and look at it, from close to. I've never seen one of these places before."

"Look your bellyful," the man said. "I hoped you'd see sense when it came to the point. I'll get the picks along."

The man kept his eyes upon Hi, who took a pace back to consider the front of the building. He did not see the temple: it was all a blur of angry gods topped by a foam of flowers and the spears of palms in a glare of light as red as blood. He knew that the man was watching him: he knew that the man had killed Wigmore so that he might be alone in possession. The facts of the murder were all bright in his brain. Wigmore, the scholar, had found the place and cleared it. Then this man, the wanderer and waster, had come thither, by some Fate or chance, and had murdered Wigmore. Now that he himself had come thither, the man wished him to help in the finding and the raising of the treasure. If he refused, he would have a bullet in his brain within ten seconds. If he accepted, he would have a week's or a fortnight's toil: then the bullet. If he tried to escape, what hope had he, save to wander in the fever forest in the fever season till he died miserably or was lost in the marsh?

"We'll start in that door where the tree was," the man said. "It may not have been the main entrance, but the stone is all worn away there by people's feet: it is a used entrance."

"All right," Hi said, with the words sticking in his throat. He did not know what he was to do; there was nothing that he could do. He felt suddenly that there was nothing for it but to plunge into the forest, cost what it might. "I'll never get out of it," he thought. "But anything to get away from this fellow."

The building faced him, running north and south across the clearing. They were standing close together nearly opposite the central point.

"Well, have you looked enough?" the man asked. "You'll have plenty of chance to look at it in the next ten days or so."

"I'd like to go along the side of it once," Hi said. "I'd like to pace it."

"Pace away," the man said. "It's 120 yards, but you'll want to know for yourself, I suppose."

"Have you measured it, then?"

"Yes."

"Well, I'd like just to pace it and see it close to."

He turned south from the man along the line of gods to the end of the temple, which had not been cleared of creepers; the forest came to it and cloaked it there. He turned here to look along the line of the building. What struck him most was its silence, its blood-red colour where the facings had fallen, and the fact that every inch of it bore life of some sort. The man was watching him and playing with his rifle; he was sitting on the stone trough which contained the tools, much as a cat, having a mouse in a shelterless space, will drop him, withdraw a few paces, look at the sky and lick her fur. Hi pretended to examine the carving: he felt that the man must know what was passing in his mind. "I must start pacing," he thought.

He lifted his eyes towards the other end of the building. Dudley Wigmore was standing there, facing him, with his right hand upon the building, and with his left beckoning to him to come. It was very strange: he was there and yet he was not there: he certainly saw him: then lost him: then knew that someone sad was there who wanted him to go there. "Right, I'll go," he thought; so he set out, pacing and counting.

When he came to the central door, abreast of the man, he was hailed. "You needn't go any further, chum. The other half is exactly the same, another sixty yards."

"I'm going to the end," Hi said. "I believe your figures are wrong. I believe you're four yards out."

"A pace won't beat a yard-measure, chum."

"I'll talk in a minute," Hi answered, still counting. "Just a minute, if you don't mind: I don't want to lose count."

He went on counting mechanically, thinking of a strangely different mark of a vanished race not far from his home in Berkshire. Someone had told him long before that that monument was 375 feet long. He counted his pacing of this temple wondering if it would not prove to be the same, and if it were the same why it should be. All the time he was terrified, lest he should be shot in the back: the sweat was dripping from him. Hope kept surging up in him that he might escape: despair kept urging him to fling himself at the man's feet and squeal for mercy. All sorts of thoughts, of home and Carlotta and the things he wanted to do, seemed to be protecting him. His life was from second to second; "eighty-one," he was alive, "eighty-two," no bullet, "eighty-three," not dead yet. Dudley Wigmore was there: he could see his expression; very sad, yet hopeful. Dudley Wigmore was not there; the end of the temple was there, in a great corner-god, helmeted in the snake and eagle, whose mouth crunched the leg of a man. By this time he was up to the hundred. Suddenly Dudley Wigmore was there again, showing him the forest beyond the end of the temple: the ground was sloping down there in a cover of greyish thorn and greenish scrub, topped by what looked like ilex. He went on pacing, repeating his count aloud: "a hundred and ten; a hundred and fifteen."

"Hey, chum," the man called. "Hold on a minute. Wait for me a moment."

Possibly he began to suspect suddenly: at any rate, he snapped-to the breech of his rifle, rose, and began to walk steadily towards Hi.

"I'm just finishing," Hi called. "I'm sure it must be more than you make it. I make it 127 paces." He turned to see where the man was, measured his distance as about fifty yards, and then quietly, as though exploring some ruin at home, turned the corner of the building.

The instant that he was out of sight, he darted across the end of the temple into cover: he forced his way through the scrub, ducked well down into it so as to be hidden, and ran downhill as he had never run. He had gone perhaps seventy yards, head down and arms across eyes against the thorns, when something hard took him across the leg, just below the knee, so that he fell headlong violently into a thicket. It was a severe fall, which knocked all the breath out of him. He came to himself with a pain in his leg. "I've been shot," he thought, "shot and hit in the leg."

Up above him on the plateau of the temple, he heard Letcombe-Bassett call: "Chum. Heya, chum. Are you there, chum?" He heard him probe at some of the near-by cover, seemingly with the barrel of his rifle. "I've not been shot," Hi thought, "I fell over a snag." He dared not stir a muscle, he hardly dared to breathe: Letcombe-Bassett seemed so near, almost looking down upon him.

"Sing out, chum," Letcombe-Bassett called. "Where have you got to? Answer." He listened for an answer, and, having none, muttered a curse.

"You needn't pretend that you can't hear me," he called again. "You're within a few yards: so answer: don't play the giddy goat."

Hi's heart was thumping in his throat, yet he smiled at this order, it was so like the call of a cross seeker, in hide and seek, in the shrubs at Tencombe, bidding the hiders to call "Cuckoo again."

"Now cheese it, chum: come off with this kidding: where are you? Cut this right out."

There was a pause after this, while Letcombe-Bassett listened, not so much for an answer, as for some sound, which would show him where Hi was. Hi kept still as a stone, which was not easy, for he had fallen into an uneasy posture, in a thicket which was the breeding or roosting place of minute scarlet midges. These things surveyed him for a few seconds, then, having decided that he would be good to eat, they settled upon him. There were perhaps fifty of them, each with the theory that the nearer the bone the sweeter the meat. Their bite was by far sharper than the bite of the spotted-winged marsh-midge at home. But far worse than the bite was the pertinacity with which they thrust down his neck, into his ears, up his nostrils, or down to the roots of his hair, before they bit. Hi longed to beat them from him and scratch as he had never scratched. Letcombe-Bassett listened, making no sound.

"Chuck it, chum," he called at last. "I know you're there. You won't kid this nigger: I'm not that sort. You'd better come out. If I come in to fetch you, you'll sing a different song, my lad."

Seeing that threats had as little effect as persuasion, he tried again, with an appeal to reason. "Look here, kid," he said, "I'm only speaking for your own good. You'll never find your way out of this. You'll get bushed to a dead cert, just as you were before. And if you get bushed in this part, God help you. There'll be no kind white man to give you chow; don't think it. If a snake doesn't do you, a tiger will. Or if a woods Indian finds you, he'll eat you: to say nothing of the fever. Come on out of it, like a sensible kid and turn-to at the temple. . . .

"If you think I'm not offering you enough, you've only to say the word. I'll go you an honest half, share and share alike, in all we find: I can't say squarer. I wouldn't do it for many people; but I like you, because you've got guts, and so I tell you straight."

"That's why Doll Tearsheet loved Falstaff," Hi thought, not stirring. "An odd taste, but love is blind. What will be his next move?" Letcombe-Bassett paused to consider and to listen.

"All right, chum," he called at last. "I'll remember this. You needn't pretend to me that you've got clear away. I'm not so easily fooled as you may think. You're within earshot and very well within range; kindly remember that. Are you going to come along and bear a hand?" He waited for ten seconds for an answer, then said,

"I'll give you while I count seven: if you don't come before then, I'll come in and fetch you. I know where you are. As a matter of fact I can see you from here." This was thrilling hearing, though Hi believed (and earnestly hoped) that it was not true. The man gave it a few seconds to work upon his victim's mind; then he began to count.

"Very well, then: while I count seven. One. Two. Three. Four. Five. Six. This is your last chance, I warn you straight. Are you coming? Very well, then. . . . Seven. I think I may promise you that you'll regret this, my young friend. You're within easy shot-gun range, and I'll walk you up like I'd walk up partridges. I gave you a square deal, but you asked for trouble. Don't blame me, if you get it."

At that instant, from somewhere in the forest, perhaps thirty yards from where Hi had entered it, a piece of a dead bough fell to the ground, with a noise which to Hi was exactly that of one slipping on wet earth and recovering. To Letcombe-Bassett it gave a much-desired clue.

"Right," he called. "Thank you for telling me where you are; now we'll see. My Indians say you stink. You'll stink worse before I've done with you, my young whelp."

At this he burst into cover in the direction of the fallen bough; but as the jungle happened to be thick there, he gave it up, went back into the open, cast about for Hi's marks, and re-entered at the very place where Hi had entered. When once within the scrub, he seemed to neglect tracks and again tried to force a passage to where the bough had fallen. He beat the cover as he went. It was all dry, feathery, fronded cover, sweetly smelling when crushed, but abounding in scarlet midges. Hi heard him slap at his cheeks and curse: he himself felt that he was being eaten alive, yet he could not stir.

"All right," the man called. "Don't think I've done with you. You've not done me yet. Since I know you're not over here, I know you must be over there; and when I get you, you'll get the kibosh put on all this poppycock; you wait."

The man cast back along the fringe of the cover, beating it, as far as Hi could judge, with care. The wood there was all sage-green sari-sari plants, easy to thrust through but confusing to see in, as the fern-like shoots grew thick to the ground. When he had made a cast of about sixty yards, he turned, to make a cast back, a little further into the wood. Hi heard him come nearer.

"The brute," Hi thought, "he knows something about hunting; he'll cast to and fro like a shuttle till he lands right on to me. My only chance will be to trip him and try to bag his gun."

The man came slowly back, searching: Hi heard him kick at the undergrowth, shake aside boughs, slap at the midges, and whistle between his teeth. Sometimes he sang, in a voice no bigger than a hum, the first line of a song:

"There were three flies; three merry, merry flies."

He would stop here, as though he knew no more of the words, hum through the tune, or whistle it, in a groom's whistle, between his teeth, and then sing the refrain: "Whack fol lol tiddly ido." All the time, he was drawing nearer, beating the cover; presently he was at the end of his beat, and turning to beat back a little further into the forest. "I'm sixty or seventy yards into the forest from the clearing," Hi reckoned. "He has gone roughly through half of that. Now he's getting really near, and this time he may see me."

The man seemed to think that he was drawing near to the quarry. "Do you hear?" he called, "you're not dealing with anybody; you're dealing with me. I don't give up when I begin a thing: I do it. This cast or the next you'll be sorry, my little sucking swine." He came back, upon his new line, beating as before, and muttering to himself: "Oh, not in there? No, but not far off and not much longer. Damn these flies. If I'd a dog I'd damn soon flush this puppy. Come on out of it, you young swine. My good golly, I'll take your pelt off in return for all these midges: so much I'll promise you."

He came slowly along, drawing nearer to Hi. He seemed to take hours over each few yards of ground. Hi understood now how it comes to pass that hunted men, with prices on their heads, will sometimes give themselves up. He had not come to that point yet, but it was no longer out of his thought. The man came near to Hi, passed him, still muttering, beating and singing, and so slowly went to the end of his beat.

"Now for it," Hi thought. With the utmost care he moved his hand, so as to smear it, for one delicious instant, over his face: it was the only relief possible: the next instant, he heard the man turn and come swiftly straight towards him. Could he have heard or seen him moving?

"That's where you are, is it, my cock," the man called. "Right you are."

Hi was tempted to leap and run for it. The words went through him like shots; but he gripped himself, and said, "No, this man deals in bluff; he's bluffing now to make me stir." He lay still, while the man came straight towards him. There was no song of the flies now, he was walking with some fixed intention as though to a mark. He stopped at about nine yards from where Hi lay. Hi could see both his leggings and boots.

"Now then," the man said. "Now then, my sucking dove; you're somewhere just about here. I know you must be. I'm quite content to stay here all day, waiting till you squeal. I've done as much for a rabbit I'd got no quarrel against. I'd do more for you, let me tell you. You won't tire me, when I'm fixed on a thing. Are you going to surrender and ask my pardon? Well, if you won't answer, you're wise; for you're going to get a bullet in your guts before you're much older: you can save your breath to squeal with."

He came two paces nearer through the scrub. Hi could see the fronds of the talpas moving above him as he forced his way through. Just beyond the talpas was a space of earth littered with yellow fungus. "When the beast comes on to that," Hi thought, "he'll be bound to see me; he must see me."

The man wrestled through the talpas on to the bare space and kicked the fungus aside. "Yellow stink-horn," he said. He was within six feet of Hi; he had only to stoop to see him.

Then at that instant, with a sudden startling leap, somewhere to the right of the man and behind Hi, something big arose in the cover and ran for it. The man was prepared for a jump of the sort: he leaped to one side with a cry: "Ah, there you go. So you think you'll try that." Hi saw him clearly for an instant, standing tense, trying to see the leaping thing, whatever it was. Then, as he could not see, he leaped into the covert after it, shouting, "Stop, or I'll plug you." Two yards further on, he may have had a glimpse of a quarry, for he fired, jerked out the shell, snapped in a second shell and fired again, quicker than Hi had thought possible. Hi heard him mutter: "Got him. That touched him where he lived; but I've got to get to him, to make sure."

The man stood for an instant, trying to see. "He's down," he muttered. "Or is he down?" The noise still came to them of something moving: perhaps after all he hadn't got him. Hi heard him jerk out the shell and snap in another. "Well, I'll soon make sure," he muttered. "It wasn't a bad shot for nine-tenths guess-work, if I did get him. I'd have given something to have seen him cop the spike. These stinking kids think themselves someone at school: then they come here as though the earth belonged to them: they have to learn what they amount to."

He moved away into the wood. Hi heard him there beating shrubs at about a hundred yards from him. At that distance he was not likely to hear small movements in the bush; Hi was able to change his position to a thicker patch of scrub and to deal with the midges. After an hour of searching, Letcombe-Bassett became silent. "He's resting," Hi thought, "or waiting for some sign. He thinks that if I'm alive I shall think that he is gone and get up to go; while, if I am dead, the carrion-birds or those beastly 'betes-puants' will show where I am."

Letcombe-Bassett was in fact waiting for just those reasons. He had nothing better to do: he enjoyed snap-shooting and would gladly wait all day for a shot: he had besides found cause to believe that Hi had not budged. Presently, he came nearer to Hi and called, "All right, son, my Indios will be here at twelve with chow. We'll see how you feel with some Indio trackers after you." This was the last threat for the time: after this he came slowly up the hill, kicking or beating at some patches, though not searching them as on his way down. He passed within fifteen yards of Hi, somewhere out of sight in the talpas and sari-sari. In a few minutes, Hi heard him burst through a patch of crackle into the clearing.

"He's going to wait for the Indian trackers," Hi thought. "Or is that just a ruse of his? I wonder how long it is to twelve."

CHAPTER XVII

He reckoned that he had breakfasted before seven, and had been at the ruin before nine: perhaps it was eleven now. Almost at once, he heard the chant of Indians and the drone of a pipe coming towards the clearing. "My luck is out again," he thought. "Here are the Indians: this is where I shall stop, then." He heard Letcombe-Bassett hail the Indians: he was still close to, at the edge of the clearing. Hi could hear the goobies clatter as the men trotted across to him. He heard the man address them, explaining what he wished them to do; and the grunting of the Indians as they understood and assented.

He was tempted to rise and run; but the memory of the swiftness of the man's shooting held him back. "He would have half a dozen shots in the first half minute," he thought, "and then the Indians would run me down. I've no chance that way; but this way I may get one bang at an Indian, if not at him." He squirmed down into his patch, while the man led the Indians to the spot where he had entered cover some hours before. "Leu-in, hounds, eleu, ed-hoick," the man called. The Indians came into cover, just like hounds, and began to cast, with little cries and ejaculations, like the whimper of hounds, feathering yet not quite owning to it. "Ed-hoick," the man called. "Yooi, pash him up. Hoik to Chaunter: hoik. Hoik to Dowsabel. Yooi, yooi, yooi; fetch him out."

"We all know you've been terrier-boy to the North Surrey," Hi thought with bitterness. "You need not advertise the fact."

The hounds came eastwards in a very wide cast. "It's a drive," Hi thought. "They're going to make a semi-circle, and drive me up to the gun. He's going to stay in the clearing, to pot me when I break."

He had not time to consider the matter, for the Indians were moving swiftly to him, some above him, some below, and one straight for him. They were on the work they did best in the world. They were doing it with enjoyment, with little quick cries, one to another. "No power on earth can stop that Indian from seeing me," Hi thought. "He's coming straight for me." In an instant the Indian had thrust aside the scrub, so that Hi saw him plainly. He was a short, squat, plump young Indian brave, in a cotton shirt; he had long black hair sleeked down with fat; he had a gold half-moon in his nose; he carried a spear, and bore a blow-pipe on his back. Their eyes met. Hi had never seen him before, that he could remember. He was a broad-faced, high-cheek-boned man, with hardly any nose, like most of the tribe. He looked at Hi and Hi at him for one marvellous second, in which they understood each other. So will a man and dog meet, understand and pass on, with no word said, yet the dog wagging his tail. The Indian smiled and passed on, and Hi knew that it was all right.

The little quick cries became a little louder, that was all, some sort of a message passed down the line, to let the Indians know.

Presently the Indians moved up into the clearing to report that the white man had escaped.

Their going was like the lifting of the cloud at the passing of the line-squall. Hi knew that there had been an overwhelming change in his fortunes, brought about by no merit of his own, but by something fortunate that happened. He had been upon the rack for hours: now he was suddenly free. He cleared his face and hands of midges, though their bites no longer seemed to matter. He rolled over, with a sigh of delight at being alive, and fell asleep.

Sometimes in childhood he had dreamed a recurring dream, of a most beautiful grave spirit of a woman, whom he knew as his "Elder Sister Ruth." In his dreams, this spirit sometimes came to his bed, looked at him with eyes so beautiful that it was hard not to wake, and then, sometimes, some blessed times, took him by the hand and led him into the air, through the window and away, over the tree-tops, to strange lands, or to the stars. Even if such dreams were broken they were a joy to him: when they were not broken he thought of them for days.

He had not dreamed of Ruth for years; indeed, he had seldom thought of her since his going to his prep. school; but now he dreamed of her: she was there, that heavenly spirit, calling him "Christopher," her name for him, just as she had called him, for the first time, in that night-nursery at Tencombe, in the nook where his cot was, when he had wakened (as he thought) to see her beside him, lit by the flicker from the fire. It was such joy to see her there, after those days of friendlessness, that the tears streamed down his face. He knew that it had been hard for her to come to him, and that it was hard for her to speak; yet what use were words, she understood.

For a moment he lay still in his happiness; then, thinking that he had not seen her for years, he gazed at her, and found that she had not changed; but that he could see more in her face than in the past. She had a calmness and wisdom of beauty that was not subject to change: all peace, courage, goodness and happiness were in her face, and a hope so bright that no danger made a drawback.

All this was joy to him for a moment, until, in his dream, the thought came to him that she only appeared to him in dream; that this was a dream, and that it would fade. She smiled at his thought. "No, it is not a dream," she said, "look about you."

Marvelling, he sat up and put out his hand upon the soft grey-green frondage of the sari-sari. That dry, feathery touch was real: that smell of mint and turpentine from the crushed fronds was real. The red-hearts in the glow of the sun were real; so were those little green wrynecks questing their bark for food. On the ground was the broken yellow fungus, and beyond it lay the two brass rifle-shells, with ants examining them. A little gust of wind came down the forest, the sari-sari bowed to it and glistened and dappled, like the grass under the wind on Blowbury. A buck of the forest, delicate and proud, appeared, wide-eyed as a hare, noble as a Persian prince; he scraped with his forefoot and tossed his head in challenge.

"You see, it is real," Ruth said. "Shall we go on, then? We will set out together: it is not far."

"O God, Ruth," he said, "I've wanted you. I've wanted you."

She knew that, without his telling: she helped him to his feet. The light became more glorious than he had ever known it: all the leaves upon the trees seemed to be edged with fire. The light upon Ruth's face came from the beauty of her spirit: he knew that. This other beauty was a part of the happiness which she brought.

Instantly they set out through the forest side by side, so easily that they seemed to be moving upon the wind: the boughs gave way before them: they passed the hawk in her ravine and the wild-cat in his range: the deer gazed at them, but were not startled. In a glade of grass where a brook ran Ruth stopped him, because, in the brook, was a nest full of the eggs of a waterfowl, and in the grass were little blue mitai berries, known as the berries of our Lady from being ripe near Lady Day: of these he ate and took store.

After this they came to a jut of earth on which a dead tree stood with its roots exposed. Many mice in their holes here watched him with little bright eyes. At the foot of the jut was a shrub with hard, thick, dark-green leaves, and a rough bark, seamed with fibres like veins, as fragrant as incense from creamy gum.

"Put this cream upon your face and hands," Ruth said, "then you will not feel the bites of the insects."

He smeared himself as he was bidden and instantly the burning in his skin was soothed. He saw Ruth gravely considering him with eyes so beautiful that he felt that he could not bear their gaze.

"Will you be always with me?" he asked.

"Always."

"Oh," he said, "if you would help me to save Carlotta, who is in danger and trusting to me."

"She is in no danger," Ruth said, "but the trumpets are calling."

As in a dream, the words "the trumpets are calling" seemed fraught with meanings from beyond the world. He gazed at Ruth, as though by gazing he would come to a knowledge of the truth. He saw, as it were darkly, a confusion of men doing terrible things to each other while the trumpeters blew. Then all this cleared away, he beheld nothing but Carlotta in white, looking upward, with a look of happiness such as he had never seen, save on Ruth's face. Behind her, he saw the pinnacles of a church, glittering, as he thought, from the light catching the crockets, until he saw that the glittering was from winged spirits exulting in such beauty.

"It is not as man thinks," Ruth says, "but as God wills."

He felt the scene merge again into a dimness, so that he could not see, only feel, that he was moving away again, with Ruth near him, over country which would have been difficult but for her presence. She led him through thorns, which he never felt and through waters where she bare him up. Once, after the endless way, he would have sunk, had she not sung to him, as once before at Tencombe, a song so beautiful that it was as though the world were singing. What happened to him in these hours he never knew, save that he was miraculously helped: in a sense, those hours were as though they had not been: in another sense, they were among the intensest hours of his life.

It was after three o'clock in the next afternoon when he came out of the wood into the plain of San Jacinto. The forest ceased, the light became stronger suddenly: then, instead of the waving gloom stabbed with glare, he saw the plain, going on into the north in rolls of freedom: he saw the homes of men and heard the lowing of cattle.

Soon he came to a road running east and west; he turned to the east along it, till, at a wayside cross, he sat down, wondering whether he could go any further: the world seemed to be swaying beneath him and in front of him.

Half an hour later, a horseman hove in sight, closely followed by a three-horsed brake full of men and women, who were singing to a mandoline and a reed-pipe, under an awning of green and white stuff. The rider saluted Hi as he passed, then, being struck by his appearance, which was that of a corpse and a scarecrow combined, pulled up and caused the brake to halt. Some of the men dismounted and asked Hi, in Spanish, what was the matter. A plump and pale young woman, with eyes like big black plums, came down to look at him. Hi heard them decide that he was English and a caballero; but, then came a discussion of the question: how had a caballero gotten into this pickle?

"Where you been?" the girl asked, in English. "In the forest?"

"Yes."

"Lost?"

"Yes."

"Ay de mi. For how long?"

"I don't know."

"Dios mio. He had been lost in the forest. Regard the mud: see also the thorn-marks and the bitings of bichos."

"Always some are lost in the forest: they go blind, then they go mad. They will drink fire, thinking it water."

"Remember that man of Matoche: he who had nothing but a book."

"Also that other: the Americano: for whom some Americana must still mourn. He had her locket, the poor man."

"And this is but a boy and a caballero."

"Yes, and very gentle," the girl said. "His manners are so modest."

She turned to Hi, and spoke again in English. "You go San Marco?" she asked. "We take you to San Marco?"

"Is that near Anselmo?"

"Near where?"

"Anselmo."

This the girl did not know: she repeated it among her friends, who all seemed puzzled. Then one man said:

"Anselmo?"

"Si," Hi repeated. "Anselmo."

"Si," the man said, with a swift jabber of assent and explanation to the company. "Anselmo." He seemed to add that it could be reached through San Marco.

"Yes," the girl called, "you get Anselmo there."

"I'm not very tidy for riding with you," Hi said, shewing the wreck of his clothes, torn in forty places and mired to the throat.

"That doesn't matter," the girl said. "Can you climb up?"

He could not climb up; he found that he could hardly stand. The girl and one of the men helped to steady him on his feet; then the men in the brake got hold of him and heaved him in, with cries of:

"Welcome the stranger."

"Since thou mayst be Jesus, welcome: yet if thou beest not, welcome."

The girl, who had spoken English, made room for him beside her, and as the brake drove on, she put her arm round him and called him, "My dear." She had been drinking a little, but she was a very good young woman.

"I talk English, my dear; I love the English: some of them, what? We had two English in our house. Mr. and Mrs. Watson; do you know them? To-day, we been to a wedding."

Here one of the musicians handed her a wicker-covered blue glass liqueur-bottle with a tin measure which could be screwed over the stopper.

"Isn't Paco dreadful?" she said. "First we had wine: then we had brandy: now he's going to give us all the Milk of Venus. We shall all be drunk, Paco."

"No, no, not for you," Paco said. "But for the Englishman." They gave Hi a swig of the Milk of Venus, which revived him wonderfully: then they took swigs of it themselves till it was all gone: then they threw the bottle at Uncle Philip (as they called the rider), hit his horse on the crupper and made him buck. The plump young woman was very kind; she put her arm a good deal more tightly round Hi and said that she did love stars.

"You know, stars in the evening: they're so like angels."

Hi said that she was like an angel.

"A bit fallen angel; I don't think: what?" she said.

A man with a mahogany-coloured face, "rather like a frog," Hi thought, since his eyes turned up and his face was all going to throat, began to sing a doleful ballad, with a chorus in which all joined. As all felt better after this, one of the other men sang a song which went with great spirit, though it made the ladies blush. As he was pleased with its reception, he sang all the blushing parts of it a second time. Then the frog man produced a bag from under the seat: it contained three small bottles with brightly coloured labels showing ladies of a free disposition. The labels were printed with the words: "Smiles of the Muses." There was much applause in the brake when they appeared.

"Ha. Smiles of the Muses. Three bottles."

"Ha, the good Hernando, who knows what is good."

"Always the good Smiles of the Muses, to drive away care and settle what went before."

The brake pulled up by the wayside, so that no Smile might be spilled. The good Hernando dispensed something like a quarter of a bottle to each of the company. It was a syrup or cordial, about as thick as olive oil. It smelt, when opened, of all the flowers of heaven. At a first taste it reminded one of strawberries and of honey: then it warmed the throat: then, as it trickled along, it made a feeling glow all the way down.

When the brake drove on again, the mandoline struck up a Smile of the Muse: the reed-pipe piped to it and the company sang. The song had not much body to it, being indeed a catch about the eyes of a lady being as lovely as stars. It went on, during some miles of the way, till in the dusk of the evening the brake halted in San Marco, which was a town of six farms and a chapel.

Here, as weary as Hi was, he noticed that something had happened: someone had come in with news which brought all the town out of doors. When the news reached the wedding party, it changed their tone. The younger men hurried off to the group about the messenger, who stood on the chapel steps answering questions. The frog-faced man, the good Hernando, helped Hi down from the brake. Uncle Philip and the girl urged him to enter a lime-washed farm-house, with a smell of wine-press about it near which the brake had stopped. Hi was so dizzy with fatigue that he hardly knew what he was doing, yet he shrank from bringing his filthy state into a clean home.

"You come to the harness-room," Uncle Philip said, through the girl, "for a bath, and to get out the thorns and jiggers."

They brought him a half-cask and hot water: after his bathe they gave him a clean cotton sleeping suit and a bed with Christian sheets. They brought broth to him, when he was in bed, but he was asleep before it came: he slept for fifteen hours.

In the afternoon of the next day, when he woke, he found his clothes washed and mended. Uncle Philip and the girl brought him a coat, a sombrero and a pair of new shoes, which they pressed him to accept with a grace and sweetness of welcome which moved him almost to tears. "Guests come from God," they said.

"Hosts, too," he thought.

"If I ever can," he said, "I will bring these things back: be sure. I can never, never thank you enough."

When he had dressed, he came to the girl.

"What has happened?" he asked. "I've been lost for a week. What has happened in the country?"

"There is war," she said.

"In Santa Barbara city?"

"We do not hear of the city, save once in the week, when the ore-train returns with the empty trucks. No; but one from the west came here yesterday to call us to war. There are thousands, he said, marching to Santa Barbara."

"What for?"

"For our religion, so he said."

"Is that Don Manuel?" Hi asked. "Is it Don Manuel's army that is marching?"

"I do not know. It will be some army."

"Where it is?" Hi asked. "Do you happen to know where it is?"

"It was near here, within a short ride, yesterday," she said, "going to Anselmo, the place you asked about."

"That is it," he said. "If the army comes from the west and is marching east it must be Don Manuel's army, going to save Carlotta. Is it a White army?"

"Yes."

"Thank heaven," he said, "Ezekiel Rust got through. You do not know, do you, whether the Reds have harmed one Señorita de Leyva?"

"No."

"I suppose all the people here have gone to the army?"

"No," the girl said. "One or two have gone."

"Aren't you Whites here? Are you Reds?"

"We have the work to do: it is the people in cities who have these quarrels."

"But in this quarrel," he said, "surely everyone must join."

"The work has to be done. If these city people worked, they would not have the time to quarrel."

"Oh, wouldn't they," he said, "that's all you know of men. But, look here, how can I get to Anselmo?"

"You are not going to fight?"

"I've been trusted with a message to Don Manuel. If he is to be at Anselmo, I must try to get there to meet him. You're sure it is Anselmo?"

"The men from here went there last night."

"And how can I get there?"

"The ore-train to Piedras Blancas, going to-night," she said, "would take you to within ten miles of it, so Hernando says."

"Could I go in that?"

"Uncle Philip will speak to the engine driver."

"Oh, thank you. At what time would the train reach the place within ten miles of Anselmo?"

"Who knows, with a thing so dangerous as a train? Perhaps at midnight: perhaps at dawn. Sometimes it is two days."

"Good heaven. Is the engine-driver likely to refuse to take me?"

"Hernando says that soldiers were searching the line yesterday."

"What soldiers?"

"Red soldiers: State soldiers from Meruel. They were looking to see if the Whites were coming by train."

"Has there been any battle yet?"

"We have heard of none. They expected none till they are close to the city."

"Thank heaven," Hi said, "perhaps I shall be with them in time, after all. And, oh, will you ask your Uncle Philip to beseech the engine-driver to take me? Say it's very, very important: for a woman's life may depend on it."

"He ask all right."

"Suppose he refuse," Hi said.

"He not refuse, unless he got soldiers with him. But Hernando says they may explode the line to stop the soldiers."

However, at eight that evening, when the engine-driver took Hi as a passenger, the line had not been exploded and no news had come of a battle. The engine-driver was a Scot from Lanark, who had seen a detachment of the Western army away in the west two days before. "They came to the siding at Zamorra," he said, "to lift the oats stored there for the teams. Their captain was with them, a very big man, fierce-looking, with fine hands. What's this, they call him? Manuel."

"Yes, Manuel."

"The damned marauding son of a gun will get his neck in a noose before he's much older."

"Will he?" Hi asked. "He has the right on his side."

"Be damned to the right on his side. He's setting up a civil war here, because he don't like the laws of the opposition. Yon's a damned precedent. However, he'll be soon hanged and his moss-troopers the same. Now get in, lad, to your nest: she's starting."

Hi leaned out to shake hands with the girl, Uncle Philip and Hernando, who had come to see him off. He thanked them again and again.

"If you come these way again," the girl said, "you look us up, what?"

"That indeed I will do," Hi said. "And I wish I could thank you or repay you."

The train's jerk at starting flung him from his farewells into his nest among the ore, where he passed this the last night of his journey to fetch Don Manuel.

CHAPTER XVIII

Shortly before dawn the next morning the train stopped at the quarry-siding of Piedras Blancas, where the cooks of a squadron of Meruel Reds were preparing broth and maté with water from the railway tanks.

"There you are, lad," the driver said, as he bade Hi good-bye. "Here's a wheen good law-and-order men to give yon marauding Manuel his paiks. More power to ye, sons," he cried, raising his voice. "And hang yon idolatrous Deeck Turpin on a sour apple-tree."

On leaving the train, Hi slipped through the crowd of quarry men and soldiers, out of the siding to the road. Men and horses were coming from their billets in the village. The cliff of the quarry loomed out white: the stone dust made the village like moonlight or a flour mill.

Turning rapidly away downhill, he came to a grassy bank, where he breakfasted on food which the girl had provided. As he ate, all that expanse of the plain came into light and colour from the morning: he could see.

There, far away, was Santa Barbara, glittering under a smudge of mist, which hung over the violet of the sea. There, less than half way to the city, was the hill to which he had been struggling all these days. That heave of hill, topped by the church tower, one pinnacle of which was a statue of Our Lady, was the hill of Anselmo, distant. . . . He could not say how far distant it was, in that deceptive light: "Ten miles," they had said, but it might well be fifteen. "Oh, for a telescope or a pair of glasses," he said, "then I could see if the White army is there. That is where it must be."

As he turned towards Anselmo, he heard the sergeants of the Meruel Reds calling the roll at the siding.

"Those fellows are here for no good," he thought. "I'll get along to Don Manuel before I am stopped."

The sun strode up out of the sea to give to the country a beauty, unspeakable to one who had been for a week in the gloom of the forest. To the joy of the light was added a beauty of overwhelming blossom, so great that the soul of the earth seemed to be exulting in the sun.

"I shall reach Don Manuel after all," he said. "I shall be actually with him when we save Carlotta from the prison. And, oh, thank God, after all, I have helped a little, for Rust has gotten through."

After an hour and a half of walking, he was so far down into the plain that Anselmo was almost merged in the tree clumps at its base. It seemed to be less than two miles to the tower. The track led through clumps of ilex into groves of timber, among which a brook ran. As he passed into the cover of the ilex, he looked back at the land from which he had come, at the foothills like an advanced guard and the mountains like an army of kings. On the track by which he had come, he saw horsemen coming in twos at a rather quick trot. "There are those soldiers who were at the station," he thought. "They are coming this way, too. Can they be coming to join Don Manuel?"

Why should they not be? They were State troops, but in civil wars, troops sometimes pass from the State to its rebels. "They can't be coming to attack him, anyway," he thought, "for there aren't a hundred of them, and Don Manuel has thousands, so they said. If Don Manuel be in the village there, they'll meet their match."

It came into his mind that if these men were coming to attack, or if Don Manuel, being at Anselmo, came out to attack them, his own position, between the two forces, would be perilous. He therefore hurried through the cover, and pastures beyond to a copse of Turkey-oak which hid all sight of Anselmo hill. As he went, he listened for some sound of Don Manuel's army, the noise of many hoofs, the call of bugles, the shouting of orders, or even a shot from a picket. As he heard no such sounds he concluded that the army was not there. "Perhaps it has gone on to Santa Barbara," he thought. "I may be just too late for it, through sleeping too long yesterday."

Then he thought, "It is more likely that they are all in Anselmo town on the other side of the hill. And more likely still that they haven't yet reached Anselmo. They've been coming a long way on very bad going; they're bound to have crocked a lot of horses. That's it, no doubt. I've got here before them. In which case, good Lord, those Reds behind me will probably take me prisoner. I'd better hide in this copse till they've gone on or shown their hand."

He had not gone far into the copse of Turkey-oak, when he suddenly found that the further half of the copse was full of soldiers. His first thought was, "Here are the Whites," but a clearer view showed him that they wore dusty reddish Meruel uniforms such as he had seen at the station at dawn.

"Meruel Reds," he thought, "I wish I knew which side they are on."

To hesitate would have looked suspicious: he walked boldly on.

"I shall jolly soon know which side they're on," he thought. "They're Reds. I'll bet my burial money."

Those whom he saw were single mounted troopers, each holding three unmounted horses. All were craned forward on their horses' necks intently watching something that was being done outside the copse towards Anselmo. Beyond these horseholders, some dismounted troopers with carbines at the ready were at the edge of the copse, also intently watching. Two officers who were there staring at Anselmo through glasses, caught sight of Hi. One of them challenged in Spanish and at once moved up to him, to ask who he was, and what he wanted there.

"I am English," Hi answered, "I am going to Anselmo."

"What for?" the officer asked, in good English.

"To see George Elena?"

"Who is he?"

"A horse-breeder."

"What about?"

"To borrow a horse to get back to Santa Barbara."

"Where do you come from?"

"I've been lost in the forest."

"How?"

"Well, I lost my way."

"Oh, you lost your way, did you," the officer said, becoming somewhat harder in his manner. "Why do you wear that coat and hat? you are not a native here. Why are you disguised?"

"My own clothes were ruined in the forest as you can see," Hi said. "Some kind people at San Marco, where I came out of the forest, gave me these to make up."

The other officer moved over to them, to ask what his brother had asked.

"So, a sacred pekin," he said. They talked in Spanish for a moment, with looks at Hi which were not favourable.

"Zubiga," the elder officer called, to a couple of orderlies, who jumped forward at the order, "Take this man in charge." Then turning to Hi, he said, "You will stand aside a little. We will see later."

"Mayn't I go on to Anselmo?"

"No: sacred pekin, you mayn't."

They left him with the orderlies, while they returned towards the edge of the copse to watch what their scouts were doing. "They are sending out spies," Hi thought. "I've come just too late. Don Manuel is up the hill in Anselmo, and if I'd only been here an hour sooner, I'd have joined him before these devils arrived. Now I'm diddled again."

After some minutes of suspense, the squadron from Piedras Blancas entered the copse. The officer in charge of it took the salute of the two officers who had stopped Hi; he spoke to them both, went to the edge of the copse, to watch what was being done, talked for a few minutes there, and then came to Hi. He was an elderly man, with a frank, fearless face, and the pug-nosed look of a lightweight boxer.

Like all the officers of the army he spoke English.

"When were you last in Anselmo?" he asked.

"I have never been there."

"Never; yet you know people there. Do you speak Spanish?"

"No: unfortunately. I've only been about a fortnight in this country."

"Where were you last night?"

"In the ore-train coming from San Marco to Piedras Blancas."

"Where were you yesterday?"

"At San Marco."

"Did you see or hear anything of a rebel army at San Marco?"

"No."

"How old are you?"

"Eighteen."

"What are you doing in this country? How did you come here?"

Hi told him as much as he thought sufficient: it did not ring quite true. The officer seemed puzzled.

"Were you in Piedras Blancas this morning?" he asked.

"Yes."

"You saw these troops?"

"Yes."

"Did you see troops yesterday?"

"No."

"Yet you saw these this morning, you say?"

"Yes."

"And at once decided that you would bring the news of what you had seen to Anselmo?"

"Not at all," Hi said. "I'm not a spy. I happen to know that the Elenas in Anselmo have horses, and as they know friends of mine in Santa Barbara I hoped to borrow a horse to ride home on."

The officer frowned.

"There's something not quite right, somewhere," he said, "I don't see what brings you here. What friends have you in Santa Barbara?"

"Mr. Winter of Quezon. Mr. Weycock of the Sugar Company knows me."

"English people?"

"Yes."

"All right," the officer said. "Stand easy."

He stood easy for a few seconds, considering, then he returned to Hi.

"You say you were taken to Ribote and then lost your way in the forest? What were you doing when you were taken to Ribote?"

"Going to Anselmo."

"What for?"

"To see the Elenas' horses."

"You say this was ten days ago?"

"Yes."

"Why should you see the Elenas' horses?"

"My father is a horse-breeder in England."

"If you're lying," the officer said, "it may be a very serious matter for you."

"I am not lying," Hi said: he hoped that he wasn't. A couple of scouts rode in to the copse to report: the officer left Hi to examine them: he went with them to the copse-edge while they explained something. Hi could see them gesticulating, while the officer tried to get at the truth. After a minute's thought, he called the other officers, explained the situation to them, and gave the order to mount. Seeing Hi, he called to the orderly in Spanish to bring the boy with him. "Mount him on a spare horse," he said.

"Sir," Hi called out. "Will you not let me go on to Anselmo?"

"No, sacred pekin," the pekin officer answered. "And make less noise."

When the squadron had mounted, with Hi in their midst on a spare horse, the files moved away out of the copse into the open. They moved across a scrubby pasture in a direction parallel with Anselmo hill. Flankers rode out to their left, and all eyes were turned to the left, not to Anselmo, but to a roll of rising ground beyond it. "That is where Don Manuel is, then," Hi thought.

As they drew clear of the trees, Hi had for a moment a good view of Anselmo. It was like one of the little hill cities which he had seen in Italy, except that it was smaller than any, and stood upon a smaller hill. A clump of trees grew on the hillside so as to hide most of the wall with gray-green leaves. From the edge of the wood the white church tower rose, topped by its statue.

When this was about a mile behind them, the troops came over the roll of ground into sight of the plain stretching on into the west. There, rather more than a mile away, was a big white estancia with a haras or horse-breeding stable beside it, below three conspicuous windmill pumps. About half a mile beyond this, moving slowly towards Santa Barbara, was a large body of mounted men, with flankers thrown out on both sides, and many spare horses.

"There they are," everybody said at once. "There it is," Hi said to himself. "That is Don Manuel's army, or a part of it; and that big breeding stable is the Elenas' place, where I ought to have been ten days ago.

"And now," he thought, with a quickening pulse, "I shall probable see a battle; and these hundred odd Reds will get licked as they deserve."

However, the officer of his party had no intention of engaging. He hung to the rear of the moving army for rather more than a mile: then, at a crossing of tracks, he turned away directly to Santa Barbara and gave the order to trot. It was perhaps ten in the morning when they left the cross roads: it must have been mid-day when they halted at the Inn of the Little Foxes, where a trooper, bearing a red pennon, stood at the door: the inn being a headquarters of some kind.

The commander went into the inn to report and to ask for orders. He was gone for a quarter of an hour, during which a shot was fired a mile or two to the west. It was followed by several shots, of different qualities, answering each other. After this, though the firing often almost ceased, and sometimes sounded from further away, it never quite ceased and on the whole drew nearer. It was all independent firing.

It reminded Hi of the sounds of pheasant shooting at home in the unpreserved downland coverts where birds are scarce.

When the commander came out, another officer was with him. This one seemed to be a general, preparing to ride. He was flicking his spotless boots with a silk handkerchief, and walking with an arch of the legs caused partly by tight breeches, partly by affectation. "Where is this English fellow?" he called.

"There, sir," the commander said. "Bring him up, you." Hi was led forward.

"I believe, boy, that you are a spy," the general said. "I've a good mind to shoot you. Most soldiers in my place would shoot you. As it happens, my orders are not to shoot aliens, but to send them in for trial; which I shall do. You will go in to Santa Barbara till your case can be sifted a little. Any misfortune which happens to you you will have brought upon yourself." He called in Spanish to some troopers to take Hi to the waggons which were about to start under escort to the city. He also gave them a few written words about Hi's case for the escort commander. As Hi now knew what answer any officer would give to him, if he replied, he held his peace. The troopers gave him into the charge of the escort of the waggon, who told him, in English, to get into a waggon. When Hi asked which waggon, for there were half a dozen tilted army waggons all of one pattern, the man told him that he did not care which waggon, but that if he did not get into one straightaway he would break his face. "Get into that one there," he cried, "and don't show your face outside the tilt or you'll get a butt in the lip."

"You can't come in here," an Englishman, inside the waggon said, "this one is full up."

"What are you waiting for?" the escort called. "Get in."

"It is full up," Hi said.

"Full up," the man replied. "Who says it's full up? You sacred suspects should all be shot if I'd my way. I'll see if you're full up. Get in. Make way for him, you. Now get in." With a cudgel which he carried he poked the suspects till they made room; then Hi was thrust in among them.

The waggon was full. It contained an Englishman with a Spanish wife and three little children; an elderly American in the pineapple trade; an imbecile of doubtful nationality who dribbled at the mouth and gurgled in the throat; a strong young native woman in hysterics; an old woman who was drunk; her grandson, who had eaten something which had disagreed with him; three native men, one of them very old and infirm, the second shot in the body, unconscious and plainly near death, the third in a dreadful condition with fever. On the top of the discomforts of Hi's entrance, the waggons started.

"Why couldn't you have gone to one of the other waggons?" the Englishman said. "You could have seen that this was full, one would have thought."

"I had to do what I was told," Hi said. "It's not my fault."

"At least you can give a lady room," the man replied, "you can see that there's a lady here in an interesting condition."

"I am sorry," Hi said, moving as far as he could, "I did not see."

"Any man of decent feeling would stand up," the man said. "But perhaps you don't come from the fobug St. German."

"Where is that?"

"Oh, perhaps you don't understand Latin; it's where manners is."

"Well, I wish we were there," Hi said.

"That touched you where you live," the American said. "This kid ain't to blame for coming here. Though I'll roast this gol-derned Government for putting him."

"Ay, ay, ay, de mi," the young woman called, as she rose to a sitting posture and clawed with both hands in the faces beside her.

"Come off with all that, Angelita," the American said. "You, mister, catch a holt of that hand and I'll catch a holt of this; then she won't do us an injury." Hi caught one of the arms of the young woman as he was bid, but she was strong in the arm and writhing all ways at once. "Gee," the American said, "this young woman will ask her husband how about it when he comes home from his Lodge; she won't wait till day dawns."

As Hi hove down the arm of the young woman, the imbecile began to coo at him, with symptoms of affection. Presently the Englishman, who was a tall, thin, hatchet-faced man, with little moustaches waxed at the ends, said: "That captain-man ought to be shot for sending a lady in such a state in a waggon like this. I have been here five years and this is my reward. My wife now is going to be sick. It is the fresh air beating upon her, in her present state."

The old woman, who was drunk, here shoved her grandson to the tail-board of the waggon; the fresh air seemed to have beaten upon him.

"This is a nice way to send a lady to the city," the Englishman said. "That boy ought to be ashamed of himself. As for that captain-man, I shall complain to the Government. It is a marvel that she doesn't miscarry."

"She'll run a darned good chance of that," the American said. "The Whites will be here this afternoon. There'll be fighting in the streets to-night. So if you know a good snug cellar in a back street, get to it, pronto."

Here the three children of the Englishman began to cry; their mother, who was a big woman with a white fat face and jowl, boxed their ears for crying. The drunken woman, having soothed her grandson a little, drank from a bottle; then, rising from the floor to her feet, tried to dance, lifting her skirts to her knee. All this time the waggon was swaying forward at a good pace on a rough road; the children were weeping, the Englishman was growling, the young woman was writhing and hysterical, the old man was motionless, the dying man gasping for air, and the man with the fever was shivering. Hi and the American were trying to keep the girl in one place. The imbecile, who had decided that he liked Hi, kept pressing close to him and patting the back of his neck. Hi, who had no free hand, kept warding him off with his elbow; but the creature, perhaps mistaking this for a return of affection, pressed back, cooing.

The girl suddenly shook herself free and shrieked at the top of her voice. She did not know what she was doing; all her young muscular body was out of control. Hi remembered tales in the Bible of people who "had a devil"; this young woman had a devil, or the devil had her. "Look out, kid," the American called, "she's into the hay-lot, your side."

"Come back," Hi called. "Be quiet, señorita; it's all right. We're all friends here."

"Friends," the American said, "I guess we are. It's these darned Santa Barbarians who are the enemies in this land. They'll knock my apple season galley west. Lie still, Angelita, lie still."

"It's all these hidalgos," the Englishman said. "They cause the trouble in this land. What this land wants is to be opened up to free competition and progress. It wants white men. These priests and these hidalgos are fallacies; they ought to have been exploded long ago. If the English Government doesn't step in, it ought to be made to. My wife is a Pinamente; one of the oldest families, if we had our rights; and here these soldiers, these fine jacks-in-office, send her in a waggon like this."

"I feel for her," the American said, "being of a darned old family myself."

At this moment, above the noise of the waggons, as they bumped and lurched along, there came the whine and beat of barbaric music. The waggons drew to the side of the track, while the music grew louder and went by. Some hundreds of horses in twos went by, with a scuffling up of dust and the stink of sweat, horses and hot leather.

"Pitubas moving out," the American said. "I told you the Whites are coming. They'll fight this day and the Whites'll whip."

"How do you know?" the Englishman asked.

"Because I've been in the fighting business; had three years of it, and I know fighters when I see them. Man for man, the Whites will put rings round these yellow devils."

"You lie," the old drunken woman said suddenly, in very good English, blinking like an owl. "Damn your soul, you lie." She blinked, but said no more; as it happened, it was all the English she knew. The waggon halted by the side of the track as other music drew nearer.

"Their darned national anthem," the American said, beginning to sing to the tune.

> We will rally to the banner of our fathers,
> In the land that we lo—o—o—ove so well;
> We will rally to the banner of our fathers,
> In the land where our lo—o—oved ones dwell.
> Red the blood that we shed for our faith,
> Red the flag that we cherish to the death,
> Red our hope for our enemies' confusion
> In the land that we lo—o—ove so well.

"Perro de Rojo," the old woman screamed. "Abajo, perro de Rojo," she leaped up to a kneeling posture and spat in the American's face.

"Now, now, momma," he said, "That don't go. You didn't ought to spit at people, even when you've bit 'em and hate the taste."

She snarled at him like a wild beast; then, seeing foot soldiers marching by in the dust stirred up by the Pitubas' horses, she wrestled her way to the tail-board of the waggon, from which she cursed them for being Red.

"Come back into the waggon, mother," the American said. "Gee, kid, catch a holt of mommer. These Reds will shoot her if she don't let up." An officer who was passing struck her with the flat of his sword in the face: "Keep in," he said. "And you, driver, get on with you into the city."

The waggon moved on slowly after that. Troops were passing, horse, foot and a few guns, with waggons and gear. They were in the suburbs by this time, among houses, in a stream of people who were setting into the city, carrying whatever they could from their homes in the threat of war. At the gate, there was delay and confusion; the waggon was jammed in the crowd, waiting its turn to pass. When they came through the gate, a big mulatto, with a bright green ostrich plume in his hat, looked under the tilt at them, and said, "Suspecteds. Take all Suspecteds to the Church of the Sanctity of Lopez, once called by the slaves of superstition Trinity."

They had not far to go to this church. They passed a public square used as a camp for refugees, then they entered what seemed like a city of the dead, where none stirred out from the shuttered houses. As the guards herded them into the church once called the Trinity, Hi heard the distant fire of rifles, popping more constantly from the region through which he had passed.

"Skirmishers' independent fire," the American said. "If it comes nearer, it's a sign the Whites have whipped; if it dies down, it's a sign the Whites are whipped. Say," he continued, to one of the Red officers at the church-door, "we here are American and English citizens. Don't you think to gaol us, but send us to our Consuls." He repeated this pointedly in Spanish. "We're not going to stand for being gaoled," he said.

"This is no gaol," the officer explained, "but a shelter till affairs are resolved. Whom do you wish to see?"

"The American Consul."

"And you?"

"The English Consul," the Englishman said.

"And you?"

"I want to go to my hotel, the Santiago," Hi said.

"It is closed."

"Then to the English Club."

"That, too, is closed."

"Then the English Consul."

The officer made notes in pencil upon a piece of paper. "Word will be sent at once to your Consuls," he said. "Now enter."

"I'll be darned if I enter," the American said.

Half a dozen troopers flung him violently into the church; Hi and the Englishman were flung in on top of him, and the doors were closed and locked upon them. Two English-speaking guards in the pulpit called out to them to be quiet.

"But we insist on seeing our Consuls."

"Consuls sent for," the men said. "Hold your rows."

"I'll bet the Consuls aren't sent for," the American said. "I know my darned Barbarians by this time."

CHAPTER XIX

It was about half-past one in the afternoon when the church doors closed: the sound of the rifle fire continued, in an irregular popping as though the people some miles away were letting off fire crackers.

"That's not fighting," the American said, "that's still only skirmishing. These darned people can neither make war nor keep peace."

The church was of a Renaissance model, with rounded windows high up in the walls, and a ceiling painted with simpering ladies in clothes like rolls of blue smoke. All the sacred symbols had been wrenched or cut away from the decorations. A big coloured print of Don Lopez stood in a gilt frame over the altar. It represented him in evening dress with a red sash across his shirt. It had a dreadful likeness to a pig whose throat had been cut. Under him in gilt letters was the legend:

Liberty from Superstition.

There were about a hundred men, women and children of the suspected imprisoned there: most of them were stunned, some were terrified: one or two, like the young girl, hysterical. What shocked Hi was the atmosphere of suspicion: all there were afraid that the next person was a spy. They looked at each other, but hardly spoke, hardly even whispered. They watched the shot man die and the fevered man shake, without interest and without help: I was I, he was he; self was become terribly important, and sympathy a dangerous thing.

"They've been through the mill, these people," the American said.

"How do you know the Whites will be here this afternoon?" Hi asked him.

"Cut it right out, son," the American said. "I've been through one of these picnics once before here. This place is plum full of spies. You'd best not talk."

"But do you know if the Reds have killed anyone here?"

"Killed? I dunno. I guess they won't kill till they see which way the weasel pops. If they whip, they'll rip around. But you stay quiet."

The advice was good, for even as they talked a man edged a little nearer to them, with the look of the eavesdropper. When he found that the two fell silent, he sidled up to Hi, indicated the portrait over the altar, and said: "Look at that. I call that a dam' outrage: don't you?" Something in the look of the man reminded Hi of the brothel-touts who had beset him at the landing stairs before 'Zeke drove them away: it flashed into his mind that this man might be a spy: so he answered, "No, I call it 'Liberty from Superstition.' " The man was puzzled by the answer, but seemed to consider Hi's youth, and then moved away.

Soon after this, an armed guard appeared at the door, under an officer, who explained that the married couples as well as all women and children there in prison were to be moved "in the interests of morality" to another church, where they would be alone. As some of them expected to be murdered outside the doors, this caused a piteous scene, of screaming and begging for mercy, but by persuasion and force the removal was made. Among those removed, to Hi's great relief, was the Englishman with the Spanish wife, the pride of the Pinamentes, and their three children.

While the doors were open, some sweepers from the barracks brought in a cask of water and a basket of army bread for the use of the prisoners for which those with any appetites left were glad and thankful.

The American tried to find out from these sweepers what was happening outside. They would not answer him except by shaking their heads: when the guards noticed the questioning they ordered the prisoners not to speak to the sweepers on pain of being shot. "These Red Runts are plum scared," the American said. "They wouldn't bring us food unless they were afraid of being whipped. They're keeping both sides the fence."

Hi was cheered by this, as by nothing else. After three minutes in the church, he had felt that he knew and loathed every detail of it. He tried walking up and down the aisles; but the sense, that he was a prisoner, took all the interest out of walking. He tried lying down to sleep, but the sense that he was a prisoner, the knowledge that he had failed, and the excitement of the coming battle, kept him awake. He tried to pray that the Whites would rout the Reds; but the excitement and anxiety were too great, he could not put the prayer into words. Time seemed to stand still, all reality seemed to have ceased; he lay in a horrible nothing, anxious unspeakably. Everybody there in the church was in the same state. When Hi listened, he felt that everybody in the city was in the same state. One of the strange things of that afternoon was the silence in the town about them; it seemed like a town of the dead, save for the pacing of the guards outside the doors, and the occasional passing of patrols. At about half-past three, the distant firing, which had hardly varied in volume for two hours, increased and changed. Plainly some much heavier metal had come into action.

"Two batteries of four guns," the American said, after listening. "Number three gun in one of 'em is slow in getting off. They've only four batteries in their whole army: and one of them's in pawn, for the Dictator's new state coach."

"The firing is nearer than it was," Hi said.

"There's more of it," the American said.

There was more of it for half an hour: then suddenly it increased to a rolling, rattling racket much nearer at hand. This went on with the utmost fury for twenty minutes, during which all the windows in Santa Barbara rattled and trembled. Hi could hear shouting in the noise of the firing: then the shouting ceased and the firing dwindled away to a popping till it almost ceased, too. He looked to the American for an explanation. "That was an attack," he said. "But I guess they've grown tired of it."

It seemed as though that were the case, that they were tired of it. The light began to move from the floor up the wall as the sun went down the sky. The day of battle and suspense seemed coming to an end. Then suddenly, within a quarter of a mile of them, seemingly somewhere on the sea-front of the city, there came a clattering of horse-hoofs and shouting.

After this, there was silence, while everybody waited in suspense for a quarter of an hour, when a sudden shattering volley from close at hand sent the hearts into the throats. Ricochetting bullets struck the near-by roofs, there were falls of plaster and of tiles and the cries of women, while the space down by the sea-front began to roar with firing: hot and hot, so near at hand that presently the stink of the powder drifted into the church.

The firing went on for nearly an hour, dwindling as the light dwindled, till by the time the church was dark, save for the moonlight, it ceased altogether.

"The Whites must have entered the town and won," Hi said to the American. "That firing was in the town."

"It was in the town all right," the American said.

Hi rose from his seat and began to pace up and down in his excitement. The thought of Carlotta being set free was more than he could bear. The guards lit a couple of candles in a side chapel, peered to see who was walking, and called to Hi to keep still. The town outside was deathly still for some time after the firing had ceased: then all the streets began to ring with the trotting of horses, coming into the city from the direction of the Medinas Gate. They came in at a fast trot on at least three roads, so that the clatter and clink filled the air.

"Here the conquering heroes come," the Americans said.

"The Whites?"

"It's the side that's won anyway, or they wouldn't come in in order."

"All the White army is cavalry."

"Our darned Consuls might get a wiggle on without slopping over into speed."

"I don't suppose they know we're here."

"It's their job to know we're not here."

The cavalry, whoever they were, went to their stations or bivouacs and ceased to clatter. The town lapsed again into silence. Presently, in the quiet, within a hundred yards of the church, a sentry challenged someone, waited for two seconds, and fired. Someone cried out and fell, while the sentry jerked out the shell, which tinkled on the stones, reloaded and snapped-to the breech.

"The sentry's night to howl," the American said.

Soon after this, when the town was silent save for the pacing of the feet of sentries here and there, and the occasional slow passing of horse patrols, some volley-firings, of three or four rifles together, began in the direction of the cathedral. These volleys were repeated at short intervals for twenty minutes.

"What is that sort of firing?" Hi asked.

"It can only be executions," the American said. "They're shooting people."

"Deserters?"

"Yes; or prisoners."

"Prisoners of war? Surely not?"

"Any gol-darned prisoner's good enough to shoot in this gol-darned Republic."

"Then it means that the Whites have won?"

"Well, it would seem so."

"I hope to God they have."

"Well, kid, don't hope it publicly till you know it's a fact."

"Don't you think that the Whites have won?" Hi asked in a whisper.

"We'll know soon enough."

At about ten o'clock, when most of those in the church had begun to think that nothing more would happen that night, a strong guard marched into the little plaza outside the church and halted there. Hi suddenly saw a great increase in the light outside, for the newcomers had lit flares there. The doors of the church were opened and a strong squad of armed guards entered. A prim-lipped man, with the look of a "spoiled priest," who seemed to be in charge of the guard, gave orders that the altar should be brought from a side chapel, and placed as a table near the door. When the altar had been placed, and its candles lighted, he seated himself upon a chair there, asked for the register of the prisoners, and began to read it through. From time to time he looked into the body of the church, where he could see hardly anything, but a few white faces, the twinkle of the two candles in the nave and the glistening of some of the gilding. Hi heard two or three of the prisoners near him praying beneath their breath with the intensity of terror. He watched the prim-lipped man just as his rabbit had watched the snake. The man seemed to be waiting for some one who did not come. Beyond him, Hi could see the dip at the church steps, a market-flare burning, and moving shadows. The prim-lipped man marked his register with a pencil.

"Say, sport," the American said, stepping up to him, "we ain't your nationals. We demand our release or our Consuls."

All the other English-speaking people there, eight in all, joined in, in this appeal. The prim-lipped man listened to them all with courtesy, then he said, in English, with an Irish accent:

"In the very unsettled state of the city, you are safer here than you could be elsewhere."

"That may be or may not be, but I guess our countries are pretty well able to protect us. We are unlawfully detained here. We've been here pretty well all day. We've protested, and demanded our Consuls. What are you going to do about it?"

The prim-lipped man listened again. "You will understand," he said at last, "that I am not responsible in any way for anything that may have happened to you in these disorders, nor for your being here now. I am sincerely sorry that you should have been inconvenienced. I must ask you to blame the time, and those guilty for the time, not the Republic. In a few minutes, the commandant of this ward will be here, when I promise you that your cases shall be heard. In the meantime, let me see each one of you, who claim not to be of our nation."

The eight came forward to the table in a body, and explained in turn who and what they were. The prim-lipped man accepted each claim. "You will understand," he said, "that in these disorders we have to use every care to protect those domiciled among us. As the disorders are now over, I do not think that you will be inconvenienced beyond to-day."

"Will you tell us, sir," Hi asked, "what exactly has happened here?" The American's hand pressed Hi's arm.

"Happened?" the prim-lipped man said. "Order has been restored, or is fast being restored. The Republic has been saved." He looked at the papers, to see what Hi was charged with, then dismissed the eight to one side.

"Is this man a White?" Hi wondered. "Are those guards White? They wear no white upon their uniforms, but neither do they wear any red. Supposing Don Manuel were suddenly to appear with the commandant: oh, that would be joy."

Almost immediately after this a carriage drove to the steps of the church and halted there. Hi heard the guards called to attention and ordered to salute. The prim-lipped man turned to them.

"This is the commandant," he said.

Some footsteps sounded upon the church steps, one of the feet clinked with spurs. Hi craned forward to see who entered, feeling sure that Don Manuel would be among the party: something within him told him that he was there, coming victorious to set his servants free. "Oh, Don Manuel," he thought, "if it is only you, I don't think I'll care what happens to me for ever after."

Three people entered together into the light of the altar candles. The truth came upon Hi with a stunning of heart and head: these people were Reds, the Reds had won.

The three who entered were:—a big, flashy, free moving, swaggering type of cavalryman, wearing a scarlet sash across his uniform: the big negro with the green feather, whom Hi had seen taking the Piranhas' horses; and a woman, who also wore a scarlet sash across her shoulder.

"Gee, kid, there's the were-wolf," the American whispered to Hi. "Now there'll be blood."

"Who is she?"

"Anna, the were-wolf: an anti-cleric: been fighting the church all her life. She's a Red from Medinas."

"Then the Reds have won?"

"You bet your sweet life."

The woman and the soldier seated themselves at the table with the prim-lipped man; the cavalryman asked some questions, the prim-lipped man seemed to be explaining about the foreigners. The woman looked through the registers: Green Feather, with a drawn sword, stood at the door. As the woman, Anna, sat nearest to Hi, in a good light, he had occasion to notice her very particularly.

She was perhaps seventy years old. She had a face without any mark whatsoever of kindness, or mirth, or hope, or charity. Her eyes were grey, hard and stony: her mouth was a slit, drooped at the ends: her ears were enormous: her hair, which was of a dirty grey, fell untidily about her brow; she kept thrusting it back with a fat red hand, the thick fingers of which were black at the end. She had ploughed and sowed against her enemies for fifty-three years of hatred: now she had her hour.

The prim-lipped man rose from his chair and called:

"Will those English and American subjects come forward?" When they had come forward, he said:

"The commandant of the ward wishes me to say that during these disturbances, in the state of martial law in which we live, foreigners not vouched for by the municipalities in which they sojourn are required to repair on board the ships of the nations to which they belong, or to such other ships as will receive them. Which of you have carnets signed by your municipal authorities?"

None had any such papers.

"None?" the prim-lipped man said. "Very well, then, you will repair on board the ships of your respective nations. A guard will take you from here to the Mole, where boats are now engaged in taking those qualified to go. I will give you here this paper to sign, opposite to your names."

When all had signed their names, the commandant called an officer, to whom he gave charge to embark the eight at the Mole. The officer called them out to the plaza below the church steps, where troops were halted. Some of the soldiers stood in groups of four facing a blank wall where a flare was burning.

"Firing parties," someone said. "Some poor devils in the church are for it."

Hi, looking back, saw the white columns of the portico, with the yellowness of candlelight inside the door, and the blackness of Pluma Verde standing like a death. A squad of troops formed about the eight: the officer gave the order to march. One of the eight began to hum a Dead March.

"We are well out of that," someone said. "They'll clear most of that bunch up against the wall."

"These darned foreigners: why can't they agree? They're like a lot of children."

"Children? They're like a lot of savages."

"Well, we come out at the thin end of the horn, whatever they are. We'll not get ashore again till Lord knows."

"Surely," Hi said, "they'll let us go ashore again, when the troubles are over."

"When will the troubles be over?"

"I suppose in a week."

"Not in a year, kid."

The American had been talking in a low voice to one of the squad of soldiers: he now spoke to the company.

"See there, now," he said, jerking his head to the right, as they came out upon the water-front, "the Whites got into the town here. They got in at the gate there. The man says that they fit like hell along the beach, till all the lot of them was killed."

"All the lot?"

"Yep."

"And Don Manuel, too?"

"Yep. Not one man left alive."

"Oh, Lord."

"There goes some more of 'em, who weren't in the battle at all."

Behind them, from the direction of the church which they had left, there came a sudden volley of three rifles. After a minute there came another volley, presently a third, then many more.

"These darned Reds," the American said, "it's their night to howl. Those were the poor devils we were with a few minutes since; give them a prayer, sons."

They gave them their prayers, as they marched on in the moonlight along the deserted water-front. All the houses there were dead, with blank eyes. The rhythm of their steps echoed from the walls, the sea washed on the shingle beside them. The shootings still went on near that church of liberty from superstition.

"Blast them," one of the eight said. "Don't they pardon anyone?"

"It's their night to howl," the American said:

> They're all the way from Bitter Creek,
>
> And it's their night to howl.

"Do you think I could send a message ashore, when we get to the ship?" Hi asked.

"What for?"

"To ask after friends and to get my things."

"There'll be darned few messages passing after this."

"Well, what are we to do, then?"

"What did the cat do?"

"I don't know. What did he do?"

"He went back, when he couldn't stay no longer."

"The Consuls will help us get our things," a man said.

"The Consuls, hell," another answered. "We'll not see a stick nor stitch of anything we had. This land is going to have the bust-up that's been preparing for years. It will be a year before it's settled. Perhaps a year after that we may be allowed in again to settle our businesses. Thank God, I saw a little of this coming."

By this time they were at the Mole, where Hi had landed with such hopes a fortnight before. The water was gleaming over the lower steps. Some men were standing under the Mole light: some soldiers came to attention there as the party drew near.

"Halt, there," a voice called.

They were called one by one under the light, and sorted out to three boats then lying at the steps, from a French barque, an English ship and an American schooner.

"Will there be any more to-night?" an English sailor asked. "Shall we send the boat in again?"

"We do not know."

"Well, if any more are to come off, dip your light there and I'll send the boat in."

"How?"

"Dip your light. Lower and hoist your light, to let me know you want the boat."

"It is good."

"Is it good?" the sailor muttered, as he shepherded his six down the steps to the boat. "You're about as likely to do it as my Uncle Joe is to have kittens."

Four ordinary seamen in the boat pulled them clear of the Mole into the harbour, towards the sailing-ship anchorage. The firing-parties were still firing in the town. Away beyond the Farola, a house which had been fired began to burn up brightly. "That's just about where the Piranhas' house is," Hi thought. "They've killed the Piranhas, too."

"What ship are you taking us to?" a man asked.

"*Solita*, Liverpool," the mate said. "I guess the lid's off the *Tenderloin* to-night?"

"They're playing hell all over."

"Give way, sons," the mate said. "Come, put your weights on."

They pulled on over the sea in the moonlight towards the grove of masts. All were silent now, from weariness and bitterness; there was no sound except the gurgle and wash of the water, the grunt of the oars in the crutches, and sometimes a church-bell, or a volley of shots from the city. The mate who was steering began to croon a hymn as he watched the *Solita's* riding-light:

> Give me that old time religion,
>
> Give me that old time religion,
>
> Give me that old time religion,
>
> It's good enough for me.

Singing thus at his hymn, which could be made to last for a day in case of need, he brought his boat to the gangway under the lean iron flank of the *Solita*. The Captain looked down upon him from the poop rail.

"Is that you, Mister?" he asked.

"Yes, sir: I brought six more."

"Come on up there, you."

When the six stood on the deck, the captain spoke to them.

"You are on board a British ship," he said. "The rules are: no smoking and no matches between decks. Any of you caught striking a light below there will sleep on the fo'c'sle head. Write your names here. Anderson, show them where they belong."

One of the boat's crew helped them down a perpendicular iron ladder into the gloom of a 'tweendecks which smelt of decayed malt. A spare starboard sidelight cast a green light on one side of this space, so that Hi could see many bodies lying on sails. On the other side of the space two planks upon casks made a table on which some food was spread, in bread-barges.

"You can get your supper if you'd like," Anderson said, showing the bread-barges. "Or you can turn in on the sails, if you'd rather rest. Your lot makes it forty-one that we got. We'll be able to have some fine sing-songs. The steward says we shall probably sail within three days for New York. There's fresh water in the bucket there and a dipper to drink by. Any matches you've got, you've got to give to me."

When Anderson had gone, Hi drew away from the six to a lonely space on the sails, where he dragged a hatch cover over himself, so that he might think alone. He had had his first wrestle with life; he reckoned that he had been an utter failure. The future was dark enough, but it was nothing to the darkness of the present.

"I failed," he thought. "And I've probably killed 'Zeke. And 'Zeke has brought Don Manuel to death; and the Piranhas are probably killed too, burnt out, anyway. And I've probably settled Carlotta's fate as well. They are certain to kill her; all by not avoiding politics, as Winter told me. They might all be alive now, if I'd not stirred."

The mate, who was walking the deck near the hatch, partly lest the boat should be needed, but mainly to detect any striking of a match among the refugees, sat upon the coamings for a minute, humming his tune of the old-time religion. "Ah, the old-time religion," Hi thought, with the tears running down his face. "Nothing but religion's any help to a man in my state. Oh, God, I have made a mess of it."

And Carlotta?

Ah, Carlotta.

CHAPTER XX
APPENDICES AND NOTES

On the fate of Carlotta de Leyva.

Carlotta had been killed a week before this.

The day after her arrest, some hours after Hi had started on his journey, Don Lopez ordered Carlotta to pray to him while he sat throned in public on the high altar of the Mission Church of Santa Barbara. On her refusal, he ordered her to be enclosed in a house of common prostitutes.

The mistress of this house, an Englishwoman known as Aunt Jennings, refused to admit her, saying, "That none but a dirty dog would have thought of sending her."

When this was reported to Don Lopez, he ordered that Carlotta and Aunt Jennings should be taken by the hangman to the new town, and that there their throats should be cut. This deed was at once done by Don Lopez' son, Don José, assisted by the two half-breeds, Zarzas and Livio.

This was the first of the many crimes committed by the Red party in the year of madness, 1887-1888.

Carlotta was put to death at about the moment of Hi's arrest by the Pituba officer, before he was taken to Ribote.

On the fate of Don Manuel and his army, or what happened on the day of the battle.

When Hi saw the White army near Anselmo, it was moving from its bivouac towards Santa Barbara, expecting to fight that morning. It was delayed in its march by Pituba skirmishers, so that it did not come into position above Santa Clara until after three in the afternoon.

Don Manuel had expected that a part of the Federal army, the San Jacinto Horse, and the battalion of Independents, would declare for him, and either join him or help him. Their officers were known to be Whites and their men were hostile to Lopez. Unfortunately, Colonel Velarte, of the Horse, who was a friend of Hermengildo de Bazan, the White leader, disliked Don Manuel and refused to help him. The Colonel of the Independents felt that the Whites would be ruined if he did not help Don Manuel, but would not help unless he were given the command. While affairs were in this state, the day before the battle, Don Livio disarmed both these battalions and put their officers under arrest, so that the Whites were not helped by any Federal troops.

When the battle began, Don Manuel had with him between six and seven hundred horsemen, armed in various ways, undisciplined, without artillery, and almost without ammunition. The Federal troops opposed to him numbered about four thousand, including the Meruel and Pituba regiments of horse, three battalions of Eastern foot and two batteries of horse artillery.

The battle proper began when Don Manuel's men came on to the little ridge above Santa Clara church. At that point they came under shell-fire from the batteries, which had been registered upon the ground during the morning. As Don Manuel saw that his only chance was to charge the guns, he charged. His men got into trip wire laid before the guns, and were shot down there by the foot soldiers or routed by the lancers. Some fifty or sixty of the Encinitas men followed Don Manuel to the right of the field, broke through a squad of Meruel horse, made a dash for the city, entered the southern gate, and summoned the fortress to surrender.

Here, through the wit of Don Livio, they were ambushed and driven on to the water-front, where they fought till they were lost. The last of them made a stand about the green boat or lighter which Hi had seen on the morning of his setting out with Rosa. When their last cartridges were gone, they took to the water and were killed in the bay.

Don Manuel, because he took to the water after the others, when the light was worse, contrived to reach the English barque *Venturer*, whose Captain (Gary) received him and brought him to safety. Some five weeks after the battle, he landed in the United States.

Of his army, it is thought that about one-half escaped alive from the battle, and that of these perhaps a third were killed in the pursuit or in the proscriptions which followed. The Federal loss is not known, as the returns were falsified. It is thought that the Reds lost many men in the skirmishing, both before and after the battle.

The battlefield, which was then mainly race ground and market gardens, is now covered by the suburb of Santa Clara. It is a couple of miles from Medinas, on the northern road from the city; at a little distance the ridge (now covered with houses) which was the White position, may still be seen.

On the fate of Donna Emilia and her daughter Rosa.

Donna Emilia died in misery shortly after the outbreak of the troubles (in May, 1887). Her daughter, Rosa Piranha, though proscribed in the September massacre, was saved from death by the devotion of her old nurse. The house which Hi saw burning, as he walked to the Mole, was not the Piranhas' home; that was spared though sacked. Rosa returned to it when the troubles were over.

In May, 1888, she entered a community of enclosed nuns, to whom she made over all her earthly possessions. In this sisterhood she has lived ever since.

On the fate of Hi, after he went on board the *Solita*.

As the aliens in the ships were not allowed to land again in Santa Barbara during the troubles, Hi, with his fellow refugees, went in the *Solita* to New York, where he landed.

As his parents felt that he had better stay there, he remained in the United States, where he underwent the adventures and hardships usual to youth. After some months there, it happened, that he met Don Manuel.

As he felt that his life was linked to Don Manuel by ties not easily broken, he joined the band of White refugees sworn to destroy Don Lopez and his faction. With these outcasts he wandered and suffered for some months, till that campaign began which led to the killing of Lopez and the establishment of Don Manuel as Dictator in his stead.

For some years after this, Hi remained in the Western provinces, in Don Manuel's employment, at work upon the problem dear to him, of perfecting steamboats for river traffic of different kinds. In 1891, when Don Manuel began his great scheme of controlling the San Jacinto River, some of his ideas were put in practice. For the next seven years, he was busily employed on the San Jacinto, in partial or complete charge of the boat service by which the workers on the dam were supplied. The following letter from him, written in early May, 1898, to his mother in England, will fill in some of the blanks in this history:

"On the 15th we had our great day with the opening of the dam. His Excellency, with his staff and a lot of senators and Congressmen, came to the pier at Curucucu, where they took our boats for the last ten miles up to the dam. After the formal opening, there was a banquet, at which H. E. made a very nice speech. He said he did not think the work would ever have been done but for my boats, which perhaps was partly true.

"About a week after the opening they finished the last stretch of the railway so that now the waters are linked with both coasts and my seven years' job is at an end.

"As I had nothing to do, I was one of the first to take the train to the east through the forest; and I took the opportunity to go over the scenes of my old adventures. I got Dick Binge and Tommy to come with me. I started by going to San Marco, where the marriage party was so kind to me. I found Uncle Philip still living, in the same farm. His niece had married Hernando, the man who dispensed the cordials in the waggon. They were living at a farm near by and doing well. I had promised them when I parted from them to return the clothes they gave me. I couldn't quite do this, but I was able to get them a couple of pedigree cows from His Excellency, which I hope will thrive up there on the hill.

"After seeing them, we went with a guide two days into the forest to the temple where the cousin of the Hundred Yards Blue nearly plugged me. The place has long since been opened up and explored. From some of the Indians thereabouts I learned of the end of Letcombe-Bassett, if that were his name. It seems that a few days after I escaped, he worked into the temple by himself and made a certain number of finds. A big stone fell across his legs and pinned him there. He called to his Indians to lift the stone, but the Indians wouldn't, because they hadn't liked his ways, so he stayed pinned there for three days and nights, till he died of thirst. So Dudley Wigmore was avenged. We had a look for Dudley Wigmore's bones, but the jungle had taken charge of them. I learned later that one or two of his things and some of the treasure from the temple were recovered and sent to his old mother at Shepton Mallet. This was done by one of Wigmore's French friends, years ago, during the troubles, soon after I was there. The rest of the things found in the temple are in the museum at Santa Barbara.

"From this point, as so much of the forest had been cleared and a lot of the bog drained, it was easy to make the next stage to the ranch, where the corpse looked through the window. Here I learned what had happened; it had long been a puzzle to me.

"The troop of Pitubas who had burned the Ribote house made one or two forays into the Gaspar country, to burn the houses of other prominent Whites. Word came that afternoon that they were coming to burn this particular ranch. That old ruffian, Don Pablo, who would not let me go to Anselmo, ordered the people to vacate the ranch, and to join his body, which (he said) would then attack the Pitubas. They hurried the women away to safety; then, as they rode out to join Don Pablo, someone in a panic fired a shot, and everybody began to blaze away at nothing. These were the shots which I heard.

"A young Englishman employed in the ranch stayed there after the others lest a telephone call should come through with news of Don Manuel. While he waited, he saw the Pituba spy and shot him through the window; being then thoroughly scared, he took horse and galloped away. I heard him go.

"The telephone call came through while I was there, as I am not likely to forget.

"The people who challenged me and shot my horse, as I left the place, were the Pitubas, who burned the ranch to the ground that night. I found it rebuilt and thriving. That old ruffian, Don Pablo, owns it: he is a Senator and a grandissimo: I saw him there. He looks liker a portrait of a beadle than ever: a beadle or a town-bull.

"From this point we rode through the forest to the place where I went astray in the rain; and thence up the pass to the crater; and so, by degrees, to the Ribotes' ranch. The old man and wife were still alive. The old man was failing and the old woman had had so many troubles that she did not care to see me, but I paid for my horse, I am glad to say, at last, and heard their news. The daughter had become an enclosed nun and the son, Anton, had been killed in the anti-clerical rebellion five years ago. I was grieved indeed not to see those two again. The house had been divided against itself, like so many during the troubles. From there, I rode on to the little town where I had been jailed. It has become a very prosperous place since I was there. They have built a new town hall and a new jail. They have also changed its name from Ribote to Tres de Mayo. Some don of state had built a lovely palace on the site of the Ribote mansion, which was burned while I was there.

"From here we rode on and camped in the clump where the officer made me a prisoner. Of all the places which I visited, this was the only one which did not seem to have changed. In the morning, we rode on and came to the falls down which I had been swept when I escaped from Brother Bright Tooth and his friend. As there was very little water in the river it did not look the same, but I could see the place with the overhanging bank where I came ashore. Just at the place where I took the water there is now a railway bridge; the track by which I rode on Bright Tooth's horse has now the railway beside it. The hamlet where Bright Tooth and his mother lived has changed beyond all recognition into a thriving market town, but I found the German. He had become very stout and enormously prosperous. He remembered me quite well and told me all about Bright Tooth and his mother. The mother, he said, went into Santa Barbara during the troubles and was ended when the troubles were ended. Bright Tooth and a friend of his, I hope the friend who was with him when they tried to nobble me, were garrotted under His Excellency for murdering an old woman at Medinas.

"From this point, it was only a short stage to Carpinche, which is now a port for big forest timber. There were ships of up to a thousand tons in the harbour there. I watched them heaving the great red-hearts and green-hearts in through the holes in their bows. Not that the forests are being skinned. They are being planted as well as being cut.

"We took boat here—not a sailing boat, for those have passed away and market produce goes now to the city by train. We went in one of the ferries which ply every hour from Carpinche to Santa Barbara, calling at La Boca. I landed at La Boca to try to find word of Giordano. He had gone back to Italy, they told me, some years ago and was living there near Florence; very rich, they said. Pedro Ruiz was still marketing and gardening. I saw him at last in the flesh and bought some plants from him, which I hope I shall make grow for the sake of old times. The padron of my boat and Chigo had both gone back to Italy: few Italians stay here more than seven years.

"From there I came on to the Farola, where I had the long wait that anxious morning. As I landed in the late afternoon, I was the only person there, except a few anglers fishing for snappers. I could see what used to be the Piranhas' house, so leaving the pier, I walked up to it. It is now the house of enclosed nuns in which Rosa lives. They are contemplatives, so there was no seeing Rosa: none of us will ever see her again, I suppose. I am too active to take to the monkish way of life myself; but I have seen monks and nuns out here, from time to time, who have made me see something of what they see. When you once see the beauty of holiness, no other beauty seems living. Rosa is happy. I went to the house just when they were singing their service, in that chapel which used to be the Piranhas' chapel, where Donna Emilia and her husband are buried. I felt very queer, to think that Rosa was singing there and I so near her, listening: and suddenly I knew that she knew that I was listening, and was sending me a message of great happiness.

"In the city, I learned of some of the rest of these people. Don Inocencio was killed in the troubles: murdered the day after Don Manuel lost the battle, like so many other Whites. Allan Winter is still out at Quezon: Weycock is in the Shipping Co. I saw him at the Club: he is a man I cannot stick. Don José is one of his clients, they say: he would be.

"I asked Colonel Peñedo at the War Office if he could find out for me about the Pituba officer who would not let me land and afterwards jailed me. He was a Captain Avellano, it seems; a well-known Red and as brave as they are made. Don Livio, that mongrel scoundrel, was responsible for sending him to Ribote to burn the Ribote house. It seems that he had no written orders to stop the boats at La Boca: in doing that he was probably just being cussed. He was a gallant man in his way: he was killed fighting for Lopez a year later, "fighting like a wild tiger cat, one against twenty," so Peñedo said. The Pituba officers were usually pretty tough: so I hope he may rest in peace.

"Of some of the other criminals and waifs, upon whose tracks mine impinged, I could learn nothing. Anna the were-wolf got herself shot in the troubles by wanting to be too revolutionary: the Reds did not kill the Whites so that Anna and her friends might rule.

"I haven't mentioned Ezekiel Rust, because I have so often written to you about him. He and his wife Isabella are still out at Encarnacion; he runs the haras there, in very good style; she seems fond of him: both are well. He always wants to come back to England, to see Tencombe again, but I beg him not to think of it. Many there would recognise him, and although the evidence against him cannot now be strong, he would be certain to incriminate himself, and it would be too pitiful if the poor old chap should get himself hanged or (more probably) shut up as a criminal lunatic. Where he is now, he is a valuable man. Where *he* is now, Keeper Jackson is, I hope, a valuable ghost. Why not let it rest at that?

"I asked about that picture-dealer on the water-front. It seems that he got a lot of things from the de Leyva collection, chiefly the bronzes. Then Don José tried to get them out of him, and as he wouldn't sell them, Don José took them, with all his other belongings, and had the man deported. I suppose this is Don J's nearest approach to a virtuous act. Of course, this was years ago, only a few days after the troubles began.

"H. E. had me out to dine at the palace, to ask me about another job, opening up the Burnt Lands by canals, and would I design the boats? It seems tame, after the San Jacinto: like falling off a log; but I want to be in everything that H. E. is in. He thinks that the B. L. can be planted in patches, if there are catchments. He is the most hopeful soul I know.

"By the way, in the palace, I found the Aztec, the Ribote brother. He is a sort of Secretary for Clerical Affairs, rather a big gun. I did not remind him of our meeting.

"Well, this is a long letter: I must stop.

"Words cannot describe the changes in the city since the bad old '87 days: no town can have changed more in the time. My love to Bell and Father. I hope to be back in June, for a couple of months: so don't fill the house up."

A note added by Highworth Ridden:

"The above was written by me to my mother soon after the completion of the dam, when I revisited Santa Barbara for the first time since the troubles. I left the pier on that morning of the troubles thinking to be back in ten days: I did not return save for that time as a prisoner for more than eleven years.

"What I did not and could not write to my mother, I write now, after another eleven years. It is about Carlotta. It is difficult to set down what she was to me. 'Calf-love,' I suppose most people would say. Well, there is a generosity in calf-love that gives it a grace: not that mine had any grace. I saw her on only one day twenty-two years ago: I have thought of her every day since; not as a lover of course (for years past), but as a spirit apart, unlike anyone else that ever was. You who never saw her cannot understand this. She was the most exquisite thing: in life marvellous, in the unspeakable end, heroic: and always so beautiful, so gracious. All who knew her felt this: she had cruel enemies, the mad, the diseased, the godless, the savage and the greedy hated her.

"I went to the chapel of Carlotta, which H. E. built. Her tomb, with her recumbent figure, is there: it is very beautiful. Her sculptured head on the stairs leading to the Plaza is liker her. Gamarro's painting of her is not like. Bedwyn's pencil sketch is like. But she was like the light, no one could have painted her.

"I tried to do something for her once, and though I failed, I am prouder of that than of anything else that I have ever done. Whatever she was, she made men know that gleams come into this world from a world beyond, which is better than this.

"H. F. R."

"When I set out from the hotel on that morning of the troubles, I took with me a scrap of the hermosita which she had broken for me. This being in my pocket-book, was stolen from me at Ribote by the Englishman who got me out of jail. The rest of the spray, being in my trunk at the hotel, was, as I supposed, lost, during the troubles, with all my kit.

"But in 1899, being at the Club in Santa Barbara, I met the then proprietor of the hotel, who said, that he had recently found some trunks and bags in a disused cellar: that these had evidently been put away during the troubles and never claimed since, and were now to be sold. I went to see them, and among them found one of my tin trunks, in which were some ruined clothes. With the clothes, in some hotel blotting-paper, I found the hermosita spray which Carlotta had given to me, and the envelope, addressed by her to Donna Emilia, which I had picked up and kept. So that I have what few have, one of the last gifts and one of the last writings of a lovely soul.

"That is all that one can say of her, that she was a lovely soul. I have met no one in the least like her. I can but thank God for her, knowing that she came from God.

"H. F. R."

A note upon Carlotta, by Arturo Grau, author of "Memoirs of Those Times."

"I felt when I met her, what I have felt ever since, that in her mortal body an angel walked, who needed but a small instrument though a perfect one.

"Those who met her, felt despair at their unworthiness beside so much perfection; yet felt exaltation at the thought that such perfection could be in this world. I can truly say, with so many others, that she altered my life for me."

Another note upon Carlotta, by Roberto Mandariaga.

"None can describe her, nor would one understand, if she were described. She was like a light sent from God."

Another note upon Carlotta, by Roger Weycock.

"She was a little, sprightly thing with a lot of colour. She was very much of a lady by birth, being a de Leyva; but for this she might have passed for bold. She seemed to me to be very fond of her own opinion, which was not always wise. She had been the spoiled darling all her life; old de Leyva's pet; the Chavez group worshipped her. Someone had told her, in her youth, that she was like a little fairy. She seemed to me to be always acting the fairy. I do not of course pretend to justify her murder, which must ever remain a blot upon an unconstitutional but, on the whole, rather great administration. At the same time I, who saw her, can testify that she was not the angel from Paradise which some, who never saw her, would have us believe. She was a pert young woman, accustomed to her own way, who had the tragical fate to run counter to a much stronger way than her own. The character of Carlotta de Leyva, as worshipped (this is scarcely too strong a word) at present at Santa Barbara, had no original in the young woman whom I met; it is an invention of the poets (of the sentimental-idealistic school, of whom Tomás de Medellin is the chief exponent), backed by an able but quite unscrupulous propagandist press, whose interest it is to blacken Don Lopez by every means in its power."

Another note upon Carlotta, by Guillermo de Medellin, father of the poet.

"I saw her almost daily for many years. As a traveller in both hemispheres, I have met many thousands of people; some of them distinguished, a few great, none like her. I have met some with more compelling power; that, after all, was not what she had; she had blessing power, as though she came from Heaven.

"She was one whom many loved; surely all to their great good. No hatred or other evil could exist in a mind full of her memory.

"Once, when she was a little girl, five or six years old, I asked her what she would do when she grew up. She said that she would build everybody a palace. 'What,' I said, 'with your little hands?' 'No,' she said, 'my lover will build it for me.' This I have so often, often thought of."

The poem "Carlotta," by Tomás de Medellin, is well-known in Santa Barbara. It is a formless but interesting jumble of writing about her, in sonnets, ballads, lyrics and dramatic dialogues. It contains most of the fables about her which the imagination of the race has seized upon. I quote here some translation from portions of the poem.

The Sonnet of Camilla, Mother of Don Manuel, on hearing of her son's betrothal to Carlotta:

> Lord, when Thy servant, doubting of Thy grace,
> Went in despair from what she judged Thy frown
> To search for comfort in an earthly town,
> Despairing of all help in any place!
> When she was sure, that not in any case
> Could her demerits touch the longed for crown,
> But rather sorrow, that would bring her down
> Where no light comes, nor joy, nor Bridegroom's face:
>
> Then, in the chaos, lo, a plan revealed.
> Lo, in the sand, the lilies of the field.
> All thy blind servant's darkness of untrust
> Proven more wicked than her tongue can speak.
> To her unfaith thou turn'dst the other cheek,
> And, to her greed, gavest gold that cannot rust.

Lines, on the same occasion. This poem is known in Santa Barbara as "The Vision of Camilla concerning Manuel."

In the dark night I saw Death drawing near
To make me go from here;
In all my sin, with all my work undone,
Leaving behind my son
With no more stay nor path
Than what the wild horse hath.

I saw the souls of all my earthly friends
Laid bare, their aims and ends;
How some might love him, many help, but none
Be wisdom to my son.
Wisdom that is a road
Where no track showed,
A dawn, when no lamp glowed.

Thus in the night I heard Death come, I heard
The mouse shriek at the bird;
My sins came huddled to my bed, the bell
Dead hours did tell:
There was no light: only the tick of time:
Life, strangling in the slime.

Then in the multitude of souls I saw
A bright soul, without flaw,
Wearing a star upon her brow like heaven
In the green light of even.
However black (I knew) the night might turn
That star would burn.

She reached her hand to me and cried: "Death calls,
Time strikes, the hour falls.
And like a flight of birds the souls prepare
To whirl into the air,
To bring to be what none may understand.
I shall but light the hand . . .

> Lo, here, the light upon my brow shall lead
> Thy son until he bleed;
> Until he fail, and falter, and despair.
> Even in his blackest night I shall be there
> My star will be his guidance: he will know
> What light is, from its glow."

A sonnet upon Ezekiel Rust.

> Son of Isaiah Rust, of Churn, his wage
> Was eighteenpence a day, working for Squire,
> With rabbits twice a year, and sticks for fire,
> In a stoopt cottage, broken-backt with age.
>
> His life was among horses from his birth,
> He uttered cries which horses understood,
> He handled squire's stallion in his mood.
> Strange blood being in him from the ancient earth.
>
> Often, when moons were full, he ranged the Downs,
> Much like the fox, but liker to the hare
> Who forms in the thymed grass in the hill air,
> And sees from the hill edge, as the stars rise,
> The glare in heaven above the market towns
> And turns back to the midnight, being wise.

The Meditation of Carlotta in Prison.

> This that I understand,
> This that I touch with hand,
> This body, that is I,
> To-day will die.
>
> O given Spirit, now taken,
> Keep to this truth unshaken,
> That the good thing, well-willed,
> Becomes fulfilled.

The Meditation of Highworth Ridden.

> I have seen flowers come in stony places;

And kindness done by men with ugly faces;
And the gold cup won by the worst horse at the races;
So I trust, too.

The Comfort of Manuel, on Setting Forth defeated in the *Venturer*.

Bad lies behind, worse lies before.
What stars there were are in us still;
The Moon, the Inconstant, keeps her will,
The Sun still scatters out his store,
And shall not Man do more?

When the worst comes, the worst is going:
As a gate shuts, another opes:
The power of man is as his hopes:
In darkest night the cocks are crowing.
In the sea roaring and wind blowing
Adventure: man the ropes.